An Empty Cup of Kindness

George M. Cochran

For my children, Heather, Scott, Timothy and Carter,
thanks for growing up to be great people,
and to Joan, without her attentive caring,
"Cup" would not have been.
Thank you!

Chapter One

A gentle rain fell through the night, teasing Calcutta's parched earth. Awake through the early hours, Mary Templeton Powell had finally fallen asleep, as the last rivulets of rain gathered silently. The shutters on her windows floated with the breeze, dividing the soft flashes of lightning that moved out across the Sea of Bengal. Just below her window, darkened puddles of rain rested and waited for the reddened fingers of India's sweltering sun to color their mirrored surfaces.

Mary had spent another night of torment, dreading this morning's sunrise. The warm shafts of daylight began to saturate the sheer bedroom draperies, and the light broadened across the cool marble floor. The sun's radiance hadn't yet found the foot of her bed when her inner sense of time obligingly awakened her.

The distant sounds of the city came to life, accented by the early morning train to Nepal. The pitch of its shrieking whistle was compelling.

Mary's eyes opened, as she began gathering her thoughts, searching for the reason she felt fatigued and terribly anxious about this day. She had pleaded with herself to stop obsessing about this second appointment with Dr. Satara at the hospital. Yet, she had spent the last week anticipating this "nightmare" and had continuously reviewed every possible discussion she could have with the doctor on this Monday morning, December 30, 1999.

Mary was up and showered. Brushing her black shoulder length hair tightly back and gathering it with a rubber band, she reached for her lipstick, but chose not to wear any. She looked up for a brief second and started to look at herself in the mirror but turned away. She felt anything but attractive and refused to confirm her frame of mind with her reflection.

She dressed quickly. Leaving her apartment, she closed the door carefully behind her, holding the latch back, to keep from making any noise. She took the steps, not wanting to see anyone, especially the chatty doorman.

Calcutta's congested back streets were seething with its natives, but Mary's western features were an obvious exception. She hurried, attempting to join the "traffic of humanity" that crossed her path. Push-carts, bicycles, and small carriages edged past her rear door in both directions adding anxiety to the distance between her apprehension and the finality of her last medical tests.

A sure-footed Indian man maneuvered his rickshaw past Mary, then stopped abruptly. The passenger of the rickshaw was startled and began to complain. The diversion allowed Mary to step in behind a well-dressed Indian woman in a flowered sari, and her little boy.

The woman was very aware of the child; she held his hand firmly as they walked. But he would fall behind her pace from time to time. His attention was drawn by his curiosity, and his size made it easy to step into the spaces that wavered within the crowds. Then he would have to quicken his step to catch up. Mary observed his inquisitive fingers gliding across every texture within his reach. His head followed the motion of his fingers.

She treasured children. She would capture their purity in her paintings, which were extraordinary. And with every opportunity, she observed their spontaneity. This child, an arms-length away, was no exception.

The boy turned his head, stretching his neck and looking over his shoulder, He questioned what was behind him. His curious glance met Mary's eyes. She quickly took her hand, held it high, and "cupped" it, moving her fingers up and down, to say "hi." He mimicked her as best he could and then added his cheerful smile. His mother, with a gentle tug, reminded him of their mission.

This child was offering his innocence. And he was a distraction that Mary more than welcomed.

Mary was living in Calcutta, not because of an engaging mystery of the Far East but because of her husband's appetite for international business. John Carter Powell, corporate raider, was on an inexhaustible crusade—in pursuit of "the deal." He had said to her many times, "We're off... Rio for six months... you will love it there! Hong Kong for just five weeks... but it's important! Johannesburg... I'm not sure how long we're going to be here."

More than a decade had passed since Mary Templeton had presented her first and only show at the Hartford Art Gallery in Seattle. It was a dream come true, and it was Mary Templeton's very *own*. Her talent was unique, which became apparent to all that attended the black-tie gala.

The CEO of one of his ventures had invited John to attend this auspicious affair. John saw the occasion as an opportunity to test the waters of Seattle's well-to-do and to determine if any of the gallery's patrons were significant players in the rapid growth of the software industry in the United States. John was "taken" with Mary's presence. He saw her as a very attractive woman, with a slender build. Her black hair framed her soft facial features. Her black evening gown, with a simple strand of pearls, was elegant.

John felt that her bearing was distinctive: *You would not point her out as a painter*, he thought. *Alluring... yes... in fact captivating... but not an artist.*

His assessment touched on polish, wealth, and importance—mandatory attributes in his line of work. Men were all around her. John had been introduced to Mary, but she wasn't paying any attention to him.

He sought out the curator and purchased two paintings but with two provisions—that Mary would receive a note immediately, stating that he had purchased the pieces—and that he would be pointed out in the crowd to her.

A few minutes later, after she had read the note, John affected surprise when she approached him. They spoke for a very long time, with John creating an endless list of questions on the "what," "where," "when," and "why" of the two pieces, saving "who" (are *you*) for a late dinner that same evening.

John was definitely different from anyone she had been with before. He was older, a very confident man. His manner was perhaps a little too formal, at times, but she had found him exciting and was beginning to have a deep affection for him.

They had begun seeing each other frequently. If John were anywhere near, he would fly to see her for days at a time.

The time they spent together was exciting. They often met with Washington's politicians, along with its powerful corporate leaders. In addition, she was fascinated with the lifestyle that he seemed to adorn so well—generations of English refinement.

And her perception of their relationship was that it was very "European," rather than the traditional, Seattle concept of, "working class man meets artsy woman." But social graces aside, he had a willingness to share his life with Mary, "the woman he loved," and would consider having a family.

A nobleman had found in Mary and her art something he wanted to share forever.

Accepting John's proposal to travel with him was a means of breaking away from the ordinary—the boredom of the familiar. And Mary was young and led so easily by the opportunity to explore the world as an artist.

It hadn't been quite a year when they were married in Madrid. Mary wrote her mother and father of the wonderful news and sent a photo of John and her standing in front of a tiny church in Madrid. Mary's letter from her mother caught up with them months later; there was a photo of Mary as a three-year old.

She was standing alone in their kitchen, in her father's black snow boots, which climbed all the way up to her thighs. She was holding two large house paintbrushes and had a very determined look on her face. On the back of the photo, written in her father's hand, was, "We love you both." Just beneath it was, "Me too! Be good, Mother."

Just one month later Mary had received a phone call from her mother telling her that her father had died. Mary was told that it was all right not to come home and that all was settled.

Over time, Mary had written to her mother. She would ask about her cat, Lilly, send photos of the many places she and John had lived, and ship many paintings back to her. She would also call, once a month, faithfully, but Mary would never see her mother again.

John and Mary had traveled together to the major cities of Europe and the Far East, with John closing one deal after the other. His obsession for accomplishment was "seasoned" by the competition with his father. As the eldest son, John's mission in life was to prepare for the "inevitable." His father was very successful and could send John into a tirade in five words, "Have you done anything lately?" And as smart as John was, it always worked.

But in time, Mary's art had become her principal distraction. Ironically, it took her away from the boredom of being alone more and more frequently while they were residing in Johannesburg.

It had taken many years, but John had changed significantly. Mary had been introduced to his other side: He was distant, cold, uncaring. His business relationships became a "matter of fact" with little if any emotion. He treated Mary no differently. And although she couldn't prove it, she was certain he was having affairs in his absence. Affection was "doled out" to her with a demitasse spoon.

Surprisingly though after returning from one of his London trips, John had asked Mary to join him on a brief trip to Turin, Italy.

His business had taken a few weeks to negotiate the details of a merger. When they had returned, Mary received word from her Aunt Catherine that her mother had passed away. (Aunt Catherine and Uncle Paul had been very close to Mary's mother.)

John had accompanied Mary immediately back to Seattle. Yet, the guilt she harbored, for not *being there* for her mother, would never leave her.

John had managed to leave such a negative impression with Aunt Catherine that she suggested to Mary that she should come home more often and stay longer but that John could stay in London to watch over the Queen Mother, who was ailing at the time.

The "journey to nowhere" had continued. John's being away was becoming too obvious. She would ask "why?" His standard response was that he had many things going on and that she would be happier to paint.

His father would summon him from time to time, and he would go to London alone. Returning, he would never mention anything about his trips or his family. When Mary would ask if all were well, he would respond with, "A curious lot... my family." And that was it.

It had been less than a week after one of John's London trips. He and Mary were leaving their apartment for dinner when the phone rang. John had answered it. Mary could see John's face change to sadness. She went to him to offer her concern, thinking that something was definitely wrong. He walked, deliberately away from her, and he began to ask the caller questions regarding time and place leaving her standing in the middle of the room.

He hung up the phone, not looking at her, and in a strong voice said, "Father has died. We'll be off to tomorrow evening. I'll make all the arrangements." That night at dinner, he remained unusually quiet and never once discussed any of the phone conversation.

Mary went with him to London to the funeral. She was surprised that she was included since she had never been introduced to the family.

John's family seemed to have it all: stately mansions, butlers, maids, and chauffeurs. The entire family, including third cousins, was on call, waiting to scrutinize Mary from head to "the articulated word." Every move she made was another test.

There were many "closed-door" business meetings with his sister and mother, and they could be heard many rooms away. Their last discussion ended with John screaming an emphatic, "Goodbye Mother."

With the library door slamming behind him, John returned to their sitting room stating, "We're off... How does Rio sound... just wonderful this time of year?" After the ceremony, they went directly to the airport.

His caring for anything had become more and more mechanical, no sentiment, just cold gestures—flowers a day late, and a phone call in the middle of the night, or no flowers at all, and the wrong year written on a card for a birthday or anniversary. It was almost amusing, but the cards always finished exactly the same: "Best wishes, your loving husband, John."

She would look forward to his being home but began questioning "why?" At breakfast, she read the back of his newspaper pages: *The London, New York, LA, Bombay, and wherever—Times.* He would lunch with business types until cocktails and then get home, only in time to shower and dress for dinner with any number of business acquaintances. He would say his "goodbyes" and be off again "to who knows where." (Mary wanted her husband, a marriage and a child—not the cold rhetoric that was replacing them.)

It was Mary's thirty-seventh birthday, May 22. These birthday occasions had become John's "signature evenings" since they automatically became "an event," or better yet "an excuse," to invite business associates. So, for Mary, with the exception of the cake, it was difficult to see any difference from any other evening they spent together.

The party had begun as all of the others: the sommelier had been kept very busy that evening with all the quests enjoying the fine choice of wines, that John graciously bestowed on the occasion. Mary blew out the single candle that was centered on the top of her ornate cake—as John's guests completed the traditional song, applauding.

Then as they seated themselves, one of the guests made a comment that *time* passes much too quickly. Mary responded by asking to stage a performance. I'd like to recite a few short lines on that subject... a characterization, if you will, of my dear loving husband's 'proper behavior' delivered with his 'proper English accent.'"

Mary began to transform into her charade. She raised her head in an aloof manner, her attention shifting to each of the six guests, separately, and ending with John. She stared into his eyes.

Then she reached for her almost empty glass of red wine, with two of her fingers scooping it up by the stem (her thumb supporting it as she threw back the few remaining drops across her tongue). She immediately returned it to the table—assertively. Clearing her throat, she began:

"May I offer a visual analogy from 'Time Passing,' borrowed from my old friend, David O. Selznick in his classic film, starring Bette Davis. (Mary turned to the others.) In your mind's eye, envision... if you would, *time*... your own life, depicted as a daily calendar... its pages, set in motion by the hot dry winds of a sirocco, revealing the many years that have escaped each of us. She paused, motioning for her glass to be refilled. Pages of our own time are emptied of their meaning... brushing past our awareness... dispatched into our past.

"The cold passage of this day, sends into darkness... a black hole... in space... devouring time. One might think (she turned back to look at John) that fond memories adorn the gilded edges of these pages... but not so. Instead, the pages are sheer weight... and but a burden... lifted from my stay in purgatory.

"Page after page... year after year... there awaits a single date with *time*, and scrawled across their pages will be a single word... *enough*. Has it passed? I am numb from waiting. Will it ever be?

These are questions... only this wind would reveal." She bowed her head. The group applauded—passing questioning glances at each other. Mary looked up, smiling like a Cheshire cat, and added, "Thank you. Thank you."

John responded, "Here, here you have mirrored my manner quite convincingly, darling, a bit deep... but well done." Mary continued with her portrayal, sarcastically: "Those spent pages of time were my listening to you, a direct descendant of the cultured tongue, and I was but a lonely parrot... mimicking my master's voice... darling." She smiled, as if to bait him for more, but John knew to change the subject. "Happy birthday to Mary," he announced. They all raised their glasses.

John had been traveling strictly alone. Mary had been left behind. She filled her days with her work, but his absence was becoming the subject of too many heated arguments.

Unexpectedly, though, he had made a surprise visit to Johannesburg, for the weekend, for their ninth anniversary. He had arrived there, from Calcutta, in a particularly arrogant frame of mind. He boasted of maneuvering the principles in this last corporate software merger, and he thanked Mary for its outcome—since he had planted the seeds for this reward years ago at her first art show: "I've been using your Seattle friends for some time now. You see my darling... art *does* pay."

He was beginning to have his usual gin and tonic when Mary began her plea for harmony in their marriage.

"John, please, let's take some time for us. We so desperately need time together, please." He finished his drink. "Just come back to Calcutta with me. It's that easy."

"I don't think I can... but if we don't find each other again soon, I'm going to leave you." He held up his empty glass. "Would you like something?"

"No."

"But why would you leave? I mean... I don't understand you at all. 'You've got it made,' as you Americans say." He placed fresh cubes in his glass and poured gin over them with a splash of tonic.

"Are you sure... a white wine perhaps?"

"I don't want anything," she said resolutely.

"I know I'm away too much. I know I'm a bit 'pissy' at times, but you have to weigh it all against our lifestyle. You certainly are very comfortable."

"Emotionally, I'm not comforted—but tortured."

"Oh! not one of these... again and again... and then again."

Mary fired back at him. "I am tired of this journey and you always being away—and with 'whom,' I might add. There is nothing for me in this marriage. I can't deal with this isolation anymore. You don't care about us... at all."

"No, and that's why I'm here... because I don't care. This must be your 'feminine logic,' expressing what I don't care to understand. And as far as a 'whom,' that's your own paranoia. Are you coming to dinner? You *are* dressed. Let's not do this bickering again."

"Yes, let's do this until you understand, and no, I'm not coming to dinner."

He finished his drink in two gulps, and as he walked away, added, "Mary, I'll be late this evening, and I'm leaving early afternoon back to Calcutta. You've got some time to change your humor."

Mary had been searching too hard for a reason to continue. It had all grown too old; she was drained by waiting—and awakening alone. The next morning, in the early hours, she heard his key in the door and waited for another delivery of the next volley of his excuses—as to where he had been.

Before he was to leave for the airport, Mary started up with John again. "I just can't deal with this anymore. Don't you *see*? Can't you feel my needs?"

"What are you, John? And more importantly... what am I? Is this my role... to accept your behavior... you cold, insensitive son of a bitch. I thought *frigid* was reserved for women. Is this your androgynous side that you have introduced me to? What kind of breeding do you come from? You must have been conceived in the cold of winter... in the coldest room of that museum you lived in, during the "ice age.""

"Most likely... perhaps that's it... in a nutshell." He sat down, sinking deeply into an over-stuffed chair, staring out the window. "That just *may* be it."

And she went at him, savagely, leaving no room for his proper English quips or a convenient disappearance.

Suddenly, though, John confided in her—tenderly, and he suggested as a place where they would begin as a family. "You are my only love. I know that I've been wrong... but all of the mistakes are over now." He offered these commitments, in docile tones, as his apology. Mary was taken by his sincerity. She needed his love and *wanted* their marriage to work.

John had put off his trip. His travel had dwindled to a few weeks here and there. The relationship seemed much like their beginnings. She dropped all of her defenses and, making a difficult, emotional decision, became pregnant. John was surprised but realized that he had never seen her as happy.

They had moved to Calcutta in her fourth month. But no sooner were they settled, than he began to find excuses to be away. She was concerned that the affairs had started again. She asked many questions: "Where are you going? Could you get home in time? Where could I reach you? Who are you with?" She asked these questions as an expectant mother, not as a prying wife, and she asked for his willingness to stay near—as a father.

Mary had been delighted with thoughts of having a family. Her child would definitely have many early art-school classes. She had been taking very good care of herself, anticipating her "little present."

She had completed six months of her pregnancy. John was in New York when she was rushed to the Gandhi Memorial Hospital—hemorrhaging. Her pregnancy had terminated with the stillborn birth of their son. John sent flowers, but he didn't interrupt his business trip for her. He had returned the doctor's emergency call, and had explained to Mary the importance of his not being able "to break off the negotiations."

"Chin up," he had said to Mary. "It's most likely for the best." This emotional wound was deep. It would never heal, and John had left her alone to suffer the tragedy of death—the death of her child and the death of her innocence. He was just half of one day away, one more plane ride, a minor investment of time. But this trip had no future for him; his son was dead.

She had experienced every woman's worst fear, yet his condolences had been expressed as a convenient business assessment: "It's most likely for the best." She would never forget his response, and she realized the stupidity of believing him, in their reconciliation, just before they had moved to Calcutta. This reality was part of her pain; it had intensified when she had searched, in vain, for the last expression of warmth from him.

Her determination to paint was relentless—fueled by the need for a distraction. Yet each fragmented attempt to "find herself" was scraped off the canvas then started again. Each stroke of her brush amplified the sorrow that had flooded her mind. Canvas after canvas took her further away from the children's purity of heart, into the reality of her own loss.

The last painting she had attempted was a "tightly-cropped" composition of a woman and her child. Mary had suddenly stopped working, recognizing her own expression of despair in the subject's face. The woman was dressed in black. She was clutching the child that she held, tightly, to her bosom. The infant's face was delicately veiled in soft, rolling waves of blue translucent silk; its features were concealed from its mother's view. Mary never saw her baby. This infant in the painting—was her child.

Mary had succumbed to the truth and reluctantly admitted that she had remained too long in a marriage with a man that was incapable of affection. She had discovered hate—an emotion she had never experienced—never painted. She could feel its presence in her soul. It had a face. It was John's.

This month, John was away in London. "Straight through the holidays," he had said to Mary.

Now Mary is facing this medical diagnosis, deliberately, alone. Walking towards the same hospital, that housed so much emotional pain, was difficult. Going inside was almost impossible.

She had shared nothing with John these last few months—not even the time of day. *And tomorrow's date will hold the last agonizing hours of a century,* she thought. *It will be another year without meaning... consumed by the loss... and yes, it will be another one thousand years... alone.*

Mary, once again, became aware of the current of strangers—with the fragrant envelope of Calcutta's moist and tactile air surrounding them. She watched India's people scurrying through each other's space, homogenizing this—"their scent of tranquility."

She noticed the mother and her little boy that she had walked behind on the street. The mother slowed her pace allowing her son to stretch his leg high, reaching for the first of many steps, as if it were a game. Mary breathed more deeply, *exhaling* this moisture-laden air as it ascended towards the entrance to the Gandhi Memorial Hospital. Her labored breath was suspended in the shafts of sunlight, revealing her effort to confront the reality of Dr. Satara's appointment.

A large marble-top desk shielded the white-uniformed receptionists, each responding to a frenzy of questions.

A young man was standing behind the desk, glaring intensely at Mary. Her eyes found his, as if he had been watching her for hours. It seemed impossible that he would speak to her with all of the racket surrounding them. His shirt was unbuttoned; his sleeves were rolled up. His closely cut hair seemed wet, conforming to his head in some kind of *1920's* fashion.

"May I help you, Madam?" he asked, catching her off guard.

"Yes," she answered, in a low voice. But sensing her answer to be distant, she replied more forcefully: "Dr. Satara's office, please."

The young man turned to answer a question shouted out by one of his coworkers. He answered the question abruptly, as if he considered the interruption impolite. Then he turned back to Mary. "He is in emergency surgery, but you may wait in his office, on the second floor." He pointed left. "It's six doors down, on the right."

Mary turned, thanking him, while heading for the steps. As she moved an elderly woman with a hunched back was supported by the strong arms of a younger man—perhaps her son. The old woman's eyes penetrated Mary's eyes. The woman winced as she crossed the lobby; each step was more painful than the one before. Her eyes now closed tightly. Her movements were feeble. Mary looked at her again, remembering that kindness and sadness have but one face in any culture.

The stairs, bustling with humanity, seemed to have been brought to Mary's feet. She, again, noticed the women and her young son. The woman had picked him up and was carrying him. His face rested on his mother's shoulder.

His tired expression nestled comfortably into her sari. He looked directly at Mary as if to say, "I remember you." Then he smiled.

When Mary reached the last step to the second floor, the crowd dispersed. Some moved to the left—others to the right. The child and his mother turned, continuing to climb the steps. He cupped his little hand aside his face and waved goodbye. This time Mary mimicked *him*.

She followed the directions, counting each door, needing to know how many there were: o*ne... three... and finally she reached the sixth and* last one. It contained a frosted-glass window, fully illuminated from the light within, and looked as if it had been used in *The Maltese Falcon*. The hand painted calligraphy, on the door, presented the offices of, "Drs. Satara and Jaipore." She opened it and went inside.

A single figure, a frail older man, sat on a hard, wooden armchair in the corner of this modest waiting room. His hands rested in his lap. The jacket he was wearing was traditional for his culture, but he wore it open at the neck. His skin was soft and wrinkled—validating his years. His eyes were expressive and very aware–contradicting his slowed movements. A very large window, at his back, occupied most of the wall. The warm morning light fell directly onto his figure. He seemed to be part of a canvas, the light accentuating his image. He acknowledged Mary's entrance by nodding—then, returned slowly to his thoughts—as if to resume his place in the composition.

The silhouette of a nurse appeared on the glass door to the inner office. She stuck her head out from behind it just far enough to look at Mary and ask, "Dr. Satara or Dr. Jaipore?"

"Dr. Satara, please."

"He is in surgery. It was an emergency. He will be back directly."

"Thank you. Do you know how long?"

"I am sorry... I do not, but I can say that he has been there for some time now."

Mary said, "Thank you," once more and took a seat directly across from the frail man.

She began thinking of age and the older woman she had seen in the lobby. She thought of her own mother who had died alone, in a hospital room, halfway around the world, in Seattle. *No one knew she was ill until she was hospitalized.* I *was away with John somewhere, some unimportant somewhere—and was in*accessible *to my mother's own life. Aunt Catherine had tried, but couldn't reach me in time.*

She could still feel the guilt for not having been with her mother when she was so seriously ill. *But no one knew,* she continued to tell herself. *Still, that was no excuse.* And she thought of all of the conversations, all of the time they spent together, and all of the many questions she would never be able to ask—the things that would, now, *never be*—from her earliest mentor.

And the caring I witnessed just moments ago should have been me attending to my mother. But I did nothing, and so, she thought, *what you give is what you get. Is that it?* she asked herself. *Will I find out that I too have little time left? Is that it? Will I find that John will not be there for me? Will I, too, be alone, to experience what my mother had gone through... no one to hold her in those last days? Is that it? What selfish act had I been committing when my mother died?* The sadness of it all consumed her. *I deprived my mother, of just a few moments, of my own shallow life.*

She sat directly across from the old man she had seen in the waiting room—his posture one of age—his silence one of wisdom. He seemed to be the grandparent observing her as he waited—motionless.

The sun, now hot, poured through the window, casting the old man's shadow out onto the wood floor. He never lost patience—even as the hours passed and his outline grew shorter and shorter. The shape of his *being* ebbed, absorbing into his character. It was as if he were in a trance—and could manipulate "the magic of time." He remained silent—never once looking up.

The nurse reappeared at the door, and Mary felt sure it would be her turn. The nurse glanced at her, then turned to the old man and beckoned him into the inner office. He struggled to rise, supporting his weight on the arm of the chair. The nurse moved forward, reaching for his outstretched hand, and led him away. He nodded at Mary—closing his eyes, slowly. This was his way of saying good bye. The door closed behind them. No sounds were heard, as their figures moved off the glass—just an empty, illuminated rectangle remained.

Mary sank deeper into her chair—her hands clasped, her head splitting. Her eyes returned to the empty chair. The old man left no trace that he had ever *been*.

Her mind drifted home to Seattle... *a magical place to grow up as a young girl... Aunt Catherine and Uncle Paul cared for the family home, all these years, as if it had been their own... I could never sell it.*

Their exchange of letters became endless stories about the house, Mary's dog, Rusty, and the changes that the city of had made.

The waiting... and more waiting... is unbearable... *another ten minutes, then twenty, then thirty. How much time will be spent waiting for answers to these questions.* She was fearful of this meeting with the doctor—this "official representative" of her fate. She thought, again, about the old man leaving, nodding his head, and the little boy and his mother's love. Her insecurities caused her to look around the room for support, but her anxieties pushed her thoughts into places she did not want to go.

The inner office door flew open. Dr. Satara appeared, wearing the classic white full-length lab coat, repeating her name in his Indian accent. "Marrie... Maarrie, would you please come in? I am so sorry for keeping you so long a time. Please follow me."

His face was youthful. He was as tall as Mary. His features were soft, almost feminine, which were typical of many East Indian men. He walked through another room that seemed more like a lab than an office. He carried with him a stack of files as he, briskly, maneuvered around the many cabinets—through another door and into an office. It was a very small room with just enough space for a desk and two chairs. He rested his body against the side of the desk. Then he sat, as he opened the file with **Mary Templeton Powell,** hand-written across the cover.

He asked if she would mind sitting in the chair, just opposite. She balanced herself on the edge, and then leaned forward—placing her hands on the desk.

"I have received the results of our second tests with Dr. Jaipore," he said. "How do you feel?"

"I feel anxious... very anxious."

"I mean physically?"

"I need you to tell *me*. It has taken too long, to get to this moment. I just think... well it's been torture... to say the least."

"The results offer evidence that you have a serious, degenerative problem... "

"Is there surgery?" she interrupted.

"No, I'm afraid this condition requires a different path."

"What do you mean... different path?" She stopped him.

The doctor looked strained. He began again, his accent rolling in waves, almost song-like, as he fumbled through his attempt to explain. She had thrown him off-track. It was as if he were searching for the place where he had left off. "I would like you to see another doctor, preferably one in the United States, so the technology and the opportunity for the best possible medical care can be offered to you. I want you to go as quickly as possible."

She couldn't help thinking of the contrast between the *content* of his diagnosis and the lyrical *delivery* of it.

Mary, frantically, thought about going home—of more tests—of the horror of dealing with the questions he was not addressing—of not knowing anything for certain. For she was still waiting for answers yet to come, from this young doctor who continued to stammer poetically.

"Tell me *please*?" she demanded

But he offered only rhetoric in response. "Our cultures differ in many ways: Communicating this in any language is very difficult. These tests, along with those of the other doctors, all find... ," he paused then spoke tenderly. "The fact is that we are not able to treat this diagnosis, as well as the doctors in your country. You must present your condition to doctors in the United States. We can help... but not nearly as well as the facilities in your country."

Mary's mouth turned dry. "I don't understand!" Adrenaline shot through her body as she turned her head and looked away. She parted her parched lips. "Am I dying? What is it?"

Dr. Satara reached for her hand. His voice just audible:

"A pancreatic condition... possibly. We're not in agreement," he continued, in his diagnosis that was musical, seesawing in pitch: it was the East Indian sounding out another's tongue.

"The results are not conclusive, but I do suggest the beginning of a potentially irreversible condition. I don't know about *time*. Yes, it is serious. But death? I don't know. Please go home for assistance. The facilities here are inadequate for your condition. Go home. Take advantage of the technology there. They can help."

Mary sat there looking at him, her hand touching his. She felt linked to this "disciple of technology," who vaguely offered the answers she had obsessed over for this last week. He continued speaking—but she stopped listening when she heard one word: "husband." "You told me that your husband was away," Dr. Satara had said. "Would you like me to talk to him?" Jerking back—she took her hand away.

"No, don't you ever. I'll talk to him... don't ever," she said. She wanted to cry but couldn't. She thought his opinion was more than *vague*. It was frightening. It was just enough of,

"... we aren't sure" and too much of, "... you need help." It felt like, "... *go* away." *He was wrong,* she thought. *It is wrong. They must be wrong! I haven't been feeling well, but...*

"You're originally from Seattle, aren't you?" he asked, interrupting her thoughts. "I'll send your medical records there."

He wants to be rid of me, she thought. *Even in this, I'm rejected.* And Mary retreated into her own world, too emotional to speak out loud to him: *I got up this morning, just like all the rest of these wretched mornings in this place. I took a shower, brushed my hair, did a thousand things that each of us do every damn day.*

Then I was carried to this place by a tide of humanity... to you, the Doctor... to convey that I and no one else... that I am dying, or I'm not, or I might be. Oh my God, I have to do this all again. Will I be selected, out of that 'wave of humanity'... to be left behind... Is that it? Was it any

different for my child? No, he had no time either. He had no time for me to love him. I just... I can't... I don't know what to do. Do I just get up and leave?

Mary groped for stability—something—anything—that would help her through these next moments. *It's impossible that there could be a someone. John doesn't exist.* Dr. Satara took her arm and began to walk her out of his office. He would offer her anything to finish this appointment. He was lost. He knew he was wrong to feel this way. He cared for her medically—but could not find the discourse. It was more than he knew how to deal with.

"A car to take you home?" he asked as he summoned the nurse and told her to make the car available immediately. "Are there others in your family who could help?"

But Mary found only anger now, fueled by her fears and anxiety. She needed his understanding, but all she could hear was her medical chart speaking to her. She cleared her voice, preparing to sarcastically respond to him—as if to punish him for treating her this way.

"There is no one who can help me, Doctor? So who shares my fear, the anguish, the anxiety... this ambiguity that you offer as your science? You're asking too much, to say that I must cope with 'maybe' and 'might' until I do this all over again in Seattle.

"You're rid of me... my life... with a handful of postage stamps. Whom can I turn to for support? Is the old man, whose appointment preceded mine, the answer... whom I shall never see again! What about you... your science... my husband... I know... my parents!"

Helpless, he answered, "If your parents can help, that's wonderful."

"They're dead," she said.

Mary reached inside herself... *I need time to sort it out... sort it out slowly... sort it out.*

"Somehow, I just can't say 'thank you,'" she told the doctor. "I hope you understand."

Dr. Satara clasped her arm firmly and guided her down the stairs to the lobby. Though he continued to speak, she stopped listening to his "melodious narrative." She began visually consuming the people: their expressions, the textures, and the light, everything that was squeezed into their shared space. Each element was evaluated, becoming a candidate for a new painting.

Mary was hiding again, in a place in her mind that she created. No one else was welcome. *Were there those who were missing? Was this image, that she was living, complete? Did it need the emotions that the old man in the office evoked, on the faces of all who saw him? What did she want to say? How would she say it?*

The space, she drifted through, became the movement of her hand, holding the artist's brush. The lobby, the walls, the windows were the edges of this canvas. Time became a few seconds frozen—with one face expressing the pain of so many. Mary was now in control. These facial expressions were the *subjects* of her creation. (The lobby doors had remained open, allowing a means of escape from Dr. Satara's science, a world she chose not to accept.)

Now, outside in the heat, she thought about the fragrance of warmed oils filling another canvas with the brush strokes of a thousand synapses, bursting. Each stroke summoned forth the intensity of her emotions. *But would any other person understand? Have I conveyed these moments as best I could? Is this the agony? Was there ever ecstasy? Did it matter?* (She explored these answers, from her world within, and felt protected by it.) Then, she questioned, *would there be another barren canvas? Would it matter?*

Eventually she had to emerge from these creative lapses if only to glean material to bring back for interpretation—then she would choose a medium for expressing herself—by brush, by tool, or by pen.

For Mary, her work exposed her innermost feelings. It was as if for each piece, she were mandated to present her art for evaluation: Mary, the artist, was presenting her confessions to those strangers who knew nothing of her. Those strangers that came to *see* then stood gaping at her naked expression.

In her mind, Mary could see them as she stood within the walls of her imagined art gallery. These were the walls that supported her work. She visualized these strangers, looking through her framed compositions as if they were made of glass.

They witnessed, first hand, their shallow assessments and clung to each other for support. There was a nod by one, "I like it," by another, and a sigh of indifference by still another as they walked past the paintings representing her life. Those who judged her *looked*, but they didn't *see*... they didn't *recognize*. They lived for this moment. And she realized that she was being judged by the "visually dead" but "financially powerful"—in the very same way that John had judged her.

She wondered why she had continued to make this futile attempt to communicate her need for passion for so many years, especially to the chairman of their committee: John Carter Powell. She had married him then dedicated her life to the hope that he might touch her, emotionally, as she had never been touched before. *But what a fool I was. I was an incurable romantic, clinging to an expectation that I would never realize.* They arrived at the doctor's car. He opened the door: Without saying good-by, she got in and stared, directly, forward. She barely noticed as the doctor said his goodbyes, giving her address to the driver. Instead, she thought of John:

There were times I made no sense to him. My "antics," he calls them, "are unlike any he knew," but because of my recognition at the Seattle Gallery, it was acceptable behavior. I was an acquisition—assisting him in his world as part of an illusion... an image... not created by strokes of a brush... but by the essence of power.

I showed promise as an artist but had nothing to do with his world of business associates and his family. "Who was she?" They would ask before John and Mary had married... "The Templetons? Are they the Canadian Templetons?" I must say, John is their match; he plays a game and reduces lives into an elixir then consumes them as a toast to victory. He is maniacal.

It was so easy to walk away from him, but it hurt, so much, to leave the promises I made to myself. I feel as if I have failed as a wife... and even more so as a mother.

And what will I do with another unfinished canvas? Paint over it? Is there enough time? Throw it away? I couldn't. What a waste of paint... of myself!

The car pulled up to Mary's building, and she got out, not saying a word. She entered the lobby and walked past the doorman, who smiled, offering "A very nice morning, yes?" She couldn't answer.

Gitry, Mary's housekeeper, greeted her at the door. Mary went directly to the phone, asking Gitry to get her bags down from the closet.

"Will you be away for some time?"

"Yes, I think so." Mary replied, dialing her friend, Manisha, who worked for one of the Indian government officials. She had always arranged everything for them. If anyone could reserve a seat on the next flight out of Calcutta it was she.

Manisha and Mary had shared many things together. They had met in the maternity ward at the hospital. Manisha had given birth to her second child, a wonderful healthy little girl—that she had named Rose. And now, Mary thought about her child—that she had named Paul. But he was dead—though she had wanted this child to love forever. It was her tragedy alone.

John sent his flowers and "took care of the details." But Mary had been hurt, even further, by John's deliberate absence at his son's interment. Manisha and her husband, Upen, had attended—as well as the two Indian grave diggers. Mary had taken a small Bible to read from. She tried several times to start—but couldn't. Upen reached for the Bible as Manisha held Mary. He read so tenderly. The two grave diggers offered their compassion, as they placed their shovels down and walked away. As far as she knew, John had never been to the graveyard. He never spoke to her about it—never said, "I'm sorry." There was nothing—just that phone call.

His words, "chin up" and "it's most likely for the best," would remain in her memory forever.

A woman answered the phone at the Minister of Commerce's office "Can I help you?"

"Yes, this is Mary Templeton calling for Manisha Saha." Mary waited a moment.

Manisha picked up her phone and asked, "How are you? How nice of you to call. Are we getting together? Upen is working late tonight"

"Well, I need a small favor," Mary said. "I would love to see you, but I have an emergency and need to fly home on the very next flight to Seattle. Can you help?"

"Of course. Did you say the next flight, though? You must mean *available* flight, at this time of year."

"Yes."

"But you said 'emergency.' Are your Aunt and Uncle all right?"

"They're fine. I... well, I just returned from Dr. Satara's office, and he said I should return to the States and have a physical and tests for some of his concerns."

"Is it something bad?"

"No, I want to be comfortable about it, though, so I'm going to do it. I've needed to get back to Seattle for more than a while."

Manisha, knowing her well, sensed her concern and decided to let the subject rest for the moment.

"I'll get back to you in a few minutes."

"Thank you," said Mary. She hung up and sat on the edge of her bed for a short time. Mary began selecting things from her dresser and closets, making a neat pile on her bed.

Gitry carried in two large bags, placed them on the bed, and began filling them. A moment later, the phone rang. Gitry answered it.

"It was a Mrs. Ames," she reported. Mary asked that she tell her that she was indisposed and would return her call later. A few moments later, there was another call. "It is Manisha," Gitry said.

Mary raced to the receiver.

"Hi... I spoke to my friend here, and she helped in taking care of your request," Manisha told her. "Tell me if this is all right. There is nothing today, but tomorrow, December 31, there is a flight at twelve noon out of Calcutta to Bombay, then to London. There is nothing to Hong Kong for two days except standby. If you leave tomorrow, you will spend the birth of the new Millennium in the air. What fun!"

"Book it, please. Flying West is just as hard as East. Besides, I must leave as soon as possible."

"Are you OK?"

"Yes, I'm fine," she lied. "But don't tell Upen... because I am not telling my husband."

"You mean... you're finally leaving John?"

"In a word... yes."

"I am sorry. Do you want to talk about it?"

"You mean more than we have? He is not worth dealing with any longer. He's in London. I plan on calling him there."

"You and Upen have been so good to me. How are Rose and her brother, Jiral?"

"She is beautiful. And he is very excited, awaiting his fifth birthday. We went to see Paul, Mary. The grave is very neat as always. I felt as if we must have just missed you."

Mary's eyes welled up. "Manisha, I can come to see you."

"Thank You."

"I should have come to see you to get the tickets. That's how little time I have. Thank you for being my friend. Can you stop by the cemetery, now and then, to see Paul?"

"Of course I will. I'm here for you. In the meantime, I'll take care of 'the bureaucrats.' How should I pay for the ticket?"

"John's American Express should make the ticket payment easy, and thank you, Manisha, for caring about Paul."

"Oh Mary stop. Give me the account number, and I'll make arrangements for you to *confirm* in London. As far as that leg of the trip, there's no change in planes, and you'll be arriving in London around 11:00 p.m., in time for New Year's Eve. How exciting! Are you sure you're OK?"

"I'm fine... just fine. I need to run as fast as I can away from him. It's over. I don't have a schedule to give you. I just need to go now. We will talk, Manisha."

"I don't know how you have managed through this time. Upen never understood John not coming to see you at the hospital, Manisha added. I will always hate him for that."

"Well, making me an "Aunt Mary" was the greatest honor I have ever had... that and you, Manisha. You and Upen... and Jiral... and my sweet Rose, have been the family I have always wanted... I am going to send Gitry over to your home with boxes of charcoals, along with all kinds of colors for Jiral to begin his art training, I'll send pads as well... lots of stuff."

"I want to thank you... "

Mary smiled, "Let the children start now. They are so free, so full of expression."

She reached into her desk drawer and pulled out a credit card, read out the numbers, and slipped it into her purse. "Thank you, Manisha. Please say nothing. Be happy. I'll miss you... I'll call."

"I'm not saying a word, Manisha assured her. If you have any problems with the ticket agent, call me directly. Or if customs gives you a problem, tell them you are calling Mr. Patel's office. They won't know that it's me you will be talking to. I'll send the tickets by messenger tonight, but get to the airport with extra time for customs. We will miss you. We love you," she sniffled then excitedly asked, "Mary, where are you going to be? I almost forgot."

"At my home in Seattle." And Mary gave her the telephone numbers for her home and for Aunt Catherine's.

"Don't worry. We will take flowers to the cemetery... for Paul."

Mary said goodbye with tears clinging to her cheeks. "I love you." Then she placed the receiver in the cradle and turned to Gitry, wiping her eyes with a tissue.

"I'd like to show you the canvasses I'd like crated. Please ship them to this address," she continued, handing her a slip of paper. "See if you and your brothers can ship them no later than Monday of next week."

Gitry stared at her for a long moment—as if she knew that she would never see her again. Mary looked back at her and Gitry gave her a warm nod. A look of understanding passed between them as they walked together into a room that she used as a studio.

Mary placed aside three very large pads and many boxes of charcoals. "These are for Jiral and Rose. They will love them." Mary then walked to the corner of the room, picking up a canvas approximately two feet square. It was a painting of two children. Their faces filled the canvas—a little girl and an older boy. The little girl's face nestled under his chin. Their eyes expressed an excitement that Mary had captured months before her tragedy.

Gitry said, "I love that so much: Your nephew Jiral and niece Rose. It is so lovely—her eyes and his smile! What beautiful children."

Mary held it a bit higher. "I was saving it for Manisha's birthday, but would you mind wrapping this for me, Gitry, and taking it along with the other things?"

"Of course," Gitry had answered. "I would be so happy to see her face when she opens it but... one thing?"

"What's that?"

"I mean no offense... but it is unsigned."

"Oh, thank you, Gitry. I'm so glad you noticed."

Mary immediately reached for the appropriate brush and oils. She placed it on her easel. "How does 'Aunt Mary' sound as a signature, Gitry?"

"I don't know what else should be there," she answered.

"Done, thank you again. Wait a few days before you make the delivery. Let the oils dry... OK?"

"Yes, Mary."

"And bill all of the shipping to John's company. Do not tell Mr. Powell you are doing this. It's a lady's little secret."

"Oh, yes, Mary, I understand," Gitry said, smiling.

"A messenger is delivering my tickets tonight. Please make sure I get them."

Gitry assured her she would, and Mary went back to packing all the possessions she felt were worth taking with her on this journey.

She wasn't surprised at how little there was—as she closed her suitcase, ending this part of her life. She suddenly became excited. *A trip home... and an extemporaneous one, at the very least,* she thought. And she felt like a child, remembering the excitement of a journey, needing to forget for just a moment—everything.

That afternoon passed quickly. After a light dinner, she returned the call to Mrs. Ames, accepting her invitation to tea, next week. "Won't it be wonderful to see each other again?" Mrs. Ames had asked. Mary was more than aware of the gossip that Mrs. Ames "thrived on." Her network could communicate faster than a FedEx package. John would know she was leaving before she got to the airport. It was a quiet evening. The sounds of the streets seemed abandoned compared to their usual clamor.

When morning came, she awakened at the same time as always—her own sense of time, kept well inside of her. Throwing the sheets aside, she felt the excitement for the long journey she would make this last day of the century.

Chapter Two

Mary reached for the envelope on the hall table, checking that all of the tickets were there. The doorman carried her bags to the car. She handed Gitry another envelope with her month's wages and a generous gratuity.

"Don't forget to pack the canvases well, and give Jiral and Rose a hug," Mary said.

"I'll miss you," Gitry said as they exchanged a last, warm embrace.

At the airport, Mary checked her bags and went through customs effortlessly. She waited for her flight in the Ambassador Lounge and took a seat immediately next to the door, thinking it would be convenient. Seasoned travelers packed the room, staring into their laptops and their many international papers. She quickly withdrew into her own thoughts until a waiter approached. She asked for a cup of tea. (As he walked away, she couldn't help thinking that his suit needed some help from the cleaners.)

Her thoughts drifted back to Seattle once more—and her childhood there. She recalled all of her memories in detail: She pictured her cat's ribbon, with a tiny bell, around her neck. Her cat, Lilly, had died many years ago; she had lived a long time, growing up with Mary from grade school to college. When she married, she left the cat with her mother. Mary always wondered if Lilly missed her when she left to live another part of her life that did not include her. When Mary would return, on the few occasions, Lilly would come to her as she always had, as if to ask where she had been for so long. Mary would pet her and Lilly would purr, questioning, "where did you go?" Mary would talk to her.

One of Aunt Catherine's letters was all she had that told her of the cats being gone. Once again—she wasn't there.

"Your tea, madam."

"Thank you... "

Agnes Templeton was her mother, and Ralph, her father. Now they were both gone, and Mary was always away—too far away from them.

Her father, so young, left her with such strong memories of his presence. A man she never really understood. He was very creative, always striving for perfection in all his work.

He was successful and respected, yet distant. He was warm. He was giving. He loved her, held her, hugged her, and said profound things to her. But she didn't know who he was.

She remembered him taking her to his studio so many times as a child. The place was vast with "toys" as he called them.

But these toys were his equipment that he used as a film director and producer. He spent endless hours on production. His creations were thirty seconds of time. They were commercials for the largest advertisers in the country.

His work was also the subject she hated most, since it seemed to incite many arguments between her parents. She and her mother rarely saw him in daylight hours. But he had been a kind man, driven by his compulsive personality to achieve the many goals he was always reaching for.

Every time he attained one, he would say, "It's hard to recognize the accomplishment." And then he would redefine the next challenge.

Mary was *sure* she had become him in many ways. It was just so hard to see the reflection in the mirror she was now using. Now she had become this woman on the edge of the question of mind and body—of science and emotion. Her very *existence* is the question.

Suppose I get rid of the weight of all these years of painful decisions, and go home... home to a new life, another goal. What might happen then? I must find out for sure. First, there will be more tests... more questions... more people poking at my body and telling me they must scan this, and I must drink that.

But I'll do it to prove you are wrong, Dr. Satara.

"Madam, would you like more tea?"

"No, thank you." *What a wrinkled suit,* she thought.

Mom, where are you? I need you. You drilled me into submission in so many ways: about how to feel, what to do, but not 'this.' We never talked about this. Or maybe we did. Maybe it was locked up in the story about Aunt Florence when she died. We talked for hours about who she was and how she meant so much to you. But is 'this' what I need, to unravel the thinking that hurts me now? Maybe the secret is how I feel about your death and your life. Is that it, mom? That's it. That's it. It's about you and how I feel about my not being able to see you... to talk to you... It's how you left me.

Mary's eyes welled up, and the waiter returned. "Do you need some assistance, Madam?"

"No, I'm sorry. I'm fine. Check, please."

He left it beside her empty teacup. Mary removed some money from her purse and left it on the table. *I wasn't there to hold your hand, mom,* she remembered once more. *You left this earth with no one... not even the cat... no one. I feel so guilty. I feel so sad, so useless. You are gone. I just... what might you have been thinking those last months? You told no one. You asked for nothing. You didn't tell me. And so, I'm doing the same thing, rushing home to... to tell no one... to find out these doctors are wrong. Yes, they're wrong. I'm fine... just fine. Mom. I'm sorry. I'm going to the cemetery to visit you soon. I'm going home to you and dad. That's where I belong now. I wrote you something... I'm coming home.*

Her thoughts were interrupted by a voice, over the PA system, announcing that her flight would be boarding for Bombay and then on to London. The waiter was standing at the far corner of the room; he stared at her as she collected her things.

The plane raced down the runway rushing past the terminal, taking to the air as if it were escaping from Calcutta. A great groan came from the undercarriage as the wheels folded into the belly of the plane. They climbed quickly, as though being chased.

The engines strained with a high-pitched scream, and sirens announced to clear their path. The streets—then buildings became obscured by wisps of clouds.

Then the clouds dissolved into a white canopy that shrouded Mary's exodus. She thought about Paul—and apologized for leaving him. She thought about John—and wanted to go faster. The winds that she had spoken of, that evening had finally revealed this date along with that single word scrawled across the page—*enough*.

The plane had leveled off as Mary began observing her fellow passengers, nestling into the trance that all travelers seek—a place in their mind that consumes time. Thoughts vacillate between the past and the future, none of which touch on the reality of the many hours in the plane.

It's a perfect place to relive any experience. Occasionally a cough or a sneeze, rallies to be heard, but the interruption doesn't shake the passengers' minds back to the boredom of the flight.

The landing in Bombay filled the cabin with activity, shaking all the passengers from their cerebral comfort. A few disembarked. Some got up to stretch. Others stayed cemented in their seats, demonstrating their commitment to get on with it—to—to the new Millennium.

Mary slept, losing track of time. The windows had been darkened by the night for some time when a voice on the PA system awakened her.

"Good evening, ladies and gentlemen! This is your captain speaking... Happy New Year! We would like to invite you to our pre-New Year's Eve party on board this evening, with complimentary champagne since we will be a little early for our scheduled landing and a little more than an hour before the official twelve midnight. I will be turning the seatbelt light off, so you may feel free to move around the cabin on this very special evening, the birth of a new century. Again, on behalf of Air India and the crew... Happy New Year!"

The sounds of the announcement-chime punctuated his greeting.

Mary's eyes peered over the edge of the seat in front of her. Craning her neck, she sees one, two, three, even a dozen people who seem to be on the same page of time—each reviewing their past differently—each voice contributing to a choir of emotions, celebrating the end of another year of life.

Time is spent by each of us, and in our own way, she thought. *It is a store of seconds The gift of life is offered to each of us, to spend freely, without thought for the finite quantity remaining. In our youth, we immerse our hands into its reservoirs, allowing it to effervesce between our fingers so smoothly, touching our hearts and our minds as our day to day unfolds. Hands push us ahead, advancing our lives.*

Mary turned her head quickly and looked out the window.

*This is too profound... not necessary. It should be so much simpler... my life... who I am... the me of me... I'm just looking at where I have been and where I can be in just a few short months... but wait... it's not as simple as it was. It **could** be that I'll be... no more... that I won't exist. I may be dead. But this is a dream, a very bad dream... wake up... wake up... wake up!* She reached for a tissue and held it to her moist eyes.

It's not a dream. It's real. I'm so alone... just as my mother was.

A flight attendant made her way down the aisle, offering champagne to the passengers. (It was Mary's 39th New Year's Eve.) Mary decided to wait. "A little later, thank you."

Mom, I loved you so much... but not enough. I felt too much... or did I? I'm so confused. Who am I, this person now holding an hourglass? The grains are escaping; there's no way to slow their decent—no way to turn them all around. These grains... what shall I do with them? Each one is a second—a possession to be spent slowly. These grains do not flow over my cupped hands but are now to be spent one at a time. But this is too much for me to hold in my own mind. I wanted to share all, no give all of who I was to John, but nothing came of it. I so wanted to be that person.

The tears fell quietly from her face onto her hands, now folded in her lap. A well-dressed man rose from his seat, a few rows ahead. He walked down the aisle, carrying two coffee cups, looking directly at Mary.

She quickly blotted her tears, thinking he was definitely walking towards her.

"Excuse me," he said, his warm face leaning over hers. "Happy New Year and Happy Millennium. May I offer you a cup of champagne? It seems they forgot the glasses. Well I'm glad I brought *two* cups. I see they missed you. That's not very nice."

Michael Bowland had flown around the world so many times he could get free tickets anywhere first class, for the first decade, of the Millennium, compliments of any global airline. Michael was quiet—except when he didn't want to be.

He would think deeply but liked to laugh. He was well-dressed, except when he didn't care to be. He was amused half the time and amusing all the time—with anyone, anywhere. He could make you laugh and more important, he would laugh with you.

He was a gentleman in his fifties, handsome with graying hair. He was wealthy but would never flaunt it. He was, at the very least charismatic, from a distance an executive, up close a friend.

He very rarely associated with anyone on flights, but this was an occasion that was unusual. He had observed a woman that was exceptional. Her black hair was soft; her features were even better close up. She was impeccably dressed and just gorgeous. Their flight was unique compared to any other New Year's Eve for the next 9999 years.

This was an opportunity he didn't want to let pass. So asking her to have a cup of champagne with him was a question worth asking, even if it were answered with a "no."

"Yes, I... well yes thank you," Mary said. "I'm sorry. I'm just... "

"No need to explain. It's the magic of a good time... to place a tear in your hand. Just don't fill them up!"

Mary felt like a little girl again, as he patted her hands with his napkin. She felt his sincerity and allowed him to help her.

"Would you like to sit down for a while?" she asked.

"Thank you," he said. "My name is Michael Bowland. May I ask yours?"

"Mary... Mary Templeton."

"Your name, your inflection, suggests you live in the middle to West Coast of our country," he said, whimsically, but with an air of confidence.

"Close," she said, clearing her throat and wiping a tear, trying to compose herself. "Two more guesses."

Mary thought that he was an attractive man. He seemed so warm. And it was as if he really wanted to share the occasion with someone. She sensed his gentleness. She was curious.

"Muncie, Indiana. That's it."

"Nooo," she said, laughing, with a little sniffle.

"Hmmm, well, I'm going to get serious here. Wait... yes, I'm sure now. Seattle. How did I do?"

"What street?" asked Mary, and happy for the diversion.

He leaned toward her. "I couldn't read that part on the flight attendant's roster. I didn't have my glasses on."

"Are you with the CIA, the FBI, or the KGB?"

"I'm with the MOB... My Own Business. I travel a lot, building things."

"Are you off to build something in London?"

"Well, no. I'm in between jobs, if you will. I have a few meetings in the states coming up. It seemed efficient to travel now. Since I'm alone, it really doesn't matter. Besides, it's a great time to fly, a wonderful way to spend the only holiday that's pinned to a specific number... *twelve:* 'The Easter Bunny hides his eggs any old time. Santa comes while we're sleeping. The 4th of July is an all-day picnic. Rosh Hashanah is at sundown. But New Year's Eve is *12:00 midnight...* the one moment when the seconds, minutes, and hours hold hands. There are more to come."

She observed his motions. He was confidently animated, a bit silly, but humor was welcome. "A good laugh could cure so many things," Aunt Catherine would say. She sipped her champagne. "Do you *like* that kind of exactness?" she asked him.

"Not really... no. I'm trying to be interesting," he said. "But it's not working is it? We could talk about the subject of art, he said. How do you feel about the Dutch school for the chiaroscuro of light... compared to the Impressionists?"

"You're very funny... at least, for my sense of humor."

He leaned towards her, whispering. "It's a good place to hide."

"Yes, Michael. We all find places to store our emotions. Our thoughts can be very complicated."

The plane shuttered and the pitch of the engines whining could be heard well over their conversation. Mary's mind returned to her sad thoughts of the minutes before, and her facial expression changed. Her smile disappeared.

Michael turned just at that moment, away from her, missing it, as a passenger brushed by his shoulder. Then he faced Mary, as he answered. "Yes, we do. But that's why there are attics, so we don't have to carry all that weight when we travel. The ole steamer trunk is full of 'on-hold emotions.'"

"Hmm, on hold," she said. "I'd need a switchboard."

"You just need an old trunk," he suggested to her.

She liked that. "On hold... in a trunk," she repeated. "OK!"

"In a sense, we let those moments in our lives remain motionless... dormant... until we climb the attic steps and pull the light chain that sends the bulb shaking back and forth, casting a thousand shadows throughout space, as the bulb swings side to side," he said, growing animated. And he continued:

"Emotions are suspended within the closed trunk, as they endure the cold of winter, the sweltering heat of summer, and the realities of our past, waiting for the key to unlock the memory of who we are. It's like the lyric, 'While We're Out a Makin' More.'

"Then in a brief moment we place more inside the trunk, close it, and turn off the light, not to return until a distant tomorrow."

"Where does this come from? Mary asked. That was very nice," and teasing him, she added, "but you forgot the cobwebs, and dust-laden surfaces... untouched by time."

Suddenly she grew sad again. "And I don't like *time*," she told him, turning away. "I just don't."

The flight attendant stopped by and offered the last of the champagne to them. They raised their cups, brushing against each other slightly.

"Your attic is in New York?" Mary asked.

"Yes."

"So then, you're flying there tonight?"

"No, I'm off to distant lands once again. My tickets and I don't always agree. The destinations are very adjustable because of my business." Michael feigned seriousness, raising his hands and touching his temples with his fingers. "I've got a message coming in from my 'sensitivity center.'"

"From *where*?" she laughed.

He paused. "I have a *thought*... just a pleasant thought...How about spending the next five years with me? It's a small offering of a celebration about tonight; five years all in one night. Well that and ushering in an entirely new century. When it's done, we will no longer be strangers but old friends... in a new Millennium."

And Michael explained, "We're flying to the West, and it is New Year's Eve. These two ingredients allow us to chase time zones and celebrate a minimum of five or six years all in one night."

She leaned her head back, her eyes never losing contact with his. "Talk about commitment," she said. "We just met... and judging from your twelve o'clock... just minutes ago. And now... five years?" She stopped, for a moment, to think it over.

"Yes! I like it," she added. How do we do that... since I'm guessing that it's some fiendish plot from M.O.B. Inc.

"And more important I don't age, do I?"

"Not one hair," he said. "I promise."

His expression saddened. "I wanted so much to do this once before on a simple New Year's Eve, but it didn't happen."

"What?" she asked.

"I've wanted to chase time *this way*," he answered, quickly. "Technically, there are five or six New Year's Eves between here and Seattle, depending on air speed. But emotionally there are as many as you would like to recognize if you simply turn back your watch an hour at each 12 o'clock. Or if you have a bezel like mine, you just rotate it, celebrating every hour. Each setting offers another year, giving us time."

Time... extra time, she thought.

Michael continued: "All in one night, for the rest of this evening, we can accumulate years of excitement in just a few well-spent hours. And by the time we have ushered in the Millennium... five times... I'm sure we will have gotten it right. Are you interested? It's going to happen anyway. And our assignment, should you choose to accept it, is to... capture it... hold it... enjoy it. And the greatest part is that the minute you get home, you can put it in the trunk."

"Can I wait a while before I do that?" she asked.

"As long as you like."

She smiled and added, "I was *going* to read my book."

Well I hope it's about some terrific guy who meets a wonderful woman on flight. It's New Year's Eve 1999, and they fly to Seattle, celebrating many years together... launching a new Millennium"

"That's it!" she said. You've read it?"

"No. I saw the play."

Mary took her book and slipped it into her flight bag. (He smiled as if to say thank you.) "Why not!" she said. "What's your next carrier?"

"Well, let me do a little math and get my tickets. I'll be right back, OK?" And he placed his hand on the seat in front of him without getting up, as if waiting for her permission.

"I'd like that," she said.

Michael smiled and then returned to his seat. Mary returned to her thoughts: *Five years more... who is this man who's giving me such a precious gift... unknowingly. He's offering me a state of mind that feels so comfortable. I like it. He touches my feelings.*

The plane's wheels screeched, as they touched the runway in London. It had begun to rain.

Chapter Three

While Michael went to arrange their flights together, Mary walked towards a bank of telephones. She sat staring out at the storm that had grown more intense since their landing. The heavy rain pelted the very large windows. The flashes of lightning and crackling thunder seemed appropriate for the conversation she knew she had to have with John. For it was senseless to continue to be miserable. The obstacles that stood between them were impossible to push aside. Paul's death had polarized their relationship completely, and the only way to convey to him, her decision to leave, was to use his style of frankness.

She rose from her seat and walked to the phone. She lifted the receiver and placed her coins on the metal shelf. Reluctantly, she picked up one of them and dropped it into the slot. "May I help you?" an operator asked. She searched for courage. "Operator, I'd like to call the Hyatt Hotel here in London, please."

"Just a moment, please," the voice at the other end answered. "That number is 99-58769."

Mary placed another coin in the slot then pressed out the number. She heard a ring... then, "Hyatt London. May we be of service?"

"Mr. John Powell's room, please," she said.

"Thank you," said the clerk.

There was a slight pause. "I'm sorry Madam. He is not in his room currently. But could you hold for one moment?"

"Yes," she answered, in a distant voice.

"I'm connecting you with the concierge."

"This is the concierge's desk. Mr. Parker speaking. May I be of service?"

"Yes, this is Mrs. Powell."

"Yes, Mrs. Powell. Mr. Powell left word to forward his calls to the Oak Room. Hold on, please."

She had thought out this conversation a thousand times, and now it is about to be delivered in just a few minutes.

A man's voice answered. "Oak Room."

"Mr. Powell, please."

"Just one moment... I'll page him."

Each connection became impossible to bear, as the anxiety of her thoughts intensified. *Everything about him was distant, even this call. How much longer would it take? He was impossible to reach.* But in a few minutes, a part of her... a very hurting part of her... would jet away. *It had to happen.*

"John Powell speaking."

She could hear a party, an "English" party—so level, so controlled. There were others, like him, feeding on each other, slowly exhausting their use of one another. It was "the business of business."

"John Powell," he said again, his voice growing deeper, wanting to intimidate the caller.

His voice, arrogantly, insisted on a response.

"Hello, hello... John Powell here."

"It's Mary."

"Well, what a surprise," he said. "You're up very early, aren't you? It looks like I'll be through by Monday, next. Wonderful thought, to be getting back. Just leave the car at the airport."

She could hear laughter coming through the other end of the phone; the airport's sounds filled the void at her end.

"Mary, are you there?"

She heard the rain striking at the window. "I'm in London," she said through a clap of thunder.

"What? Couldn't hear you. London, you say?" He was shouting. "Where?"

"Heathrow."

"I'd send a car," he said, speaking loudly and deliberately, "but it would seem easier for you to hire one there." She could feel his cunning mind assessing the reason for her call.

"You should be here just after midnight," he said. "What a wonderful surprise to see you tonight."

She could wait no longer. "No, I'm not here to see you at all, John," she said.

His response now became razor sharp. "Then, what do you mean? This isn't going to be one of Mary's elusive moods is it?" She could see his lips snarling, his face pushing into the phone, muffling his words so others would not see the real John.

"I really don't need that feminine attitude you seem so fond of: 'The *90's* woman held in bondage.' What is it you *say*, 'suffocated?' Not that crap now, especially in the middle of New Year's Eve. Darling, come and join the festivities rather than lamenting some hysterical feminine condition. This is a very important evening. The Marshals are here. Mary, you're going to have to deal with it. Be a big girl and give this crap a rest."

"Hold on!" He put his hand over the phone to say hello to someone passing by. She could hear his muffled greeting. "Good evening. Happy New Year! So good to see you. I'll just be a moment."

She heard his hand move off the receiver as the muffled sounds of the party returned.

"Why are you here in London, then, if not to see me?" He questioned.

"That's it, John. I'm *not* here to see you at all... ever," she said, emphatically. "I'm going home, John."

"To Seattle?" he interrupted, hatefully. "Well, it's not to see Mommy, is it then?"

She began crying softly but held her voice steady. "You hateful person. You poor, poor man. I'm going to Seattle to my home, John. My home."

"I'm not so poor, Mary," he answered loudly.

"I'd say a penny for that thought... for that's your 'net worth'... emotionally. I'm going home, John, to where I come from, to find out who I am... to my place, not yours, John. I'm officially giving notice. I quit. I am no longer a part of your shallow life, no longer an icon, the wife, the 'whatever you think I am,' the 'whatever you think you own.' I'm through. You're the only cold-blooded 'nothing' in my life.

"I don't understand myself for thinking I could make 'us' happen, for sharing anything with you, nothing! It's been my mistake, but not anymore. I'm leaving you and Calcutta... specifically, you. You are worth nothing to me. You are disposable refuse. You see yourself in meetings around the world, in great places. I see you in garbage dumps."

"Garbage dumps?" Mary you've crossed your little artist's line. I can't believe this. Have you seen a doctor... a psychiatrist? Stay in London, and I'll arrange something for you. Get a grip, woman. Leaving me... why?"

"I'm not leaving now, as much as... "

"What?"

She raised her voice over the noise of the storm. "As much as letting you know that we deserted each other's feelings many years ago. It's something that should have been mended, somehow, *then,* but wasn't. It was left unattended to for too long and there was a chasm created by the two of us, driving us further apart. Time. Precious time has been wasted. You're married to your real love... your business. We failed. I failed."

She was crying louder now. "I just can't invest in this misery any longer. I've got to go." Her tone grew cold. "Goodbye."

"Mary, don't hang up," John commanded.

"Why, John? Is it inconvenient for you? It's not in 'the plan?' It's too much of a surprise that I am miserable? You don't care about me as much as how it works into the bigger picture. You'll create a reason for my absence. You can say, 'She needed psychiatric help. I tried to help her but... ' Well, maybe, emotionally. This psychiatric help I need can be translated into a need to be loved. And clearly now, John, a thaw from your ice age will never happen for you. That is impossible. That is why we as 'we' cannot exist... anymore."

"I'm... I just... " he interrupted.

"You're less than I need. You're just nothing, John. I am so sorry. But it's over. Maybe if I were one of your projects, you would begin to understand. Even then, you would have to be giving, John, *giving*... something you cannot do. Paul and I needed you, John, but you never came to say goodbye to your only son. We hate you for that. While there is a breath in me, I must say goodbye. There's not enough time to repair the hurt you've caused me... just not enough time."

She depressed the button, on the receiver... then lifted her finger. The operator's voice returned.

"That's nine pounds, Madam."

Mary placed the coins into the slot; her head bent downward, one at a time. The tears fell from her cheeks as she dropped in the coins, placing each one so deliberately as if to pay for the sin she had just committed. When she deposited the last coin, she placed the receiver back into the cradle feeling emotionally ripped in pieces. She had just done the impossible. She had freed herself and lightened the baggage that had remained in the "attic trunk" for too long. *Where am I now?* She wondered. I am still miserable, but I am free to reach for my own life.

Michael moved away from the counter. He was excited. It was New Year's Eve, and he had met an interesting woman. Now this rare combination of events was allowing him to fulfill a dream. But before tonight, this dream had only been a nebulous *something* that he thought would never happen, after his wife's death.

His wife and daughter were both gone. They had been taken so quickly, in their innocence, by an automobile accident. They were so young. They had so much to give. In a way, it made no sense that they were not with him, especially tonight. He missed them so. *Was this right, to share this time with Mary?* He wondered. *But how could it be wrong? It was so long ago that we talked of doing this very same thing... chasing time on New Year's Eve. Now I have a chance to watch it work... to live the might-have-been... to break away from the past.* He was determined. He wanted it to happen and tonight would be the beginning of a new century. Perhaps this was the perfect place to start. There was no stopping it.

The airport was crowded and very loud. People were moving in all directions. A voice blared continuously over the PA system, making one announcement after the next. Michael saw Mary standing near the telephones and waved to get her attention. She didn't acknowledge him. He walked closer, calling out her name as he approached. Still, she didn't respond.

"Mary!" he said, walking directly in front of her. "Mary!"

She looked up.

"It's done," he said.

"Yes, it is," she answered, catching herself. "Was it difficult to change?"

She sniffed, trying desperately to compose herself and to avoid any mention of her previous conversation.

"Are you OK?" he asked.

"I'll be fine... just give me a few seconds."

"We should start walking to the gate. It's right over there," he pointed. Then as he took a deep breath, asked, "Well, would you like to know how it all works?"

"Sure."

"We'll be on the Concord in a few minutes to New York. It's a special New Year's Eve flight. We'll have our first celebration over London. So, we don't have much time."

"The Concord," she said. "WOW! That's nice. Was there enough to cover the full amount of my flight change?"

"Well, between a price change out of London to New York and some other airline 'mumbo- jumbo,' no. But they owe me a few favors, and sensing you're a 'today's lady,' and wouldn't want *me* to pay for you, I had them charge back any difference to your account, which was minimal."

"Good, John needs to spend a little bit more on his travel account."

"I assume that's your husband and some of the reason for your sadness?"

"Very much so."

"Well, I'm sorry for your trouble. Are you OK?"

"I'll be fine. Please tell me more about the plans."

"Are you sure?"

"Yes, thank you," Mary answered, as they walked towards the gate.

Michael explained, "There are two or three time-zone changes across the Atlantic, and then there's one in New York City... that's three, or four, if you want to accept the optional time zone before Atlantic Time... outside the USA. We will be given *time*... a gift... a celebration... all in one very special evening. Happy New Century to you!"

"I'm going to think a lot about all of this," Mary said, "not just you but the time, as well. Yes, I like this part. Shall we go?"

As they boarded the plane, the pilot's voice filled the cabin with an announcement: "This is Trevor Blake, your pilot. Happy New Year on my behalf and the crew of British Airways! And for those of you who wish to celebrate again, and then again, please join us at the stroke of twelve... once for each degree of our globe that we circumnavigate.

"Now, we are in the first of our time zones—Greenwich Time—and out over the Atlantic. In approximately twenty-two minutes, I will make our count down into the new Millennium. If you're asleep, don't worry. You have two additional opportunities to celebrate before New York. We should be landing in New York City for yet another New Year's Eve. We'll celebrate the beginning of the year, 2000 with our friends, the Americans, done in New York style. Please, delight in our complimentary champagne. Oh and yes, please, welcome the next hundred years."

Mary turned to Michael. "I've never thought of having an action-packed evening... chasing time zones... playing with time she said, buckling her seat belt... To 'play with time,' is something H.G. Wells would like. Now I'll have a small collection of New Year's Eves, each with memories, as you said, placed carefully in my trunk. It is a 'gift of time.' I just never thought of this. You're a smart guy, Michael. I like this. Thank you."

Mary sat quietly as the Concord rushed down the runway, *away from John,* as fast as they could. She chose not to look out the window, as she did not want to look back at anything. Michael was busy, "organizing his space," but she felt him glance at her frequently.

A few minutes later, he asked, "Don't you look out the window? It's pretty normal to, you know."

"Well, you're right," she said. "But I just disappeared into my thoughts for a few seconds, and I missed the take off. Besides, London, by night, looks like any other city. But then, *you've* been fidgeting, organizing, preparing, as if you were the Mad Hatter on his way to an important date."

"I am," he said. " 'I'm late, I'm late, and I am on a very important date'. I am, I hope. Ahhhh... am I?"

"Yes. Your timing is perfect for a date. To be honest, I feel like a school girl, excited with my expectations... thrilled with the possibilities. So now, that's the little girl in me. The big girl in me says, 'Show me.'"

"Ooops," Michael sighed. "I've got my work cut out for me."

"You're on," she told him.

The plane leveled off, and the flight attendant quickly passed out the champagne.

"Can we have two cups, please?" Michael asked.

"Sure, in just a second," the attendant said.

"Four minutes till New Year's Eve," the captain announced... four minutes to the Next Millennium.

Mary wanted to leave it all behind—all of it. She knew she could escape for just a while. Certainly tonight offered her something she never expected.

Michael gave her a very serious look. "I'm not... I hope I'm not overstepping into your personal life," he began. "I mean, I don't mean to be a man intruding on... "

"Michael," she said, sensing his concern, "I'm past the stage of separation. I've been in a marriage that has consumed too many painful New Year's Eves... most of them alone. I am not divorced, but to me that seems academic. A very long time ago, I freed myself of wearing a ring, symbolizing the bond." And she showed him the empty space on her ring finger.

"Please understand," he said. "I'm looking at this as fun, trying always to be a gentleman, but... "

"Then let's not waste any time on the past," she said, and then she changed the subject. My father would have used this plane as some kind of metaphor. He would have said, 'Our time is here now, the past exhausted, tired vapors left behind, chilled by time.' I loved my dad very much."

"He sounds like a bright guy... a little heavy, but... "

"Well, not so. He also would have said, 'what's taking so long for those damn cups.'"

"Now I *know* he was my kind of guy," Michael said.

The flight attendant arrived with two more split bottles and the cups.

Michael quickly opened a bottle. With the cork still in his hand, he poured the champagne as the bubbles rushed to the top of each cup.

"Thirty seconds and counting to midnight, Greenwich Mean Time," the captain said.

"This is exciting," Mary giggled.

"Ten—nine—eight—seven—six—five," the captain counted. Happy New Year! God Bless our new century, and the Queen." The toast resounded through the cabin.

31

"Our first New Year's Eve, with many more to come," Michael said, as the captain and crew began to sing "Auld Lang Syne."

When the song ended, Michael turned his attention back to Mary.

"So, in the great world of events, what do you do to busy yourself?"

"Well, once upon a time I was an artist. I was full of creative thoughts, expressing them through my brush, by my chisel and with the written word. I used to call the chisel part—sculpting. John, my former, on the other hand, called it 'a waste of time.' He was rarely supportive. I really liked working on big pieces; something about the scale, between me and them."

"I would have guessed something like diplomat, or your own business such as... well... importing?

But an artist... that's a pleasant surprise. It's so very different. By the 'written word,' do you mean poetry... like Joyce Kilmer and his 'Trees?'"

Mary paused. "That part of me, as an artist, is the part that rarely escapes from within. My expressions are from my heart, my soul, reaching... for understanding. They're for me and for those that have touched me. They are my deepest truths exposed.

"On the other hand, painting requires an audience, which makes it difficult, since my work is, let's say... esoteric, relatively unnoticed, except for an occasion in Seattle. But my painting has remained with me, for the most part. John, again, my former husband, was hardly aware of it, and could only *smell* the oils. He could never *see* or *feel* its meaning."

"What about you? What kind of mischief are you into?" Mary asked, changing the subject.

"I'm kind of a sculptor as well."

"You're kidding!"

"I work on very large pieces... very large. So I understand the relationship you speak of between you and your work. But millions see my work every day, by air, and by foot, they come to see and interact with it as well."

"So, you sculpt?" She asked, beginning to wonder at his explanation.

"Yes, big time. I have a lot to do with building dams and bridges... also boring holes in mountains. Stuff like that."

"So," she said, "That's where the 'exact' thing comes from."

"Well, it takes many years to build them; the projects affect many people. My current endeavor will start construction next year and won't be completed until about the same amount of time it will take us to get to Seattle, say 2005 or 2006."

"You're an engineer?"

"I have engineering degrees," he answered quickly. "But my real job is financing the construction, through bonds and substantial loans between countries."

"You're the piggy bank," she said, finally understanding. "Or at least you know where it is."

"It's always in the same place," he said. "Washington."

"So why did you choose Seattle?"

"They keep loose change and 'the key' there.' I'm meeting with the 'keeper of the key' and his committee in a few days."

"So, you don't have to be there tomorrow?"

"No," he said, "no meetings for a few days."

"It's great that this all worked out... I mean your schedule."

The PA system chimed as the pilot announced. "Ladies and gentlemen, it's eight minutes until the New Year."

"Are we ever going to drink this champagne," Mary asked, "or is it some kind of a prop?"

"To *us*," said Michael, raising his cup. "To *you. Chind Anni*."

She smiled, "One hundred years."

"Yes, one hundred brand new years."

Mary said nothing, as their cups touched to their toast. One sip, and then another, for each of them. She placed her head back with a sigh as Michael looked at her.

They remained quiet for a few minutes, feeling very comfortable with one another. The plane shuttered enough for Mary to bring her head forward.

"It's nothing," he reassured her. "They always do that. It's a thing the pilot does to make you drink more champagne. They try to flatten it out by shaking it up... along with you... so you tend to drink a little faster."

"It works," she said, as she gulped the last of her drink. "May I have some more?"

"That's why they're the pilots, and I sit in the back," he said.

"And you get to drink."

"Yes, but I have to let them think they're terrific because I don't want them to figure out that I'm also with (he looked around) the most beautiful woman in the plane. If they figure that out, I'm sunk."

"Why?"

"They're pilots; handsome, tall, dark, bright, and rich. They're authority figures. I don't stand a chance."

"You mean with me?"

"Well... "

"I'm flattered. Well, if it helps, the pilots have to stay there with their toys... their lights, bells and whistles because *you* don't know how to fly this plane. Do you?"

"I do. But they would have to torture me."

"You're a pleasant man," she told him. "I mean... comfortable to be with. I need that. I'm glad we're doing this. But tell me more about your life, Mr. Bowland. Tell me what it's like standing at the foot of your dam, looking up a thousand feet to the top of power lines and turbines and with water spewing from the gates that you so perfectly placed by design and by good ole American dollars."

"Well, I was born the only son of Don and Andrea in 1948 on December 15th."

"You just had a birthday... Happy Birthday."

"We try to forget them at this stage... all us old folk."

"Well, I'm close enough to understand," she said.

"You're just a child in my eyes... a baby."

"Thanks. But my high school prom is more than history."

"Well," he said, "the next thirty years will bring even more to think about."

"That's a long time... thirty years. I don't know about that, Michael."

"Let's see... You'll be about fifty-five, less this accelerated trip. That's a minimum of five years, plus you've won the bonus round, so take away six... that's twenty-nine."

"I'm twenty-nine? I like your math. But I hope your math, when building dams, is a bit more accurate."

"There is nothing wrong with that calculation. It's in Venus time... yeah! That's it... twenty-nine. I'm 216 in Martian time. I picked up the concept from a book I read a few years ago. It was one of the relationship books about the differences in men and women. The author used the planets of Mars and Venus to suggest that we come from two entirely different worlds. Have you read it?

"No. Where I have been?"

"I purchased the book, wanting, only to disprove the author's theory. But by page forty-three, I knew that I was totally off base, and was definitely holding a passport from Mars.

"More champagne Mr. Alien?" she asked him.

"Hey, it's two minutes to twelve," he said. "I'll open the other split."

She held the cups while he popped the cork. Around them, other passengers were preparing for the toast.

The pilot interrupted them, making an announcement. "Once again, this is your master of ceremonies this evening. We're going to have a countdown to twelve. If you would like to join the continuing celebration, we have one minute and thirty seconds to go. I am speaking softly and might remind you all that some of the passengers are sleeping. So when we do the toast, we will try to be tastefully quiet for their sake.

"There are optional New Year Eves coming up before New York," the captain continued. These time zones, generally, are not recognized as official time zones, except for air and sea traffic. But technically, it is fifteen degrees to the west of our last one, so I will mention it. Our Concord can traverse earth miles at this latitude faster than the clocks consume sixty minutes in time. So, it is thirty seconds to midnight for the second time this evening. I won't bother you again until we officially approach the Atlantic Time Zone so Happy New Year, again."

"That's two years since we met," Michael said.

"I feel as if it were seconds ago. Two years I'm away from Calcutta already. I was there for almost a year, which felt like two centuries. I'm away a few hours... and two years... gone. You are a treat."

"Seven—six—five," said the captain, softly, "three—two—one. Happy New Year!"

"Happy New Year!" echoed the passengers in whispered tones. The gentleman across the aisle reached over and toasted the two of them. The woman in front reached back and did the same. As they toasted, the flight attendant passed by, offering refills and asked if they would like glasses.

"The *cups* are perfect, thank you," said Mary.

Michael held his cup to hers, "Happy New Year, Mary."

"Thank you, Michael," she said. "Thanks for being here tonight. Happy New Year!"

The two continued to have unending discussions. Michael's small talk seemed to come from thin air. He was a master of making it interesting... an ability that she enjoyed. They laughed about his stories, of visiting building sites in distant worlds, and the horror of translating a phrase or gesture into different cultures. He told his story of the time he visited a shop in Cheng Chow, China. He was there to personally review the topography for a possible network of roads that would connect it to the coast, the Yellow Sea.

"I noticed a little store about ten-feet wide in the village. They made pipes, the kind you smoke. I took an interest in it because of my father, who was alive at that time, and loved to smoke... using his extensive pipe collection.

"I casually walked in and didn't get two feet into the shop, when the proprietor greeted me with the traditional bow and nod. I did the same." (Michael demonstrated the action.) "I picked up a beautiful hand-made, European-styled pipe. In a flash, he moved right up... very close to me... and uttered the sound, 'boouelluoud,' very fast.

I was taken back for a moment, thinking I was supposed to understand what he said. (Moo Goo Gai Pan and Chow Mein, are all I know in Chinese.) I looked directly at him and parroted his word... repeating it, as best I could and just as fast... 'boulloud.' He seemed frustrated and nodded his head, saying the word again... emphatically this time and moving his hands... 'boouelluoud.'

"I slowly mouthed the word back in his face about 12 inches away." Michael did the same to Mary, as he sounded out, burr ellllll wooouuuuddd, boouelluoud. He was a not happy at all, and he grabbed the pipe from my hands and pointed to the inside of the bowl with some other Chinese chatter." This time, Michael gestured that they say it together. "Boouelluoud," they both repeated.

"Well, it hit me like a ton of bricks. He was trying to say, Burl Woods, as if I knew that all the time.

Raising his shoulders, he shook my hand and said as clearly as I am this second, 'on sale.' What else could I do? I had to buy it. When my Father opened his gift, he looked at it and said, 'a boouelluoud pipe.' No, just kidding." They both laughed for quite some time.

"This is Captain Blake again. We are minutes away from the edge of the Atlantic Time Zone, so through the magic of technology, we have become a part of the very few people that have experienced this many New Year Eve's tonight.

According to our schedule, we should arrive in New York City in time for all of you to capture this magic moment once again since the Eastern, or New York Time Zone, allows us another New Year's Eve. Only this time, since I will be off duty, I will join you all in a toast to 2000. On behalf of British Air, thank you for flying with us and Happy Millennium!"

The flight from London to New York was so much fun, she had forgotten her past. They were having a great time, and it wasn't over yet.

They landed at 11:18 p.m., New York time.

"You're not tired, are you?" Michael asked.

"Not yet... there's too much to do. Besides, I slept on the last flight... the first year I met you."

They exited customs at Kennedy. Michael looked for United Airline's gate 38. He apologized to Mary for the brief stay, but added, "As long as we're here in, we might as well celebrate New Year's Eve." They laughed.

The many bars within the terminal were packed with happy travelers who were about to have their first celebration for the evening. It seemed so special that Mary and Michael were about to have their third.

Michael moved off ahead as Mary stood in place, people watching. The faces she saw were those of her own people. She felt relief. It was the security of being home. The noise was unbelievable with people who were electrified—anticipating "2000." Televisions were everywhere, with each screen an image of Times Square, and hundreds of thousands of people jammed into a few blocks. She remembered that she was on the other side of the world a few hours ago, walking through the streets of Calcutta towards the Hospital. Now, because of the Concord, time zones, latitudes, and Michael, she's in New York and is far away from her anxiety. A total stranger has comforted her, but he has no idea of what he has done for her. And she knew there was more to come. For the first time in a very long time, she wanted to express herself to someone who could appreciate Mary for Mary.

Michael waved his arms, calling to her. "Over here, Mary! Come over here!" She began walking towards him so fast that they bumped right into each another.

"Excuse me," he said.

She stared at him for a brief second, out of breath, and she stood there, as he said... .

"New York City in the nick of time. Let's jump into this joint."

Mary smiled. It was just something her father would have said. He would have been just as confident as Michael was about the place; the fun, the good times they would have. She followed willingly. *It's impossible to imagine all those years captive, and this man out there all that time?* She thought. *I hope this continues to be a fairy tale. But then it can't be a fairytale. This time I'm living it. This time my expectations are real.*

They pushed their way through to a single space at the bar.

Michael turned, shouting to ask if she wanted the same "libation?"

"Yes," she shouted back.

Michael got the bartender's attention by making him laugh and smile. Within seconds, he had a bottle of Cordon Rouge in his hand and two cups. He asked Mary to hold the cups as he poured the champagne. They moved away from the little space to a corner of the bar. There were many people, but somehow there were just the two of them. Michael possessed some kind of magic. They didn't have to scream; he spoke so softly to her.

On all of the televisions, a man announced, "Yes, five minutes left of 1999. That's 9999999." The volume within the masses went up. As the cameras panned through the crowds, the youthful faces screamed in delight. "It's one New Year's Eve for them... our third or fourth this wonderful evening," she said.

"One minute to the last blastoff of the century," the MC announced. Michael looked at Mary, motioning whether or not he should pour more champagne into her cup. She smiled, feeling happy for the first time in many New Year's Eves. "Ten—nine—eight—seven—six—five—four—three—two—one. TWO—ZERO—ZERO—ZERO. YESSSSS! Happy New Year! Happy 2000! Happy Millennium! Happy Century!"

The crowd in the bar went wild. Michael leaned over and kissed her on the cheek. She kissed him back. They parted and stared into each other's eyes... inches apart. Mary felt excited for the first time in a long time. Michael said, "That's three fabulous years I have known you, Mary."

She looked at him, wondering how she had gotten to be so fortunate this night. She needed this distraction tonight, wherever it went. She felt like a woman again—alive, because of Michael. It wasn't anything you could touch. It was nothing on canvas, nothing you could see. But it was as Michael had said, "At the magic number twelve, time will hold hands."

"Michael, we've only a few minutes till takeoff," she said.

They walked towards their gate with Michael tucking a bottle of champagne in his coat. As they passed through the gate, with his magic, it reappeared. Handing it to the flight attendant, he asked her if she could chill it and serve it at the appropriate time. She did so without asking a single question, breaking another rule, but it was a special night for everyone. They sat in the third row, 3A and B. Mary melted into the seat.

Once again, the excitement filled the plane as fellow travelers gathered in the race—chasing time. Mary noticed some of the same people who were also on the flight from London. The passengers nodded to Michael as he did in return. She thought about the *different* meaning that this gesture has in Calcutta. There, it didn't mean "hello, how are you?" as much as "hello, I remember you, but I don't want to talk to you now... maybe later, if I feel like it." She didn't think it was right, but she had become used to it.

Michael and Mary chatted through takeoff as the plane leveled out. Mary seemed to fade into comfort with Michael at her side.

Michael looked at her as her eyelids settled. Her head slowly leaned towards him and came to rest on his shoulder. He was happy she was so close to him.

It was the night he had wanted to experience for so many years. And his thoughts dashed back in time to his wife, Candise and their daughter, Margaret. Again he thought about how he and Candise had talked about "chasing time" on New Year's Eve. But a set of events had placed Candise and Margaret in the wrong place at the wrong time, killing them both instantly. Michael would cringe when he relived these thoughts. If there had been a second before, a second later, things might have been different. He wanted to change it all. But it could not be.

Michael's was thinking... *life is not so funny. It's much too serious. Laughter, humor and the whimsical are only tools to suppress the pain that lies latent within us. Some of us are able to sustain the pain without the anesthetic; instead, we have the comedic mask that anesthetizes the truth at the core of who we are. Could I ever remove the mask? Could I expose my vulnerability? Would I dare reveal the inner sanctum of my emotions? Is that forever? Hmm... New Year's Eve, a new Millennium. I realize, now, that it's a journey I will cherish forever.*

And he felt so good about sharing it with Mary. As he looked at her, resting on his shoulder, he thought, *I know it's right. I feel really terrific now that she's here. I want to do more. Thanks, Mary. I hope you feel as good about tonight as I do.*

The captain's voice came over the PA system. "Good evening ladies and gentlemen. We are about to catch up with ourselves once again this evening as we embark on the edge of the Central Time Zone in about fifteen minutes."

Mary stirred a little, moving her hand close to Michael, but not touching him. He looked at her finger, without the ring, and wondered who she was, where she had come from, and what kind of life she had had. *Is there some great mystery, or is it as simple as she put it? Why is she going to Seattle, now? Could it be a vacation... or a visit home? But, now, just after the holidays? Well... I don't know, but I would like to find out. Seeing more of her is the only way that I could answer the many questions that I have for this interesting person.*

"Ten minutes," whispered the pilot

Mary opened her eyes, sitting up quickly. "Have I missed it?" she asked.

"No," he assured her.

"How much time until our next celebration?"

"Nine minutes."

She got up. "I'll be right back," she said, excusing herself.

She's very attractive, he thought, *this lady I found this special night. Hmmm.*

Mary was back quickly... just like the schoolgirl she said she was, her face was freshened, her hair brushed, and she was full of energy. She was greeted by the flight attendant, who handed her and Michael a glass of champagne.

"Thirty seconds to go," he said.

Mary sat down. They looked at the glasses and laughed. "There's no time to change to cups, he added. Three—two—one. Happy New Year, Mary."

"Hey Michael, it's the fourth year of our relationship."

"Mary, I'm beginning to like this a lot."

"Yes, Michael, me too. So when do we do this again? Over *where?*"

"We should, comfortably, celebrate New Year's in two more time zones, around Denver and Seattle. But it won't be based on our watches, in terms of mating theirs to 'twelve o'clock,' since this plane can't fly fast enough."

"Should we turn your watch bezel each time? Mary asked.

"That's what's so terrific." Michael said. "We get to choose. But in terms of recognized zones, the USA, as you know, has only three, and the plane, technically, can't match twelve in each zone. But we can easily say five years and an optional sixth one 'for the gods' as they say."

"That will be our last New Year's together. I don't like that part," she said. "Well, I mean, tonight," she said.

"Yes, I know what you meant. But... "

"Do you mean something else?" he asked.

"No, I just... "

"What's wrong?" he asked.

"I'm just, well, some parts of this become sad," she said. "New Year's Eve is a little bit of many emotions... all converging at our magic number. But I must admit, I never thought I'd have this many options all in one night. I don't know that I have done this deliberately."

"What?"

"Well, my responses to each twelve o'clock were different wishes... each of them important... all things I would like to happen."

"Tell me what they were," he prodded.

"You know you're not allowed to tell. If you do, it won't happen. I know that I never had this before, ever."

"Well, I'm not telling, either. I'm not talking about the gold mine, or the 125-million dollar lotto, and I'm especially not revealing my lustful thoughts and needs for a Big Mac beamed up by Scotty right now."

"Well, that's it," she said. "You get coal."

"Coal?"

"Yes, in your stocking. If you're bad, and if you reveal your wishes, you get coal."

"But Superman can make a diamond out of coal."

"It can be done," she said. "But the time is important. I think the coal has a better chance of lasting."

"OK, I give up. I was only kidding about the gold mine. The real thing I wished was... "

"Shhhh," she said.

"*Cups,*" he finished. "We need *cups.* I'm going to get them now."

Michael got up and dashed toward the flight attendant's station. Mary watched him as he worked his charm on the attendant. She laughed as they both moved into the service area for a moment. He emerged, victoriously, turning back to her to say something she couldn't hear. He raised the cups high above his head, as if they were the World Cup. Some passengers took notice but shrugged off his exuberance. It was New Year's Eve.

"So much for wishes," he said, as he climbed back into his seat.

"Well, forget the gold mine," she said.

"We'll save these for our next New Year's celebration," he said, referring to the cups.

"So, where do you go from here?" she asked. "After the airport, that is?"

"I'm staying at the Serento, in the city, for a while," he said. "Then up to Vancouver, back to Seattle, then New York. The good news is, then back to Seattle. I was hoping I might get to have dinner or something with you."

"Most definitely. Yes."

"Most definitely... great," he said. "When were you back here last?"

"Years ago. It's my parents' home."

"Oh? How old are they?"

"No, they're gone," she said.

"I'm sorry. I... "

"No, it was a while ago. I'm... well, time makes it easier, but there are moments."

"It's my nature to think like this. How do you take care of the house?"

"It's simple. My aunt and uncle live down the road... a mile or so. They just do it because we're family... a kind act to my parents. These are very proud people. They want nothing for themselves. Each month a check is deposited for heat and electricity and something for maintenance. They pay the bills and keep a careful eye on it all."

"You're fortunate. My neighbors would probably rent it out for parties or a halfway house for mass murderers. I'd find it with doors hanging by one screw and the kitchen charred black from too many flambeaux bananas."

"Stop... I'm sure your neighbors aren't quite like that."

"That's my brother and sister-in-law," he said, "weird, very weird."

"You are a character."

The cabin quieted as the effects of the champagne came to rest on the many that had enjoyed a second New Year's Eve.

"I think I'm going to take a cat nap," Mary said. "Is that OK with you?"

"Sure, I'll keep watch for the dragons," Michael said.

"I feel safe now. I do," she said, warmly. Mary sank into her seat, moving her head towards Michael, her hands cupped together. Within moments, she was asleep.

Who was she, this beautiful woman, chasing time zones, accumulating years of memories with him? She knew so little of him, he thought. *There's fairness there. But what a beginning! If this is a date, I don't know that it could be better.*

A few more hours, halfway around the world, and we'll land, having celebrated the beginning of 2000, more than the entire population of the earth... well, give or take a few thousand people. I'm having a great time, with a great lady. I know what to expect... just companionship, I guess. But there seems to be much more. I can't let it end here.

She has agreed to a date in Seattle. OK... so let's just make that happen as soon as possible. I'm going to expand my stay in Seattle and push off the meetings in Washington a while. That will let me see her, I hope. This time, this evening, we know so little of each other, but another time... another evening. She is definitely an interesting person... a very interesting person.

Candise, Margaret and I had so little time together. We had been married only four years. Margaret was three; she was a beautiful child and much the image of her mother. Candise would have loved this trip. I can see that now that I am living the reality of our dream. What a tragedy. How does a guy who flies around the world, in some of the most miserable conditions, have eventless journeys and they, coming home from Candise's school... die? It will never make sense to me.

I would have made you laugh... silly things, Candise. She loved me... so long ago. All these years, and I'm still thinking the same thoughts... all this time.

But tonight it happened, Candise. It was wonderful. I know you love me still. Have you watched this evening unfold? It's been what I thought it would be. I know this is not fair to Mary right now. But I'm glad I've done this. Is this right? I'm not sure. But I know my memory of us will not end. I feel, that for Mary and me, this is a beginning. Thank you, dear. Give Margaret a hug.

"This is your captain speaking. We're creeping up on a time change to twelve o'clock again... flying over Cheyenne, Colorado in sixteen minutes and then one more time into Pacific Time... just before landing in Seattle, ahead of schedule."

Michael moved his finger to touch Mary's nose very delicately. He tapped once, and then again, as she moved her hand to brush away the disturbance. Their hands met. She opened her eyes and realized that he had awakened her. She held his hand tightly, looking at him with a sleepy smile. Their hands stayed locked together.

"That's a nice way to wake up," she said.

"I didn't want to make it abrupt. The captain just announced the next New Year's Eve. I thought you would want a moment to wake up before our toast."

"Thanks. I have cobwebs in my mind right now. How much time?"

"About twelve minutes."

"I think another trip to the Ladies room is in order. I'll be right back."

As she left, the attendant came around filling glasses again. "May I?" she asked.

"Yes, please," said Michael. "But in the *cups*, please. We won't be using the glasses."

"No problem, sir."

Mary got back to her seat with one minute and thirty seconds remaining and saw the filled cups.

"You've been busy," she said.

"Yes, we're ready for our optional year." he answered, "one for good measure. Do you realize it is the year 2005, and like I promised, you haven't changed a bit."

"Well, a promise from you is something to cherish," she said.

"Ten seconds," announced the captain.

"Five—four—three—two—one. Happy New Year," the pilot said, quietly.

A few people raised their glasses. Most were asleep.

"A very happy and very healthy New Year to my old friend, Mary," Michael said.

"Old?"

"Well, in terms of old friends... "

"Happy New Year, my fine and distinguished old friend," she said. "Thanks for the cheer. It's the very best I've ever had... a gift I shall keep forever."

Their cups met, and they drank their last toast.

"Do you mind my using your napkin?" she asked.

"No," he said, handing it to her.

She reached into her purse for a pen and began to draw.

Michael excused himself as she continued to draw.

She busied herself with a beautiful sketch of an airplane with cups for engines. A banner flew behind, with her telephone number on it.

He returned, as she finished the last few strokes, and she handed it to him.

"This isn't complete," he said.

"Well, I couldn't fit the address and the zip code on the banner. Sorry."

"No, not that," he said. "I would like you to sign it, please."

She retrieved the sketch and signed it, tastefully, in the bottom right-hand corner. "There."

Michael reached into his wallet and offered his card to her, asking to use the pen. I'm writing the hotel name down, but if for some reason you can't get me there, call this number. He quickly scribbled a phone number on the back of the card. It's my mobile phone. I don't give the number out to everyone, and sadly, I haven't quite gotten into the habit of carrying it everywhere with me. So, if that doesn't work, try contacting my secretary, Heather. She always knows where I am. She can get you through to me. I'll call her and tell her that your calls pre-empt anything and everyone... from now on."

"Well, if you call me, you can use the answering machine, if it still works, and you'll hear the voice of a younger Mary... from another time."

"How are you getting home from the airport?"

"Well, my home is about forty minutes from the airport, so I'll hire a car," she said.

"Would you want me to drive you home? Or better yet, we could share the ride and drop you off?"

It didn't take too much convincing for Mary to concede. She was getting tired.

Chapter Four

The voyage complete, the passengers found their weight upon their feet once again. Courtesy at this stage of travel was minimal. People would use the appropriate phrases, "excuse me," "I'm sorry," and "pardon me," but it was really, "let me out of here," and "why don't you understand that you are in my way?"

The passengers expressed their conditioned response to the engines shutting down. Un-snapping, standing, reaching, and unlatching as fast as they could—then reaching into the overhead compartments to collect their belongings. Michael and Mary joined the ritual a bit late—inching along then stopping. A petite, elderly woman asked for help in getting her bag from the overhead compartment. It seemed to have filled the overhead space in every direction.

Michael offered his assistance. "May I?"

"You're so very kind to help. Thank you."

"You're very welcome."

He turned to Mary, whispering, "She is returning from the National Bake-Off contest. Did you know that?"

"No," she smiled. "I'm ready."

"She won first place for her macadamia nut cookies. And in 'the spirit of the moment,' she also kidnapped the Pillsbury Doughboy, and with the heat in that overhead, the un-speakable happened inside her bag."

Mary burst out laughing. "What... he suffocated?"

"No. Look, she's punching him down."

"That is *very funny.*" Mary laughed, again.

The flight attendant expressed, "Thank you for flying United. We hope you had an en-joyable flight."

As they walked, Mary began explaining that they were chosen to be the leaders of the *Baggage Claim Game.* Michael said, "Now *I'm* ready."

She continued explaining that they were about to become part of the lowest levels of public interaction—a game she called *Baggage Claim.*

"Interestingly, it's a job most men assign to women," she said, looking at him with her eyebrows raised. "That part is called 'find me if you can.' Now we need to search for clues. The game's icon, she said, is a two-dimensional illustration of a suitcase with a hand grasping its handle. The bag is white and depending on what country and city, the field around it is brown or green."

"It's there," she exclaimed.

"I didn't know that was a game. I thought it was a reminder. Like, did you forget that thing that looks like this?"

"No, it's there for the game... *Baggage Claim.*"

"You see the passengers behind us?" Mary asked, as they both turned.

"Yes."

"This procession is dedicated to retrieving their luggage, so they have to play. A few might get lost as they disappear into the terminal's cavernous space. However, most of them are dedicated to the art of *Baggage Claim.*"

Michael pointed towards a machine scrubbing the marble floors, scurrying along with its attendant. He was enjoying their little "bit of fun" that Mary had started. Michael contributed to her fantasy, explaining that the "scrubber man" was a kind of a police force that would search for those that had strayed from the game of *Baggage Claim.*

She looked at him. "Good. Great, I like that."

"I'll meet you at the Baggage Claim then," Michael pointed, laughing.

"I knew it," she said, "minus two points... for you."

He frowned. "I'll take care of the car."

"What else would you do?"

"I'll send a porter. Just point out your bags. See ya in two seconds."

"Minus six points," she said as they separated.

In her thoughts, she felt that, in the big picture, he had accumulated over 1,000,000 points tonight, so it was acceptable.

There it was, the last icon: the luggage carrousel. It was missing the calliope. A few of the familiar faces, she had just celebrated with, were ready for the challenge.

The ownership of space became obvious as all of the passengers presented themselves, assertively, beside the empty carrousel, staking out the best possible vantage point to retrieve their prize. Some were cunning and seemed to be thinking, "Please don't notice that I placed my carry-on on your feet. Thank you."

The porter arrived. "May I help you, ma'am?"

"Yes," Mary said. "Here are the stubs." She chose not to play but to observe and send in her "professional trainer" for the challenge.

The stainless steel leaves expanded and contracted, turning around and around. It appeared vacant as the carrousel went about its business—distributing nothing, until one very large piece of green luggage appeared from behind the wall. A clothes-line rope was tied tightly around its middle. No one was willing to claim it; it was tacky—very tacky.

The carrousel was very noisy, insisting on the attention of the players. The reflections from the harsh ceiling lights undulated across the polished aluminum surface. The squeaky sounds of the many wheels propelled a closed chain of endless plates in motion. Around and around it turned with the same very large piece of tacky green luggage, with a rope tied tightly around its middle, appearing, then disappearing behind the wall. The machine's lonely groan reverberated within the enormous space. There was no scent of tranquility, just one of plastic; not one of man, but one of man-*made*.

The contestants were silent—their attention riveted to anticipation. The flight number appeared on the illuminated board. An awful buzzer pulsed loudly as a warning, STAND CLEAR. The game begins. In defiance, the contestants (in this game of Mary's) lunged closer to the action. Exciting the crowd, the luggage began spewing from the top of its volcanic shape.

There was bag after bag of measureless configurations, made of leather, fabric, plastic, wicker, fiber. There were cylinders, squares, rectangles, and circles. All shapes rolled, slid, and chattered down the incline, moving past the traveler's feet as a procession of choices. One by one, these shapes traversed past their impatience.

The porter collected Mary's bags as if they were his own, recognizing every piece before it arrived at his feet. Hundreds of others were busy pecking at shapes.

A "contestant panics," choosing the wrong bag, and becomes disgusted, knowing the sign above her head warns, "Some Look Alike." Another is breaking the biggest rule: reaching across the front of a person about to snap up their last bag. The people playing "baggage claim," ultimately allowed the relentless carousel to return to its starting point—with only the aluminum surface and the one tacky green bag.

Michael said, "Compliments to the group, the game is over in fewer than eight minutes... just above the international average... Bravo." The one green bag is a descriptor as to how the game works. It is not owned by any passenger. It's just there, never to be removed... cemented to the polished interleaving surface.

"This game needs a more specific name, how about *The Carrousel 6 B game,* played by the dedicated passengers of flight 326.*"

I'm a little tired of this game and the machine, Mary thought to herself. *It's too much like the full time job that I had, for too many years, with John. It... no he... has no heart.*

It's just not fun, no matter how I try to change it. I hate that bag... that one miserable bag. And I hate John. Hey, she thought, *if John were a piece of baggage, I wouldn't claim him. He could be the green bag forever... great thought. I am tired. I just want to be home now. In another hour, I can sleep.*

The porter summoned Mary to follow him out to the street. Michael was standing, motioning Mary to come as the car pulled up. The driver loaded the bags into the trunk, and then opened the door for Michael and Mary.

"Where to?" he asked.

Michael and Mary looked at each other, with Michael saying, "You first."

"It's 682 Canyon Drive," she said.

"Is that near the lake?" the driver asked.

"Yes. Do you know where is?"

"Yes. I... well, my mother lives up near there. No problem, ma'am."

Mary and Michael sat back in their seats again. She turned her head, looking out the window as they drove. Everything had changed. But she still had a very strong sense of being home.

Michael moved over to the corner of his seat, bringing his leg higher to sit at an angle. While cupping his hands around his knee, he placed her in his vision directly, her face silhouetted against the window.

Her hair was pulled back behind her ears, allowing her profile to seem suspended in the darkness. The features of her face were petite. Her eyes were intently alert, consuming her environment. She seemed to be recording every nuance of information around her. The lights of oncoming traffic illuminated her presence. She closed her eyes slowly; the headlights were too intense for her. She sighed and turned to Michael.

"Michael, this day... how long it's been... so many things happened, all at one time. I feel it's been *one day*, and then I feel it's been *all the years* you promised. I've not been home yet! *Yet* I've never been away.

We must all feel that, *emotionally*, within us. It must be that we have a sense of reality as to who we are and where we've been, but how *fast* we get there is not real. It's... well, anyway, we're here. And according to our calendar, it's the year 2005."

"For you, it's home," he said. "For me, it's a place in-between... a place I'm still traveling through. I'm still in the unreal. The difference is the importance of the journey and the relevance to my life. There must be some fortune-cookie that says, 'The road home is filled with experience. Thanks for flying United.'"

"I like that. I feel I can rest now that we have a perspective on this," she answered, and they both laughed.

"There used to be another building here," she said suddenly, looking out the window again. It was a very large, old brown one, with large turrets... kind of 1900-ish."

"I'm sorry to interrupt," said the driver, "but that was the Smith building. The family went bankrupt or something. It was sold for taxes and a developer built that glass tower. I have a customer I drive there every now and then."

"Thanks," said Mary.

"You folks been away a little bit longer than a vacation?" the driver asked.

"A lifetime," said Mary.

"Two," added Michael.

"Many changes these last few years," the driver said. "I don't know, maybe it's my age. It just seems that there isn't much that hasn't changed, including me."

"I understand," Mary said.

"We're getting close, ma'am," he said. "It's nice to have a full moon to see a little better."

"It's just so wonderful. I feel so wonderful to be home. Please make a right onto High Ridge Road," she instructed him. "It's coming up soon."

"I know that turn, the driver said. Thanks."

"Then onto Canyon," she told him.

The car turned onto Canyon Road, the sparsely placed homes glowed in the moonlight. Mary was excited. She moved to the edge of her seat, leaning forward in the car as if to get closer to her destination.

"Six eighty-two, ma'am," the driver announced.

"Yes, yes," she said. "Yes, this is it. Just slow down a little. Could you stop here please?" She asked. The driver came to a stop. She inspected everything from the mailbox, the walkway, the porch, and the garage—*to* the roofline with a billion stars above it. She paused, looking at her bedroom window on the second floor, a little night-light illuminating the sheer drapes that hung neatly, suggesting the presence of caring people inside.

"I hope the secret key is still a secret," she said, to no one in particular.

"We can park if you like, driver. Thank you."

The driver pulled into the driveway. The car's headlights illuminated the white double door garage immediately in front of them, and a portion of the house. The driver got out and opened Mary's door, asking Michael to point out her bags. Michael began to help as Mary walked up the flagstone path towards the front door.

A simple balustrade enclosed the porch with columns accenting the entrance. The house was built back in the forties and had all the traditional trappings of that era. The natural cedar shingles were darkened by their age. The house was trimmed in white and had louvered shutters, which were nothing like those that hung in her bedroom in Calcutta.

Her favorite ingredient to its charm was a large circular leaded-glass window, centered just below the peak of the roof. The glass had been designed by her father, and Mary would go along with him- through each stage of the creative process: She had watched him draw the rough sketches, review the glass samples, then *complete* the final stage of the beautiful window of two Dutch children (a boy and a girl) walking through a field of tulips. Each was carrying tiny baskets of cut flowers. It was difficult to see in the moonlight, but she knew its design piece by piece.

She walked up the two steps, onto the porch, towards the dining room window and reached behind the shutter. Her fingers reached back in time, across some chips of peeled paint, and found a nail with a key still hanging there, waiting for her return.

She placed the key in the simple lock, turning it ever so slowly. The oval glass door opened easily, as she stepped into the only real home she had ever known. She reached for the hall light switch, and if it still worked, the attic light switch—installed just for "the Dutch children who lived upstairs" as her father would say.

She ran outside, and then turned and looked up. There it was, lighted and suspended in the darkness, as brilliant as the day her father had installed it. It was so comforting to feel the welcome that surrounded her. Mary ran back in the house and walked through each downstairs room. With her hands extended, she touched the surfaces and the textures surrounding her as the little boy in Calcutta had done. But Mary was touching her *past*, and she could feel the warmth it all offered.

She made a full circle, and met the driver entering the foyer with her bags. Michael carried the last piece, placing it alongside the others.

"That is one *beautiful* piece of glass up in the eves, Mary... a very lovely Tiffany window."

"It sure is," the driver agreed. "If that's it, I'll be in the car, sir. Have a good night, Mrs. Bowland."

"Thank you. I'll just be a minute," said Michael.

"Well, Happy New Year," said Mary." She moved toward Michael and hugged him, kissing him on the cheek.

"Happy New Year to you," he said. "When will I see you?"

"You have the napkin with this number on it. Give me a call when you're rested."

"If you would like to call, I'm at the Sorrento."

"I need to sleep," she said.

"But I must *say*, you made me feel very special tonight," he said. "Good night and sweet dreams."

Mary waited by the door until they had pulled away.

Mary Templeton was home. She sighed with relief, thinking that if it weren't for Michael, it would have been impossible. She was as far away from John and Dr. Satara as she could get. This had been quite an evening. Mary turned off the porch light and attic lights and walked up the stairs to her bedroom. Everything was perfect. Her bed was a welcome sight. Before Michael had reached the main road, she was in bed and ready to fulfill his request for her sweet dreams.

Michael was tired. He sat back and loosened his tie.

"That's the Sorrento, sir?" the driver asked, reassuring himself.

"Yes, thank you."

"Where did you fly in from?"

"India, Bombay."

"Well welcome home. You must be tired. This time of night, it should be about forty-five minutes to your hotel. I'll leave you be... to rest."

"Thank you. I am exhausted."

Mike Bowland, he thought... *That was fabulous... half way around the world... chasing time with a very beautiful woman. My life... what I'm about, is definitely a little off the wall. I'm not the same as the guy across the street or the man behind me in the plane. It's just not... But who knows me... really knows me... not many. For so long, I've avoided contact with anyone who gets close; it's become a mask I never remove. It is said, 'a person lives as long as someone who knew him lives.'*

It's part of the Chinese philosophy that I think is true. Two people share an experience. The experience may be brief, like a ride on a roller coaster... or a night like tonight. Still, the experience could be a life together as husband and wife. And the surviving person, who has shared the experience with another person, perpetuates their memory after the others' death. Everyone gets the opportunity to extend the lives of others through the memory of the experience they shared... clinical but deep.

For me, Candise and our little girl, Margaret, will live as long as I can remember. How beautiful they were... how warm and cuddly Margaret was with her little giggle when I tickled her. If her Pooh Bear were real, he would know her best. She took him everywhere. He absorbed her tears... received her hugs. Pooh stood vigilance, all night, protecting her from that damn alligator in Peter Pan. His memory of this would be timeless. Where am I going with this?

I have been here before... this place in my mind. I'm remembering I didn't like it. I try to reassemble the emotion, and I come up feeling lonely, rejected, not loved. I'm not sure what that means, except it's not a good feeling.

I'm tired... very tired. Am I at peace with myself? I don't think so.

The sounds of traffic and the city noises were becoming hollow. An ambulance howled past their cab, headed in the opposite direction, in the darkness that surrounded him. Michael's thoughts were becoming very distant. He leaned further back into the seat.

The lights flashed in his face as oncoming traffic briefly illuminated his presence, appearing and then disappearing in the reflection of the driver's mirror—so dark—then so bright. One minute he was there—then not. And this was the same way that his *image*—then his *thoughts* had, intermittently, materialized in bursts.

This person I am thinking about needs to confess to one other person... a Mary, perhaps. She just may be accepting of these fragmented pieces that need a lot of mending.

Her caring nature could relieve all the angst that fills all the voids of who I am. Can she do that? I think so! Does she want to? Maybe. Is it time to go in for repair? Do I trust her? Hey, I'm going to try... just try. I'll give her a call... definitely. Michael was awakened when they arrived at his hotel.

Morning came so quickly. Mary's eyes reluctantly opened. Although she acknowledged where she was, other parts of her mind raced across last night, trying to figure out what time it was. *If my watch says it's nine o'clock in the morning, and if I'm thirteen and a half hours away from Bombay... but who cares? My body feels like it's been through hell. I'll go with my instincts and just lie here a while.*

I must call Uncle Paul and Aunt Catherine ASAP. Now that's exciting. Uncle Paul is a wonderful man... so kind and so giving, and Aunt Catherine... a carbon copy. Both of them have always wanted to help. They have been an enormous support through my entire life. When Dad, then Mom died, they were always there, as if I were their only child.

Aunt Catherine is truly a matriarch, a leader of troops, and not one to fool with. She is her own person, and while you're at it, you best not mess with her husband. They are a 'tag team match' with a very special marriage and relationship... made in heaven as the saying goes.

Mary found herself up and about, wandering through the house, enjoying the rediscovery of every item in every room. She touched, then held, so many precious things: pictures, curios, and books—that brought her back to her childhood. She recalled moments of high school and college, her mother and father, and Uncle Paul and Aunt Catherine.

She picked up the phone and dialed the number as if it were just yesterday that she would be calling to see if mom was there for coffee.

The phone rang once, twice, three times, before Uncle Paul answered. "Hello." His voice was so comforting to hear. "Well, hi, Uncle Paul... " She could barely get out his name before he recognized her voice.

"Mary! Where are you?"

"I'm home. I am really home," she said.

"You mean at the house?"

"Yes."

"I'll be right over. Is that OK?"

"Oh, yes, that's wonderful," she told him.

"Catherine is over at the Thompson's. I'll be there in two minutes... bye!"

Mary was beside herself with excitement. She ran up the stairs to brush her hair. She opened her suitcase and grabbed a pair of jeans and her trusty paint-stained sweatshirt. She pulled on the jeans, and then took long strides down the short hall, still tucking her shirt in. As she neared the landing, taking two steps at a time, she saw her Uncle Paul turning into the driveway.

She dashed out onto the porch, closing the distance of half the world to a few feet. He walked briskly towards her, his hair "white as snow." With a friendly, father-like smile, he offered his arms. His head was back, and he was as proud as he could be that she was within his reach. Mary tucked herself, tightly just under his chin, and then she kissed him on his whiskered cheek.

"What a wonderful surprise!" he said. "Catherine will be so happy to see you... not to mention how great you're making *me* feel.

"Let's go in," he suggested. "It's a beautiful day, but a bit chilly. How long are you staying?" His eyes moved upwards, questioning, yet wrinkling his forehead with a smile. "I kept the house just as you left it. I hope you like it?"

She reached for his hand, squeezing it softly. "Like it! It's perfect!"

They walked through the front hallway into the kitchen, and Mary offered him some tea.

"Let me run the water in that sink for a while," he said. "I haven't done it in a few days. I think it's a good idea."

"*Tea... tea,*" she wondered out loud.

"It's in the cabinet... one of those preserve jars on the left."

"Got it," she said.

The water was on the stove. The gas jet lit immediately, as if her mother had just used the burner an hour ago. The flames wrapped around the pot, warming the air around them, as well. The kitchen had an aroma that was everything she remembered.

There was something about the wood and the smell of paint on the cast-iron-baseboard radiators that sent her back to this place—back to *her* home and no other—back to being a schoolgirl. She felt content, and she had not felt this in a very long time.

The kitchen had been renovated back in the late seventies. There was a lot of light from the skylights. The bleached oak wainscoting skirted most of the perimeter of the Spanish terracotta floor. A large fan, with no lamps, hung down from the beamed ceiling. Her dad hated the light that came from those "beacons," so it had remained a simple fan.

All of the incandescent lighting came from indirect sources that bathed the entire room with soft illumination. Her father was obsessed with lighting things, people, and spaces because of his sensitivities as a film director. "Light was like a religion," he would say. "The fragrance of heated bulbs on the set was like being in church." He loved it.

One of Mary's paintings, she had done as a child, hung over the table where they were seated. Its subject was Lilly. She sat on top of the stone-wall that was in the back of the house. Her orange-striped tail wrapped around her body. Above her, spanning the entire width of the piece (about forty inches), was a beautiful rainbow with blue clouds suspended in a white sky. Her father loved that painting for a "gazillion reasons" but mostly because of its honesty and the bragging rights about his daughter's talent.

This moment was not a dream. Mary was home. It was true. The excitement was shared for both of them; their faces were filled with happiness. Uncle Paul's eyes were kind; they were hazel in color. He glanced at Mary, and she became more aware of his eyes that she had painted. She had captured his character before in many canvases, conveying what was his nature—kindness. These paintings were *giving* and *loving* visual narrations—They were gifts to those that were fortunate enough to *feel* their meaning.

"How long are you staying?" he asked again.

"Forever," she said.

"That's long enough for me," he said, a little surprised. "Where's John?"

Mary turned away at the sound of John's name—her face reddening—her facial gestures tightening. "He is in London, and that's where he'll stay."

Concerned, Paul had difficulty phrasing his next question. "Are you," he began, turning his head so that his eyes looked directly into hers... "divorced?"

"No., not yet," she answered, "but it can't happen soon enough."

"I'm sorry, Mary," he said, overwhelmed with compassion for his little girl.

She fidgeted with her tea bag. "It's OK. He... me... well, it's just better for me, and that's what matters."

Paul lowered his voice in a fatherly fashion. "Yes, that's what really matters," he said. "Is there anything I can do?"

He closed his eyes in sadness... turning his head to the side... his whiskers touching his shirt.

"No, you've done all of this for me," she said, waving her arms around at the house. "Without you, I would not have this home."

Paul stood and placed her head on his chest, holding her to him. His strong hands grasped hers tenderly, and Mary wrapped her arms around his waist.

"I think of you as my own daughter... my very own," he said. "I'm sorry. It's the only real selfish thought I have had these last few years. If this house hadn't been here, I would have had nothing to do most days. I would come and sit in this chair, thinking that you would come home soon to your aunt and me. I would talk to Rusty. He would lie right over there. This home will always be here for you... always... and so will Catherine and I."

"And Rusty?"

"Rusty got to be a little older than most dogs. We held on as long as we could then finally put him down for a long rest... about two years ago... in the fall. I couldn't have been any sadder and just can't replace him... neither can Catherine. He was a good friend." I don't know if she had the heart to mention it in her letters?"

"He was a great dog," Mary said.

The pouring of the kettle filled the silence as the steaming hot water splashed across the tea bag into the cups. Mary's thoughts returned to last night.

"Oh, yes," she said suddenly. "Happy New Year. I almost forgot."

"Happy New Year, honey," said Paul. "Two thousand... that's a lot of years."

"Thank you and Happy Century! Want some sugar?"

"This is fine," he said, coughing. "It's the end of my cold."

"No sweets for me, either. The many years in Calcutta have made me a purist when it comes to tea... even Lipton."

"How was it there?" he asked. "How did you adjust to their culture?"

"Not easily... the Indian culture is complicated. But the Americans and English were impossible: They were the nouveaux riche, who gave dinners and parties, attempting to spread their shallow existence over too much turf. John was groomed for the part because he was born one of them. I, on the other hand... well, you know."

"You must have had a field day with some of them. I guess they wouldn't know a real person if they saw one... so many people with so much insecurity."

"I'm not sure why I went in the first place," she said.

"Well, it was a different time," Paul said. "Sometimes in life you end up where you start out. It just takes a little longer to get to a place where you've been. You've made the journey. It's done now. But John... is he over this, too?"

"He doesn't have a choice. It was my decision. It's just over. I am not going back, and he is not welcome in my life at all. He has been a waste of time. Whatever happened—however it happened—he left me emotionally hanging as an ornament. I was something he owned. If I were one of his business associates or a project, I'm sure I would have been paid more attention.

I buried myself into painting, then writing some prose... things that expressed myself... just *stuff* filling the emotional void that I was not willing to admit to. It was denial, but it's over. I feel free," she added as she slowed her speech. "Sad, but it had to be over."

"Stuff? What's stuff?" asked Paul. "Oh, it's kind of a creative license for 'artsy types' to call their work 'stuff.'" Well, he said proudly, "If it's anything like these paintings we've stored here, I wouldn't mind hearing or seeing *more* 'stuff,' please."

Mary sipped her tea, holding the cup with two hands. "Well, of course," she said. "There are *cases* of more stuff being shipped here in the next week or so, so be on the lookout."

He leaned back, immediately accepting the mission then cleared his throat. "So, emotionally you're home licking some severe wounds. Are you OK otherwise?"

"Fine," she lied.

"Are you sure?" he asked.

She quickly changed the subject. "What time is Aunt Catherine getting back?"

"I imagine as soon as she gets through with two cups of tea and a little storytelling... well *that*, and she's picking up some vegetables at a new produce market on Lake Street." She should be about an hour or so.

She looked at him seated so comfortably in his bentwood chair; the wicker supported his strong back. His snowy white beard followed the contour of his gentle features—his appearance was consistent with his kindness.

She had never forgotten the way he nodded his head, while closing his eyes, to show understanding. She remembered that John never nodded. If he did, it was like a string puppet, *affecting* emotion as best he could. But this man, her Uncle Paul—in a nod, in a wink of an eye, or a gentle smile—comforts her.

He raised his head, finishing his tea. "May I show you something?" he asked.

"Sure," she said. "Is it wonderful?" she laughed

He reached for her hand. "I *think* it's practical, but I'm *sure* it's wonderful. We'll need our coats."

Mary's arm stuck in her sleeve as she pulled on her coat, and Paul lent her a hand. They walked out the front door, across the porch, and down the steps toward the garage. A gentle breeze blew a few leaves across their slate path, towards the surprise. Uncle Paul lifted the hinged arm that held the double doors shut. The two doors were separated only by inches.

Motioning to Mary, he said, "Now you stand here and close your eyes."

"Is it Christmas?" she asked.

"Well, kinda," he said. He opened the doors, swinging them back against the building. "*Now*," he said, in a voice that revealed his own excitement. "*Here's* a gift of love... fond memories... and practicality. Take a look at this."

"May I open my eyes?"

"Yes, please"

"Mom's Buick!" she exclaimed, raising both hands to her head. "Immaculate. You kept it!"

"Yes, I did," he said. "And I might add that it's just as your mother left it."

Mary touched it, running her hand over the trunk, then the side window, and across the door. "It's as blue as my memory, as clean as the day I left, and as beautiful as my dreams. Thank you!"

"It's my pleasure," he said, with a big grin spreading across his face. "I have thought about this moment a long time. I'm happy you love it so much."

"It's ready for the new Millennium."

"And," he said, "It has 23,000 miles on it. I changed the battery a couple of times, had it serviced regularly, and kept up the registration and insurance because we would use it now and then... but rarely. Start her up."

He reached into his jacket pocket and pulled out a key, placing it in her hand.

Then he depressed the chrome button on the door handle and the door unlocked. He moved away, and then he opened it, giving her room. She kissed him on the cheek, as she stepped forward and sat in the driver's seat.

She looked in the rear-view mirror and saw tears in her eyes. *So many years have gone by* she thought. The last time she had looked into this mirror, she was a young girl. Now she saw her mother.

"What do ya think?" he asked.

Mary was speechless. She placed the key in the ignition and turned it. It started right up.

"Let's take it for a spin," Paul said. "I'll come around."

"Let's do it," she agreed.

Uncle Paul got in the Buick and backed it out slowly. Mary rolled down the window to adjust her mirror as the wheels rolled over dry leaves. The sound of crackling twigs beneath the tires heightened its moment. The fragrance in the car (that reminded her of shades of her mother's perfume) had been held, tightly inside. The scent was ever so faint—but there.

"Where to?" he asked.

"Any direction but East," she said.

"That's fine with me. Let's go see if Catherine is back."

Mary placed her foot on the gas gently, as the grand old car's engine revved. They were off, down the street, past the homes that seemed the same and yet different. The trees were more mature, the homes were bigger, and there were more of them. There were also more walls and more white-picket fences.

They arrived at the intersection of Canyon and Middle Patent Road and made a left, then crossed Cedar Hill and made a right. A mile ahead, and there it was—the O'Connor's home. It was a lovely little place with just the right elements to use in a Courier and Ives Christmas card.

A little smoke was escaping from the chimney as they drove up the drive and parked just behind Catherine's sporty Oldsmobile.

For Catherine, seeing the Buick in the drive could mean only one of two things. But seeing Paul exit the passenger's side meant only one. Catherine was out her kitchen door and almost running before the two had shut the car doors.

"Oh my God, it's you! My darling child! Paul, I wondered where you disappeared to without a note! You must have been in the same hurry to give her a big hug!" she gushed, as she embraced Mary. "Well, I'm speechless. Happy New Year, Mary. What a wonderful way to start a new century!"

Then Mary pulled Uncle Paul into the hug, squeezing them both hard. "It's so... I just love the two of you," she said. "I do! Happy New Year, for all of us!"

"How long are you home for?" Catherine asked.

Paul laughed. "She said 'forever.'"

"That's just right for us," said Catherine. "We missed you so much. The letters were wonderful. Sometimes I knew you weren't happy... in a few of them... but that's for later."

Paul walked ahead of them and opened the kitchen door. "Let's go, ladies. The heat's getting out."

Aunt Catherine and Uncle Paul's home was, in many ways, similar to Mary's parents. Their generation had its sameness, but without question everyone had his own character. They all expressed themselves in varied ways but always ending up with a comfort level called 'home'—overstuffed sofas, café curtains and the kitchen clock ticking as it had for decades.

Catherine placed her arm around Mary's shoulder as they walked into the kitchen. Mary turned her head and nuzzled into her aunt's arm, her face pressing against her knitted sweater. Its touch was soft and comforting.

Catherine's rosy cheeks needed no make-up. Her kind eyes announced their own beauty, and her walk was as solid as the person she was. Catherine needed no titles or list of accomplishments to introduce her. Catherine Frances O'Connor: her person, the woman, our friend, had been part of Mary's life since birth.

Her bath powder had a fragrance reserved for a mother and aunt who would never reveal the secrets of its formula. It would cast a magic spell over the children who came close enough to be hugged and kissed. Mary had always thought of her mother and aunt whenever this enchanting fragrance wafted past her, when she and John had traveled together and had been in the lobbies of great hotels in Europe or in a shop in Rio.

As they walked in, Uncle Paul squeezed Mary's hand, officially welcoming her back to their home. The kitchen had not changed a stitch. A small oak table with turned legs and two spindle-back chairs remained steadfast. Aunt Catherine always sat on the right—Uncle Paul on the left. This table, in the kitchen, was the center of their universe. Just beside the table, there was a double casement window, dressed with café curtains; the bottoms were pulled back at distinct widths, expressing a rare difference of opinion on where they should be placed.

The window supported many practical and beautiful things. It held a large magnifying glass, with a brass handle, so Uncle Paul could complain about the size of the type the newspaper was using. And Aunt Catherine kept her collection of translucent blue glass figurines grouped across the sill. All elements were part of their life's art.

Each piece was removable but was always returned with a slight twist, as part of an ongoing "adjustment in their harmony." There was even an old plastic ruler—that seemed to survive—even though most of its numbers were erased.

And there was a blue cut-glass sugar bowl with an assortment of pens and pencils, easily available for use for Aunt Catherine's crossword puzzles and Uncle Paul's bill paying.

The light that came through their window was the adhesive that tied all these elements together. The only two variables of composition were Catherine and Paul, as they moved within "their art." Mary felt privileged to be part of their spirit while observing them from within.

They had created a statement that artists strive for: a purity of expression through the selection of shapes, colors, and textures. Their "collection" was "a complicated statement made simple," since it was presented within the perfect environment—and entitled "home."

It was so right, so visually expressive. As an artist, she humbly respected them for their taste. As the child, in their eyes, she just loved being there.

Catherine moved directly to her place at the counter and started to remove some fresh beets from a grocery bag. She turned, recalling Mary's statement, "home forever." *I like that,* Catherine thought, *but then what exactly does that mean?*

"So," she asked Mary, "*John...* is he forever, too?"

"He is out of my picture... no longer a part of me."

Catherine held out her arms for a hug and Mary came to her. "I'm very sorry, dear," she said, holding her.

"You don't have to say a word," said Mary. "I just feel so good right now that I don't have to be part of any of that life... his 'owned wife.' This is the end, *finie...* done... finished."

"Is he coming here?" asked Catherine. "You know I am ready for him, anytime."

"I doubt it," she answered. "And I'm sure you can deal with him. He does know I'm home. We had a... let's say... heated discussion, over the phone in London last night... that 'spelled it out' as he would say."

"I don't see what you saw in him then or now," said Catherine. "But those were different times, different needs. I tolerated his behavior because of you."

"I know exactly what you mean. At first it was escape," Mary said. "Escape to the un-known world... to the newness that youth requires. Then it became an emotional prison, and the price was *time...* too much time attempting to repair the 'un... repairable'... with too few tools to fix it. His emotional 'suit of armor' was impervious to sensitivity or expression.

"For me he became a fixture, just standing there in our own personal museum. Our marriage became a 'relic of the past.' His only interests were 'the competition.' He was driven to compete at business... then at golf, and he was always prepared to joust with his next op-ponent.

"When my demotion occurred from 'fair lady of the realm' to 'stable hand,' I left. Now I'm back. I'm home and happy."

"And as your husband said, 'sometimes in life you end up where you start out. It just takes longer to get to a place where you've been.'"

"He said that?" Catherine laughed.

"Yes."

"I've been telling him that for years," Catherine said. "My mother... God rest her soul... must have told me that every day when I was a young girl."

"Well, we both love him," Mary said of her uncle.

"Yes, we do. Where did he go anyway?"

"He went upstairs just a minute ago," Mary said.

"How are you feeling? The trip must have been exhausting... all the way from Calcutta."

"That's true. But more than that... I'm not sure what time it is, or for that matter, what day it is."

"I've never been that far away, except for the time we went east to Chicago. I reset my watch two hours. Paul refused. He said he wasn't going to be there long enough."

"Well, I had quite a time last night with a very unusual man, Michael. Do you have a tissue?"

"Yes, there are tissues on top of the fridge. And now about this man?"
Mary stood on her toes and reached for two tissues. It was the most wonderful time I've had," she said. "We chased time zones and celebrated five New Year's Eves in one night. It was his idea, and I just... well... it was so touching."

"How romantic."

"Yes, it was," she said warmly... remembering. "Very."

"You must have enjoyed his company?"

"Yes. He is very unusual."

"How so?" Catherine asked.

"He is warm, caring, and giving... very funny... always putting a spin on a phrase. But I think his other side is very deep... a part you would like to know more about. As a man, he seems sensitive and emotional. There's something about his touch."

"Touch?"

"Well, I met him on the plane to London. He came out of *nowhere* to *me*. He was sitting up front. He walked down the aisle to my seat with two cups of champagne."

"*Cups?*"

"They didn't have any *glasses* on board, so we all used *cups*. He asked, in a very pleasant way, if he could join me. I had been crying. A few tears had fallen on my hand. He placed a cup on the tray then proceeded to touch the tears with his napkin, saying it was quite all right to cry on New Year's Eve because it was the perfect night for emotion.

"He said something about, 'not too much,' and 'not to fill up my cupped hands or something.' It was funny... kind of absurd. It made me smile. Then I lost my thoughts because I was staring at him... at his warm face. I was taken away from my sadness and consumed by his presence in just a few seconds.

"I feel like last night was a gift, a surprise gift, which I never expected to receive... 'five more years' all in one night. I find him very interesting, intellectually. I enjoyed his persona."

"Well, I love Paul, his persona, and his whiskers," Catherine said. "You know that. We stayed up till nine and watched the ball drop in Times Square and then went to bed. But I do love him."

"We were there at JFK as you watched!" Mary said, excitedly.

"Well, Happy New Year, again, dear, and many more." "I'm ready for the next one hundred."

"And again, Happy New Year to you," said Mary, glancing at her watch. "I don't know what time it is."

"It's 11:30 a.m., New Year's Day, 2000. Oh my God, 2000! But what are your plans? What are you going to do?"

"Just enjoy life... do some painting... writing," she said, setting her watch. But she changed her tone, trying hard not to reveal the truth behind the questions, reaching for the inner strength to mask her expression. "And, I," she said, stammering, then coughing, "excuse me... should have a physical. I haven't been feeling well these last few months." She wondered if she was convincing. Not certain, she held the tissue to her face, shielding her expression.

"How so?" asked Catherine, looking directly at her.

"Tired. I think it's more the emotional strain."

"Hmmm." Catherine took a hard look at Mary's movements, as a mother would look at a child's body language while they explained what they did wrong.

"What was my mother's doctor's name again?"

Catherine had started to fold the grocery bag, then, stopped. "He specializes in certain things," she said, beginning to wonder about the question. "You probably need an internist or whatever. These doctors today specialize."

"Yes, but I would trust his recommendation," Mary said.

"Sure," said Catherine. "I have to check my little book for you. It's been a while since I took your mother to those visits. I think he moved. But it's been a long time. I do miss your mother, Mary. She was the only real friend I ever had."

"Thank you... mine, too."

"How tired do you feel?"

"Ohh," she said, yawning. "Right now I'm pretty tired from the big night I just celebrated."

"You should take a nice nap. Would you like to lie down in the spare room?"

Mary got up and walked to the kitchen door. "No, I think I would like to go home now... unpack and settle in."

"Paul!" Catherine yelled upstairs, as she snapped the bag to finish folding it. "Paul!" His low voice came from a distant part of the house. "Just a minute!"

"He sounds intent," Aunt Catherine said.

The floorboards creaked as Paul walked across the floor above them. Then he walked down the steps to the dining room. He entered the kitchen with his wonderful smile.

"Hi, I had to get these things together for you if you're going to stay home now," he said.

"What things?" asked Mary, wiping her nose.

"Well, here's the checkbook for the house," he said. "You've got a nice balance there, so keep an eye out."

"Balance?"

Paul scratched his ear. "Well, you rich people must think it costs a fortune to run a home in this part of the world with the size checks you sent. We just used what was necessary and Catherine connected it to a savings account, so you'd get some interest.

"The only big thing we did was keep the phone on, since I'd be there working, and Catherine would give me a call to get home or stop at the store. So anyway, that's why."

"Then here are the keys to everything else. I have a set as well, in case you need me for something.

All the bills are paid, including the taxes. I just can't believe the taxes."

"Don't get started on that," said Catherine. "Please... another time."

"You two are just wonderful," Mary said. "Unbelievable! I love you both. Thanks!"

"Mary's going home for a while, to take a nap and to settle in, Paul," Catherine said, rinsing her hands at the sink, "But not before we give her a little care package of some soup and a little of that pie I made."

"Oh, that's great. Thanks," said Mary.

Catherine had it ready in a jiffy, wrapping it in a brown bag. "Now keep it flat. Place it on the floor of the car."

"Thanks again. I better get going."

Catherine dried her hands on a kitchen towel, and they hugged, exchanging 'Happy New Year' again.

Mary walked down the driveway, her package in hand, while Uncle Paul and Aunt Catherine waved from the doorway.

"I'll be by a little later for my truck," yelled Paul.

"Mary says she's feeling tired. She wanted to know her mother's doctor's name," Catherine said to Paul quietly, as Mary drove away. "I'll call her later."

"She's had a rough few years, she tells me."

"Well, I hope that's all."

"Come on, now, Katie. She's home, and that's all good news." They waved again as the Buick pulled away and Mary headed home.

Chapter Five

The absence of any sound was forbidding as Mary attempted to assemble her thoughts, coming out of a deep sleep, searching for a path out from her stupor. Her eyelids fluttered as she stared into the corner of her pillowcase. Muted pools of color filled her vision with the closeness of the pillow as if she were seeing the surface of some planet—light years away. She had no sense of time. It was a moment of not knowing where she was.

For many of the darkest nights of her life, in Calcutta, Mary had wrapped her head into her pillows, smothering the sounds of car horns, police sirens, and train whistles on the streets, many stories below. In her sleep, she had returned to this reflex. Her senses dulled, she wrapped the pillow tightly around her ears. She barely felt the fibers of the woolen comforter on her face. There was no warmth, nor cold. She sensed the tips of her fingers scratching across the surface of the pillow, crossing her ear, through her hair. She yawned, feeling its resonance only, as if she were submerged under water, having pressure against her eardrums. She fought her fatigue attempting to assemble herself into fully awakening. She began to push herself up—lifting her head out from the pillow. The phone rang, ripping her from the quiet. She recoiled away from the sound, with her body shaking for a brief second before she reached for the receiver.

"Hello?" There was no one on the other end. "Hello?"

"This is an international operator. Would you hold please?"

"Yes," she answered. Mary moved her hair away from her ear, shaking her head and grasping the receiver tighter. Then she pressed the phone closer to her ear, straining to hear *any* sound. And then the worst sound—the sound of John's voice came to her.

"Hello? Mary, are you there?"

It's him, she thought, in disgust.

"Yes, John."

"I'm delayed getting home, but will definitely be there by middle of next week," he said. "Will you be back before me, or when could I expect you?"

There was a long pause. "Mary?"

"John, I haven't changed my mind. And I doubt that I ever will. I am staying home now... as I told you... staying at *my* home."

"Well, if you won't be coming home, may I visit?"

"You may visit anyone you wish, but not me," she answered. "Don't you bother. I don't want to see you. In fact, if you decide to do a magical appearance, it will probably send me into a tirade. Allow me to make this perfectly clear... stay away from my life... my work... my thoughts. Stay away from me. Our marriage is over. But if you feel like traveling *somewhere*... go to hell."

"May I call?"

"Goodbye, John. Goodbye. Goodbye. That's three phone calls you didn't have to make."

"I do love you, darling," he said.

"You *love* me? Are you reading from a script? Those words could never come from you. It's impossible. You have no clue of the meaning of the word. 'Love' is a word you use for convenience."

"Well, in keeping with the brevity of four-letter words. I hate you. Got it? H-A-T-E," and the worst part of hating you... for *you*... is that I've decided, I really like it. I feel just fine hating you... darling. Goodbye, John."

She placed the receiver back in the cradle of the phone. Her arm was outstretched. It remained there as she pressed the phone into itself, as if pushing John back to Calcutta—committing, intensely, to her decision.

The phone rang again; her hand was still on the receiver. It frightened her, and her arm recoiled again in surprise. It rang again while she composed herself—then a third time. She lifted the phone slowly, placing it to her ear. "Hello?" *This better not be John again*, she thought

"Hi, Mary, it's Michael."

"Well, hello Michael. How are you today?" she asked curtly.

"You sound tired," he said, "well actually... angry."

"I am very angry," she said. "But not with you. I'm not very happy at this moment. I'm sorry."

"Why did the chicken cross the road?" he asked.

"I don't believe this... why?"

"To get Mary off the subject."

"Almost."

"What did the elephant say when he crossed the road and smooched the chicken?"

"What?"

"Mary sent me."

"Can I send the elephant to London?" she asked.

"No, but he's got relatives."

"Well, let me know who to talk to."

"John called," he guessed.

"Yes, I just hung up. In fact, my hand was still crushing the phone when you called."

"Great timing," he said. "It could have been worse with call-waiting."

"What's call-waiting?"

"It's when your phone can receive two phone calls at once."

"I'm glad I missed that one. Mine still has a dial."

"No crank?"

"That's me. *I'm* the cranky one."

"Speaking of breakfast, lunch or dinner... when may I see you again?"

"How long are you in town?"

"Not sure... but I can wait."

"Well, how about lunch tomorrow in the city?"

"Great! Where?"

"Well, you're *staying* where?"

"The Sorrento."

"I'll meet you there at 'twelve-ish.' You think of a place. In the meantime, anything is fine."

"Great. That's wonderful... can't wait to see you."

"Tomorrow then. Bye."

"Bye."

After talking to Michael, on one hand and rehashing her anger with John on the other, she sensed her body's rigidity—the position of her hands and her head was fixed. She looked directly upward. Her feet were crossed—motionless.

A flash image ripped through her mind. She saw herself in a casket. Her body was cold and in this same rigid position. Her hands were crossed and folded across one another. She struggled to reject the image, but her eyes were held, tightly, closed—quivering. A flash of heat rocketed through her body. Her thoughts smashed, head on, with the reasons for her anxiety. Her fears conjured up the prose she had written about a frightening ride on a merry-go-round. The first lunge forward expressed the horror of being alone. This strained movement forward was the beginning of an unstoppable expedition into fear. There was a sense of forbidding as the torque of the motors began to move the wooden horses slowly up high—then down so very low—with the floor turning in an opposite direction. Her grip strained the leather reins.

The merry-go-round... the merry-go-round... each turn another day... each fluctuation up and down... a triumph or dismay. She fought to suppress her thoughts of her life, of her death... until this second. She tried to banish this fear to some hidden corner of her mind. *But the merry-go-round just builds up speed and gives no heed to those that step in its path.* She kept this all... in her darkest thoughts, contained behind the doors. It was the "never talked about," the "never opened door"—this fear of locked entrances, just as she walked down the hallway of the Ghandi Memorial

Hospital, counting doors—walking towards either the beginning or the end. This emotion was again running hot, now uncontrolled, through her mind. Her fears had been sealed until this moment. There was no stopping them, no emotional tools to cope with the realities of their impact on her life. She saw herself dead again. Then in an instant, she was like a child atop a hand-carved, gallant steed with a flowing mane—then she was dead again.

Building up speed, she could feel the acceleration. She was riding faster and faster with the wind blowing her hair back. She looked out to see caskets—and her mother dead and her father dead. Then there were blurs of space and color. She saw Paul and a door, with her mother and her father behind it. Now she is spinning around even faster and faster, but each fluctuation of "up and down" seems to be saying—enough! *I need one word to change my thoughts,* she pleaded to herself: *child... my child...mom... life... death.* Suddenly a key seems to be forced into each of her hands. And there are two doors. But which door should she open? The fear of unlocking the reality created another avalanche of emotions within her. Which key is life? Which key is the unspeakable? Her fingers trembled. *Where can I send myself? This is not real. I can create anything, anywhere. But a reality is behind each door. Am I on the inside locked in or on the outside locked out?* Confusion and frustration consumed her thoughts—and with lightning speed.

Her palms were sweating. She could feel the keys in her hands, cutting into her flesh. Her eyes moved beneath their closed lids—left, right, up, down. Then there was a pattern of opposites: "a ying and yang," an "in and out," a "yes and no," a "right then wrong." It was the past—no, the future.

Who am I? Why me? Is this true? I feel nothing in my body except the pain in my hands.

My mind races over the past: chasing down back alleys, touching, groping, sensing the cavernous depths of fear.

How do I get back? Should I go back?

Can I just wake up and rid myself of this place I have put myself in?

Open your eyes! Sit up!

I can't move.

I'm stuck, pasted to this place.

Am I dead?

I'll move a finger... a toe. I can't feel them!

I'll take a breath... or I'll cough! I can't!

I'll listen for the clock. I can't!

Mary, time to get up! I can't!.

Hurry now, you don't want to be late.

It's my Mother's voice... but she is dead.

Is she?

I hear a child crying. Do I?

She ripped herself upward out of her nightmare. She sat erect, gasping for breath. Her eyes opened wide. Her hands were wet. She looked in disbelief. There were no keys. All of her fears were amplified by being alone. She sat there not knowing where she was going—immobilized by anxiety.

"What will I do? How do I find the path? To where?"

Minutes passed. One foot found its way to the floor. A short while later, the other foot followed. She stood and walked to the bathroom sink. She turned the faucet on full, cupping her hands, splashing cold water onto her face, over and over again. With the faucet still running, she placed her hands on the sides of the sink supporting herself for a moment.

She turned the water off. Finding a towel, she held her face into it; she slid it, slowly, away and looked at herself in the mirror. It was over. Her thoughts quieted. She was back—far away from her fears. She felt more like herself. Her thoughts turned to Michael. This was comforting.

The aroma of Aunt Catherine's soup permeated the kitchen. Any other awareness helped her focus and escape from her anxiety attacks. They didn't come too often—but they were always a frightening experience. They would go away if she moved around. This movement would dilute the fears by replacing them with pleasant thoughts.

After filling a large mug with her soup, Mary walked towards the living room. She stood in the doorway looking into the room with a wall of cherry-wood cabinets at the far side. In the center of the room was a fireplace, and above it was a very large framed pencil-sketch of Mary, seated on her father's lap. Her mother was holding her hand; they were centered above. Her father's dear friend, John Thompson, had sketched it of them back in the *60's* as a return of a favor. Its detail was incredible. The expressions were captured by a simple pencil and the enormous talent of a "really nice guy" her dad had always said of him. The Baja carpets, the walnut armoire, and the jade chess set were still immaculate.

She chose to sit in her father's favorite chair—an Eames. She warmed her hands around the hot mug as she carefully sipped the delicious soup.

Her father's photo albums filled three broad shelves. They were just within reach, each album contained hundreds of pictures—"a visual story" of their lives. She placed her mug aside and reached towards an album. She felt so confident about their contents, knowing every image as well as she did. She always enjoyed skipping through decades, reviewing a moment frozen in time with the clichés that everyone used as they paged through: "They were so young," "Paul was so thin." And below a picture of Catherine, was a remark that she had written about herself that was so telling of her personality: "If I had known that you were going to keep these pictures so long, I would have worn a nicer dress."

Each page was filled with life. Their laughter and good feelings were conveyed through thousands of caring moments about them. It was as though they had all been "lead characters" in their own play.

There was another album to see, then, another. Then she would break the pace with a second mug of Catherine's soup. *Mom and Dad really did look so young... so happy... so content.* Hours went by as the imagery stimulated parts of her memory that had been quietly waiting for many years. She began to fall asleep. Her eyes were closing while the album she was holding slipped to her side—startling her a little. She closed the album. It was time to go to bed.

Chapter Six

Morning came quickly enough. For a few minutes, Mary wondered what to wear for lunch with Michael, but it seemed to come together easily enough.

Her adventure was about to begin—a trip into the city! She certainly hadn't done that in a long time.

Mary backed the Buick out of the garage. She drove directly to the hotel, or at least almost directly. First, she made a few wrong turns—along with a couple of "almosts," but she managed to pull into the Sorrento's garage two hours early. She wanted to explore the buildings and streets that had changed. She looked up at the walls of glass. Now there were sleek lines and simple designs. *Were they beautiful or boring? Time would tell.* At this moment, they were beautiful.

The streets were filled with many people dressed in business suits and a variety of other American attire. There were no turbans or saris, not one rickshaw—just a lot of Americans. There were many differences from her last time in Seattle, but the teenagers had made the most drastic change—wearing their clothing, so big, it was as if they were wearing clothing for two. Their crotch was at their knees. It was almost a joke. Was this the return to the *twenties'* zoot suit? Teenagers must have been rebelling against convention. She knew what that was about. She took a deep breath and continued to walk down past the hotel onto University Ave. She was excited. The stores were just opening as Mary found the Hartford Art Gallery. "*Perfect,*" she thought as she reached for the door handle just as it swung toward her. A very pleasant man greeted her as he opened the door.

"Good morning," he said.

"Good morning," Mary answered.

"What a wonderful January day."

"It is," she agreed."

"If you would like any information, I'll be with you in just a moment."

"Thank you."

Mary glanced quickly at the quantity and size of the pieces in the gallery. They were impressive... *a Chagal... a Klee... and look at that... a Henry Moore.*

I'm so glad I found this again, she thought. *What a treat.*

She walked toward another *Moore.* It was a black shape—so large yet so graceful. She could feel the effort the artist had to put forth to bring it into existence. Its presence demanded attention.

Looking through the sculpture, across the room, she noticed a dark rectangular shape that turned out to be a doorway to another exhibit. The entrance seemed to change with the lighting that escaped from within. Drawn to it, she moved away from the mass of the sculpture. She seemed to be the only one in the entire gallery.

The light from the room began to touch her as she moved into its space. An amorphous crystalline shape was centered within a pulsing pool of light. Its mass had been placed asymmetrically towards the back of the room. The walls were graduated from white, at the rear, to black, at the entrance. Its presence was simplistic, existing as a core element, but the use of light, which emanated from within, changed as she walked towards its nucleus. And she noticed... *with every movement I make, the shape changes, spewing a spectrum of intense light around in space, reflecting off the walls. One very talented artist brought science and art, light and our own selves together.*

It was a long time ago when Mary had had her own show here. *Her* work, she felt, didn't use science as much as emotion and different levels of awareness, to stimulate the viewer's senses.

And it was here, that she had met John. He had swept her right out of her own life and into his. She had been overwhelmed with his intensity, his persuasiveness, and what she thought, then, was his character. However, now, she knows him as a man who is a cunning predator. *It has taken many years to escape his grip, but now, I am back.*

The man who had opened the door returned.

"Are you enjoying the exhibit?" he asked.

"Very much... thank you."

"A very unusual collection of diverse artists are here right now."

"Yes... I really enjoy this piece, especially."

"This one communicates everything for everyone," he said, stammering.

"What do you mean?"

"No two people can speak of the same experience, since it's not the same one or even similar. I find it frustrating. I've, well, it's silly... but it makes me a little annoyed from time to time since it won't allow us to share beyond the obvious. To me it's a very curious piece but not deep enough."

"We can do the unthinkable," she suggested.

"And what might that be?"

"Well the one thing that the painting would hate the most is to have it communicate with itself, and we simply walk away and enjoy the rest of the exhibit. We never return to question its existence. We just walk away. I have done this before. It makes you feel your independence. It's very healthy," said Mary.

"Are you an artist?"

"I've been reaching for that description for my entire life," she said.

"I can tell that you accomplished an *understanding* of your art years ago. I mean that as a positive."

"Thank you. I had a show here long ago."

"That must have been. I've been part of the gallery for ten years. May I ask your name?"

"Mary Templeton."

"Mine is Scott... Scott Withers."

"Happy to make your acquaintance."

"Are you still painting?"

"Very much so."

"Good. Very good."

"I can't say I remember your show, but if you would like me to re-introduce you to the senior administrators for a possible 'something' for you, I'd be glad to do so."

"Just like that?"

"Yes, sure. With artists, you never know when you're finding a treasure... never *when*, never w*here*. So I say, if you would like... "

"Thank you," she said. "I feel wonderful. You made my day."

"Here's our card with the main number," he said. "Ask for Jacob Reinner or Janice Winthrop. I would start with Jacob. He's a nice man, very sensitive. Janice needs more time to understand the sensitivity of our resources."

"It says you're the curator," Mary said, reading the card.

"Yes, I am," he said. "But it takes more than me to make it all come together. I've decided to spend a lot of time in the gallery, people watching, attempting to feel what changes we should be making. This is very important. So, let's *start* this way and I will help."

"I'll call... send up a flare... come back... whatever it takes. I have an appointment just around the corner. Thank you very much I might add." And they walked towards the exit.

"Well, it's been a pleasure, Mary. Stop in and let me know what you're up to. I'll check back in the records for your show. I would love to see your work some day soon."

"Thanks. You will... very soon. Many of the newer pieces are on their way back from Calcutta."

"Calcutta! You were painting there?"

"Yes I lived there for quite some time."

"You must have had a veritable reservoir of subject matter," he said

"It was the children. I found them to be the emotional key to revealing the honesty of the East Indian culture."

"Now I am more than intrigued."

He opened the door wide for her. They exchanged goodbyes.

Mary walked back to the Sorrento. The lobby was vast. She gazed upward into the atrium as she walked toward the main desk.

As she walked past a man hidden by his newspaper, she was startled to hear Michael's voice call out her name. He pulled the paper down from his face.

"Hi!"

"Hi, how are you?" she asked. "Is it just me you keep picking up, or are you an international picker upper person?"

"Just you," he said. "But I perceive it to be a full-time job."

She sat next to him. "So, have you researched the world of food and come up with some epicurean experience for lunch?"

"Yes. I found the Umbrella Club yesterday. The service was excellent, the portions just right and the taste... mmmmmm. I said to myself, 'I have to get back here as soon as possible.' But I wasn't sure you would want to, or I should say, I wasn't sure if you would like it."

"It sounds good to me. Let's go. But why would I not like it?"

"Well, let's head in that direction," he said. "I'll show you."

They walked out of the hotel, retracing the steps she had just taken from the gallery. They crossed the street and turned right—past the gallery. Mary saw Scott standing near the window and waved. He returned her wave with a 'thumbs up.' Mary smiled.

"Do you know everyone?" Michael asked. "He seems to be your best buddy."

"I hope so," she said. "I drove in early this morning hoping to browse around, and I found myself reaching for the door handle of the gallery, just as it was opening. That man I just waved to is the curator. I had a very lovely conversation with him about an opportunity to show my work."

"Well, that's terrific. When?"

"Oh, it's going to be a while. I have to make a few calls and go through a lot of hoops before they commit... if ever."

They continued walking, making another turn that revealed a small park-like area between two large buildings. Its fountain seemed inviting. Mary stopped to gaze intently at it. The sunlight made the water appear "white hot" against the darkened evergreens.

"Oh how nice," she said surprisingly. "The polar bear's *still* here. I guess, since it's not very big, they managed to leave it alone."

The park was tiny, by anyone's standards, but it was beautiful. The ivy walls bordered a short stone path, which led to this polar bear sculpture. It was placed atop an ice floe, raising it many feet above their heads. It had a smooth patina and was sculpted in brightened aluminum. It was totally monochromatic but reflected its diverse surroundings.

They approached an unusual bench which faced the bear. The bench was a piece of art as well, fabricated in a similar metal to the bear. There were figures of a woman and a man, much like paper cutouts and about a half-inch thick. They were facing each other, and having an exciting conversation. The figures were folded into acute angles that created the bench. The man's shape faced the woman. His mouth was open, as if he were speaking. Mary sat atop the girl's figure as Michael motioned with his hand, asking, "May I?" Then he sat on the edge of the figures' knees, sliding back towards its full figure. The design had the man's arm reaching over the woman's back—as if he were holding her.

"I feel we should mimic the artist's design," Michael said, "And I'm sure *she* would feel we should."

"How do you know that a woman did this?" Mary asked.

"Well, Cheryl is an old friend of mine, a real talent. It's like you said, 'I just know everybody.'"

Michael chuckled and asked if she'd like to have lunch right there and in the next few minutes. She turned and saw the Sabrett stand and said. "The Umbrella Club! I get it. Yes... excellent! I'll have a hot dog with mustard and sauerkraut... and a diet soda... perfect. Can I help?"

"No, I'll ask for take-out," he said, walking away.

She had never seen him in daylight. His walk was confident. His manner was smooth, and gentlemanly. Michael was considerably taller than Mary, but the difference felt just right when they walked together.

Michael chatted with the hot dog vendor as he prepared their order with a 'majesty of movement.' The mustard was applied with a single motion. They were laughing as Michael picked up the cardboard carrier box and returned.

"I wonder how many lunches have been eaten in front of this bear," said Mary.

"Many! Look at the size of him!" Michael replied.

"I hope you're rested from our journey. It's very difficult to adjust." He popped open a soda for Mary. "It seems the older I get, the more difficult it is to adapt."

"I'm feeling fine," she said. "The conversation I had with the man in the gallery is the second thing I've done for myself in two... no, three days."

"And the first?"

"Leaving John and that miserable city. It offers a stimulant to my otherwise 'turned off' life. I feel up and positive... wanting to do things... share things... good things... great things."

"Well, aren't you lucky? That's... " he paused, looking at her, "good for you."

"Do you mean that?" she said.

"Absolutely."

"I haven't had this awesome all-American dish in so long," Mary said. "It is just the best. The Indians have no idea how wonderful this is. Could you imagine... if you put together a few hundred of these stands in or on any path to a temple? The volume of sales would be awesome."

"Is that what you want to do? Because they would have to be veggie dogs," he teased.

"No. But that's the way I think. In any case, let's walk. You're right! Veggies. Hmmm," she said.

"Sure," he said. "Where to now?"

"Who knows? Let fate take us to the best place ever."

They discarded their trash and turned left at the Sabrett stand, thanking the man for his presentation. He smiled. See you tomorrow?"

They walked for hours, exploring Seattle's sights. Mary noticed a professional building with a sign, listing the doctors. One was Dr. Kainer, the same doctor that had treated her mother. She made a mental note of the location, allowing her not to have to include Aunt Catherine in helping her find it. Turning the last corner, they found themselves in front of the hotel. They walked through the doors and back to the seats they started from. They both collapsed into the chairs with a sigh of comfort.

"Would you like a drink?" Michael asked.

"Sure."

They went into the cocktail lounge and found a table in the corner. Mary ordered a Budweiser with a frosted mug.

"I just can't believe how perfect that sounds," said Michael. "Yes, I would like the same."

"It's been so long since my last Bud," she said. "I have to confess... years."

"I've rented a room here for a month," Michael said—out of the blue.

"A month? How come?"

"Well, I have business in L.A. and in Vancouver over the next few weeks, so I made a nice deal with them for a room. It gives me a sense of place. Besides, I thought you might want to see me again. So I would kind of 'be around'... maybe. What do you think?"

"Sure... a month... makes sense to me."

"My American Express bills look like the national deficit," he said. "But that's the cost of doing business."

"Vancouver. I've never been there," said Mary. "As close as it is, I just never went in that direction."

"Want to go?"

"Not this time... maybe another," she said.

"If for any reason you would like to stay in my room while I'm away, I'll give you a key. It saves the drive. I'll be glad to let you do that anytime."

"I might take you up on that. What kind of schedule do you have? I don't want to inconvenience you."

"I'll leave you a key and an itinerary."

"What's in Vancouver?" she asked, changing the subject.

"An engineering firm with a couple of really smart guys who are designing a portion of the project in India. It's a small suspension bridge that crosses the Tungabhadra River near Kurnool."

"That's a mouth full." *But sculpting in metal is on a very large scale,* she remembered.

The waitress arrived with the Bud and poured it.

"Happy New Year," they said, toasting each other.

"So tell me, why do I feel so comfortable with you?" Michael asked.

"Because... "

"Because?" he questioned

"Well, it's because I feel so comfortable with you."

"You do?"

"Sure. We have both traveled halfway around the world to find each other. And it was on the way back from... and not here and not there... but on the way back from. *That's* a because."

"Because you didn't find me there, when *I* was there, and I found *you*, when we were leaving. Is *that* a because?" he asked.

"Kind of... but it's more because we found ourselves... then found each other. You just found me, and now I found you. *That's* because. "

"Well, I like because... 'because it's *you*'"

"You got it. That's it, because... "

"What are we up to this evening?"

"Dinner and more conversation," he said. "Dancing... hand holding... and... "

"I don't know about this hand-holding thing. It sounds a little intimate for me."

"Well, I meant when we were dancing."

"Well, that's different."

The waitress returned and asked if they wanted another beer. "Yes, please," he answered. "And I've got a question. Besides this fabulous hotel, and the wonderful people here, who cater to our every need, where would you go for dinner?"

"Well, you know this is 'Pill Hill,'" the waitress said.

"You mean First Hill," said Michael.

"It's called 'Pill Hill' because of the many hospitals and medical services that are here. So unless you would like Jell-O and aspirin, I suggest going over to Capitol Hill and Broadway and try any one of a number of great places. They're all pretty busy. There are a few places near the REI store, or where it used to be. But ask a cab driver. We're still not used to it not being there. Enjoy."

"The Buds are on me," said Mary. "Besides, I feel good about my first purchase in the US being a couple of American-made beers."

"Thanks."

They left the bar and walked out to the front of the hotel. The doorman asked if they needed transportation, and Michael wanted to know how far it was to Capitol Hill.

"Just far enough for a cab," said Mary.

"Yes, madam," said the doorman. He blew his whistle and a yellow cab pulled up.

"I'm new in town," Michael told the driver when they got in, after he asked him to take them to Capitol Hill.

"I'm old in town," said Mary.

"That's nice," the driver said.

"What I mean is, what do you recommend as far as restaurants up in that area?"

"To tell you the truth, I just paid my tuition, and for me it's a little out of reach. But if you like tacos... "

"Well, not really," said Michael.

"Well, I do drop a lot of people off at this little place called Pete's," the driver said. "It's kind of New York-ish, but with Seattle overtones or so they tell me. I guess you can take a look in there. You do have a lot to choose from up in that area."

"OK for me," said Michael. "Mary?"

"It's been a long time, but I have been there. Anything would be great."

It didn't take long for them to arrive at a little storefront bar and restaurant with red checkered curtains and the oldest doors they'd ever seen on a building. The handles were long, worn, and polished by the many who had dined there. Michael reached for one of the handles and opened the first of two swinging doors that created the entrance for a trip back in time: the hexagonal tile floors and the smell of beer seemed all part of the setting. Then a waiter approached them immediately and asked if they wanted a booth.

"Yes, of course," the waiter answered for them, before they had time to answer for themselves. He led them to another room and then into a third. "Would you like a drink?" he asked after they were seated.

"Two Buds," they said, in unison.

They looked around and noticed a few couples here and there but not much of a crowd.

"Was it with 'Claude,' 'Vincent,' or 'Leonardo' that you were here with?" asked Michael.

"Ralph," she said. "My father, for lunch a few times. It was a long time ago. Did you know that Jimi Hendrix lived here in Seattle?"

"Yes, and not to be a smart guy, but isn't he buried here?"

"Yes. He was the best. I was a kid when he was hot."

"We were all younger," said Michael. "So, for the sake of knowing everything I *can* about you, tell me about your life... growing up in this area."

"Boring," she said. "Very boring."

"I'm sure it wasn't. That's the way we all respond to our own childhood."

Mary explained, "Actually, in my life... in my own little life, I've been more prepared, more skilled... with a healthier perspective on what I've confronted, or even created, than most people. This is a gift from my parents. Not all people are that fortunate.

"My parents were very creative. They were intelligent and hard-working characters in their own time... in their own convictions. They passed this tenacity on to me. I didn't appreciate it then. And perhaps if they were alive, I would still resist their daily demonstration of 'who they are or were.'

"But I have sensed so much of them in me, so much so, that I feel guilty for the feeling of resentment that seemed to saturate my responses to their most insignificant gestures, requests, and interests... when I lived at home. It was the 'child in the child,' the 'child in the young adult,' and the 'child in the young woman' that rejected the institution.

"I had a genuine lack of respect, yet I was the child who refuted who they were as people. My parents only wanted to give to me, but I fought it and questioned every nuance of their parenting. Was this typical? Maybe. Was it smart? No. And even worse, I have not, nor will I ever have, the opportunity to express that kind of love to them. They must have really loved me to tolerate the injustice I offered in return for their gift. The arrogance I must have shown, to stand toe to toe and question everything."

"Well, maybe that's it," said Michael. "You are so much *like* who they were. What they created, out of love, is themselves. Just maybe who you are is what they expected to see... a stubborn little talented kid who can stand on her own two feet, 'toe to toe' with those who are their own Achilles heel.

"Maybe they wanted you to be the creator of the yardstick... the controller... the master. And now, the person that you have become can only be tested by *them*. You *passed* the test. They have replicated themselves and can now rest easy since there is one of their own, representing their beliefs in your world today."

"Maybe that's it," she paused and said nothing else. She didn't want to bring up anything negative.

Michael said, "The one ingredient children constantly bring to the equation of child rearing is obstinacy. They think they have to prove to their parents that they have a voice. They're looking for the ultimate pat on the head... the love and attention. A 'good boy' or a 'good girl' title is hard to earn."

He continued, "For me, as a child in school, I would get a C in math. My mother would say, C's aren't good enough.' I'd then get a B. 'That's not good enough,' she'd still say. And then the ultimate, A would appear. And she'd say, 'Can you do that again?' Just once wasn't good enough. And so it went, through college.

Each time I brought my grades home, she'd say, 'Why did you get a C in biology?' She wouldn't recognize the A's in civil engineering. When I graduated, she asked, 'And now a job?' Not *just* a job, but *the* job.

"So I got the job and then the next one until I was responsible for an entire project. And I took her to see the building, the complexity of the project, and the enormous amount of money, people, effort and responsibility. They would call me 'Mr. Bowland.' There were so many phone calls and meetings. She observed it all. I took her out to lunch. She didn't say a word about any of it.

"Yet, when it was time to leave, she said I ate too fast and to take it easy. 'Be healthy. That's all that matters,' she said. I took her home. There was no pat on the head."

"What's your real response to entropy?" Mary asked.

"Entropy is a five-dollar word with a no cents return," he answered.

"Is that a put-down?"

"Never," he said. "It's not part of anything I can control or organize. Therefore, it's out. I try to prevent it from happening in everything I do, but it happens anyway."

"Well, personally," she said, "a well-organized disorder is the ultimate lifestyle. People, who *need* to be organized, never obtain enough tools, or files, or bins to organize themselves. They ultimately *find something* but better yet, *can't find, something* because it's impossible. They're *too* organized. This further proves that in a small way, we are evolving into a new and improved disorder. What do you think?"

"I think, therefore, I am," he said. "That's what I think, and that's what my old buddy, Rene Descartes said."

"No. It was Nietzsche who said that... *not* Descartes," she said, taunting him.

"Maybe Bacon, but I think Descartes. Well, we'll see."

"But I bet you, you're *wrong,*" she said.

"Bet *what?* I don't care if I win, but you must know *you're* wrong."

"You're despicable," she said, teasing. "Nietzsche. And I, too, don't care if I'm wrong as long as you're wrong. You *despot.*"

"And you might be honored to know... the very last one. You will eat, now!" he said.

"Yes, you 'smooth talkin' man of men. How about what I see, being placed on every table? I think it's Saltimbocca alla Romano. But I'm so used to seeing minced, chopped, diced, and cut vegetables; a whole piece of something is too much to bear."

"You know it by sight?" he asked.

"Go away for three years too, and tell me you don't dream of food like this. I would sketch this as a doodle while doing something, anything to relive the experience of my own culture," Mary answered.

"I guess I've always had the 'quick fix'... a trip home... a fast something before coming back," he said.

Just then, the waiter appeared and asked if they were ready to order.

"Yes," said Mary. "Is that what I think it is? Saltimbocca alla Romano?" She pointed to a dish on another table.

"Yes, it is," the waiter answered. "It sure is. It's one of our specials. Would you like to hear the rest of them?"

"No, I couldn't deal with that many decisions," she said.

"It's OK. I'm the despot," Michael said. "But what's a female despot called?"

"There's no such thing as a female despot," she said, looking at Michael. "Just Saltimbocca Alla Romano, please," she told the waiter.

"I'll have that as well," said Michael. "With another round of drinks, please."

"OK, you're set," the waiter said. "But if I may ask, what is a despot?"

"It's a man with strong opinions, and I am the very last of the breed," Michael said. "But evidently, it doesn't come in a female size."

"No offense," the waiter said, "but guys your age have it tough. Women you grew up with all have it out for you."

"Well, how about you? How does it work in your generation?" Michael asked.

"I'm not sure yet," he said. "But I do know one thing. She likes you... a lot. I'll get your dinner."

As the waiter left, Michael looked questioningly at Mary. In a quiet voice, he asked, "Is that true?

Do you like me... really... really?"

"Despots don't talk like that," she said, mimicking him. "'Really, really.' I like the old despot better."

"OK then... you will like me, and that's it."

"Yes... a lot."

"Well, now, that's better. 'It's good to be king.' That's a quote again... but from Mel Brooks, not Descartes. Do you think, in his wildest imagination, that Mel Brooks ever thought he would be juxtaposed against Renee Descartes in the same sentence?"

"Excuse me... that's Nietzsche... not you-know-who."

"So, what color is your favorite color?"

"Red... for the blood I will shed if you're right... and it's Nietzshe."

"I've got the feeling I can't win for losing. But we'll check it out."

"It's fun, anyway," she said. "It really doesn't matter."

"No, it doesn't. But just so you know, to help support your level of correctness on this subject," he began, then, held his hands in front of his mouth to muffle the words, "I got a kdkjh in philosophy."

"A what?"

"A mfmmfmf."

"Sounds like F to me."

"No, it's a D."

"Well, I got a B. So there." she retorted.

"The professor said my own philosophical thinking was a little on the warped side. And he was going to save my Blue Book exams to see if he ever would have another student with the same thought processes. But in the interim, the grade was D," he said.

"Was the D for despot?"

"Was the B for beautiful?"

"Great save."

They continued to laugh and joke through dinner, telling stories and devouring the food, which was an enormous hit with both of them. They said goodbye to the waiter and walked outside the restaurant just looking at each another. Michael reached for her hand as Mary offered hers. He placed both his and hers into his coat pocket to keep them warm.

"Would you like to walk for a few minutes?" he asked.

"Sure."

As they strolled down the street, they passed a variety of restaurants, including more Italian, French and Japanese. For a moment it resembled New York, but without the traffic.

"Well, it looks as if we have many candidates for many other evenings of dining pleasure," Michael said They walked slowly, stopping in front of the shops to peek in the windows. "I like the jacket and pants very much," she said.

"It's very feminine... very tasteful... not too dressy." Michael added.

They walked for quite a while, window-shopping. Occasionally they would bump into each other and laugh. "There are times I can't walk a straight line," said Michael

"Well we can't drink beer anymore... only champagne," Mary said, as they neared the entrance to the Sorento. "That was wonderful. It was a great ending to a fabulous day."

"A night-cap?"

"For the first time, no," she said. "I want to get home before these eyes want to close."

"Well, where is your car?"

"In the hotel lot."

"Let me have the ticket."

She reached into her purse and handed Michael the stub. He took it to the doorman, then stood with her while the valet brought it around.

"Nice car, sir," the valet said. "Great shape."

"It's the lady's," he said.

"Well ma'am, it sure is a great car."

"Thank you. I love it."

"You must."

Michael held the door for her while she got in. "Thanks for a great evening," he said, sticking his head in the car.

"Me too," she said. "It was wonderful."

She kissed him on the lips, and he returned the kiss, pressing a little tighter, offering a strong sense of wanting to express more of his emotion for her.

"You call... I call... whatever," she said. "I'll be home."

"I'll call tomorrow," he said.

A cab pulled up behind Mary's car and flashed its lights, impatient to drop off its passengers.

"Well, you have to go," Michael said. "Good night and thanks."

"Good night."

She drove off as he walked back into the hotel.

Chapter Seven

Uncle Paul paced himself carefully as he hurried to answer the phone. Catherine must have gone to the store, he thought, as he grabbed the receiver. "Hello?"

"Hi, it's me, Mary," she said, sounding up and full of energy.

"Well, hello stranger. Where have you been? I gave you a call yesterday. Where were you off to?"

Catherine's car pulled into the driveway as Mary began to explain.

"I went into town and enjoyed seeing all of the changes that our fair city has been through these last few years. I met Michael for lunch... then dinner and didn't get home until late."

Catherine walked into the kitchen, motioning to Paul. "Is that Mary?" she whispered. He nodded, *yes*.

"Well, that's nice," he said. "When are we going to meet this tall, dark, and handsome friend of yours?"

Catherine motioned with her hand that she wanted to talk with her. Again, she did the same, being very persistent.

"Just a second," he said. "Mary, I think Aunt Katie wants to talk to you. I'll speak to you later." Aunt Catherine grabbed the phone. "Mary?"

"Hi."

"Sunday night we'll have an early dinner. Have your friend come over."

"Well, I'm not sure if he'll be around or not."

"Well, you check on that and get back to me. I'll make a pot roast with brussel sprouts. Do you think he'll like that?"

"Who wouldn't? I was just telling Uncle Paul that we had dinner in the city last night. It was a lot of fun."

"I knew it was you. That's why I grabbed the phone from your uncle. I was excited about asking."

"Well, I'll be talking to Michael today, so I'll let you know about the particulars later on. And by the way, what time do you want us there?"

"Six-thirty for him. You can come over any time."

"Thanks. So, how are you?"

"Well, your uncle took a spill today down his ancient ladder. I told him to burn it five years ago, so now *I* am. Do you need some kindling? I'm so mad at him. He hurt his foot and raised the skin on his shin. All this, for a ladder that can't support itself and a man who won't listen. This ladder goes back to when your father and he bought it together, at the beginning of this century."

"Is he OK?"

"Well, I'm sure he is. He took a hot bath, and he's still grumbling, so I think he's OK."

"Well, I'll talk to him later. Say 'hi' and you take care. Bye, Aunt Catherine."

"Bye, Mary."

The rustling of leaves and some chattering noises outside the kitchen window caught Mary's attention. The shafts of sunlight coming through the window made it warm and bright. She lifted her hand to shield the brightness from her eyes, just in time to see two squirrels chasing one another. One darted up a low branch. The other followed, then jumped onto a large rock, then hopped to the ground.

They seemed as if they were having a good time, but just as the fury of their motion seemed endless—they stopped. One clung to the branch, motionless as if it were frozen. The other began scratching at the earth, intently excavating. It would dig as if in a frenzy for a few moments, then stop and look around with its tail quivering—shaking—twitching, sending squirrel body language out for the other to see. It would dig some more, and then stop, shake its tail, and freeze. Then it would work and look around.

Finally, there was the prize: a well-hidden acorn. The other squirrel ran quickly to his friend's side and began to dig at a great pace, its claws penetrating the hardened earth with ease. The first ran off through the dappled light and sat in a very proper squirrel-like stance. He held the prize in his paws, biting quickly into the nut, swallowing, then biting. Little flecks of the nut fell to the ground. The squirrel stopped, looked, and then busied himself, chewing as fast as his little mouth could move.

It leaped once again, then seated itself in the center of a shaft of direct sunlight, perfectly placed as the light wrapped around the furry creature. The light offered warmth. Its color was a deep orange, exaggerating the texture of the squirrel's fur and the leaves that surrounded it.

This was captivating for Mary. She hadn't taken time to watch much of anything in such a long while, except for the baggage machine and the sculpture. But this was real. This was of her own choice: sitting and watching a squirrel eating an acorn. It was a simple act of life.

The scene didn't need a motor, electricity or a welding torch. She and the squirrels came together and all that was required was time—precious time. It was a "special delivery" visual message about the simplicity of life and its beauty. It was a treat... a real treat. It was definitely a way to avoid calling the doctor's office. But she had to—today.

Ahhhh, enter the ominous! A shadow broke the sunlight, passing across the squirrel. As it looked up, it saw a crow descending. Its wings were opened wide; its talons were extended. The squirrel ran as the crow landed, then the crow strutted about looking for more of what the squirrel was eating. If the squirrel had something to eat, so could it, it seemed to be thinking. But the squirrel didn't seem to mind the interruption. The two creatures looked at each other, accepting each other's presence: The squirrel twitched its tail, and the crow turned its head back and forth. Finding nothing, the crow turned and looked at Mary in the window.

It moved its head left, then right, before it hopped, stretching its wings. There was a flap, and then another, as it ascended, finding its way through the maze of branches up higher to the cyan sky, then out of sight. The squirrel placed the acorn back in its mouth, then hopped away. Mary turned to see the other one, but it had gone as well.

She moved back away from the window, and as she moved, the sun traveled with her. It stopped as it met her face. The warmth was rewarding. With Her eyes closed, she leaned her head back and ran her hands through her hair. Taking a deep breath and stretching, she enjoyed this little piece of time and space. It was all free, as free as her spirit that was awakening her senses.

It was two thirty when the phone rang.

"Hello?"

"Hi, it's the Umbrella Club representative."

"Well, how are you today?"

"I've been really busy putting together this three-dimensional puzzle with some missing pieces. I started early this morning to work with the time zones we're so familiar with. It's been a long day."

"Well, I just made one call today to Aunt Catherine and my Uncle Paul's house. They have invited us for dinner Sunday evening. Tell me you're in town."

"As a matter of fact... yes. And I would love to."

"Great."

"Do they drink?"

"Rarely, but a red wine is good. She's making a favorite of mine... a pot roast with brussels sprouts. Is that OK for you?"

"Well... well... well, a pot roast. It's been a long time, and I love it, especially at home."

"She said to be there at 6:30. I'll meet you there. Do you need directions?"

"The last time I was up there, I had a driver, so who knows."

"I do."

"So tell me."

She gave him directions to their house at 1066 Wildwood Road.

Thanks. So I'll see you there at 6:30. Does that mean 6:30 or 6:15 or 6:45?"

"In their generation it means 6:29 to 6:31."

"OK. See you then."

"You'll see my car in their driveway."

"No problem. Bye."

She had suppressed all the bad news for many days now and had to move in a direction that she did not want to face. She reached for the phone again. "Operator, may I have the number for a Dr. Kainer in the First Hill area? Thank you."

"The office number is 884-9900."

"Thank you."

She placed her finger in each of the circles of the rotary phone. Each rotation and return was a step closer to the reality that she had no choice, but to go through with this. It had to happen. She had to make the call. The last digit found itself at rest. There was a click and then a ring—followed by another ring.

"Drs. Green, Kainer and Marsh. Hello?"

"Is Dr. Kainer in? Well, actually I'd like to make an appointment, please."

"Just one moment, please," the receptionist said.

A nurse came on the line. "Hello? This is Diane Michele. Which doctor would you like to make an appointment with?"

"Yes, Dr. Kainer. This is Mary Templeton."

"Is this an urgent matter? The doctor's booked up for at least two weeks."

"Well, I've just returned from the Far East this week with some very distressful news regarding my possible degenerative health condition. And I would like to see him as soon as possible."

"You said degenerative?"

"Well, I'm repeating what my doctor had told me, and for that reason I have returned to the states... to my home. Also, Dr. Kainer had taken care of my mother's illness many years ago. Please, I'm very upset. I don't want to wait too long."

"He can see you Monday morning at 10:00 a.m."

"Thank you. May I have your building number, please?"

"Yes, that's 110."

"Thank you."

She placed the receiver back in its cradle and began to cry. The fears she could not share; the thoughts she couldn't keep in her mind for very long, were so horrible. Her fingers clutched the book on her nightstand, so tightly, her fingertips turned white.

I'll fight this. I'll win. I'm strong-willed. I don't even know if the diagnosis was right. What do they know? It was time to be quiet. She went to her bathroom and soaked in a very hot bath for quite a while. Grabbing her book, she slid into her bed and read until she fell asleep.

The radio announcer reported that it was 9:27 a.m. on this very fine January morning, with the temperature, unseasonably, warm and with bright sunshine throughout the day.

She took more time than she thought in the shower but she couldn't shake her state of mind. Dressing as if she were late, she rushed down the hall steps, took another quick look in the mirror, and then reached for a heavier coat. Finding its weight uncomfortable, she reminded herself, *this is Seattle, not Calcutta.*

Mary opened the garage doors, got in the car, and turned the key in the ignition. She wasn't sure about where she was going, but she backed out of the driveway and found herself headed in the opposite direction of Aunt Catherine's.

She took a left turn at the intersection, then drove a few more blocks. And there it was—a place to go for a while—a place to rest one's mind. It was St. Andrews Church, a wonderful old church, with a tapering steeple, that she hadn't seen in a long time. She parked in the lot and walked into the foyer of this perfect place. No one was there, just Mary and all her thoughts. The wooden walls were classic walnut and cherry. The inside doors were the same that she had passed through as a child—a teenager—and a young woman.

Was this the place to come? Is this where I begin a journey that takes these thoughts and feelings and exposes them to realities that I thought would never be?

She seated herself in a pew, sliding to a dark corner. She folded her hands, one within the other, just as she had done on the flight home, just seconds before meeting Michael, and just seconds before he had walked down the aisle offering cups and champagne. And, while she was drying her tears.

I have to think, she whispered to herself. *I must think about my life. Is it finished?* She pressed her hand across her mouth, as if to stop her thoughts. But the words kept coming. *Over. Done. Complete. Is that all there is? Will I be like that depressing Peggy Lee song, 'When I was a young girl, the circus tents were hung from the stars' or something like that? Then there is the big question... 'Is that all there is?' Well, if that's it, then it's too soon. I feel depressed, sad, frightened... mostly frightened. It's not death. It's not dying and it's not existing that's frightening. It's that 'nothing,' that I can't deal with.*

She slid closer to the end of the pew, looking up the aisle. Her anxiety lessened.

I walked up this aisle as a young girl, holding my first communion flowers. She gazed intently up the aisle, as if she could see herself again as a child. *Patsy Downey and I were always the first two in every procession because we were the shortest. We would look at our parents, smile quickly, and then turn so that we would not be caught talking during those serious services. We'd look at one another and giggle at nothing. The priest's nose was 'good', Patsy said. 'God gave him a very big nose to smell sin.' How silly, but we were kids. And kids are wonderful. My little Paul was wonderful.*

Maybe I should approach this day by day. Maybe today's not the day to deal with this. Maybe I'll find a way to deal with my problem in stages. Like right now I feel good... physically. So I'll ignore my thoughts for now and move forward. I'll think of good things. Get ready for dinner tomorrow night with Michael, Aunt Catherine and Uncle Paul... the three people I love. I just said I love Michael. Well... like him a lot, and maybe... he cares for me. I like that... but so soon? Is it too soon... or is it too late? No, it's not too late. I feel good about him. Suddenly a voice came from beside her, making her jump.

"Hi."

"Oh, you startled me, Father."

He's so young, she thought, *Or was it that she was so much older?*

"Can I be of any help? I'm sorry. I haven't seen you here... have I?"

"No, I just returned from the Far East a few days ago. But as a young girl I was an active member of the congregation with my parents. We live a few blocks away. My name is Mary Templeton."

"I'm Father Reversion. Is there something troubling you?"

"No, I've just stopped in to... oh it's been a long time."

"Welcome back. I hope to see you again soon."

The priest walked up the aisle, knelt at the altar for a few seconds, and then got up and walked into the rectory.

Mary left the darkened church, walking out into the bright sunlight, squinting.

She started the Buick and went directly to the Flower Hill Cemetery. *There's something about old cars that age, like wool, with a touch of sweetness, that never leaves the interior. It's all a part of their character.*

The cemetery appeared on her left. She turned into the drive. It had been a long time. She drove down a little hill and up a bigger one. There's n*o one here... no one. I'll drive along this ridge to the fountain and stop.*

She got out of the car and walked up a path with her hands in her pockets. Her coat was open, her hair blowing in a chilled breeze. There they were—Ralph Templeton and Agnes Templeton—Mom and Dad. The graves were well taken care of, the stones much alike. Mary spoke aloud, but softly...

"Hi, Mom and Dad. It's been a while. I just came from the church. There's this new priest there.

"He's a *boy*, I think. But then you said that of Father Milliken, Mom. He was the one with the nose... remember?" She sniffled and laughed a bit. "I know you told me to stop saying that, but... Dad, are you OK? You probably want to go to the studio. I know what you mean Dad! I understand. Aunt Catherine said that Uncle Paul fell off that ladder you and he bought twenty-five years ago. She's real mad at him for not throwing it away. She's going to burn it.

"I'm back now for a while, well... forever. And I left John... and I met Michael. And Mom, I miss you... I miss you too much, and you too, Dad. Do you know I'm here? Worse than that, you must have known I *wasn't* here all those years. I'm just so... I don't know, Mom. I have no excuse.

"Dad, I'm sorry. Don't be mad at me. It's a 'girl thing.' Dad ask Mom about it, OK?"

She broke down and started sobbing. "Mom, I'm miserable. I just don't know how to deal with this. What can I do? You must know about everything... about John, Dr. Satara, Michael... and about your grandchild, Paul. Please take care of him. I prayed you would. There is no one that can take care of him any better... at least until I'm with you. Forgive me. I hope it's not for a while, you understand. Hold him close. Tell him I love him. Mom... Dad, I've got to get through this. Help me, please. I am your little girl. I'm having a real bad time with lots of stuff. I wrote something a while back that I'll bring next time for you to hear. I love the three of you. You know that I do. I'll be back real soon."

Mary walked back to the car with tears in her eyes, not caring where they fell. She felt good about talking to her parents—so good that she had asked about Paul because, in her mind, they were taking care of him. She was *so* comforted about finally making the visit that she had wanted to make for many years.

The afternoon went by quickly. Even the geese were busy flying back and forth from the lake and making lots of noise. There were fifteen or twenty at a time. The lake was a place worth visiting but not today. Mary needed to work—to do something creative.

She wanted to do some pencil sketches for a painting she had begun to think about. She lit a cozy fire and began, as usual, with rough lines and smudges on a large tissue pad. She would work with a pad for a while, keeping certain elements by placing the tissue under a fresh page and tracing it. Then she would crumple up the old one and toss it into the fireplace with each piece bursting into flames. She spent hours concentrating, intensely, enjoying her work.

Whoosh—and a page was removed from her sketch pad, crumpled into a ball, and thrown into the flames. A few logs later and then another page was tossed away. Each one had a special feeling of progress, knowing she was closer to the completion of her painting. It was gratifying to create something that hadn't existed before.

She loved the process. It was like seeds, snatched from the nebulous expanses of her creative mind and later nurtured into an emotional expression.

Mary thought, *this is why I live. This is a big part of why I left a world that was suffocating me. I am at the beginning of a new life with happiness.*

She sketched a few important lines. Then there was a rub, a pause, and a thought. A good feeling consumed her. Now, she would save this last tissue to use for a blueprint for her painting.

She pushed the tired log back, deep into the hearth, closed the mesh curtain, and retired for the evening, feeling that she had accomplished something good.

Tomorrow night was their dinner party.

Chapter Eight

Mary spent most of the day refining her artwork and preparing the canvas for paint. She worked diligently through lunch, thinking, mainly, of her work. At one point, she realized that Aunt Catherine must have started dinner and that it was time to be transformed into something more than an artist with paint all over her hands and arms. She went up to change.

She was excited for many reasons and was spending more time dressing for dinner than she had anticipated. For Michael to meet her aunt and uncle for the first time was one thing. Finding the right dress and making it all come together perfectly was another... because... well she liked that "because."

Hmmm... what color?... how long?... is this too obvious?

Her creative self was now sensitized, by her needs as a woman, to feel as attractive as possible for Michael. This was not a challenge but a state of mind.

Each dress and skirt was carefully considered. Those that were rejected were tossed on the bed. Suddenly the right combination of what she was feeling rushed over her. A silk skirt from Paris, a blouse from a few weeks ago, and her old and faithful opera-length pearls—would all be perfect.

Her black pleated skirt fell loosely around her legs and flowed as she walked in front of her free-standing mirror. Her image disappeared as she walked out of her own reflection, then back, to feel the skirt moving freely against her thighs. She liked the touch of the fabric crossing her skin while it visually sent a message of being a woman—a women with spirit. The blouse was red but tasteful, like a candied apple with highlights that shimmered as the skirt flowed. She felt tempting until the shoes... *ahh the shoes. What would be more perfect than black? But I hate all of my black shoes, especially these.* She held them up to scrutinize them. *Maybe if I change them... a little tiny button or something. No, I can't deal with that now.* She decided to bathe, do her makeup, and think about the shoes later.

The water was hot, yet soft. The nozzle was set for a gentle spray, almost a mist, and the water fell upon her as a blanket of warmth. Each drop in motion massaged her face, rolling down her breasts, down her legs and feet. She could have stayed forever, but the reality of an old hot water heater reminded her of her date this evening. Reaching for the handles, she turned back to the thoughts of her shoes. She would have to make a decision.

She dried her hair and began to apply her makeup. This was a process that she never quite got used to. She always wore a minimal amount and felt that it was something like painting—and using herself as a canvas. The shading and tasteful eyeliner were all a building process. Now, one last look in the mirror and she thought, *I liked it better when it was a little steamier in here... a little impressionistic. Oh well, that's me... the best it's going to be. The shoes... now for the shoes.*

She went through the closet that held a thousand memories and just as many items, including boxes of shoes stacked neatly on the floor. She sat and patiently opened seven or eight of them Then she saw the little prize. But would they fit? A simple pair, black with low heels from a decade ago, waiting for tonight. She slipped her feet into them, ran over to the mirror, and tilted it downward. Feeling that they were comfortable, she was ready now to bring it all together.

There was one last thing before the commitment: It seemed every time she reached this point of dressing, she remembered a page from a wonderful book she had read. She had forgotten its name but remembered that the woman in this novel was pampered by the maidens who helped her dress. After she bathed, they would stand beside her, spraying her fragrance into the air, and she would walk through it, never applying it directly. From time to time Mary would imagine that her maidens did just that as she, herself, sprayed her perfume into the air, allowing it to fall upon herself in the most classic application of style and elegance. *Yes, that's it!* She felt ready to dress in the silk blouse, the pleated skirt, the comfortable shoes, and her pearls. She took one last look in the mirror and smiled. She felt ready for Michael.

Mary went down the steps, grabbed her coat, and was out the door. Minutes later, she was walking into Uncle Paul and Aunt Catherine's house. "It's me," she called out, as she opened the kitchen door.

Aunt Catherine greeted her with outstretched arms, giving her a hug. Catherine took a step back as Mary removed her coat. "You are gorgeous. You must *like* this man," she said. Then she frowned. "I *do* have a small, but important question from an old lady and another time. You are married, aren't you?"

"I am. Yes, but I am not. Since I doubt I'll be getting married again, I'm a woman who senses a gentleman who cares about her. I'm simply responding to something I've always wanted to do but never did in my 'so called' marriage."

"Well, you know what you're doing, I guess. It's just different times, certainly for my prehistoric thoughts. I want you to be happy... so Uncle Paul was sent on a mission for dessert. He'll be back soon."

"Can I help?"

"Certainly. I'm sure you remember where everything is, so if you don't mind, you could set the table."

"OK."

"The roast will be done about seven. Everything else is in the wings, ready for the oven."

"I'm sure it's under control."

"I saw your car at the church yesterday. I was passing by, coming back from the store. I hope you enjoyed seeing that it hasn't changed."

"Well, the priest has. He's so very young, or... "

"Don't say it. If you're thinking that, can you imagine what I think at my age? It's like going to Boys Town. But I *do* say, I have the most genuine respect for his manner. It seems to come from a much older man inside him."

"I told him my name, but I don't think he knows us as a family."

"Well that's good for now since we missed church today, and by the time he figures it out, I won't feel as guilty."

"Well include me in that guilt for the last bunch of years."

Mary walked into the dining room. "I'm going to use your Lenox... is that OK?"

"Yes, that's what I had in mind. I got a new set of flatware. We never did buy the silver, except for a few sterling serving pieces."

"Well, that's OK," said Mary, speaking from the other room. "Silver spoons remind me of 'you-know-who,' and I just don't want to think about him."

Aunt Catherine removed the lid from the pot roast as steam and the aroma escaped into the room. "How did you happen to be in church on a Saturday, Mary?"

Mary halted, as she was about to place a plate on the table. She thought quickly. "Well, I... I wanted to see if it had changed, like you said. And I took a few minutes to go to the cemetery to see mom and dad."

Aunt Catherine placed the lid back and thought about that. "Hmmm," she said, raising her voice a little. "I had been up there over Christmas. They keep it very trim. I like that. You must feel a little relieved, having been there?"

Mary paused, again, as she folded a napkin. "I guess you know me really well, don't you?"

"Well, honey, it's that you're so easy to really know and love that makes me see things. You *are* OK, aren't you?"

Mary turned back to the kitchen doorway, wanting to walk in and hold her aunt and confess. Instead, she gripped the back of a chair and cleared her throat. "I'm sorry. I was going to sneeze. Yes, I'm fine," she said. She decided to change the subject. "I'm excited about bringing Michael home to see you both. It's... well, it's just great."

Mary heard the car door slam. "Uncle Paul is home,"

"He probably bought out the bakery... knowing you're here."

"I hope so."

The kitchen door opened wide as Uncle Paul walked in, carrying an armful of white bags and a box. Hi everyone," he said, from behind the packages. "I got something you'll love. But it's a secret until after dinner." Mary took the bags from him, placing them on the counter, then gave her uncle a big hug.

"What time is he coming? It's Michael, right?" asked Paul.

Six-thirty," Aunt Catherine and Mary answered, in unison.

"Is he an 'on-time' guy?" Paul asked.

"Yes, I believe so," said Mary.

"Well then, I've only got about twenty minutes to change from a frog to a handsome prince."

"At your age, if you haven't made it to king, you might as well get back on the lily pad," said Aunt Catherine.

"Well, I know where I stand."

"Yes, in our *way*, so skidaddle upstairs and do your magic. I placed an ironed shirt on the bed for you."

"Thanks. I'll be ready."

Mary went back to the dining room to finish her work while Aunt Catherine checked out the rest of the menu, in various stages of "almost ready." Mary kept looking out the window to see if any cars were driving by. She had no idea what kind of car or color to look for, so each one became a candidate for Michael's arrival.

When 6:28 p.m. came and there was no Michael, Aunt Catherine offered reassurance. "He'll be here," she said. "We're all set. So rest. Let's sit in the living room. You can get a good view from the bay window."

Mary sat in the window seat, looking through the shear curtains. A new blue "something" came up the drive and stopped behind the Buick. Aunt Catherine, bursting with curiosity, peeked out to see Michael. The two women were so intent that they didn't see Uncle Paul walk up behind them.

"Is that our friend?" he asked.

Aunt Catherine jumped. "You scared the life out of me," she said. "Well, you ladies were concentrating... "

Michael walked up to the front door and rang the chime, as Mary and Uncle Paul went to answer it. There he was with a big smile and a "Hello."

"Let me help you with these," said Mary, taking two bags from Michael so the two men could shake hands. "Uncle Paul, this is Michael," she said. "Michael Bowland... a friend."

"Well, please come in, Michael."

Aunt Catherine was standing under the arch in the living room, wiping her hands with her apron. She had a welcoming smile on her face. "Hi, Aunt Catherine," he said. "May I call you that?"

"Yes, it's Aunt Catherine or Catherine, but not Katie. That word is reserved for Paul when he's annoyed with me."

"Well, Catherine. How are you?"

"Just fine, thanks. Come in and have a seat. Paul, take his coat."

"Well, let's put these bags in the kitchen," Paul said.

"I brought a few bottles of red wine," said Michael. "I hope you like it."

"Thank you," said Catherine.

Uncle Paul disappeared into the kitchen with the bags as Michael sat down. "Catherine, where's the cork screw?" he yelled from outside the room.

"In the middle drawer in the back," she yelled back.

"Can I help with anything?" asked Michael.

"Yes. Come open your wine," shouted Paul. "We'll have a little something before dinner. I can't figure out how to use this contraption."

Michael opened the bottle as they each took a seat in the living room. Mary brought out four glasses and handed them to him so he could pour.

"My job?" he asked.

"Yes."

His hand was steady as he filled each glass, offering one first to Aunt Catherine, who exclaimed, "Oh, that's too much."

After he gave a glass to Paul and to Mary, and last to himself, he held his glass up for a toast.

"May I?" asked Paul.

"Of course," said Michael.

"In the simplest of terms... welcome... welcome to our home."

"Thank you," said Michael.

"Michael," said Aunt Catherine, "Mary tells us about the wonderful romantic journey you made last week. It's something I never would have thought of myself. I guess because we come from the Model T era rather than the jet plane era. New Year's Eve in a Model T could take years."

"It did," said Michael.

"It *did?*" asked Aunt Catherine.

"Yes, it did take years... five years... one for each time zone. It wasn't 2000 again but another year, another moment we shared in time."

"So, it's the year 2005 plus," said Paul. "Wow, how time flies."

"I'm sorry, I felt the time, but I guess I didn't explain it well," said Mary.

"What a wonderful thought," said Catherine, "to spend so much time together in one evening. I like it. I think it's so sensitive. So that's why Mary asked us to meet you, the author of this special thought, a timekeeper of sorts."

"Aunt Catherine," scolded Mary, embarrassed.

"No, I'm sorry. I just think it's something you may never do again. But to do it once must be very touching, a very real chapter in your own book. It's a passage to a very interesting relationship for you both."

"Good for you, Michael. All I know is how to make pot roast."

"Well, I don't," he said. "But I've got to say I hope I don't have to go half way around the world to have it again."

"Well, if you're good and stay on good terms with Mary, we'll have you back. But if not, well, Happy New Year."

"I'll be good. I promise."

"I need a few minutes in the kitchen. Excuse me," said Catherine.

"Can I help?" Mary offered.

"Yes."

"Can *we?*" asked Michael.

"We have work for you, don't worry," said Mary.

"I have to say this," said Michael, as the women got up to leave. "You both look very beautiful. And Mary, the pearls are very pretty."

"I'm glad that's the only difference," said Catherine. "Thanks, Michael."

The ladies went into the kitchen to finish getting dinner ready as the men continued to talk. Paul asked about Michael's career. Michael explained his traveling the world—building things that Paul might have read about but would never have thought that someday, in his own home, would be the man who made it happen. And at one point Paul said, "The most construction I ever did was to build this house we're in."

Michael responded, "But you've created your own address. All I have accomplished is creating the opportunity for the projects to happen. A big difference is that I got a lot of the credit while the men and women who 'moved the mountains' were left nameless and referred to as... 'All the Dedicated Craftsman,' and this was engraved on the project's plaque. At least you can say it was all your own effort, with a deed to prove it."

In Paul's dry sense of humor, he asked Michael if he had a deed for the dam. They both laughed.

After a few minutes, the men seemed to bond in a way that men do. It either takes a long time or only a few well-chosen sentences to clear the path to a healthy relationship.

Aunt Catherine shouted from the kitchen for Paul to place the roast on the table and to sharpen his knife. He was up in a flash, excusing himself, as Michael sat sipping his wine. Mary stuck her head out the door to ask, "Hey sport, want a job?" She asked him to carry out a few of the dishes. "Where to, ma'am?" he asked. She took his hand and showed him where everyone would sit and where the dishes should go.

The dinner began with full glasses of wine as another bottle was opened. The slicing of the roast was somewhat of a ritual; the sharpened knife cut through it with ease, offering a mouth-watering event for anyone who was at all hungry. Paul stopped while he was still standing and toasted the occasion as a special place to offer special people an exchange of thoughts and respect for one another.

Michael thought he had never been with people like this in his life. Maybe he was missing something. His own family never exchanged such words. It was something he liked and felt so comfortable with, he wanted to say he hadn't seen this in years, but in truth, he had never seen it from strangers.

The dinner was superb. The roast was served twice along with the most interesting brussels sprouts he had ever eaten. It was excellent. Everything was just perfect. The conversation never stopped as Aunt Catherine or Mary told little stories about her childhood, with Uncle Paul slipping in a few remarks from time to time. Michael tried to get a few "words in edgewise," but it seemed his timing was always off, since his mouth was full when the ladies turned to hear a response. Aunt Catherine was pleased to see a man enjoying her dinner so much. Mary, on the other hand, wanted to know how he stayed so slim. He nodded his head, looking for time to chew.

They sat for a long time telling stories, even after the dinner plates were cold. When Aunt Catherine finally picked up her plate, it started an avalanche of movement, everyone helped to get things into the kitchen. Paul went off to prepare his secret dessert as Mary and Michael finished stacking the plates and returned to the table. The smell of coffee came from the kitchen as Mary moved her cup a little closer to Michael. The lights were dimmed and a cake with a single candle came from the darkness of the kitchen as Uncle Paul began to sing "Happy Birthday" to Mary.

Michael was a little taken back as they finished the last chorus. Mary blew out the candle. They all applauded. "I didn't know it was Mary's birthday," he said to all.

"It's not," said Paul. "It's May 22, but we missed so many of them, we thought we would catch up."

"So many of them? I'm just twenty-five," said Mary. "Now, that's not so bad."

"Twenty-five... I like that," said Michael. "I was twenty-five twice. I might make it to three times... who knows?"

"Well, I hope you do," said Mary. "Even four."

"Michael, we have a little present for Mary," said Aunt Catherine. "We don't want you to feel bad, so we have a present from you to Mary, too."

Michael took it all in stride. "OK," he said.

She handed her a long package, lightweight like a candlestick. Then she gave her a heavy package, about the size of two books.

"Open Michael's first," Catherine said.

Mary unwrapped the paper, exposing five lovely sable paintbrushes. "Oh, they're beautiful."

"And now you may open the other," said Catherine.

Mary slowly removed the paper and pulled the lid off a lovely wooden box. Inside were many tubes of oils. She thought it was the best present anyone could give her. She was ready to paint.

"This present has a catch," Catherine said.

"What's that?"

"You have to finish the painting of Rusty."

"Oh my God, yes, I will. I will."

"Rusty?" asked Michael.

"That was our dog. We loved him," Catherine said.

"Deal," said Mary.

"Well, I want you all to take a piece of this cake and follow me to the living room," said Paul.

They settled into the seats they had taken earlier while Michael offered his compliments to the chef.

"I won't be eating like this for a while," he said. "I'm off tomorrow to Vancouver for about a week, and I'm sorry to say, this dinner would be impossible to repeat without all of your company."

"You're very sweet," Aunt Catherine said. "But I'm sure we can do this again soon."

They talked and laughed late into the evening. A little yawn came upon Mary, which she tried to cover without anyone catching her. But Michael saw her and suggested it was time for him to go.

"Would you like more coffee or cake?" offered Aunt Catherine, not wanting the evening to end.

"No, thank you," he said. "The evening has been wonderful."

"Paul, give me a hand in the kitchen," Aunt Catherine said.

"Sure, after I get Michael's coat."

"I'll take care of that," said Mary.

"Well, I hope to see you soon," said Paul.

"Thank you," said Michael.

Mary took his hand and walked with him into the hallway, where she helped him on with his coat. She opened the door and walked outside with him onto the porch. She placed her hand on the side of his face and kissed him, softly. She told him how special he was and how he had made the evening the second best she had had in a long while.

"Can I show you home?" Michael asked.

"Soon," she said, "but not tonight. I just have to... well, I need a little more time."

"That's fine," he said. "I'll see you in about a week or less. Is that OK?"

"I'd like that. Thank you for a lovely evening."

"I'll leave an envelope for you at the hotel with the room key, and I'll tell them that you may be coming by... if you wish."

"Yes, I just may take you up on that offer. We'll see. Thank you."

"I think... " he began, as his eyes looked intently into hers, "I think... "

"Yes, Mr. Nietzsche, you think. So go, do your thing, and let me know where you are."

"I will, and by the way, Descartes is my name."

"Get moving."

She kissed him again. He held her closely. His arms wrapped around her for a moment. "Get back inside before you get a chill. It's too cold for you out here," he whispered; and then he asked again if they could go to her home. "I think... "

"Be good now," she interrupted, and dashed back into the house. He walked off into the darkness. Mary flipped a second switch that turned on the driveway lights so he could see. Michael waved and said "Good night."

Mary helped clean up the dinner dishes as Aunt Catherine gave Michael her seal of approval.

"He's wonderful," said Aunt Catherine, giving Mary a hug.

Mary went for her coat and purse and then she returned to say good night.

"Good luck, my child," said her aunt. Uncle Paul walked her out to the car, opened the door of the Buick and gave her a hug, as well.

"He seems like a nice man, Mary," he said. "Whatever happens, we're on the same team forever."

He closed the car door, and she backed out of the drive, heading directly home. She had had a lovely evening and had missed this during all the years she was away. The four of them had simply exchanged a pleasant conversation that generated nothing more than a good feeling in the heart. There were no deals. And there was no networking, no exchange of business cards, no shallow "me toos"—just the enjoyment of being with people she loved. It was a lot of excitement for one evening. She was tired, and tomorrow was another kind of day that she had to face well rested. She placed her pearls atop her dresser and got ready for bed. Minutes later, she was pulling the comforter up to her face with a faint smile. She closed her eyes and fell gently to sleep.

Chapter Nine

Mary craned her neck to see over the car in front of her as she drove by 115 Main Street. *There it is... 110! And I'm a half hour early. Oh, let that guy leave... yes! He's pulling out of a parking space right here. That makes it so easy.*

She placed a few quarters in the meter and walked toward the building. There were no carts, no masses of humanity, just scattered individuals here and there, most of them hanging around outside the building, smoking cigarettes, exiled from the majority.

She looked for the directory that should have been hanging on the wall somewhere in the marble lobby she was in but couldn't find it. She shyly stopped a man passing by to ask if he knew what floor Dr. Kainer was on. He kept walking and pointed toward a kiosk.

"It's all in there, ma'am. That's the directory. The *world* is in there."
She smiled and said "thanks" and began reading the directions on the kiosk. *Touch here for this; touch here for that.* She slowly took her finger and touched "Doctors." Up came the alphabet. "Touch the first letter of the doctor's last name," it ordered. She touched K, and it asked her to spell the full name. She got to K-A-I which was enough for "Drs. Kainer and Green: Fifth floor" to appear on the screen.

She moved away from the screen, thinking of the contrast of the lobby of the Ghandi Memorial Hospital where there had been the scent of curry and turbans and color. *Now one finger, a screen, and the space replaced these: Now there were no people and no chatter. Where were they all?*

She found the right elevator and walked in towards a few people moving backward into the car. As the door closed, another passenger asked for her floor. A surge of anxiety swept through Mary as she thought of the visit. She tried to clear her mind of the thoughts that were beginning to cluster there. She couldn't focus on the woman's request.

The indicator light above the door read 2 and made two dings. Then 3 appeared with three dings then 4 and four dings. "Five," Mary blurted out. "I'm sorry," she added. The woman quickly touched five and the elevator came to a stop. The doors opened.

Mary hesitated before stepping out; then she said "thank you" to the passengers who were staring at her—wondering what part of this person was missing. The elevator doors closed behind her back. Mary stood motionless, looking for a sign on a door. *How many doors are there? There are seven and only two with signs.* She moved toward one, her eyes focusing on the sign: *Dr. Donald Kline. Then Dr. Kainer's must be back in the other direction towards the right: two, three, four, five, six. Here it is... Drs. Kainer and Green.*

She opened the door and walked into a room with no one there. There were just empty seats and overhead fluorescent lights. The walls were white, and there were a few well-read magazines in disorder, lying in the corner of an artificial leather couch. Mary's state of mind was 'on edge'—an edge that she had experienced before—and one that she hated. She froze, motionless, inside the room.

An inside office door opened, and a nurse came out. "May I help you?"

"Yes, I... I... I'm Mary Templeton."

"Yes, Mrs. Templeton. Have a seat for just a moment, and I'll tell Dr. Kainer you're here. It is Dr. Kainer?"

"Yes," she answered, turning her head away from the nurse.

"While you're waiting, could you please fill out this form for me? Thank you."

Mary sat on the edge of the sofa, filling in the blanks on her form. She hated forms. *I always mess up, right in the beginning, with: "last name first," and then what line is the "first line?" That was always happening.*

Now she took her time going through some questions she had no answers for and stopped. The nurse came out and asked Mary to follow her inside. She went like a reluctant sheep; her mind was overloaded with the fear of not knowing what was going to happen and where it was all going. *Reality is about to descend on me, and I hate it.*

She walked down a corridor and was instructed to step on a scale. She quickly placed her purse on a counter and stepped on the scale. The nurse said nothing as she quickly made notes on a clipboard. She then led Mary into an examining room. There was a white cube with the examining table in the center. A side table and assorted medical apparatus was attached to it. Stainless steel shelves were on the wall with a few metal canisters with lids. That was it. If you looked up at the recessed florescent ceiling fixture, you could see the bulbs through the waffled insert. It was bleak, sterile, sparse, cold and frightening. It was starting all over again, at a higher plane, but it was still frightening.

She hung up her coat and was told, "Please disrobe and put on a hospital gown." She was left alone. Mary paused for a moment, looking into the examining slab. She placed her clothing, piece by piece, on the chrome hooks on the wall. There were no hangers. She fought with the gown, first placing it on backwards then turning it around. There were no mirrors. She thought of last evening when she dressed for a different occasion. How cold and distant this was, from her thoughts of black shoes and pearls. *No make-up now... just my body, placed on a big roll of Cut-Rite wax paper.*

She sat on the examining table waiting for the next stage, feeling the cold beneath her. The room was nothing... just nothing. It was up there in 'never-never land.' with a cold empty feeling. It offered no opinion... no support to her insecurities. Once again, she would be attached to a glass slide and was about to be placed under their microscope.

Just as Mary was beginning to wonder how long it would take for Dr. Kainer to make his appearance, she heard a tap on the door. Not knowing what else to say, Mary said, "Yes."

Dr. Kainer walked into the room, carrying a clip board. He wore a white lab coat. A stethoscope hung loosely around his neck. He closed the door behind him.

"Mrs. Templeton, how are you feeling?"

"OK... I guess," she said. "How are you?"

"I'm well," he said. "How kind of you to ask. He looked up and down on the clip board. Now, this note about your condition uses the term degenerative. Can you help me understand what you mean by that? May I call you Mary?"

"Of course."

"You seem on edge."

"That's an understatement."

"Well, talk to me about it. Why are you here?"

"I have been living in Calcutta for the last few years. Approximately two months ago, I began to feel tired, very tired... too often. So I thought I would get some vitamins or something. It was that innocent. My former husband and I have many acquaintances in that part of the world. Most of them are professional people, so a simple request for some vitamins became a battery of tests with a Dr. Satara at the Ghandi Memorial Hospital."

"What were his findings?"

"I went last week to the hospital. That's where his office is, and he told me to get to the states and clarify his findings and... "

"Mary, let's cut to the chase. What, as best you can construct, did he say?"

"He said... " And she began to cry. "He said I'm going to die."

Dr. Kainer took her hand. "We don't know that, Mary," he said. "Let me know a little more. What was his diagnosis?" He reached over to the paper towel dispenser and handed one to her. Then he gently released her hand.

"It was a degenerative pancreatic disorder. He gave no indication of much of anything. It was just, 'Go away, and find your way home.' I didn't need any convincing to run from the hell he had created for me. I just flew home the next day."

"But it's been a week plus."

"I needed to compose myself. I needed time."

"I suppose your files will be difficult to obtain."

"No, I know how to get through all the red tape to have them sent."

"How?" he asked. "Shall I call?"

"No, I'll do it immediately," she said, wiping her eyes.

"Well, I would like to do some simple things for you here today and schedule you for a battery of tests, starting tomorrow. Is that OK? You will need to stay in the hospital overnight. The nurse will help you in suggesting what personal belongings you will need.

"Mary, I might add that, at this time, we don't know anything conclusive. The strength you will need in the next few days is very important, and I want to dispel any anxiety you might have about your assumed condition. The facilities here are the best in the world. I'm very proud of that. I think we have to provide concrete information to determine an accurate diagnosis.

"I think that until we have conclusively determined what's really wrong, you should relax and provide yourself with a positive outlook, as I suspect you can do. What do you think?"

"I'm trying my best, but I have a very active and creative mind."

"Do you work? What profession have you been working at?"

"I'm an artist."

"Anything I've seen?"

"Not yet," she said. "Soon."

"Well, let's make your work your obsession and not Dr. Satara's theory until we are prepared to make that conclusion."

"Thank you. You were my mother's doctor many years ago. We were all a lot younger."

"Your mother?"

"Yes, Agnes Templeton. She died."

"I'm so sorry. I don't recall the name, but when I see the file it'll refresh my memory. It's good you told me. We will reread those records."

He pressed a button on the intercom on his desk. "Yes, Dr. Kainer?" came the nurse's voice.

"Could I see you for a moment, please?" he asked.

"Yes, doctor?" she said, opening the door.

"I'd like to do a work-up on Mary. Please let me know when you're ready for me."

"Mary, if you'll go with the nurse, I'll be with you in a few minutes."

He turned again to the nurse in the doorway. "Mary is going to help us collect her medical records that are currently in India. Please tell Carol to assist her in any way to expedite our acquiring that data as soon as possible."

"I'll see you in a few minutes, Mary, and chin up."

"Thank you, Dr. Kainer," she said. "Thank you."

The nurse led Mary down a short corridor where she was instructed to sit in a chair with an extended armrest. The nurse placed a large rubber band around Mary's arm, took a cotton ball laced with rubbing alcohol and sanitized the area. She then slapped Mary's vein and said the first four of the seven words that came from her mouth... "just a little pinch."

The needle was inserted. Mary looked to see her blood being sucked into the first of three vials. "Is it my turn to feed the vampire?" she asked the nurse, who barely smiled as she placed a Band-Aid on the puncture. And as if that wasn't enough blood, the nurse proceeded to hold her hand to prick her finger, saying, "A little sting" and squeezed her finger, allowing a drop of blood to fall on a sensing strip (another smaller Band-Aid). Lifting her arm in the air, she removed the thermometer, scribbled a note in her chart, and collected the samples. Mary couldn't help thinking... *say hi to Dracula.*

She led Mary back into the examining room, instructing her to lie down and closed the door. Mary lay back upon the cold table, bringing her knees up close to her chest while holding her Band-Aid tightly. She stayed in that position for some time, reviewing the shelves that held all the mundane medical icons: tongue depressors, little packets of disposable thermometers, cotton balls and the chart of **Templeton, Mary**. A few lines of information were at the top and nothing else. *What were the rest of the lines going to prove? What would he and others write? How many pages of 'things' would it take to reveal the truth about the medical history of Templeton, Mary?* She sat up abruptly, thinking that she did not want the doctor to find her in that position.

The doorknob turned and Dr. Kainer came in with the nurse.

"I'd like to listen to your heart, Mary, so might we open the top portion of the gown?"

He placed his stethoscope on her chest, listening attentively—then placed it on her back. "Breathe deeply with your mouth open, please, Mary."

He removed the otoscope from the wall, peering into her ears, and speaking softly. The nurse wrote something on the chart, and then she placed a blood pressure cuff around her arm for the second time while he pumped it up. It surrounded her arm, squeezing tighter and tighter. *When would he stop?*

Each procedure began to fill the pages of her chart. He went on and on, touching, groping, and reaching inside her body. Gloves were on. Gloves were off. The only separation between them was a thin, white prophylactic coating wrapped around his hands. *A stranger touching me, feels weird... a doctor, yes... but uncomfortable.*

Mary looked at the nurse, who continued to write the doctor's remarks on the chart. It was another beginning. Dr. Satara had performed the same procedures in India.

"Well, Mary, we've done as much as we can do here," Dr. Kainer finally said, "Please get dressed and come see me for a minute in my office. Nurse, if you've finished, I'll take the chart. Thank you."

He turned and left the room with the nurse immediately behind him. The door closed, and Mary was left seated on the edge of the table with her robe open and with each hand at her side supporting herself. The open gown exposed one of her breasts. Her hunched over posture seemed somewhat pathetic. Her chin touched her chest. This was the beginning—just the beginning—of a journey she feared taking.

She slowly slid off the paper. Her feet touched the cold floor. Her toes curled beneath her own weight. She removed her gown, allowing it to fall to the floor, and imagined what she looked like, standing in the room naked, vulnerable, and so very fragile. She started dressing herself with very slow movements. Finally, she reached for her blouse. With no mirror, she ran her hands through her hair, *feeling* the placement.

Not seeing her own image became disconcerting. It was as if she were blind. She saw no visual feedback—no visual support. This was about Mary, and Mary could only see Mary in a reflection. She could imagine and create an image mentally, but with no confirmation.

She could only suspect what her appearance was. It wasn't that she was concerned with a hair out of place or a button unbuttoned. It had to do with *seeing*. It had to do with her thought process: no mirror... no image... just assumptions with no confirmation. *But who cares*, she thought. *So few*, she answered, tucking her blouse in. She reached for the door handle and walked the same path as the doctor and nurse. She was looking down at her feet as Dr. Kainer came from the opposite direction, and she nearly bumped into him.

"I'm sorry, doctor, I wasn't looking," she said.

"That's OK, Mary. The nurse will give you the particulars, but tomorrow morning, I'd like you to admit yourself to this hospital. The tests will take a few hours. It will take a few days to accumulate the results. I'll call you when I get them."

"Do you still want to see me in your office?"

"No, that's OK. Just see the nurse."

"Thank you, doctor."

She continued down the hall to the nurse's desk, where she picked up the information she needed. The nurse had written it all down, with her name and the appointment time at the top: "Templeton, Mary, Tues, 8:30 a.m." and in bold letters, "No food or drink after 10 p.m."

"Are you taking any medication?" the nurse asked her.

"No."

"Well, please refrain from any form of aspirin, or anything after 10:00 p.m."

Mary walked to the car, opened the door, and just sat there. Her keys were in her hand as she stared out the window. She was quiet and barely aware of what was going on. She sat there for quite some time, until a police officer tapped on the window. He gestured through the glass and mouthed, "Are you OK, ma'am?"

Mary turned and answered mechanically. "I'm OK... thank you."

He took his ticket book and pointed at the meter. It had expired. She took the keys, started the car, and turned on the blinker, entering the traffic. She drove a few blocks before making a left turn. Not knowing where to go, she passed the gallery and made the left into Michael's hotel. It was her refuge. She pulled into the parking lot and walked directly to the main desk.

"May I help you, madam?" the clerk asked.

"I believe there is an envelope for me from Mr. Bowland. Michael Bowland."

The clerk checked his mailbox and removed an envelope. "Your name again, madam?"

"Mary Templeton."

"Could you sign this, please?"

"Sure."

She took the envelope and moved away from the desk to a seat in the lobby. It felt so good to rest. She paused for a moment, and then she opened the envelope to find a key and a note from Michael:

"Hi. I'm glad you're here. I'll call you about my return... no surprises. Please make yourself at home. The room service is great. Whatever you need, please order. Love, Michael."

Mary folded the note and placed it in her purse. She took the elevator to the eighth floor, room 838. The key turned easily, and she entered Michael's room, turning the inside lock behind her. It was lovely: a sitting room and a bedroom were furnished with antique chests, overstuffed chairs, and a bar. The bedroom boasted of a four-poster king-sized bed with an emerald green comforter. It was so high, it had a set of wooden steps that were tucked beneath its side. There was an envelope, on one side of the bed, addressed to Mary. She opened it.

"Mary, hi again. I'm very happy you decided to stay here for 'however long.' There's champagne in the bar, chocolate in the drawer, and a great restaurant downstairs with excellent room service. I've been sleeping on this side of the bed, not that it matters... but just so you know... and it's mostly for the phone. I'll give you a call here or at your home tomorrow. Love, Michael."

Mary climbed up into the bed. Her eyes felt heavy. She fell asleep.

She slept for hours and awakened very rested. The quiet of the room was inviting. It wasn't quite dark as she reached for the lamp switch, stretching—having to move herself closer.

She sat up, then slid off the bed to the floor and walked to the elegant armoire. She turned a key that remained in the lockbox and opened the armoire. A few of his suits hung neatly. His shoes were placed beneath them on a wooden rack, all polished. Just aside the armoire, one of Michael's briefcases had been placed on a small table. The worn brass catch was open. The leather was scuffed from use. Its handle was frayed. *The case must have traveled many a mile, at his side,* she thought—*but not this trip.* Mary placed her fingertip in the seam, lifting the top. *I'll just take a peek inside the red file... and maybe the green one.*

She examined a very nice black pen and a Swiss army knife connected to a little flashlight and another curious contraption, about twice as large as the knife. There were tiny illustrations on the sheath. There was also a pair of pliers, a screwdriver, and a tiny hammer. *These are a few of Michael's 'toys,'* she thought, *and he's very organized.*

She walked into the bathroom where some of the toiletries Michael had left behind were placed in a well-defined line of order. *He is almost as bad as me... in the compulsive department.*

A hot bath would make her feel rested. She turned the oversized handles on the bathtub and sealed the drain. The water flowed from two spouts, filling the tub quickly. She disrobed and removed the Band-Aid. She placed her toes into the water. It was hot but not scalding. She sat down slowly as the steaming water rushed up over her body.

She placed her head against the rest and enjoyed the comfort of every pore responding to the warmth. She cupped her hands and brought the hot water to her face, running her hands through her hair. Leaning her head back and sinking into the tub, she submerged her face for a few seconds. *What a simple but wonderful thing to do... just soak... letting the tensions of the day become diluted in the hot water.* And her tensions seemed to evaporate—like the steam that dissipated into the room. She lay there for a very long time until she began to sense the water cooling. Unfortunately, it was time to get out.

She turned the drain and stepped out toward the fluffy, white towels. A wonderful terry cloth robe awaited her. (It had a long belt and a high, round collar that surrounded her head.) As she brushed her hair, she wondered if there was a little bottle of white wine in the refrigerator in the room.

She found everything she needed: a corkscrew, nuts, crackers, cheese, and bottles of everything from Absolut to Pinot Grigio. Choosing the wine, she removed the cork and poured it into a pretty glass. Her choice reminded her of the *cups* and champagne on the plane last week.

With a glass of wine in one hand and the room service menu in the other, she sat, placing her feet under herself as if she were going to cozy up with a great novel. *Hmmm, what should I order... something light,* she thought... *a Caesar salad with something wonderful... a Caesar with some salmon and 'a something else.'* She picked up the phone and ordered. Then she sat back, enjoying the wine.

A part of her felt like she was intruding in Michael's world. It was as if she were sneaking into his room with him not knowing. There was a knock at the door. *It's too soon for room service.*

"Housekeeping" was announced as Mary opened the door. A maid came in to turn down the bed and to say good night. Mary said, "thank you," as she was leaving.

Mary felt Michael's presence. His person was very strong. She began to look at his things again: on the secretary, there was a little picture frame; within it was the picture of a little girl and an attractive woman in her early thirties. She picked it up. Mary remembered the many conversations they had had about his wife and child.

This must be them... what a tragedy. This is a very strong man, having been through so much. He is a different kind of person... the type I have never met before. In some ways (with his 'toys' especially) he's typical, but the greater part of him is singular. We have both suffered the loss of a child... a precious child. He would understand when I tell him about Paul—but I will wait.

She placed the frame back as she had found it. She began to feel his presence, even more, by touching the things he touched, seeing the things he would see, and feeling the things he would feel. He had stood here in this space where she now stood.

She felt encouraged and comfortable with being there. His offering her the use of the room became a commitment to her—a statement that said, *you're welcome to my world. This is who I am. There are no guarded thoughts. Allow me to introduce myself. This is where I live.*

Chapter Ten

This time room service was announced from the hallway. Mary opened the door. "Room service, ma'am. Shall I place it on this table? Or would you like it somewhere else?"

Mary motioned toward the table and offered her credit card as payment when the waiter said, "Mr. Bowland has made a specific request to bill all charges to him directly, ma'am. I hope that is permissible."

Mary said OK and that she would resolve it with Mr. Bowland when he returned. She signed the receipt, and the waiter moved the briefcase then placed the tray on the table. He retrieved the check saying, "Thank you. Have a pleasant evening." She was starving, and it was still early enough before 10:00 p.m. not to conflict with the order from the nurse. She lifted each silvery cover, placing the lids to the side. Each plate was exciting: her salmon, the salad, and lots of "little tastes" of other things that came along as a surprise. She turned on the television, something she hadn't done in years.

The first station that came up was fine. It was some kind of *40*'s movie in black and white. She sat and began to savor one wonderful taste after the other—a bit of salmon, a little salad, a sip of wine. *Cagney, that's who that is. This is the classic one, I think. This is the one where he sticks the grapefruit in what's her name's face. What a slime ball he was. His character was wicked. John wasn't that bad and Michael, well... that's a whole other film.*

Mary couldn't finish all of her dinner, but she did manage to get through the entire half bottle of wine. The movie went on and on. The drowsy comfort of the wine and the distraction of Cagney's loathsome character successfully diverted her thoughts from the next day's appointment.

She had to get up early enough to be there at 8:30 a.m. *Let's see... no breakfast, no coffee, not a thing. So if I get up at seven, that should do it.* She lifted the phone and asked for a wake-up call.

After tidying up a bit, she decided to go to bed. She turned off the lights having left one on in the bathroom. The deep green comforter had been pulled down, with both sides of the bed presented equally.

There were two Godiva chocolates on each pillow. The maid must think we're both here. She went directly to Michael's side and got into bed. It was quite a chore climbing up into it. She slid her arm under the pillow as she began to roll over; then she felt an envelope there. It was addressed to her. Her name was written, stylishly, across the front. She opened it.

"Hi... me again. I'm very happy you're here and that you decided to stay. I'm hoping I won't find this note unopened and that you'll tell me you found it. Sleep well. I guessed on this side. I was right. P.S., I've been saving the Godiva in the top drawer of the night table. Love, Michael."

Mary opened the drawer and placed the four pieces of candy on top of the many Michael had saved. Turning off the lamp, she moved her body deeper under the covers, pulling them up to her chin. She closed her eyes, thinking Michael had slept there, right beneath her, his head touching this pillow. Michael signed all the notes "Love, Michael." *I like that. Am I more than fond of this man? Is this true? I'm in bed with him now. I feel his touch, his warm manner touching me. I kissed him twice. Well, I kissed him once, and he kissed me once. I liked it. He's so very good to me... so very good!*

The phone rang at seven. Mary reached for the receiver. "Good morning, Mrs. Bowland. It's the wake-up call you requested. Shall I call you back in ten minutes?"

"No, thank you. I'm up,"

There was hardly any evidence she had slept on the bed. Mary stood there and looked at it for a second. Then she reached over on her toes, standing and pulling the covers down a little, and hit the other pillow, thinking, *who cares? Well, I just want the maid to think I slept with him... our little secret. No one knows, just me.*

She showered, dressed, and was out the door.

It was a foggy morning. Mary walked past the fountain just outside the hotel's portico. The sounds of the water were muffled; its cherubs hid in this gray mist. An envelope of secrecy concealed her from the others waiting for their transportation. Mary decided to walk to her test. It would take more time, but she did have a half-hour to get there. She liked the idea of being in the fog. Grey shapes appeared out of a seamless cloud, then disappeared behind her. Again, she would walk to a hospital with the same apprehension, but this path was washed over in ashen grays. There was no sun-soaked breath, no flow of humanity—just monochromatic gray space.

The traffic lights seemed suspended in air. Their primary colors changed to pastels. The sun tried to penetrate the mist, brightening from one street to the next. The fog was lifting. *What a shame. It was so beautiful,* she thought.

Mary walked up the steps to the hospital complex... *no turbans, no scent of curry, no doors held open by the tide of humanity but in their stead an electronically activated door sensing my presence, opening especially for me.* "Thank you" she said.

Mary walked to the desk. A woman dressed in white said, "Good morning. May I help you?"

"Yes, I'm here, as Dr. Kainer's patient, for some tests."

"One moment please," said the receptionist, as she typed "Kainer" into the computer. "And your name, please?"

"Mary Templeton. T-E-M..."

"Yes," she said. "You're going to admitting, just down the hall. Take a right, and you'll see the sign."

Mary walked down the hall. Opening the door, she approached a nurse.

"I'm here for some tests," she said, "Dr. Kainer's patient."

"Yes, could you have a seat over there, Miss. I will be with you in a few minutes."

Mary sat and began to observe the movement of personnel. She noticed the computers, the little offices and the signs: "Don't do this," "Only do that." "Have your Social Security number ready."

Room rates... hmmm... a shared room, $475, a private room, $575, a psychiatric room, $775. Well, you'd have to be nuts to pay that much.

"Mrs. Templeton?"

"Yes?"

"Could you come over here, please?" summoned a woman from the smallest glass-enclosed office. "Good morning," she said.

"Yes, to you as well," Mary answered. "You have a tiny office."

"Did you see my stickers?" the woman asked, pointing to a dozen colorful fish decals stuck here and there on her glass walls.

"Oh, how funny! That's great," said Mary. "That makes you in charge, size-wise."

"And don't forget it," the woman said, smiling. "Well, we want you to get started, don't we?" she continued, changing to a more serious tone. "I've got a whole bunch of questions I'd like to ask."

She asked Mary everything from what kind of insurance she had to her mother's maiden name. It went on for ten minutes. She hit a button and papers started spewing out of the printer to the side of her desk. She ripped a few pieces along a perforated edge and placed one thin paper into a blue bracelet, asking Mary for her hand.

"Are you a righty or a lefty?" she asked.

"Lefty." The woman asked for her right hand and slipped on the wrist band. "Is that too tight?"

"I don't think so," said Mary. The woman trimmed the edges with a scissors.

"You'll have to wait here for a candy striper to come escort you to your floor," she said. "That's the rule. And they have plenty of them, so if you would like, please return to your seat for a few minutes."

Mary did, and then she began to "people watch," eavesdropping on a conversation between two women about one of their dates last night. "He was wonderful," gushed one of the women, excitedly.

"I'm jealous," groaned the other. "I should be so lucky... finding 'Mr. Right.'"

The candy striper arrived then with a wheelchair. "Mrs. Templeton?"

"Yes?"

"Would you please sit in the wheelchair?"

"That's not really necessary. Do I have to?"

"Yes, ma'am. It's a rule."

It was quite unusual, riding around in a chair, she thought. People stop to let you by. They look at you differently, wondering if you're unable to do things for yourself.

Mary's candy striper wheeled into the elevator, turning her around to face the doors. Just as they started to close, another wheelchair rolled in. A little boy, his leg in a cast, looked up and immediately asked Mary, what was wrong with her.

"My leg is broken," he volunteered, before she had a chance to answer. "I broke it playing in my tree house. I fell down. My Mom is so mad at Dad because he helped build the house. It didn't hurt, but I cried, and I was scared. Now we are going to x-ray it again. That doesn't hurt. Did you ever have an x-ray? It's like Superman. They can see through anything. Do you want to sign on my cast?"

"Sure," she said, as he handed her a magic marker. "And what's your name?"

"George," he said.

Mary found an unused portion of the cast. She drew an animated "smiley face character"—but he was frowning, with a broken leg, and George's name was around the circle.

The elevator stopped. The doors were slow in opening "How old are you?" Mary asked lovingly.

"Eight and a half."

She just smiled and took a long look at George.

"Get better fast," she scrawled quickly on his leg. Handing him back his marker, she told him. "My name is Mary," and as the candy striper wheeled her out, she added, "I'll see you around, George."

"Hey, that's cool. You can really draw!" he said. "See ya!"

Eight and a half, she thought... *eight and one half.*

The candy striper took Mary down the hall to the nurse's station and handed her paperwork to the nurse in charge.

"Hi, Mrs. Templeton. I'm Judy," the nurse said.

"Please call me Mary."

"OK, thanks."

Mary rose from her chair and was escorted to room 421.

"You'll place your personal belongings in here," Judy said. "Here's your gown and hair cap. If you would like to lie down, please do. I'll get you another blanket if you wouldn't mind putting your gown on, while I'm getting it. I understand you're to have an indium-labeled scan, so a technician will be here shortly to take some blood. The good part about this scan is you get to have some of it back."

"I have no idea what's going on," said Mary. "What is an Indian scan?"

"No, indium. It's an isotope. Well, they take some blood. The white blood cells are isolated, then labeled with a radioisotope then returned to your blood stream. They track these identified cells to points in your body with a camera at various times... like two hours... three hours and as much as twenty-four hours. It doesn't hurt. The only thing you do is urinate a little later. So, I'll see you in a few minutes."

Mary put on her gown and sat on the edge of the bed. The technician arrived and took two vials of blood. She looked at him and asked, "Are these for the indium scan?"

"Yes," he said. "I see you're up on your procedures."

"Yes," Mary said. "I like to know these things."

He smiled then took another vial. "A little extra for the guys in the back room," he said. As he finished, the nurse returned with another blanket.

"Well, what else is on the agenda?" Mary asked. "Do you know?"

"Well, you're scheduled for an extensive series of tests through tomorrow, which means you're going to have a chance to enjoy our famous epicurean dishes. They come in decorator colors, something similar to Crayola crayons."

"Jell-O," Mary added.

"Very good. You've done this before."

"Yes, unfortunately. But not the indium test... just walking on a bed of coals and stuff."

"Well, there's a few scans, a few liquids you'll drink, and a CAT scan. Let's see... and an extensive blood analysis, but you won't have to be present for that one. Just drop it off, and the doctor will call you in a few days. But he will tell you about all this. I'm sure he will probably show up here later today. He is always very involved with his patients. He's a nice guy, too."

"I've got to run now," Judy continued. "You can't have anything, so don't even drink any water, please."

"Another rule," said Mary.

"One of thousands," Judy replied.

"No TV?" asked Mary

"Now *that* you can have," Judy said. "The soaps are on channel 65 if you like them. The Turners are divorcing. She's having an affair with William. He's off to London with you-know-who."

"No," said Mary.

"The secretary. And the best part is that mom is in town and back on the booze."

"I think I'm in this film," Mary said.

"You're an actress?"

"I'm living it, except for the mother part."

"Well, the TV works," Judy said. "Whatever you want to watch is fine. See you in a while. And if you need me, take a walk down or push that button and I'll be here in a flash."

Mary was in a "parrot-green" hospital room and sitting in a "not so easy" chair, which could have been used for a standby for electrocutions. Taking the blanket, she wrapped it around her. She thought about the darkness down the hall and the mystery that was about to unfold as her chart became filled with clinical data, creating more questions and no answers. *Templeton, Mary, what is happening to you?*

A well-dressed, middle-aged woman tapped lightly on the door. "May I come in?" she asked.

"Please do."

"Hi, I'm part of the support program for patients. "My name is Deborah Penna," she said.

"I'm Mary Templeton."

"May I explain our program?" We can chat, or if you prefer to be alone, I can catch up with you another time."

"Well, is this a religious thing?" Mary asked.

"No, just me in case you would like someone to talk with."

"Are you a psychiatrist?"

"I'm a gist, not a rist," Deborah said. "But I can be a friend."

"Well, have a seat," Mary said. "They're coming for me shortly for some tests."

"Sure. What part of Seattle are you from?"

"Well, I grew up here," Mary said, "by Eagle Falls... near the lake."

"Nice area. It seems it never changes," said Deborah.

"I moved away many years ago... to many distant places. The last known address was Calcutta."

"That sounds mysterious."

"No, just... well, once you get over the cultural differences, which is never, it's not so mysterious as much as it's a prison. If it weren't for my painting, I would've had nothing."

"You're an artist."

"I'm trying."

"What about your subject matter?"

"It was more than visually stimulating. It was deep... very deep. I liked that, " Mary said.

"Do you sell or show? I'm not sure what to ask as I'm out of my area right now."

"I sold some of my work at the only show I have ever had. Two of the pieces were sold to the man I married. I just returned from Calcutta without him, and I'm in the process of repossessing the same two. So, I could say 'loaned.' And, I have not shown in a very long time. But I may just have an opportunity to do something about that soon."

"That must be so wonderful. You must feel so good about that. But you say you've returned without your husband?"

"Yes. I left him there, and I no longer have the baggage claim receipt. I tossed it out over the Atlantic somewhere... forever."

"I'm sorry," said Deborah.

"No, please, no," she answered. "Let's celebrate. He was all that is wrong with some men."

"Well, I must admit, woman-to-woman, I did the same," Deborah confessed. "But he lives in Redmond."

"They... men... are, fortunately, not all bad. There are a few out there. In fact, I recently found a very interesting man, or he me! I never looked nor was I ever unfaithful to my marriage, but I think that now that I have escaped, I'm open to suggestions."

"Be careful. A relationship immediately following a depressing period can often lead to a bigger hurt."

"I am aware of that. But I've known this man forever," Mary smiled.

"How long?"

"About eight or nine."

"Years? That's good." said Deborah.

"No, days."

"Well, aren't you something."

"We met on New Year's Eve, on the flight back from Bombay. He offered me a cup of champagne on the flight. We talked, and I just have not stopped talking to him from then until now. He offered a gift."

"A gift?"

"A gift of *time*," said Mary. "He asked, in his whimsical way, if I would like to spend five years with him that night into the new Millennium, and we would chase time zones across the continents to Seattle, my home, in five wonderful, action-packed, humorous, emotionally filled years.

"Each midnight brought us another year deeper into the Millennium. Each celebration was a step, in time, that I never thought I could reach. It was as thrilling then as I am attempting to express it to you now."

"Does he have a brother?" asked Deborah, smiling.

"No. He is the only one that came from that mold."

"I can see he is going to be all the support you will need while you go through this difficult time... with the tests and anxieties connected with this kind of research."

"He doesn't know. I can't tell him," Mary confessed. "I've told no one. I don't know if there is anything to tell yet... so I'm not."

"Your husband, does he know?"

"He knows I left him," Mary said. "He knows I'm home. That's all he knows about me."

"Well, you're all alone. Can I help? I'm here for you. I'm here as a friend."

"I do need help. There's something I don't know how to do." Mary's expression changed.

"What don't you know how to do?" asked Deborah.

Mary started to cry. "I just... " she blurted, sobbing, "cannot reveal my innermost fears to anyone."

Deborah slid out of her chair to her knees, embracing Mary. "It's easier to tell a stranger. I won't say a word to anyone."

"Thank you," Mary said, still crying.

"I looked at your admitting papers. They suggested a preexisting diagnosis, before Dr. Kainer."

"Who? May I ask?"

"Yes, you can ask. It's because they think... "

"They?"

Expressing compassion, Deborah held her more closely, as Mary continued. "The doctors in Calcutta have made my last few weeks unbearable with their science... the cold science of medicine. They think... they said I might be. I'm dying. I don't know how to die. I just refuse to believe *they're* right and refuse to admit *anyone* is right. I'm fine. I'm miserable... but fine."

"Oh my God, Mary. What a terrible time to be alone," said Deborah, her eyes filling with tears. "I need... I want to help you. Please talk to me."

"You are the only one I have confided in. And please tell no one... please."

"My lips are sealed," she promised. "I can feel your pain, and I just... do you know any results... what did they tell you?"

"It was so vague but enough to send my imagination swirling." Dr. Satara and John, I hate them both. I'm living with fear , anxiety , and a world filled with bad things... nothing good. That's why I came back. That's why I'm here."

"The gift of *time*," said Deborah, suddenly realizing. "I understand. And your friend's name?"

"Michael. I think I love him."

"And so you should, Mary. Love him. Very much. Where is he?"

"Away on business," said Mary, sniffling. "He builds dams... well finances them."

"He's built a relationship in less than a week. He's more than an engineer," said Deborah.

"It's going to be OK. I'll make it OK. I... "

"Will you allow me to be your friend Mary?" Deborah asked.

"Please," Mary said.

The nurse returned to the room. She looked at the two women, sensing their sadness but saying nothing. Instead, she went into the bathroom and came out carrying two glasses of water which she handed to Mary and Deborah.

"The candy striper will be here in a few minutes to take you to the lab," she told Mary.

"I didn't watch the soaps, Judy."

"You didn't miss anything."

The candy striper walked in again with the wheelchair and took Mary out.

"I'll be here for you when you return, Mary."

Mary turned her head and looked back at her new friend. "Thanks," she said.

The candy striper sped·down the halls of the hospital as if she were a racecar driver. "

He said he wanted you down there lickity split," she said. "So I'm gonna take a short cut through pediatrics." (Mary's thoughts returned to her baby.) The candy striper stopped the wheelchair—huffing. She reached up to a very large chrome button on the wall and pushed it hard with the palm of her hand. The door opened wide towards them, for a few seconds, then closed immediately as she pushed Mary into another hall.

They passed the nurse's station in pediatrics. Mary didn't like being there. *Watching* children was one emotion; being *with them,* in the hospital, was quite another.

Little children were in every room with their parents standing at the end of their beds. A little boy was walking, in his gown, with his mom. *He was so small, so precious to be part of this terror.* Children were lying in their beds, parents and family at their side. All of these little people needed love and very special attention.

Mary wanted to stop and see why the last room seemed not to have anyone in it. *Perhaps the child was alone and needed company. But then, maybe the room was empty. Why? It's best to let her fly. Get out of here. Let's get out of here, please.*

They moved through another set of doors so fast that Mary had to pull her elbows in to keep from hitting them as they parted.

"Hi Charlene," someone yelled to the candy striper as she sped past.

"Hi," she answered back, out of breath. "See you in the cafeteria later." Charlene stopped the wheelchair at an elevator, and they waited. Charlene fidgeted, pacing back and forth.

"Is it an emergency that we get there so fast?" asked Mary.

"You're new here, right?" answered Charlene. "And won't be here long, right? But I gotta tell you, this guy down in radiology is something else when it comes to cranking them out. The last time I was late he tanned my hide. I can't afford to be losin' my job, so we're flying."

The elevator doors opened. They breezed in and went down a floor. The doors opened again, and they went out the other side, backwards, through two doors and stopped at a sign that said "Radiology."

"Whew. We did it," said Charlene. "Thanks for hangin.'"

The candy striper walked into the lab and was out in seconds. "Now you sit here. They will come out and get you in a few minutes."

She walked down the hall, made a right, and was gone. Mary sat there as many wheelchairs and gurneys passed by.

At one point, a woman was placed against the wall, just across from her, and left there. An orderly arrived with another gurney and tried to pass her but couldn't, so he grabbed Mary's chair and pushed her down the hall, leaving her in a corner.

"Sorry, ma'am. Gotta go," he said.

The woman on the gurney who was across from Mary had a gray face. Her hair hung out from a shower cap in scraggly chunks. She looked to be in her late eighties. She was connected to bottles of things—packets of liquids and another bottle that hung on the side of her cart. She wasn't moving.

Mary reached for the wheels of her chair to straighten them out. They began to squeak. A technician came out of the lab as she maneuvered her chair and looked at the older woman. He seemed to be searching for her chart or her name. He looked at Mary.

"Are you Templeton?" he asked.

"Yes."

"What are you doing down there?"

"Seattle Traffic," she said

The technician wheeled Mary into the lab. It was cold. Most of the light emanated from the monitor screens. The squeak of the wheels and the technician's sneakers scrunching across the waxed floor were almost amusing.

An area to the rear of the room held an examining table against a wall with an adjustable gooseneck light that marked her destination.

The technician asked if Mary was able to place herself on the table or if she needed any help.

"I can do that, I'm sure," she told him.

He pushed the chair aside to make room in the cramped quarters, then reached for a basket that contained vials of what looked like blood. He asked her name again and reached for her bracelet to see it in writing.

"Hi, Mary, I'm Bob Mason, and I'm the technician. "What I'd like to do is administer this vial of your own blood to you. It's some of what we took earlier."

"Yes, the indium test," she said.

"Great, you know about this one."

"Only that this is the first part... with pictures and evaluations later."

"Yes," he said, searching through the little basket. "Templeton, Mary. Here you are."

He reached for the IV that had been placed there earlier and cracked open a new needle. He wiped off the area to be injected and administered CCs of the elixir into the IV patch.

The technician made a note of the time and other information, and he asked if she felt OK.

"Fine," she told him. "That's it? All of this anxiety in my mind and... "

"Yep that's it for now, but you're off to a scan in a short while."

He suggested that she sit back and rest for a few minutes.

Chapter Eleven

Back in her room, Mary met the next nurse on duty. Darcy helped her under the sheets and hung her IV on the pole. "I'll be here until 7:00 p.m.," she said. "I would like you to use the urine collector in the bathroom only to monitor volume, when you have to go."

She pulled up the covers and left.

Mary was exhausted and fell asleep.

She awoke to the sound of her name.

"Mrs. Templeton," said a loud voice. "Mrs. Templeton. We have to get you down to radiology for another look-see." This time they rolled her in a gurney and asked her to climb on top.

"I'm cold," she complained. "May I have a blanket?"

"Yes, of course," said an attendant she didn't recognize. He covered her and began to wheel her out, just as Deborah came in.

"One second, please," said Deborah. "I stopped by earlier but you were sleeping, Mary. I'll try again later when you come back."

Mary looked at her but said nothing.

The attendant buckled her in tightly, and then he took her down to radiology.

Once again the great machine would loom over her, clicking and groaning. She was placed on a cold slab which had a thin foam pad on it. Then she was strapped in and covered with a sheet to her chin. They left her alone with it. Mary noticed a note stuck on top of the cylinder.

"Please look at this. Do not look directly at... "

The last portion of the note was missing *Look at this, don't look at what? She wondered. I guess none of them have ever laid down on this contraption. No one has ever told them about the WHAT.*

Not to look at 'what'? What is there other than the note? Maybe it's your toes? I'm going to close my eyes and look at nothing. Maybe that's what the 'what' is... nothing.

"Mrs. Templeton?" Mary heard someone say, in an accent rolling in waves and song like. Mrs. Tem-ple-ton.... Oh yes... the test... has now... been completed."

"Oh my God," she cringed. It's Dr. Satara's... it's his voice."

One of the technicians was an Indian man. He was looming over her face, inches away. His hot curried breath filled her nostrils. She winced and turned her head away from the odor. He rolled her out into the hallway. It was him, Dr Satara. She only caught a glimpse, but that was impossible. She turned her head, quickly, just in time to see him walk back into the room. It's *impossible!* I'm really losing it.

She was back in her room. The TV had been turned on, and the weatherman offered his apologies for the rain. She began to think of George and his age...*eight and a half, and of her stay in the hospital in... and Paul and Manisha.* It was too depressing. It wasn't the time. She just couldn't go there now. The weatherman continued his broadcast as Mary looked for the remote to turn off the TV.

There was a tapping on the door. It was Deborah. "Well, you are awake," she said.

"Yes, for a while. This stuff can drain you pretty quickly."

"Can I get you anything?"

"No, I'm just resting, thanks," said Mary.

"How did it go?"

"Well, I don't know. It's a pin-cushion's dream... a regular day in the life of a stressed out woman with irradiated blood, cotton balls in her mouth, IVs in her body, and no knowledge of how much time is left in the game.

"Other than that, I don't like to complain. But patience was never part of the creative process. Instantaneous gratification works but not here. They're writing a book about me... one line at a time. My fear is when it's finished, I won't like the ending."

"What a mind!" said Deborah. "The most important part is the happy ending, with you and Michael riding into the sunset. That's the part you should focus on."

"That's easy. I like that... yes," said Mary. "We haven't written that part yet, have we?"

Changing the subject, Deborah said, "I'm not sure that on any given day I could keep up with you. I'm not as much creative as I am predictable."

"I understand. But for me, I'm like that feather in that old movie, *Forrest Gump.* I remain the same inside, but I'm affected by the elements that surround me."

"I'm more like a tree," said Deborah. "You plant me, and that's it. I just do the tree thing."

"What kind of tree do you think you'd like to be?" asked Mary.

"A Christmas tree. It's a happy tree."

"You mean a live one, not a cut one... right?"

"Sure... a live Christmas tree... that way, I get to be one again next year."

"I don't know if I like that or not," said Mary, slowly.

"So, what kind of feather are you?" Deborah asked.

"The kind that tickles. The kind that makes for wonderful feelings inside your heart. It's the kind of feather that floats through the air. The kind that little children blow at, with 'no hands,' to keep it afloat until it lands on a pillow... then tickles your nose. Or when Mom tickles your feet with it and you twist and turn to escape the feeling. You scream in laughter 'More, Mommy, more!'

"I'm not so big. I fit in the palm of your hand and can be held between your fingers. When you're done with me, there is an unwritten rule that you can't throw me away. You must return me to your pillow, so I can wait to be released another time. I find my way back through the hole in the seam , the whole pillow gets fluffed, and I nestle myself next to your ear and keep you comfortable while you sleep. That's me!

"Do you think I'll see you as your tree this year, Deborah? Do you think I'll get to see you all dressed up with your crown of lights, pretty as can be, sharing that special moment when your children open their presents? There's that special 'gift of life' and time of year. I missed too many. What do you think?"

Deborah's eyes were watering, her voice choked up. "Yes, Mary. I'm going to make sure I look the best I have ever looked and be the happiest tree this year because I'm going to invite both you and Michael to share our next Christmas now."

Mary, feeling Deborah's response, paused then quickly changed the subject.

"Well, do you think we'll get the orange or raspberry Jell-O tonight?"

"Raspberry," said Deborah.

"That's it. That's what I wanted."

The nurse came back explaining to the two of them that Mary would be going to radiology for one last picture that night.

"OK. Sure. Great," Mary said.

"Well, I'm going home to feed the kids pizza," said Deborah "Pizza with no mushrooms."

"How many kids do you have?"

"Two boys... twelve and fifteen. Do you have any?"

"Almost," said Mary.

"Almost?"

"My only pregnancy ended with my stillborn baby, Paul, on June 20, last year."

"I'm so sorry. I'm not doing well, am I? I seem to hit all the low spots, don't I?"

Mary reached for Deborah's hand "I was just thinking about my boy a few minutes ago; I decided I couldn't go there. So you're doing fine. I'm just consumed with too much right now. Besides, there is Michael... I hope. I'm beginning to need him more than I thought."

"You've got *his* work cut out for him."

"Yes, I do."

"I'll be back in the morning to check on you, so sleep well." Deborah reached for Mary's other hand and squeezed it softly. "I'm sorry to have brought up the other subject."

"I'm OK."

"See you tomorrow."

"Bye."

Mary waited in her room for a while before she was escorted down to the radiology department for more imaging. The same people were on duty, waiting for her, making it much easier to deal with the rigors of the test.

The camera looked unthreatening enough, but they had asked her to lie flat, to not move at all, for eight minutes, the first time; then, to lie on her side, a second time, for another eight minutes. She could only assume that now her other side would be the object of their interest.

"Hi Mary, ready for the other side?" the technician asked.

"I must be a brain surgeon someday," she said.

"Well, let me give you a hand, and we'll be finished with this for the day," he said. "I think Dr. Kainer ordered one more in the morning, but I'll have to check."

"Well, I was going dancing, but I guess... "

"You're not going anywhere," the technician said, "without me. I'd like to go with you."

"It's a date," Mary said. "Pick me up in Room 421. I'll be ready."

"You're on," he said. "Now bring your arms and hands up higher. Are you, within reason, comfortable?"

"Well... within reason. Is this eight minutes?"

"Yes."

He began to move the sensing portion of the contraption closer, compressing Mary slightly like a spatula pushing down on a hamburger.

"Is that OK?"

"Yes," she said, groaning. "Let's do it."

The technician placed the film in the top and set some kind of timer; he pushed a few buttons and said, "Now try really hard not to move."

Eight minutes of what? she thought. I'll count. No, I counted last time. I must admit, it's not so bad. This one seems OK. That must be forty-five seconds. Hmm... I've got to be able to explain this time to Aunt Catherine. I went shopping and stayed in the hotel without Michael. And as for Michael? He has probably called. I could say that I stayed there last night, went shopping today, and got home late.

Then I went to bed and well... he wouldn't call too late. He's not the type. OK... so that's my story. But what did I buy? Hmm. Aunt Catherine ... she'll figure it out. I also went to the gallery. If I get out early enough I can go to the gallery and say hi to Scott then go over to shop a little. But I need a good sleep. Do you think they'll let me sleep? Every eight minutes they're waking me up. How long is that? Maybe five minutes.

"Hey, you're doing fine. You're halfway through."

Four minutes... Michael wants to go away soon... someplace nice... an inn. Well, what do I wear? That's it, I'm going to buy some things at those new stores down the street. A little pick-me-up for Mary. I saw some nice things the other night. I liked the look, kind of funky... neat and clean. Besides, I saw that one woman in the restaurant, she looked great. I think she was a little older and her nose... this MUST be over.

"How are we doing?" she asked.

"Two minutes."

"Wind your watch," she retorted.

"It's a Timex," he said. "It keeps on tickin.'"

"OK, I'll be good."

So, hmmm... let's see. Does he mean this weekend? I guess that's good. The doctor said it takes a few days to get the results together, so I hope I feel OK. No pills or anything now... I want to be me, just me, to experience him, just him. I'm feeling that it's going to be OK. I feel pretty good right now.

"Give it up," she yelled at the technician.

"Ten—nine—eight—seven—six. Are you ready to dance?"

"Yes. But I think at my age, I'm thinking Beetles, and you're into heavy metal or something."

"Nah! I don't like that stuff. But I'm sure we both like the 'Smashing Pumpkins,'" he added as he moved the great stainless-steel whale of a machine off her body.

She stretched and tried to sit up. "I've been away, mostly in my own world," she said. "What's a 'smashed pumpkin' besides the beginning of a pie? You didn't do that 'moon flight' or that 'biosphere thing,' did you?"

"No. Why?"

"They are cool... catch my drift?"

"I know that you like them. That's good."

"Well, I'm getting it together, and I'm going home," she said.

"I won't see you tomorrow if you come back here. I've got the day off, so I'll catch up to you. Take good care of yourself," the technician said, smiling at her.

"Thank you. But you never told me your name."

"John... John Abrams."

"I used to know a John, but he wasn't as nice as you," she said.

"Thanks. I called the folks to take you back upstairs, so they should be here any second. Let me help you onto the gurney. Here you go," he said, as he helped her up.

Another candy striper arrived and started to wheel her out.

"Goodbye, John," she said.

He waved.

Back in her room, Mary was tucked back into bed, her "trusty" IV at her side. It was filled to the brim with some kind of saline solution. The nurse had come in and adjusted the drip, changed the tubes, tapped at it, snapped it and ripped it out to give her a new one. Mary had heard the story about oxygen getting into one's veins and traveling to the heart—and that's it—some kind of embolism.

Well, there it is. Right in the tube... an air bubble, moving slowly down the tube. Closer and closer, it moved down the tube.

The nurse came back into the room and Mary, nonchalantly, mused out loud, I'm just curious," she said, pointing to the air bubble. "What happens to this bubble? Do I ingest it? Ahh... "

"No, there's a little filter right here," she said, pointing, "that absorbs all the extraneous gasses in there and lets only the liquid in the IV package pass through. Otherwise, we'd have a problem."

"Well, I thought that was the case," said Mary, relieved. "I was just curious."

"Well, I've got your dinner right here if you'd like it."

"Sure. Is it seared tuna and rare sushi encrusted in sesame?" Mary asked.

"No, it's raspberry Jell-O."

"My favorite alternative... in any cuisine."

"Well, I'm sorry, but that's all we can have tonight."

"That's fine."

She ate the Jell-O slowly, enjoying the change of taste in her mouth. It was a treat. A golden delicious apple would have been the ultimate delight, but a good night's rest and a few more tests and she would have accomplished something she didn't think she was going to have the strength to do.

The hospital began to grow quiet. An occasional wheeled cart passed the door, the sound fading into the hallway—its distance seeming miles away. The chatter from the nurses' station became a melodious hum of sound, reminiscent of her childhood and the few nights she would try to stay up a little later with her parents.

Her parents' voices—the sounds—had been a resonance offering security. Their conversations had been like a child's lullaby—lulling her to sleep.

A few times during the long night, a nurse would appear at her bedside, her soft shoes making no sound across the floor. Mary felt her presence, as her sweater would brush against Mary's arm while she took her blood pressure and adjusted the IV.

Then she went off down the hall, leaving the door halfway open. Mary would move her arm, carefully, so as not to pull against the IV that remained stuck in her arm.

"Good morning. It's 6:30," announced a nurse.

Mary turned and looked at this lovely woman in her late fifties standing near her bed. The open-front sweater could only mean that she was the nurse that had cared for her through the night.

"Good morning. How are you feeling?" asked the nurse.

"OK, I guess," she answered.

"Well, you've got another test. And with your doctor's approval, you're out of here this morning. Once the doctor signs the release, we can get the IV team to remove all this stuff. You can shower and you're off and running."

"Sounds good to me. What's your name?" Mary asked.

"Pierina, with a perrrr."

"I'm Mary."

"Well, I'm happy to meet you, Mary. And I only want to see you out there in town somewhere, not in here."

"Well, I agree."

The doctor walked in. "I leave you in better hands, Mary," said Perrina. "See you later. Good morning, Dr. Kainer."

"Good morning, Pierina. Your husband, is he OK now?"

"He is fine, thank you. But he may be back here soon."

"I'll bite. Why?"

"With serious contusions to the head and neck area caused by my cast-iron frying pan."

"Well, you really don't want to see him at work, do you?" the doctor joked.

"Hmm... never thought of that," she said, smiling. "Thanks, doctor. I'll just use the fly swatter."

Mary pressed the button to elevate the bed pillows as Pierina left the room.

"Good morning," she said.

"And to you, as well. We have one more scan, and all this information will be accumulated as quickly as possible. I'll have my office call you as soon as we are in possession of all the material. In the interim, you'll be able to leave here this morning by eleven or so, depending on the lab traffic. I hope it all went well. I feel confident we're going to see some good numbers from the lab."

"I may be away this weekend," Mary said. "Is there anything I should know or do?"

"Yes, I'm glad you asked."

"Yes?" she asked.

"I'll call you as soon as I receive the results... probably the middle of next week, or if you would like, touch base when you return so we don't lose any time. Have a wonderful time. And, Mary I think we're going to be OK."

"Bye, doctor. Thank you," she said.

Mary's last set of pictures were less tolerable than the first. The new technicians didn't seem to recognize that she was human. They just went about their business in a very clinical way. On the table, off the table, on the gurney, and back to room 421.

The timing was perfect. The IV lady removed her link to the stand and placed a Band-Aid on her arm. Mary took a shower and dressed and was out of the hospital at 12:30 p.m.

She was hungry, thirsty, and full of energy, wanting to attack the stores and feeling so up about having done the one thing she thought was impossible.

She darted into a coffee shop and seated herself at a table. She then ordered more food than she could eat and drink: *yummy croissants, some bacon, juice, tea, and just one more bite of this apple muffin. Granny Smiths, I love you. I'll pay the check, and I'm out to shop.*

It was as if she had a built-in compass. She hailed a cab. At each intersection she gave the driver directions and in ten minutes—eureka! She was inside the little stores that she and Michael had passed the other day. Mary was particularly interested in the shop where she had seen that lovely outfit in the window. Michael thought it was beautiful. She was ready and needed this *up*, and no matter if she hated it tomorrow or not, there would be no returns. This was a "Bon Voyage" gift from John.

"May I help you, ma'am?" asked the male salesclerk as Mary walked in.

"Yes. I saw this little outfit the other night. It was in the window in the corner over there. It was an ivory silk organza jacket with black, light weight wool pants. I think it had a satin waist band."

"Yes, that sold right off the mannequin. I mean she just about ripped it off the helpless thing. A woman bought it who needed a can of Crisco to slip into it. But you? No. It would have been a tent on you. You're a six. I know I'm right."

"Yes," she said,

"Fabulous. I have it. Please come with me. Yes... right over here. It's so tasteful... perfect for a woman with your lines." He said while looking at Mary. "Yes... very perfect." He held the jacket high and presented it in a regal manner to her.

"Dressing rooms are to our right," said the salesclerk. I'll carry it in for you. Would you like some tea, coffee or Perrier?"

Mary answered from the dressing room. "No thank you. That's OK I just had a little something."

"Hmm, good for you."

Mary sauntered out into main room of the shop.

"To die for," he said. "Let's look in the mirror."

Mary stood inside the multiple mirrors. The salesman was gushing about her look. "

Really, I have to say this: you could wear anything in this store, or, for that matter, you could even wear that tacky stuff across the street. God forbid! And I'll go as far as including the very best shops in town. It's you. You're gorgeous. Thank you for being here. And thank you for erasing the image of Crisco lady, in this outfit, from my mind forever."

"I like you," Mary said.

"Thanks, but you understand what I mean?"

"I do," Mary assured him.

"Anything but those words."

They both laughed. Mary moved from counter to counter, as if on a mission. She was *up*. She was excited. And she had a need. She tried one little garment after another. One little thought of wearing new things for a new man, whom she felt so comfortable with, was exciting.

"I'm so happy you feel so good about this," said the clerk, noticing Mary's mood. "It's a pleasure to help a woman who has it all together. I'm telling you, this business can get you nuts. But you're wonderful."

She picked up a little lilac camisole and placed it against her body "This is adorable."

"For absolutely sure," the salesclerk said.

"I like it so much I want it in pistachio as well."

"Of course!"

"That does it," said Mary, placing a blouse on top of her other choices on the counter. "I'm done. I don't need any of it wrapped or in too many boxes since I have to carry this to the hotel. So let's make it as compact as possible."

"My pleasure," said the salesclerk.

"So just to chat while I'm doing this... where are you from?"

"As of last month, Calcutta."

He stopped packing. "You've got to be kidding? You are the most unusual woman I have ever met in this store. Please don't tell me you work?"

"No. Well, I work as a fine painter. I'm an artist."

"A gorgeous woman who paints...with taste... from Calcutta. *Kill* me. Next you'll tell me I can come see your work at the Hartford."

"Soon I hope."

"May I have your autograph?" He handed her a pen.

"Well... no one ever asked me for my autograph... sure."

She took a long look at him and started drawing on the back of one of the white boxes. "What's your name? I'm sorry."

"Lewis."

She sketched his face; the likeness was very close, and she signed it. *To Lewis, Mary Templeton.* "I'm framing it and hanging it right over here." He pointed to a wall behind him. "Thank you so much."

"Thanks for slimming me down a few pounds."

Mary paid with her credit card, thanking John silently once again for the American Express card. Then she thought she might not have spent enough... *maybe another $3800. Well, I'll let him off this time. But don't tempt me, John. Just don't say one word.*

"May I help you to a cab?"

"Please."

Lewis assisted Mary out to the sidewalk, carrying most of the shopping bags. He placed them down carefully fanning them out a little. She thanked him.

"Could you do me a little favor?" he asked.

"Sure."

"Let me wave for the cab... just a sec. His words were kind of pulsing up and down in volume. Yes... I'm waving. There's the cab... coming... but I'm really trying... to get... my... competition ... across the street ... frustrated. Yes, he saw you... and the bags. That's it. You're worth a million in depression dollars."

Mary said, "I'll be back."

A cab pulled up and he helped her in with her booty.

"Bye and thank you again."

Waving he yelled, "I'll check the papers for your show."

It didn't take long to reach the hotel. There was very little traffic. Upon exiting the cab, the doorman was quick to help her. She asked for her car and enjoyed looking at the fountain while she waited for them to bring it around. The little cherubs looked chilled on this wintry, gray day.

Her car arrived in no time. With her shopping bags on board, she was on her way home.

Chapter Twelve

Mary walked into the house carrying all of her goodies. She was very excited about everything she had accomplished. With her coat still on, she called Aunt Catherine. The phone rang three times, then four; there was nothing. Mary hung up and proceeded to bring everything up to her bedroom. She laid her booty out carefully on the bed. As she did, a voice called up from downstairs.

Aunt Catherine had arrived and let herself in. "Mary? It's me!"

"I'm up in the bathroom," Mary yelled back.

"Shall I come up?" she asked.

Mary looked at her arm. The Band-Aid, she'd have to explain.

"Sure! I've got great things to show you," she yelled, as she grabbed a sweatshirt and pulled it over her head quickly.

She walked into the bathroom and opened the medicine cabinet. Finding an old Band-Aid box, she quickly removed one, wrapping it around her finger. As she pressed down on the adhesive, she walked out into the bedroom.

"Shopping wounds," she explained to Aunt Catherine.

"How so?"

"Paper cuts from these packages... but well worth it."

Aunt Catherine looked at the bed stacked with clothes. "Wow! What a lot of pretty things."

"Thanks. Let me show you this little thingy here."

"It's lovely," said Catherine. "Silk Organza... beautiful... you must be on a roll." Well, where have you been, young lady?" she asked, her tone changing. "I called last night, and well... maybe you don't want to say."

"Well, I stayed in the city at Michael's hotel."

"When did he come back?"

"He didn't. I stayed there alone."

"Good girl."

"Yes. I did my shopping, had room service for dinner, and enjoyed feeling Michael's presence. It was really nice."

"When is he coming back?"

"I don't know for sure. He said something about going away for the weekend, so I did a little shopping."

"Did you leave anything for the other women?"

"Just the stuff I hated."

"Well, these things are beautiful. My only hope is that you were smart enough to send the bill to John."

"It's on its way as we speak."

"It's terrible how we respond when we are angry. We're bad."

"No, *he* is. And that's how you treat arrogant, pompous, emotionless pieces of garbage like John, right in his charge card," Mary said. "How about some tea?"

"Yes, that's what we need... tea."

The two women went downstairs to the kitchen. As she set about getting the tea ready, Mary could feel that it was time to confess to her Aunt, the events that brought about the emotional collapse of her marriage. Aunt Catherine deserved only good things, but this part of Mary's life had to be revealed.

The end seemed a good place to start. It was the hardest part—the worst of the worst. Mary's mood quieted. Her actions slowed. She didn't want to relive the events that would depress her, but somehow it was time to divulge a very hurting part of her life.

Aunt Catherine began to sense Mary's stress. It was as a child would move about, fidgeting—seeking a word or an action—to start to tell their parent that they did something wrong or to ask for permission to go to an event. Mary was no child but reaching for the words was difficult. Aunt Catherine made it easier. "What's wrong, dear?"

"Aunt Catherine, there is something you must know."

Mary was still searching for the words. She turned, looking directly at her Aunt. "I don't know... well... "

"Please tell me Mary, please." She began to seat herself at the table.

"John and I we... had... a...child. I lost him to a miscarriage. I... "

Aunt Catherine fell into the chair. She sat for a moment then ran her hand across her face. She seemed flush. Her rosy cheeks went pale. Placing her hand on the table, she pushed herself back up and walked to Mary. She embraced her. "Oh, my darling, when? Oh, my... a child! You didn't say a word in your letters. I remember your moving to Calcutta and this long period of nothing."

"Yes nothing... that's what it's all about... John's 'nothing'. I was pregnant when we first moved there. I didn't want to tell you then because everything was in turmoil. John and I were at the edge of our 'nothing.' I was stupid. I thought a child was a way out of loneliness, a way to keep our marriage. It was a boy. He was stillborn... just 3 pounds 8 ounces."

"Oh Mary, what a tragedy. A boy," said Aunt Catherine. "The innocence of a child... with such a burden."

"John was in New York. I was rushed to the Hospital late that evening by our house-keeper and her brother. I was hemorrhaging badly. They admitted me through the emergency ward within the hour. It was over. I never saw him. I was placed in their maternity ward. It was a very sick decision, but it's where I met one of the few friends I have, Manisha Saha. She and her husband Upen, and their children, Jiral and Rose, are the most wonderful people in this world.

"I'm afraid to ask but... "

Mary continued, "I wasn't there long... only three days. Manisha and I left together. They left the hospital with Rose, a beautiful little girl. She was healthy, pretty, and happy. It hurts to say this, but it's true. It's too true."

Mary's voice was breaking up; then, she finally broke down. (Aunt Catherine sobbed, holding her tightly.) "I left with papers... just a piece of white paper. It was a...dea... a... death... certificate."

"And John... where the hell was that bastard... you said? What did he do? When did he get home... back to you, his wife... when?"

"He did nothing," Mary blurted out.

"He was notified while I was under sedation. I received flowers with a note that read, 'I have taken care of the details. Your loving husband, John.' And in a phone call, he said, 'Maybe it was for the best.'"

"That was it?"

"Yes... nothing."

"That's all he said... maybe it was for the best. What kind of man is this? An insensitive cold... " She held Mary tighter. "Wait until I see him... if ever... to treat his wife, the mother of this unfortunate tragedy, like that... "

"He returned several weeks later and never spoke of the birth and death of our child. Never! I confronted him with his callousness... his being a miserable son of a bitch. He grabbed his briefcase and left for *where*, I don't know."

"But what about the child? What did you do?"

"He is buried in a little white casket... so tiny... so sweet, in an out of the way graveyard, on a road to nowhere, just outside of Calcutta. I would go there every day, to make sure his grave was taken care of and to talk to him. I took good care of him. He is my son. I named him Paul... Paul Templeton Powell. I don't know that John even cares to know his name."

Aunt Catherine just burst into tears. "Oh, my dearest God... St Jude... we need your help. This is sad. I don't know that we can tell your uncle. He will, well, I just don't know."

"Manisha and Upen were there when we buried him. I need to call them soon."

The tea kettle had steamed past its perseverance. The steam was obscuring the cups that were scarcely filled. Mary continued:

"John's lack of sensitivity was destroying me. I began to look forward to his being gone, hoping he would call and be a few more days. My painting became intense, the strokes of my brush, angry. The hues were deep and saturated. The subject's faces expressed my state of mind. Still lives seemed to have suggested the presence of people, but there was no one there. Also, shadows and reflections, suggested a presence where there was none. There were crowded street scenes with no faces. There were dark alleys that led to strong, negative spaces. Black shapes dominated my compositions. The movement of my brush, and my choice of paints, expressed it all. But I could not paint. My loss was too deep. My last canvas was a woman in black and her veiled infant. I will never paint another child. That image is *banned*. There can be... no smiles... no happiness... no innocence ever again.

"The moments I had with John were tension-filled... anxiety-ridden. (Her voice was unable to reveal the discontent she had had with their marriage.) The emotional suppression would build each time he would return from another successful acquisition... bragging of how he had decimated the 'poor bastards... boy, did they get screwed.' Over and over, more and more, his voice, his character, his presence became unbearable. She could lip sync the phrases, duplicate his gestures, but couldn't talk to him anymore. I thought I would paint other subjects as a diversion. It became a challenge for a while but ultimately ended with the last canvas stretched out, remaining blank. I refused to witness my own depression on the canvas any longer. Twenty-by-twenty-four inches of white *nothing*, was perched on my easel for weeks, providing a surface for the window's light to fall, casting a plaid pattern across the white on white surface. I sat staring at that shape, my mind aware of the patterns of light that fell upon it.

"My creative-self wanted to paint the space black, as black and as deep as my depression... a bottomless pit. I realized I wasn't looking *down* into it as much as looking *up* from the place I had fallen. It was time to leave, time to change, time to admit my failure... his failure. It was *enough!* I repossessed my work. They are shipping it all here. It should arrive in a few days I imagine. Other than that, I am home."

"What a shame," her aunt said. "Two lives unbalanced for so long... and your child. I'm... so... well I'm... very sad but it's support you need, my dear. Paul and I will always be here *with* you... *for* you."

"I love you, Aunt Catherine," said Mary, getting up to give her aunt a kiss on the cheek and a hug. "More tea?"

"No, I've heard as much as I can take for one sitting. Do I need to prepare for another? I hope not. How have you gotten through this? It's your mother... well the *two* of them had your strength. I've got to be going. Paul's getting home by now, and I've got a good idea of what's for dinner, but I have to make it happen. He won't be happy because it's going to be very simple.

"I don't know how to tell him. I'm going to wait until I digest this. A child... how so much happiness can be taken away... I'm so sorry, Mary."

"I needed to tell you Aunt Catherine. I'll call you a little later or tomorrow."

"Have a good time with Michael, Mary. He is nothing like John. He's one of us." Aunt Catherine hugged her again, grabbed her pocketbook, and left.

Mary went back upstairs to try things on. It was something that had become difficult. The mood was gone, but she didn't want any surprises. She looked at her finger and thought about the Band-Aid and wondered if Aunt Catherine had bought the explanation—the diversion—helping herself get through her secret. A Band-Aid to hide seemed childish at best but she felt there was no other way she could get around it.

Mary removed the Band-Aid from her finger and discarded it. She pulled her sleeve back, revealing a small mark in her vein. She thought the Band-Aid had been there long enough.

Mary kept herself busy for hours, removing tags, hanging her new things in a special area of the closet for the "new and exciting." She had a special interest in one outfit—not that it was silk or the proper dress for the ball, but she felt it was *her*. Michael had seen it in the window and approved. She tried it on once again.

The phone rang. *This must be Michael. Please... oh please... be Michael.*

"Hi," came the now-familiar voice.

"Where are you?" she asked, excitedly.

"Vancouver, still," he said. "Listen, Mary, I don't want to be presumptuous at all, but if you would like, I'll make a few arrangements for an extended weekend for us... like we said. Is that OK with you?"

"This weekend?"

"Yes... is that OK?"

"Well," she said, looking at herself in the mirror, wearing her new things. "Sure... that's great! Where and what do you have in mind?"

"A very special island in the San Juans... not too far and easy to get to. I have some nice thoughts, but I'd like to kind of surprise you with some of them."

"We talked about the surprises. And I did get your notes."

"Hey, I'm happy you stayed! Was everything OK?"

"Perfect... except my bill. I offered to pay, and they told me you left strict instructions."

"If you're that adamant, you can take me to lunch over the weekend."

"OK... that's better."

"Can you meet me at the hotel tomorrow morning about 10:00 a.m.? I'll take care of everything else," he added. "You must have been up in that area at one time or another. *Haven't* you been there?"

"Years ago with mom and dad. I was a little girl... Have you been there?"

"No, but I've been asking and checking on a lot of information. It seems to be a great place. Not formal, so don't bring the gown. In fact, I'm thinking really laid back. But I will bring a suit for one very special dinner."

"It sounds wonderful."

"Great."

"Bye."

Mary hung up the phone and spun around glancing at her mirror.

She threw back her hair and took a deep breath... *Michael... Michael... Michael.*

Chapter Thirteen

Friday morning arrived, mating all the excitement Mary had accumulated. She called Aunt Catherine to let her know she was going off to the best time she would have had in "two thousand years," and to be with Michael.

Mary arrived at the Hotel. The doorman took her bags. Mary asked that he just hold them at the door, since they were leaving shortly. She walked quickly to the elevator, just catching it as the doors were closing.

"Eight, please." An older man pressed the button and smiled at her. At the eighth floor, Mary thanked him, made the left, and presented herself at Michael's door. Feeling a little intimidated, she raised her hand to knock, held her hand still, then tapped lightly on the door. There was no response. She tried again. There was nothing.

She took her key and opened the door. The shower was just being turned off.

"Hello?" she called out.

"Hi," he answered from the bathroom. "I'm running a few minutes late. I'll be out in two minutes. Have some tea. It's all out there."

Michael's bags were ready to go. He had placed some clothing on a chair. She grabbed his pants and brought them to the bathroom door and reached in, turning her head, so as not to look.

"Do you want these?" she asked.

"Thanks. I do," he said.

In seconds, he was out the door. His chest was muscular thick with dark brown hair. His shoulders broad, his hair not brushed. It was a look she had not seen in him yet, but she liked it. Michael walked up to her and gave her a kiss on the cheek. She placed her hands on his shoulders and kissed him on the lips.

"That's nice," he said. "I like this part. Well, we've got to get moving... don't want to be late," he added.

He finished dressing, brushed his hair and was picking up his bags all in the two minutes. "Do you have luggage?"

"Sure," she said. "The doorman has them."

"Them?"

"Just two."

They stopped to pick up her bags and asked the doorman to get a cab.

"A cab?" asked Mary.

"Yes," Michael said. "You'll see."

They got into the cab, and Michael told the driver to take them to West Air.

"We're flying up there?"

"Yes," he said. "So, I can spend all my time with you."

"Well that's nice," she said. "West Air... they are all floatplanes?"

"Yes, they are."

"That's exciting."

The plane sat four. The bags were placed in the luggage compartment as Mary and Michael were helped into the plane. It rocked back and forth in the wake of a fishing boat that had passed minutes before.

"It never fails," said the pilot. "The second I put people on the plane, some vessel comes by and churns up the water."

Mary reached for the pilot's hand. "It's not that bad," she said.

"There you go, Ma'am," said the pilot, helping her aboard. Ever been on one of these before?" he asked them.

"Many times," Michael said.

"My first," said Mary.

"Well, since you have the experience, sir, you hold onto her, and I'll hold onto the plane. Other than that, it will take about forty five minutes to get there."

"Where?" asked Mary.

"I'm going to tell you everything in a second," said Michael.

The engine whined and sputtered, then started. The pilot checked his gauges. A man on the dock released the rope—signaling the pilot. The plane began to move away from the dock. It seemed strange to be in a plane on the water. They taxied out, quite a ways, taking a position in the middle of a large expanse of water. The pilot looked in all directions and proceeded to talk to someone on the radio.

"Are you ready?" he yelled, turning to them.

"Sure," she said.

"Here we go."

The roar of the engine filled their ears as they started to accelerate. Michael took her hand. It was warm.

"Just following instructions," he said.

Mary leaned her head onto his shoulder as the little plane took to the air. The ground and the boats became smaller. The plane banked to Mary's side, allowing her to almost look straight down—a view which didn't come too often in her life.

"We're going to have a great time," said Michael, speaking louder over the sound of the engine. "We're going up to an old inn up there. It's supposed to be terrific. It's a little big, but this time of year there's not too much going on, so we should have the place to ourselves. There's a couple of great restaurants... fabulous oysters, dynamite... something I use a lot... dynamite views, wonderful things, and *you*."

The pilot centered his earphones on his head.

Mary squeezed Michael's hand and turned to look out the window. "Look... whales."

"They are *big*," said Michael... must be over 70 feet long. What a beautiful area of the world. This country's got it all. And this part of it is just magnificent."

They flew over many islands and a maze of waterways, not speaking much as the drone of the engine filled the cabin.

The pilot pulled off one of the earphones, turned, and interrupted their thoughts. Speaking loudly he said, "We've got about ten minutes, and we'll be there," he said. Turning, he spoke into the microphone, beginning to make his descent.

The mountain grew taller as they descended. The boats grew larger. Their perspective was back to earth, as the surface of the water touched the pontoons. The plane touched the water—with no screech of wheels this trip. It slowed immediately. Michael leaned towards Mary.

He whispered in her ear. "Welcome to a fabulous weekend," then kissed her lips. A man and a child waved to them from the dock. The plane floated gently towards them. The pilot cut the engines and opened the door, stepping out onto the pontoon, tossing the rope to them.

"Well, that's it folks," said the pilot. "Hope it was OK."

"It was wonderful," Mary said, as Michael helped her out of the plane.

"The bags will be up at the front desk," said the pilot. "We'll take care of them."

Michael and Mary walked up the ramp to the dock and just looked at the view. The breeze was gentle. The scent of salted air was fresh. It seemed that the mixture of scents was perfectly blended, then, punctuated by the shrill of seagulls arguing over the latest catch.

Michael placed his arm around Mary. She looked at him now, knowing in her heart that this would be a very special weekend for the two of them.

"Let's see what's happening up here," said Michael. "We'll have a little something to eat and take a walk. How does that sound?"

Mary turned and started walking towards the inn. They took a few steps. She stopped, reached up to his lips, with hers, and kissed him.

They stood embraced on the dock, as if it were a photograph.

"You are beautiful. you know that?" Michael said.

Mary smiled and said nothing. They walked towards the inn with Michael's arm around her shoulder and hers around his waist.

The Inn had all the character and charm of "turn-of-the-century architecture." It postured itself on a rise, with acres of green grass carpeting the area around it, offering a warm welcome. At its feet, the gentle waves washed over the smooth stones.

The tide was low—leaving hundreds of estuaries as reflecting pools. The cyan sky and white, puffy clouds were captured as their image filled the mirrored surface from edge to edge.

"We were just there, inside those clouds, touching their softness," Mary thought. The gulls squawked at each other, then, darted high above them, rarely flapping their wings, effortlessly soaring. The path was long and well-traveled by the many who had come to share this experience. That must have been the innkeeper's dream.

It seemed as if the plane had quietly slipped away from the dock, so as not to disturb them, then taxied out into the sound, revved its engines and was off again—without them. Mary sensed her feathers deep inside herself and that they were now alone together, for each other.

They were greeted by a clerk named Richard at the front desk.

"You must be Mary Templeton, and you, sir, if she is Mary, are Michael Bowland. Welcome... welcome to our home."

"Thank you," said Mary.

"This is a lovely place," said Michael. "I had called and asked for one of your best rooms."

"Yes, sir. That's what you're getting. Room 214 . I'm sure you'll find it to your liking."

A man arrived carrying their bags. "I'm Gene. If you'd like to follow me directly up the staircase."

Gene placed their bags outside the door, turned the lock, and opened the door for them. The room was warm from the sun that filled every crevasse—every surface. This was the sitting room. Sheer curtains, tied back, revealed a window seat and a view out, over the sound, to the next portion of the island. It was magnificent. Gene was off, showing Michael around as Mary listened from the window.

"And in this cabinet, there is a TV," she heard him say.

"That's fine. I doubt we will watch it, but thanks," she heard Michael say.

Mary walked to the bedroom as Michael let Gene out. She heard the door close as Michael joined her in the bedroom.

"The place is lovely," he said.

"It sure is," she said. "What a feeling."

Michael reached for her hand. She touched his face. They came closer to each other. Mary's hand went around Michael's neck, drawing him closer. Their lips met gently as Mary held him tightly. They kissed. Michael pulled back, and in a whisper he said, "Happy New Year. I would have kissed you *then* as we have just now. I wanted to."

Mary whispered in reply, "Happy New Year, Michael," and kissed him once again.

"A drink... some lunch... another kiss... a walk... how does that sound?" he asked.

She kissed him again, taking both her hands and running her fingers through his hair. "I'd like to freshen up a little and leave the best for last," she said.

"That's perfect," he said. "On that note, I'm going to go downstairs to the lobby and do a little homework. I'll meet you in the restaurant in ten minutes?"

"Fifteen," she said.

He kissed her again and then once more, and left.

Michael's mission was easy. He just took a quick look around—making sure all was in order for their walk, dinner, and music and dancing—for the evening.

Mary was quick to find Michael standing at the desk. She was vibrant and full of energy. Michael sensed her excitement. "How about a real treat?" he asked.

"Sure!"

"Some lunch, a walk, and a pre-dinner massage."

"A massage... I love it... please!"

Michael turned to the clerk and booked them for massages at 4:30 p.m.

Over lunch, they chatted about the various encounters each had had in Calcutta. The cultural differences ranged from humorous to serious as Michael recalled an incident driving up a street, meeting the police, coming in the opposite direction, with lights flashing. Michael's animated style was hilarious, as he imitated the Indian response and language.

"They insisted I was going the wrong way. I smiled and pointed at the only street sign within a half mile. They laughed and let me by."

"It might have been a nightmare had they decided to click on the bureaucratic switch," Mary said.

"That's for sure," said Michael. "But look at this face. How about a little Lewis and Clark?" Michael asked.

"Lewis and Clark?"

"Yes, a walk."

They left the inn and found a path marked: Nature Lover, et.al. This way. The path was narrow, offering mystery to exploration. It was like a Eugene Smith photograph, part of *The Family of Man*. Two small children, a boy and a girl, ventured toward their path. A sense of light emanated from out of the darkened trees just ahead of them, luring the adventurers towards the mysterious.

This was an invitation offered to Michael and Mary as an adventure and an opportunity to share experiences within *this world*, as well as to discover *each other*. Each step was more intriguing than the last. The view and the fragrance were all part of the sensory palate with each ingredient, tastefully, constructing an experience that would become a fond memory—wrapped in their own time. Just a few steps and the entrance.

Michael reached for Mary's hand as they disappeared around the turn. Gazing upward, high atop the giant oaks and cedars, the eagles soared. One, then another, observed them as visitors to their home. Their wings stretched wide as they made their way through the branches of a thousand trees that reached up to touch them.

Each was offering a perch, as if to say, "Rest if you wish, our statuesque friends." Every step that Michael and Mary shared brought them closer together; they sensed a bond, as a breeze traveled through the canopy above them, whispering secrets only they and the eagles would hear.

The path pushed upward, closer to the eagles' world. The view was something Mary couldn't paint.

This was an image reserved for the mind; neither paint nor brush could capture it, and so it would become a part of her. The inn was distant and like a miniature building, placed at the edge of a pool of magenta. Reflections scurried across the surface of the water, bursting into dancing highlights of cyans and yellows shimmering, as the wake of a small boat crossed the expanse.

The path ended, their soaring friends still gazed upon them with curiosity. It was time to collect their thoughts and impressions and return to the inn, where they could tuck away the memories of a perfect day. Their descent down the path retraced this experience of having shared the sweet scents and sounds of nature.

"It's time for our massages," said Michael, as they walked back to their room. They collected a few things. Michael reached for her arm, gently bringing Mary close to him, kissing her.

Mary said, "Our adventure was very special."

"Yes, it surely was just beautiful," he said.

They embraced, standing as still as could be for a few moments. Michael kissed her again.

"I'll see you at the pool when you're finished. Is that OK?"

"That sounds just right."

The spa was a perfect choice: a warm shower—then ecstasy. The masseuse's hands were soothing across her back.

Mary and Michael enjoyed a full hour of pampering. The tensions drifted away as muscle by muscle was attended to.

The walk was still in the forefront of Mary's mind. The images were slowly being absorbed into her memory as she enjoyed the physical sensation of being touched. She was so enjoying it that the hour passed before she knew it.

The masseuse directed her to the pool, where she found Michael swimming toward her.

"Jump in. It's warm," he said.

Mary put down her towel and dove directly at Michael. She came up immediately in front of him. Michael gave her a kiss.

"What a treat," she said. "You were right."

After a quick swim, they went back to the room and dressed for dinner.

Mary was saving her special wardrobe for one evening only. She hadn't decided which it would be since she hadn't asked Michael what he had in mind. It was on her mind for sure but not tonight.

This evening was just as special, but her attire would be a combination of the other "little things" she purchased. *Thank you, Lewis,* she thought.

The menu offered an array of mouthwatering selections: "Oysters (a choice of eight kinds), Caesar Salad, Fresh Halibut." The tastes were all stimulating, and, of course, there was champagne—carefully opened, perfectly chilled, then poured into coffee cups.

"To us," said Michael. "Chind Anna. One hundred years—wishing you and us one hundred years of life."

"Chind Anna," she repeated.

They drank, and laughed, and enjoyed their dinner. They asked if the remainder of the bottle could be sent upstairs to their room.

"Of course, sir," said the waiter. "Our pleasure."

Mary entered the bedroom first. A single lamp was lit. The fireplace was alive with flames.

"That's nice," she said. "That's really lovely. Did you ask for this?"

"I cannot tell a lie," said Michael. "They must do it cause it's nice to do. No! I *did* ask. They said they'd take care of it."

There was a knock at the door, and the champagne arrived. Michael placed it on the table. He poured two more cups and offered one to Mary. She sipped it, and he did the same. They said nothing.

As the two of them sat in front of the fireplace, on the floor stretching out, Mary leaned against the arm of the couch. Michael moved closer to her, taking her cup and placing it out of the way. His lips reached hers, as he kissed her with the softness and adoration that he felt for her. She reached up to touch his face with her hand and placed it softly beside his ear, holding him close to her. She pressed firmly against his lips.

"Shall we stay *here*?" asked Michael.

"Yes," she said.

He got up for a moment and turned off the lamplight. The flames from the fire were all that was needed to see the expressions of love that passed between them. He lay next to her, sipping the champagne once more. Mary reached to him with both arms extended, saying, "Love me, Michael... love me forever."

He placed his hand around her neck and raised her from the floor. Their lips met once again, sending emotions screaming through his body. Michael unbuttoned her blouse, one button at a time, so carefully, while kissing her neck and ear. Mary moved her face across his and kissed him again and again. Their tongues met. She helped him remove her blouse and unbuttoned his shirt, exposing his chest. He reached for the catch on the back of her bra.

"It's been a while, hasn't it?" she asked.

"Confessions are sometimes... well, yes," he said.

"Well, the catch has been in the front for some time now," she said, guiding his hands. Michael fumbled with it for a while until Mary whispered, "Like this," and twisted the catch. Her naked breasts now touched his chest. The stimulation was intense.

They touched each other so softly and their bodies grew hot with the passion they exchanged for each another. He ran his fingers across her back, ever so softly, tasting her lips, her ear, and kissing her eyes. Their exchange became explosive—the passion, now erotic. The need they had for each other was displayed by a focus and intensity neither had ever experienced before. He couldn't get any closer to her. His whispers of love to her exploded in her mind as a commitment to her decision to be loved by this man. She touched him emotionally as no other had. His intensity was relentless—wanting her to be complete. She was the woman he needed to have, to make his life whole again. She was the woman he loved, and he wanted her forever.

Their bodies intertwined, locked together, heightening the sensitivity they exchanged so delicately. Their lives were now one, each welcoming the other to complete the missing pieces of their complex emotions. Each was so willing to surrender themselves: "This is who I am. You are what I need... I love you... yes, I am vulnerable, and yes, I want to be vulnerable for you. I trust my love with you."

The emotional bond they now shared grew tighter. This communion of their minds, body, and spirit was now at the edge of ecstasy, each wanting the other to release the tensions, the anxiety, the suppressions into the cerebral paradise. Mary clutched Michael's back, pulling him to her as he kissed her open mouth, each gasping for air, each exchanging the other's breath. Mary's body pulsed with intensity. Michael brushed the hair from her face, as she quietly rested, her hand slipping across his back, falling softly to the rug.

"Michael, I love you," she said. He kissed her again. They lay there silently, their lives made one. Neither wanted to change this moment, both hoping it would last forever. Sometime long after the glow of the embers had turned to ash, the two made their way to bed.

Chapter Fourteen

The sun peaked from behind the drapes. Michael's eyes opened. Mary's head was nestled on his shoulder and chest. Her legs intertwined with his. He felt her eyelashes fluttering upon his chest. She was awake. She moved her head back a little and kissed his shoulder.

"Good morning," she said.

"Good morning. Sleep OK?"

"Just wonderfully," she answered.

Michael pulled the covers up a little tighter under their chins. He groaned and stretched his arms and legs.

"Cooofffffee. We need coffee," he said.

He reached for the phone and called room service.

"May we have coffee for two?" he asked.

"Tea for me, please," said Mary.

"And tea as well," he said into the phone. "And some muffins, croissants, and some things like that, please."

"It'll be ten to twenty minutes. Would you care for some jellies and jams, sir?"

"Yes, thank you," he said, and hung up.

He lay back, folding his hands under his head and stretching again. Mary put her arm across him and squeezed him as she placed her head back on his chest.

"What would you like to do today?" he asked.

"Stay in bed... with you," she said.

"Sounds good, but... " he began.

She listened to his deep voice resounding through his chest as she pressed her ear against it. She lifted her head, moving her hair aside, and then placed her ear directly on his chest.

"It sounds so different... your voice," she said. "Like this," and she mimicked him.

"You need resonance," he said. "Meeeee, meeeee, meeee. And you, you, you," he sang, his voice growing deeper.

"Let's go the East Sound," she said.

"Roller blading!" he said.

"Do you know how to do that?" she asked.

"Not without very serious injuries."

They heard a knock on the door and the announcement of, "Room service."

"Talk about quick!" said Michael. He got up, ran to the bathroom, and grabbed a robe. "Just a minute, please!" he yelled.

He opened the door and a waiter entered, carrying a large tray. "Shall I place it here on the table, sir?"

"That's fine," said Michael, as he signed for it.

"Where do you want to have your coffee?" asked Mary, after the waiter left.

"Right here in bed," said Michael. He began to pour, then added sugar and milk to his coffee. "How do you want your tea?"

"Just plain hot tea," she said.

He poured her a cup and handed it to her. "Yours is easy—just tea. Mine is coffee and then the milk and then the sugar and the spoon." He took a sip and nearly scalded his lips.

"Don't scald the lips," said Mary. "We need them."

She thought for a moment. "What about bikes? Motor bikes? How about that?"

"Do they have them here?" he asked. "I thought all the motor bikes in the world were shipped to Bermuda or Hong Kong."

"I'm not sure," she said.

"Want a muffin?" he asked.

"Yes. With butter and a little jam."

Michael got up again and brought her two kinds. He stopped at his luggage and removed his "trusted friend," as he called it, bringing back with him a short-wave radio that looked as if it had seen many flights around the world. He snuggled back into bed and turned it on, running through a prolific number of sounds and voices before fine-tuning it to a local weather report.

"That's a good idea, but I'm sure we could find out the local weather from the front desk," said Mary.

"Well, I've traveled with this Grundig short-wave radio for years now. What makes it really wonderful is using it to determine what's happening before I arrive. The trick is to find an English-speaking transmission where you are going and in parts of the world like Thailand. Hong Kong is easy, but India and Tibet... I'm talking Himalayas. It gets to be a joke.

"I remember a time I thought I was listening to a forecast in Djerba. I wasn't sure about the transmission. I asked my translator, 'Hot? Cold?' He said 'Yes.' I guess that was the mistake. The translator told me how hot this year had been. Assuming the best, I boarded a train in a light-weight jacket and jeans. When we arrived a day later, on the coldest day of their year, there were three inches of snow on the ground. My luggage was lost somewhere in the back of the train. I never found out where I had listened in on. I just didn't. But I must say it's been a real friend in many instances. I really like the reach. This radio and my Swiss army knife make a decided difference in my Boy Scout attitude."

Mary and Michael kept eating, talking, and snuggling in bed for hours. It was quite a while before they got out of bed. Eventually they showered, dressed and closed the door behind them. They headed for the lobby.

"Hey, they do have bikes?" Michael asked. "Look at that sign... 'Motor Bike Rentals This Way.' Were you kidding or would you like to give it a shot?"

"Let's do it!" she said. "But I think we need warmer jackets, according to that translator you told me about."

Mary went up to the room to get their jackets while Michael arranged for the bikes. At the last minute, she remembered to look for her driver's license and was happy to find she still had it in her purse.

Meanwhile, Michael was getting directions. "How far to the East Sound?" he asked at the bike rental shop.

"About thirty minutes by bike," the clerk said. "It's a very pretty ride. Take your time and enjoy."

They met back in the lobby, and a few minutes later they were off. They took to the bikes like seasoned drivers. Mary had had countless hours of motorcycling in Calcutta. The fact that no one was around her now made for a much easier ride than she had ever had through those busy streets of Calcutta.

The two of them traveled side by side, up the road towards the East Sound. The brisk breeze in their faces was invigorating. Each turn in the road resembled a painting. The fresh air was a narcotic, stimulating their senses.

The road had been carefully sculpted into the scenery. It was a well-placed line just above the edge of craggy rocks and gentle waves, resting at the feet of tall pines so thick with growth and as deep in color. The rush of wind through their helmets muffled the motors.

The dulcet sound became part of the vibrations that ran up their arms and legs as they made their way to the East Sound. Occasionally the tree line thinned, revealing the presence of the distant mountains with places to go, and more to see—touch—and remember.

The town was small and seemed to be resting and waiting for the spring and summer guests. The flower boxes were barren, awaiting impatiens and tulip bulbs to reappear, especially the crocuses. They were not yet ready to welcome spring.

The few people who were out, moved at a pace of their own. Mary pulled over to the side of the road and removed her helmet. Michael pulled up beside her and removed his as well.

"I want to go there," she said, pointing to Mount Constitution.

"Sure, let's do it," he said.

They put their helmets back on and headed toward the mountain. The thrust of its mass became even more majestic the closer they got to its base. A road that seemed to lead up the side toward the top offered a sign. They stopped to read: "Travel at your own risk, 2409 feet to the top. Go slowly."

Mary took the lead, sensibly placing her bike closer to the inside of the narrow road. The elevation changed abruptly, and the pitch of the bikes' motors changed with it as they strained to carry them to the pinnacle of their journey. The switchbacks and stone guardrails were old, making their adrenaline rush as they thought of the sheer drop off the face of the serpentine road. The wind came in gusts, nudging them safely into the inside of the road.

They slowed as they drove up closer to the watchtower that marked the end of the trail. They stopped and parked, then decided that the tower needed to be climbed as the last few feet of their journey, so they could observe the majesty of God's creation.

Carefully, they climbed each of the weathered oak steps to the platform. The view and the excitement was incredible. They looked out from the parapet walls that kept them within the small, four-by-four area.

"It's as if we're in a hot air balloon floating over yesterday's path... a panorama of nature's best," said Mary. "Look at the eagles. They are soaring beneath us."

The tops of the evergreen trees became a bed of soft color. They could now see as the eagles see and feel what the eagles felt, as the wind wrapped around their faces in flight. Michael turned to look at Mary. Her eyes were filled with tears. He kissed her warmly. Their embrace was a bond. Her tears were contagious. He held her tightly, and she felt no fear. Michael would take care of her; she had no need to think of the height or the danger. It was his strength she felt as they kissed once again.

One of her tears touched his face. He removed a handkerchief from his pocket and dried her eyes. Mary pulled him close. She nuzzled her head into his chest, clutching his jacket with both her hands. The two of them were alone, sharing the intangible, a feeling exchanged atop this mountain, suspended by time within "their balloon" that soared above the eagles, its roof touching the clouds. It was exciting. A treasured time, place—and another well-spent grain of sand perfectly placed in her memory. She knew she'd remember these feelings forever.

It took Michael a minute longer to get on his bike. He seemed to be looking for something on the rock wall. Mary started down the mountain. Michael was immediately behind her.

The descent was uneventful as the two bikes rushed by the sign they had read a short while ago. When they got back to town, they breathed a sigh of excitement—invigorated by having shared so much that day. The day had been a canvas painted by emotion.

They talked. They laughed. They touched each other, this day, for the first time with a freedom each welcomed. Their feelings couldn't be described —'enough' was an empty word. 'Too much' could never be attained, as they explored their worlds that had been untouched for too many years.

They parked their bikes and walked back across the street, stopping in one little store after another. Each proprietor was friendlier than the next, each curious about where they came from and where they were staying. One store in particular interested Michael. He struck up a conversation about rocks and semi-precious stones with a gentleman who stood behind a large display case filled with polished geological finds. Mary drifted away from the conversation toward some primitive art hanging on the wall a short distance away. She looked back to see Michael reaching some sort of agreement with the gentleman. The two men shook hands, and she heard Michael say, "I'll see you later."

The two of them went through the shops enjoying the design and style of many crafts accumulated in such a small space. They were lured to a little area by the aroma of sausage being pan-fried by an older woman. She seemed to have no space for anything, but the few people in the store had gravitated to this aroma, salivating, needing to sample its taste.

Immediately next to the woman were small jars of jellies, mustards, and spreads, each available to test taste with the sausage.

"May I try this one?" Mary asked, pointing to a jar.

"Horseradish jelly," crackled the woman.

"Yes, please," said Mary.

The woman quickly cut a few pieces of sausage, placed them on a paper plate with a generous spoonful of jelly and handed it to Mary.

She took a toothpick and carefully chose a piece, then dipped it into the red, creamy jelly and brought it to her mouth.

"It's delicious," she said. "Michael, give it a try."

She dipped another piece and placed it in his mouth. "A little hot," he said, rolling it around in his mouth, savoring the flavor. His eyes opened wide. "Hmmm. It's re- ally good! Do you make the spread?"

"No," said the old woman. "No. We found it just like you did once when we took a trip to Vermont. I loved it so much; I have them send me cases of it so I can sell it with my other products. It seems to be a good little company with a lot of heart."

"May we purchase some?" asked Mary.

"Sure. It's five dollars a jar."

"Make it two," said Michael.

The taste stimulated their appetites so much that Michael asked where they could find a restaurant in town.

"Try Kay's down the street," the woman suggested. "Nice place, and it's open now."

Michael and Mary waved goodbye and headed off for lunch. "I could have stayed there and eaten all of that sausage," said Michael as they walked.

"Good idea," said Mary.

At Kay's they were greeted by a young girl, dressed in jeans and a neat white blouse the second they walked in the door. With menus in hand, she asked if they were having lunch, then directed them to the nicest table in the room. The windows were large and the ambiance was quaint. The entire room was constructed of wood. The timbers were hand-hewn, rising from the floor to the ceiling in a monochromatic burnt umbra. The knots and grain added a dark and light contrast to the rustic mood it created.

A waitress approached them with utensils and napkins and arranged them on the table. "Well, how are you all today?" she asked.

"Wonderful," said Mary.

"Would you like coffee before lunch?"

"Some tea, please," said Mary.

"A beer, a lite beer," said Michael. "Any kind is fine. Do you have sausage on the menu?"

"Yes, we do," she said. "Did you just come from up the street?"

"Yes," he said.

"That's my Aunt Fran. We have the same sausage she's serving. Would you like that?"

"Yes, with some fries," said Michael. "That's it. I'm starving."

"The same, please," said Mary.

"My pleasure," said the waitress.

"You're not thinking what I'm thinking?" asked Mary, when she had left.

"Yes, I am," said Michael. "I'm opening up my jar."

"Good, I'm saving mine," said Mary.

It didn't take long for the sausage to be prepared. The fries were crispy and the sausage steaming with flavor. Michael opened the jar of horseradish jelly, scooping a spoonful onto Mary's plate and one onto his own. Each piece was dipped, and then savored, as they enjoyed every morsel of their lunch. They chatted about the mountain, and the waitress even got involved in the conversation for a little while. She told them she was born on the island and had only been away once for a few weeks—and then couldn't wait to get back.

Michael motioned that he was ready to pay the check. Mary interrupted. "I believe this is mine."

"No arguments from me," said Michael.

They went back up the street, directly back to one of the stores they had left earlier. Michael reached for Mary's hand and pulled her into the doorway.

"Where now?" she asked.

"Right here," he said.

He took her up to the counter where the stones were displayed and addressed the gentleman he had spoken with previously. "How did we do?"

"You're set," the gentleman answered.

"What's set?" asked Mary.

Michael paid the man, and they were out the door in seconds with a package in Michael's hand. He handed it to Mary and said, "It's a beginning."

She opened the bag. There was a little white box inside. It held a simple silver necklace with a polished stone attached.

"It's a stone, but it's much more. I picked it up from the mountaintop where we were this morning. I asked the man if he would polish it for me and drill out a hole while we had something to eat. He loved the idea and said it would be no problem. So here is a part of what we shared up there... just you and me."

Mary just kissed him. They both looked into the store. There was the man with his thumb up and Aunt Fran next to him, smiling.

Mary placed the precious stone around her neck, double-checking the latch. The two walked towards their bikes and within minutes, were on the road back to the inn.

The day had been exciting, filled with anticipation, filled with beginnings. When they returned to the room, Mary threw herself on the bed, stretched out her arms, and reached for a pillow to pull under her head. Michael lay down next to her, his hand reaching for the stone around her neck. He touched it lightly with his fingers.

"The guy did a nice job. It really is smooth," he said.

Mary turned and kissed him. Their arms wrapped around one another, and in the quiet of the room, they fell asleep.

The nap was the perfect respite between their daylight escapades and the night's promise of more to share with each another. They shared a shower. Michael washed Mary's hair, massaging her scalp. The soap ran through his fingers and across their bodies. Michael wrapped his arms around Mary as the steaming water rushed over their faces. Their lips met in an exchange of passion. His hands were still soapy and rubbing her back.

"You are wonderful, Michael," she said.

Mary reached behind his head and pulled him closer to her. The water found new paths as it flowed through his thick, dark hair and cascaded over his eyes and her lips as they pressed against each another—passionately. The pores of their bodies awakened to the warmth of their touch.

Michael reached for the faucet, flipping the lever off.

"We're done?" asked Mary.

"We're just getting started," he said. "Let's make a date."

He pulled the curtains aside, stepped out and reached for a towel. Then he turned and wrapped it around Mary.

"That's perfect," she said.

She patted her eyes and face, as Michael reached for another towel and dried himself off.

He dropped his towel to the floor, took Mary's, and placed it tenderly around her shoulders, pulling the ends tightly. Then he allowed it to fall as his arms wrapped around her. He pulled her to his body. His hand moved to her face, pushing her wet hair back, away from her eyes. They stood there naked for many minutes motionless—not caring about time— just sharing the moment.

They decided to dress and enjoy dinner as a prelude to more lovemaking. They set a date for 10:00 p.m. to make it even more stimulating, each knowing that their expectations would be fulfilled, each willing to wait to savor the ecstasy they would create for each other.

Mary asked what night he would wear his suit. Michael hinted that he had put together something special for tomorrow night.

Michael suggested that they meet at the bar downstairs, when Mary was ready, since it would take her longer to dress. He finished brushing his hair and kissed her gently on her lips as she was putting on her makeup. Then he left.

The bar was filled with people, which surprised Michael. A younger couple, seated at the bar, was discussing the schedule for the organist and her performance that evening. Michael couldn't help but interrupt.

"Excuse me," he started.

"Hi," said the young man.

"Is someone going to play that enormous pipe organ tonight?" he asked.

"Yes, at 8:30," the man said.

"I didn't know it worked," said Michael. "It seems to have been here as long as the building."

"Exactly, something like 1900."

"Well, that's a treat."

"Enjoy it," the young man said. "The whole building resonates."

Michael turned to see Mary entering the room.

"Hey, they're going to have a little concert here tonight. The organist is going to play at eight-thirty."

"That's a bonus," she said.

They ordered drinks and took them to the table, ordering a tasty dinner of stuffed salmon with capers. More people filled the restaurant, obviously arriving for the concert.

Mary began to talk about the little organ that her church had had for many years. She had seen it the other day when she had stopped in. It was small but powerful, and she remembered how its pipes had reverberated, filling the interior of their church, always adding inspiration to the service. As a young girl, she and her friends had found it easy to whisper their secret thoughts in the middle of service.

The lights dimmed twice as a courtesy to let the diners know that the performance was about to begin.

Mary and Michael walked with the others towards the music room, where the furniture had beautiful, handcrafted teak and mahogany surfaces, all polished as if it had just been built. The organ pipes vaulted to the ceiling, which was punctuated by an impressive Tiffany chandelier—old world charm at its finest.

They were seated just as a man, wearing a tuxedo, entered the room. Standing in front of the multi-level keyboard, the master of ceremonies paused while the room quieted.

"Thank you all for coming this evening," he said. "Tonight's performance is offered to us by the very talented and, I might add, beautiful Elizabeth Dutcher, a graduate of Julliard and an important part of the Conservatory of Music at for many, many years. May I introduce Liz Dutcher."

Applause filled the room as Elizabeth took a seat at the keyboard. The room was now waiting as she placed her hands upon the keys that would trigger sounds—felt by the waters and mountains that surrounded the inn. The first chords exploded within the space, taking everyone by surprise because of the intensity and resonance felt by the movement of her petite fingers.

The sounds were elegant and perfectly pitched. The audience was in a trance.

This sound took Mary back again to her church and the little organ that reached for notes and chords which had filled their chapel. But its little voice could only be placed in the *shadow* of the resonance, created by the thousand pipes controlled by this artist.

Each trumpeting note was heard as its own, and every note was perfectly placed in harmony, as Elizabeth expressed her genius. Her art touched the audience.

Elizabeth Dutcher played on. Her talent was so well received that the audience had no awareness of time. Her hands moved quickly over the keys on many levels, pushing and pulling valves, never missing a note or inflection. The sound, escaping from the pipes and shaking the entire building, reverberated through everyone's bodies. Finally, the last note escaped the organ and rushed through each member of the audience—leaving all motionless as they felt the vibrations come to a rest within themselves. Spontaneously, the entire audience applauded her expertise. Mary looked at her face, recognizing the feeling she had of accomplishment in presenting a performance that was impeccable since she, herself, would also feel enormous self-gratification when she would stimulate others by *her* work. And this artist was one who was feeling what artists need to feel—*needed.* Elizabeth Dutcher is a fortunate woman.

The master of ceremonies returned and asked for more applause, a request that received a generous response. As the applause quieted, he thanked the audience and his talented artist, announcing that this would conclude tonight's performance.

The small audience dispersed. Some went home, others to their rooms. Michael and Mary went to the restaurant's bar, where he asked for a bottle of Cordon Rouge, "any year." The bartender asked where they were sitting.

Michael replied, "Room 214."

"I'll have it sent up, sir," the bartender said.

"If you don't mind, I'll wrap a napkin around it and carry it up," said Michael.

"Well, the house rules are... " the bartender started.

"Don't get caught!" finished Michael.

"Deal," he said.

Upstairs, Mary opened the door to find the fireplace aglow. The room was toasty warm. Michael poured the champagne into the glasses, and they both sat down to raise a toast.

"It's 9:45," said Michael. "Just right."

"I'll be right back," said Mary. She returned wearing one of his shirts.

"These are my surprise PJ's," she said.

"That's one of my shirts," he said.

"At least you get to take it back," she answered.

She slid closer to Michael, who was sitting next to the fire. Their glasses touched gently; no cups this time, just official glasses. The crisp ring of crystal blended with the crackle of the fire. Seasoned flames in ascent amplified as their motion was reflected in the glasses. Bubbles rose slowly to the surface. Mary's lips touched the rim. She lifted the stem slowly. Their eyes riveted on each another. Bubbles rolled across their tongues until they gently swallowed. Their needs intensified. Michael touched her and sent Mary back into a world of pleasure she had felt just yesterday for the first time in a thousand years. He leaned closer, then closer to her body. His head slipped down, resting between her breasts. He kissed her softly. She ran her hand through his hair, her finger stopping at his ear. Placing her glass down, she leaned towards him whispering, "It's after ten... our date. Let's go to bed."

She pulled the comforter down, then slid deep beneath the flannel sheets. Michael was moments behind her. His body traced her path; his warmth was an envelope that surrounded her. He reached for the bottom of the shirt and pulled it higher, exposing her breasts, then pressed himself against her. Mary reached for the shirt and removed it completely.

For all the moments, and all the years that had passed—a collage of negatives, agonizingly placed one day at a time in their lives—*this* moment had washed them away. The days of depression, the nights of anxiety, the belief that there was no time, that there was no *one* whom either of them could touch, was not true any longer. This love, found new, was expressed by each with an intensity that bonded them to each other. These motions are an expression filled with passion, that reaches and shares. They are emotions that have no boundaries. This is the moment, the essence of emotional honesty, a confession offered to each other.

"I love you, Mary," said Michael.

"And me you, my love," she whispered back "... forever."

They exchanged their love for hours, falling asleep with their arms wrapped around each other. Her head rested on his shoulder. It was a quiet comfort for each of them.

Mary awoke to the muffled sounds of Michael's short-wave radio. She looked at his hand, holding the radio to his ear, setting it at the very lowest volume. He was dialing through many stations looking for the local weather once again. Mary's head was comfortably tucked in the feather pillow with just one eye exposed, watching Michael as he turned.

"Good morning. It's almost 10 o'clock and according to 'old trusty,' it's going to be one of those 'gift days.' When you get up, it should be bright, sunny, and 60-ish. Let's have a picnic!"

"Good morning," she said, turning, stretching, and yawning a bit, covering her mouth as she did. "A picnic! Yes, a picnic!"

"Can we bike over to Morgan State Park for the afternoon?" he asked.

She leaped out of bed. "Let's do it!"

Michael heard her hop in the shower as he called room service.

"This is room 214," he said. "Could you put together a picnic basket for two? And could you add some cheese, crackers, grapes, and a few sandwiches or something like that with a bottle of wine?"

"Yes, Sir, can we come along? I understand it's going to be a great day!"

"Sure! I don't know where we're going anyway."

"Well, I'll throw in a little map with a few favorite places. But I must admit, we would love to be there with you two. We'll make up something very special for you. It will take at least an hour."

"Great! And thanks," said Michael.

"Michael, are you joining me?" Mary yelled from the shower.

"Two seconds," he yelled back.

Chapter Fifteen

The traditional wicker picnic basket and blanket were ready for their journey. Michael strapped them to the rear of the bikes, and they were off. The morning air was a bit chilly but invigorating. It was one of those rare days before spring, a sample of what would come. The sun began to warm the air around them. The air was filled with excitement as the gulls chased and squawked at each other—enjoying their freedom of flight after their long winter of silence. Michael and Mary crossed a little wooden bridge and stopped. Michael looked at the map that he was given.

He spoke over the noise of the motors. "According to this, we go up this road towards the mountain for a while. It's not that much further. Ready?"

They were off again. The road became a path—the path a trail. The environment became so flawless, they began to feel as if they were violating its sanctity. They stopped, removed their helmets, and listened.

"Michael, I think we can walk if that's OK?"

"Yes, I think we're making too much noise."

The pines were thick with growth. They crossed a grassy area towards the trees. Michael could see a small clearing through the branches on the other side. He held a branch back from swinging into Mary. It was as though a gentleman was holding a door open for her.

This view was magnificent. It was a painting, a photograph, a scene whose grandeur could never be captured by sight alone. It was there for the mind and for all the senses. Michael said, "Our human kind could never create an art that could express the intricacy of what lies just ahead of us."

The sun's morning light was warming all things. The stately mountain was first to accept its gift. The lake's cool waters were borrowing reflections from the mountain, adding variation after variation of its neighbor's likeness. The breeze that stirred the straw grass added to its fragrance as it wafted past them with a rush of reeds gently rasping against one another whispering, "Be quiet and listen to the silence."

Eagles flew in circles high in the sky, a deeper cyan than can be painted. At the water's edge, a tree (an evergreen with branches that remember the ages of man) reached out—welcoming them to rest beneath it.

They walked, without saying a word, then placed their basket on the ground beneath the tree. A fish leapt into the air, sending concentric ripples across the lake's surface, breaking the mountain's reflection into soft rolls of imagination.

Michael turned and placed his arms around Mary, hugging her. He said nothing. They remained in place for many minutes until the silence was broken by a flock of geese splashing and honking, while landing in the lake, churning at the surface. The serenity transformed into chaos; there was a profusion of activity for a short time as the waters absorbed the change—then returned to quiet.

Michael opened the bottle of wine. He popped the cork as she leaned back against the base of their tree. He poured the wine.

"I'm feeling this side of terrific," he said. "It's just so good to be here with you. There's nothing better... well, maybe if... "

"What? What if?" she asked.

"Well, if you were a little closer," he said.

She moved over. "That's perfect. Yes," she said.

"Well... "

She leaned over and kissed him.

"Michael, are you away on business next week?" she asked.

"Yes," he said. "I'm going to Vancouver on Wednesday. Is there something happening?"

"No, I just thought I'd ask. I've got something to take care of in town. I didn't know what you were doing so... "

"You want to stay at the hotel?"

"Well, I'm not sure what's going on," she said.

"What are you doing?"

She paused. "I've got to return some things I bought at a store."

"OK."

"And I want to see the man at the gallery."

They both sipped their wine for a moment.

"I'd like to help," he said. "If you want, I can drop some names. I think that's what the world's about. An art show is not much different from any other business. My friend sits on the board of the Guggenheim. Maybe that's good."

"That's good, believe me!" Mary said.

"Well, you see him or whatever. I'll jump in at another date if you think it's appropriate. Otherwise I'll just go to the show like everyone else, except I'll be with the most sought after artist in the world."

"Positive thinker," she said.

"No, confident thinker... about you," he said. "Oh, look at this. We're about to see something special."

An eagle swooped down towards the water, its wings spreading out, opening wide, flapping, and splashing water into the air, marking its impact. Its talons reached into the lake and snatched its prey— their grasp inescapable. The "great hunter" confidently ascended towards a craggy loft to feed its young.

"I've never witnessed this first hand, have you?" asked Mary.

"No, I haven't," said Michael.

"Which are you, Michael, the fish or the eagle?" she asked.

"Both, I guess," he answered. "I have the spirit of the eagle and the survival instincts of the fish. And you?"

"I'm not sure. I'd like to be a feather, but that's a long story."

"On the bird?"

"No, just a feather. It's special... "

"Well, what about the eagle?"

"It reminds me of John. The difference is the eagle has, built into its being, integrity and morality... ethics. John just feeds on the unsuspecting, using his father's money. He didn't make it himself. It's just his genetic gift. All that is required is the selling of your soul and a need to live in hell for your entire life."

"You are very angry."

"I am very hurt, Michael. It was a lot of years... a lot of deep wounds still attempting to heal."

"We both suffer from a lot of negatives. I think of Margaret running around here enjoying the fresh air and the space. A picnic for a child... it's more freedom than imaginable. I just loved being with her. I was her daddy, the greatest title known to man. Hey! I'm getting a little low here. I'm sorry."

"I have something that's important I want to tell you... since the subject is similar," Mary said.

"Similar?"

"I had a child within me... once."

"You had a child?"

"I had a miscarriage this last year in Calcutta. It was a little boy. He died at birth. I named him Paul."

"I'm so sorry... a child... I understand. The pain can be so bad. What was John's reaction?"

"He was in New York and never came home. He 'took care of the details' as he put it, but that was it. I had to tell you. I'm sorry I didn't tell you any sooner. I just... "

"He didn't come home to see you?" Michael asked as he thought, *how could anyone be that cold?*

"No. John has never recognized his son's birth or his death."

"Why do you suppose he was that callous?"

"We will never know. I have a few theories about his own family, but I think it's hidden somewhere in his fear of failure. Whatever it is, it didn't work for me."

He turned to Mary. "How did Aunt Catherine react? It would seem that death, especially the death of a child, would... " he paused, "especially Uncle Paul, his namesake... "

"I recently told Aunt Catherine. She was decimated. I don't know if Uncle Paul knows. My friend, Manisha Saha, and her husband, Upen, were the only people at the funeral."

"Manisha! Who is Manisha?"

"She and I were in the same maternity room together. She went home with a beautiful girl. I went home with nothing."

"You've just told Catherine and Paul after all this time?"

"It wasn't the kind of thing I wanted to write in a letter. I thought I was going to leave him then, but months went by, then a year. I couldn't, so I waited until last week. It's all bad timing."

"I am so very sorry. The loss is awful... just awful."

"I feel so guilty just leaving Paul there. I just think... it was... " Not finishing, her eyes welled up. "I'm sorry, Michael. This does happen from time to time."

"For me as well, with my two little children. Maybe they met."

They embraced. Mary whispered in his ear, "I hope so."

Michael pushed her away gently with a smile and an attempt to change the mood. "I can move mountains, but no one is ever moving *that* one because it's yours... my gift to you. Now please don't ask me to take it home because even Bloomingdale's doesn't have a shopping bag that big."

She laughed, also trying to shake off the bitterness. But it was difficult. She still had questions.

"What about you? Are you angry, Michael?"

"Sometimes I feel very angry. Most times I feel hurt, beaten by circumstances I could never control... like what we just talked about. Then in John's case, he is dealt the cards of life—and money—while mine were taken from me. The work I do, I work hard at. His is no effort at all. I feel nothing for him or those like him since it's nothing more than winning the lottery. A few do, and most don't.

As for their lives, they become shallow... meaningless, but they never affect me. Only through you have I seen the price that must be paid for the arrogance. For *that*, I do not like them. But if it weren't for you and what you are, you would have never left him. And for that, I must thank him for being the way he is. It's a strange but true story in the complex world in which we live.

So, if I may, a toast to the unsoiled. Let them remain locked in the caverns of the mint forever. But are they locked in, or are we locked out?"

"That's scary," said Mary. "I just remembered something."

"What?"

"A dream. A nightmare."

"I'm sorry. Are you OK? A toast, Mary. OK?"

"OK."

"To them."

They drank, and continued to talk about life and love, about the way their worlds knit together. They talked about Michael's stories as a child and about Mary's embarrassment as a young girl growing up with gangly legs and pimples... and with her first date with a guy who was more nervous than she.

"I understand that totally," he said.

The mountain's reflection darkened. Dancing highlights shimmered as blue-white sequins floated atop the mirrored lake. When a cool breeze kicked up, Michael asked if it was time to get back to the inn. There was the last sip of wine with a warm kiss. Then they packed up their basket and blanket.

Back in the room, Mary immediately seated herself in an overstuffed chair. She looked somewhat sullen; her eyes looked tired. He asked if she were OK, and she told him she needed a nap.

"Are you sure? You look exhausted," he said.

"I'll be all right."

"But you are perspiring, and your hands are cold."

"I just need a nap."

"Do you want me to stay here with you?"

"No, it's OK," she said. "I can handle this."

"I'll go and check on our flight out tomorrow and stuff like that," he said. "How much time would you like?"

"Well tonight is very special. You *are* wearing a suit?"

"Yes."

"Oh... an hour plus is very necessary."

He gave her a kiss and left.

Mary lay down on top of the comforter and closed her eyes. She needed rest. She slowly drifted to a quiet place in the back of her mind, storing the memories that were now a part of her forever.

The room had grown dark by the time Michael returned. He walked softly to the edge of the bed. Kneeling down, he placed his elbows on top of the comforter, then his chin on his folded hands. He whispered, "Mary... Mary... Mary... "

She opened her eyes.

"Hi."

"Hey, sleepy head," he said. "It's been a while. Are you OK?"

"Yes. What time is it?"

"It's 7:30," he said. "Time to freshen up and have some dinner."

"Just give me a minute," she said.

It was dark. The only light came from the sitting room. Michael looked at her. He studied her soft features. She turned. He reached for her hand. It was still cold. He brought her hand to his lips.

"You should have covered yourself," he told her. "You're chilled."

She began to sit up, leaning on one elbow. She reached over to Michael and kissed him. "You'll keep me warm, won't you?"

"Always," he said.

Mary sat up straight. Michael moved around the bed, still holding onto her hand. He pulled her up into his arms. "Are you ready to celebrate?"

"No," she said.

"How come?"

"Because" she said, "you have to promise to look handsome and get dressed first... then get out of here, so I can transform into a gorgeous woman, just for you. Then I'll be ready to celebrate."

"I promise. Watch me do the twenty-minute special," Michael said softly.

"Well then let's get going."

They began their mission. Michael was out the door in twenty-three minutes. Mary kissed him and told him he was handsome. She also said, "Be patient."

It was their last night. Michael organized every detail—dinner, champagne, everything that would make it a special evening. He added fifteen minutes to their arrival time for their dinner reservations because he understood her message of being patient. He was told not to worry, all was in control. He went to the bar.

Mary went about preparing herself for an evening she had thought about since last week when he had asked her to come here.

Her long black hair framed her youthful features. Her eyes were shaded with a light touch of color, her lashes long, black, and captivating. Her nails were red and exciting, matching her soft lips. She ran her slender arm through the shear sleeve of the silk organza blouse, carefully buttoning all but the top three. Her slender legs and thighs slid through the black viola slacks, fitting perfectly around her slim waist, accented by the satin waistband. She slipped her feet into simple black high heels. Her favorite pearls fell freely over her breasts.

The last, of the best, of dressing this evening was her organza jacket with a rounded collar that touched her unadorned ear lobes. *No earrings tonight.*

It was 9:00 p.m. when she took a last look at her reflection in the mirror. Her only words were, *Thank you again, Lewis.* She reached for the door latch. Mary was very aware of her perfume's subtlety and that in just a few moments it and she would deliver an affirmation of love.

Mary walked downstairs and entered the lounge. Every man in the room turned his head—every woman as well. She was stunning. Michael looked at her and couldn't believe she was with him. Michael thought to ask her if she wanted a drink, but he didn't want to share her with anyone and suggested they go to their table.

The candles were reflecting off every surface, especially her eyes. The light that fell on their face was warm. It was a glow fueled by their own emotions as they held each other's hands across the table.

"Mary, you're... I'm speechless... beautiful."

"Thanks, you're a very handsome guy too, you know.

"I'm in love, Michael, with you, totally smitten with you. Sometimes a woman needs to express herself this way and tonight this expression is all for you."

"I'm knocked out, but very much in love with you."

The waiter approached and asked if they were going to enjoy a drink this evening. He was an older man with European features. His accent seemed German, with a dash of Italian. His manner was kind and sensitive—his moves experienced.

"Where are you from, sir?" asked Mary.

"A mixture of places throughout Europe at first," the man answered. "Then South America. Now I'm here for a while. Then who knows where? I'm in love with the sea and my boat. I've cruised around the world but enjoy the solitude of my own boat. I built it or should I say ripped it apart and rebuilt it."

"Well, that sounds like an interesting life to me," said Michael.

"Adventurous maybe," the waiter agreed. "I'm sorry. I didn't mean to take your time."

"No, we love adventure, please," said Mary.

"Are you having wine with dinner, sir?"

"Dom Perignon, please," said Michael.

"Yes, sir! Immediately."

"Can you chill two coffee cups?" asked Mary.

"Coffee cups, did you say, Madam?"

"Yes, please. It's a tradition we have shared for many years."

"I like that. I'll serve our best. Yes, Madam."

Michael squeezed Mary's hand a little tighter. The waiter was back within moments. He began to unwrap the wire and seal, placing them in his pocket. He tastefully twisted the cork, ever so gently, releasing a soft pop of effervescence that had been concealed for many years.

"Shall I pour this for you, sir?"

"I'll take care of it, thanks," said Michael.

"Next sail... I'm going to do this and toast to you both," the waiter said.

Michael poured the champagne into their cups and handed Mary hers. He placed the bottle back into the ice bucket and picked up his cup to raise a toast. A couple sitting nearby witnessed the ceremony and nodded at Mary and Michael, raising their cups to them in exchange.

"Well, to you, the most... " Michael looked around, "... the most beautiful woman on this island... no in the world."

"Thank you, Michael. To us."

"I have a confession," said Michael.

"Oops," said Mary, wondering.

"Well, I ordered for us," he said, "taking a chance you wouldn't mind."

"Sounds good to me," she said.

"At first we're having our champagne. Then an appetizer of oysters, the kind you loved the other evening. Then a salad, suggested by our waiter. It's a Caesar with their house dressing; a blend of delicate anchovies, a whisper of dry mustard, a squeeze of lemon and fresh garlic, all tossed with a spiced oil but... no croutons and no raw egg.

"Our entree is a Wellington on the rare side, with a choice of veggies, then a sorbet, I believe... of lemon essence... but sweet. Then to end our interlude, we're having a very light chocolate soufflé. And all of this will be timed to our fancy. No coffee, no tea, just cham-pagne... chilled by the gods... to excite our souls."

"You chauvinist! I love it. Tell me more!"

"Well... a walk out on the veranda, a tender kiss... then up to our room for love and passion."

"No, tell me about the dressing again."

"I don't know that I can, I was lucky to get it right the first time."

"I love you."

The waiter appeared as if he had read their minds. Every course was perfectly timed. Never once did Michael have to ask or catch his attention. By the time they finished, the dining room was empty. The last of the champagne passed their lips as Mary placed her napkin on the table.

"Is it time for the veranda?" he asked.

"Yes," said Mary.

The waiter appeared. "Will that be all, Madame? Sir?"

"Yes, thank you," said Michael. "We're in room 214."

They spent little time on the veranda; both of them were eager to get back to the room.

When they returned, they found a blazing fire. Mary presented herself to him, placing her arms on his shoulders. Michael began to carefully remove her beautiful jacket. She kissed him passionately. She pulled his shirt out from his pants. He ran his hands up her thigh across her buttocks to her breasts. Mary took his hand and brought him to their bed.

The love that they exchanged was intense and continued for hours. Her fervor reached deep inside him as he caressed every portion of her body. They gasped for breath. Their emotions exploded, reverberating through their souls. Their flesh was wet with perspiration as Michael pressed himself against her. Mary responded to his deep passion by wrapping her arms around him, sliding her moist hands up along his ribs, across his arched back, towards the nape of his neck.

She held his shoulders tightly and ran her feet up and down the back of his legs. Michael's mouth hovered over hers; both of them were panting with pleasure, exchanging each other's breathing. They were one... their perspiration another stimulant... his mouth savoring her bosom. She trembled, sighing repeatedly. He could feel the reverberation in his body. She began kissing him over and over, holding him so tightly. He remained still. "I love you," she said. Michael could feel her words on his face. He lifted his body gently and looked at her. "I love you, Mary. I do love you." They remained still for a long time, while Mary, with the lightest touch, ran her fingernails up—then down his back. They rested.

The sounds of the floatplane, pulling up to the dock, awakened them. Michael turned to say, "Good morning."

"Good morning, my love," she said.

"I think that's our 'carriage' arriving," he said. "Unfortunately, it's here to take us back to reality."

"Yes," she said, pausing... ,"reality."

They showered, dressed, and packed. Mary finished a few details as Michael went down to the front desk to take care of the bill and to add a special gratuity for their waiter last evening.

Mary joined Michael in the lobby.

"We've got some time," he said. "Would you like some coffee?"

"Can we have it outside on the bench?"

"I don't see why not."

They sat next to each other, saying nothing. They watched Gene taking their bags, carrying them down the walk to the plane. In the distance, the plane looked like a toy, attached with tiny ropes to the edge of the dock. It sat in the water. Its wings gently tilted right, then left, coming around to the side as it swayed in the wake of a fishing boat moving away from the inn.

For Mary, it was impossible to leave. The path seemed too short. She thought it should be far greater than the miles between the island. She wanted it to, at least, be as long as the journey of a few hundred New Year's Eves.

The flight would close the distance between her denial and the reality of another encounter with Dr. Kainer's science and tests. Her chart would be filled to the brim with facts about "Templeton, Mary." Sipping her coffee, she turned to Michael.

He had excitement in his eyes. He was a boy. His smile was sweet and innocent. He was truly happy. He held the confidence of loving and being loved. He was an easy read. He looked at the journey home as the beginning of the rest of his life, sharing everything with Mary.

"Shall we go?" he asked.

She placed her head on his shoulder.

"What's wrong?" he asked.

"I'm very sad. I don't want to go. I want to stay here forever."

"We'll come back," he promised, "as many times as you want."

"I don't know that I can make that promise," she said.

"Why not? What do you mean?"

"Oh, it's just..." she stammered, "just that I... I don't want to leave. That's all. I'll always come back with you."

Michael put his arms around her. The pilot stood on the dock and began waving, signaling it was time. Mary looked up, turned to Michael, and began to stand. He stood pulling her gently upward into his arms. The pilot waved once more. Michael took a small step. Mary's head touched his shoulder. They walked down the path, towards the plane.

The walk was not long enough. The taxi, out on the sound, was too short. The engines were not loud enough to suppress the inner screams of anxiety Mary had kept inside. The plane cut through the choppy water, lifting with a determination that defied her will to remain. The plane banked to the right, revealing the inn and the gulls beneath them then leveled out over the lake and the path—the narrow path they walked yesterday—on *her* mountain!

The watchtower was so small, yet it was a place to see so much of life from. The eagles soared below them once more, all to become the memories she would place, so carefully, in the very special places of her mind.

The melodious drone of the floatplane's engine gave Mary a reason not to speak. Michael busied himself looking out the small window. Washington's craggy coastline offered plenty to stimulate his interest. At one point, he motioned with his hand and mouthed, "Look at the whales again." Mary touched his shoulder in response. She smiled and nodded her head. She was reluctantly leaving their weekend behind, being dragged toward the anxiety of Dr. Kainer's impending diagnosis.

The plane began to respond to the bad weather they had listened to in a report thirty minutes earlier. The flight became choppy with small air pockets just south of Everett, Washington. In one moment, they fell 100 feet or so. Michael yelled, "Wooow!" and squeezed Mary's hand. The pilot waved his hand, signaling that all was OK. Mary's eyes closed, and she said nothing.

The pilot continued his work and radioed their descent to Seattle. The plane's pontoons slapped the churned surface with a "whoosh," splashing water up and across Mary's window like rain. Their taxiing was short, but the cab ride was even shorter—for both of them.

As they entered the hotel, it seemed as if they had been gone forever. The happiness and love she wanted to express to him were difficult now. She felt guilty that she wasn't feeling good about herself, and she looked for something to change her own attitude. *Certainly Michael didn't deserve this as a parting response.*

"So, what are we up to?" he asked.

"I've got to get back home today," said Mary. "So while I'm in the lobby, I'll get my car. Is that OK?"

"Well, no," he said, with a smile. "But if you have to... "

She looked at him warmly. "When are you leaving?"

"Tomorrow, early. I'll be back the end of the week... maybe Saturday."

"Well, call me at the hotel or home," she said. "I'm not sure at this point where or when."

"I'll get the car for you," he said.

Michael went to the doorman and asked him to retrieve Mary's car. She waited near her luggage. He looked back, wondering why she seemed different. He thought for a moment that he had said something wrong and that she was angry. He walked over to her, to be sure.

"So, it was wonderful," he said. "I'll miss you this week."

"And me you," she said. "I'm sorry I am not more cheerful right now. I guess it's because it was so wonderful, and I feel so good about you. I'm sad that it's over. It's a girl thing, I think."

She kissed him, then walked outside as the car was brought around. He opened the door, and when she got in, she rolled down the window. The doorman placed her luggage in the trunk. Michael leaned through the window to kiss her again.

"If you're going to be sad every time we come home, we'll have to never go away again," he said. "I'm canceling our next 2,367 trips and weekend jaunts. I love you, Mary."

"Call me when you get in," she said. "I may be here one night. I'm not sure right now. I do love you, Michael. And thank you. And don't you dare cancel anything," she said, finally returning a smile.

During her drive home, she was in a trance-like state. She mechanically stopped, turned, and signaled for the entire ride. As she made the turn onto her street, she could see a very large truck parked in front of her home.

The driver was walking down the steps away from the house towards his truck as she pulled into the driveway.

He walked over to her car. "Mrs. Templeton?"

"Yes?"

"I'm glad to see you. I won't have to make another trip."

"For what?"

"I've got fifteen crates of art materials for you from Calcutta."

"What do I do for space?" she asked.

"They're all sealed pretty good, Ma'am. Maybe you want to leave 'em in the garage for a while... whatever you want."

"I'll back the car out, and you can place the crates in there if you like," she said. "That's a good idea."

"That's great!" he said.

Mary moved out of the way as the deliveryman summoned his partner to back the truck up to the garage doors.

She went into the house and directly to the kitchen phone. She looked in her purse, then on the wall for the telephone number for Dr. Kainer's office. She couldn't find it.

Again, she looked in her wallet and in the zipped-up portion of her purse. She found the card stuck to the back of Mr. Wither's card. *The good and the bad sealed together*, she thought. Her fingers were weak as she placed her hand on the phone and dialed one digit at a time, coming full circle, back at an agonizing pace.

The phone rang—then there was silence—too much silence. *What happened. It broke?* Then there was another ring. *Why are these spaces, in between, so long?* She dialed again.

Someone answered. "Good morning, Drs. Green and Kainer's offices. How may I help you?"

"Dr. Kainer, please," she said, her voice, unsteady.

"I'll connect you with his office."

"Thank you." *Too many rings,* she thought.

"Dr. Kainer's office."

"Is he in? This is Mary Templeton."

"I'm sorry. I do know he would like to speak with you. Are you going to be at your home number for the next hour?"

"Yes."

The doorbell rang twice, then a third time.

"Thank you," Mary said hurriedly into the phone. She then ran to get the door.

"I need you to sign this, Ma'am," said the driver. "Everything's in there; fifteen pieces. I closed the garage doors."

"Thank you," she said, her voice shaking. "This is prepaid, right?"

"Yes. Are you OK, ma'am? You seem... I don't know. Are you OK?"

"I'm fine. I just... I'm OK."

"Well, take care. Glad I didn't miss you."

Mary went back to the kitchen and sat at the table. She held her head with both hands. The reality of the moment was nearly too much. She was in a frenzy.

The phone rang, and she leapt for the receiver. "Hello?"

"Hello, young lady," said Aunt Catherine.

"Hi."

"How was your weekend?" Catherine asked.

"Wonderful," Mary said, trying to compose herself. "Just wonderful."

"You sound troubled."

"Well, I just got home, and I almost had an accident. It upset me. A giant truck was just leaving with my work... I mean it dropped off my shipment of work... fifteen crates. And you happened to call as the driver was ringing and ringing the doorbell. I'm sorry... It happened all at once. So I'm trying to keep it all together."

"That's life," Catherine added. "I don't know why it works out like that all the time. If you're waiting for a call it won't happen until you are as far away from it as you can be—like at the neighbor's."

"Do you want to come over?" Mary asked.

"Well, I am on my way to the store. I'll stop on the way back, OK? Do you need anything, honey?"

"I don't know... milk... maybe. I'm sure what's here is sour."

"I'll see you in an hour-ish. OK? Bye."

"Bye."

Mary returned to her chair and thought of the paintings finally arriving. She had her "friends" back. A feeling of excitement ran through her. She had wondered if John would find out and hold onto her work as ransom. Relieved, she just sat. She was tired, very tired.

She wanted to think of the weekend, of Michael, the paintings, anything to get her mind off the phone call, but it was too much. She was now obsessing to the point of wanting to call again. *Oh no*, she thought. *Watch! He'll call when Aunt Catherine's here. I messed up. I should have had her come later. I'll take the upstairs phone off the hook.*

Mary carried her bags up the steps to her room. She placed them to the side, thinking she would unpack later. The phone rang. She rushed to it, yanking the receiver off the hook.

"Hello? Hello?"

There was no one there, only a dial tone.

"That's not nice to do to me, you miserable invention! Not now!" She screamed out loud and slammed the receiver down. She leaned down, her face inches from the dial. The phone rang again almost as if in response—scaring her. She jerked away as if it had attacked her.

She picked it up.

"Hello?"

"It's Dr. Kainer. I hope you're feeling well."

"Oh yes, I feel really good, thanks," she said. "Well, how did I do, doctor? Tell me, please."

"We have received most of the results back a little early. That's good, and I am expecting an important piece this afternoon. I'd like to meet with you early tomorrow to discuss the results," he said. "Is that OK for you?"

"Well... yes, but what did we find out, doctor?"

"I really don't like using the phone for this," he said. "Mary, you have a good night's sleep. I'll see you at 8:30 a.m... in my office. We're going to be fine."

"Fine, you said 'fine,'" she said. "Fine. OK, 8:30."

"Goodbye."

Mary thought, *What does that mean? He said 'Fine.' It means all is swell...fine. That's OK. OK is fine. So, what am I worried about? Fine is just fine. But are doctors all the same? Is there a class on vagueness? I know. It's called, 'Dulling Your Communication Skills 101.* She went to the medicine chest and looked for the strongest gel caps she could find—aspirin, whatever, something to do—something. She took two, went down to the kitchen, and placed a pot of water on the stove, waiting for Aunt Catherine to arrive.

Her awareness of time disappeared. She rehashed the brief call and the word "fine" into a trance-like state of mind.

It might have been five minutes or an hour when the door opened and Aunt Catherine walked in with her grocery bags.

Mary heard the sounds of the paper crumpling, the door opening, and her aunt's voice.

"I'm here." Aunt Catherine announced her arrival. Her voice brought Mary back.

Mary got up quickly and walked to the stove, where the kettle was steaming and its lid rattling. She picked it up. There was hardly any water left in it. She placed it under the running water. It sizzled.

"I put it on a little early," she said, smirking.

Aunt Catherine put her bags on the counter. "I'm forever doing that," she said. "I'm surprised I haven't ruined more pots." With her coat still on, Aunt Catherine started putting groceries away. She opened the refrigerator and put the milk on the door. She removed the old container and sniffed it, checking to see if it was sour.

"It seems fine," she said. "This refrigerator always ran very cold... good for milk... bad for lettuce. Your mother always complained. But then... " She closed the door, not finishing her sentence. She took a good look at Mary.

"Are you feeling all right, Mary?"

"I'm just so tired," she said. "We had a wonderful weekend. He is a very wonderful person... and I took a few aspirin a little while ago, so I'm feeling the effects."

Aunt Catherine took two cups out of the cupboard and prepared the tea. She placed a cup in front of Mary. "You must tell me about your trip. Uncle Paul and I went up to that area many years ago. It's very romantic and certainly very beautiful."

"Yes. We motor biked, had a picnic, and enjoyed a concert by the organist at the inn. What a treat that was."

"Yes, I heard about that. I remember it has a thousand pipes or something like that."

"Yes, each one can be heard and felt right through your bones. "

Mary continued, "The dinners were so romantic... everything a woman would want. He is a gentle man with enormous sensitivity... so easy to love."

"Easy to love? Does that mean *love*?"

"Yes. I haven't loved or been loved in so many years. I love to say 'loved.'"

"I'm happy for you, dear. I hope it all works out. You do so deserve something after the bad things you have experienced. Please, I want you to have peace of mind, and if Michael helps you get there, I'll bake him a cake."

"How about a pie?"

"An apple pie?" Catherine asked.

"The Granny Smiths you used to bake? He'll be around, so I'll take you up on that."

"Can you smell it yet?"

"Thanks."

"I looked high and low for the doctor's number you asked for. I couldn't find it. But I did come up with his name. Dr. Kainer, or Keener, but I think it's Kainer. He is pretty old by now, maybe retired."

"Thanks. I just need a recommendation. But that's a good start."

"You just don't look like one hundred percent to me. You're welcome to have dinner with us tonight if you like. And if not, I brought over some chicken soup for you and a loaf of that crusty bread we all like."

"Thanks," said Mary. "I'm going to bed really early, so I think I'll take a rain check on dinner and catch up this week. I want to work on the paintings."

"Fifteen crates? You must have been really into your work over there."

"It was more like denial. I was deeply involved in my own world so that I would not exist within his."

"What a shame."

As they were finishing their tea, Aunt Catherine offered Mary a second cup, but she declined.

Aunt Catherine rinsed the dishes. "I've got to go start dinner for your uncle and finish the laundry I shouldn't have started," she said.

"Thanks, I love you," said Mary.

"We love you, dear. Now you take care of yourself, you hear."

Aunt Catherine put on her coat and hat and started to walk out. "Oh my pocketbook!" Grabbing it, she said, "I've got laundry on my mind."

She gave Mary a hug and was out the door. Mary waved goodbye through the window and retired to her room.

The sun had been down for hours before Mary walked into the kitchen to re-heat some of Aunt Catherine's soup. She cut a slice of bread and poured the broth into a large mug. Taking it to her bedroom, she stopped in the bathroom to pick up two more gel caps. Then she got into bed and enjoyed the hot soup her aunt had provided.

Chapter Sixteen

Mary slept through the night and arose by 7:10 a.m. After quickly showering and getting dressed, she parked her car in the doctor's lot and went directly to Dr. Kainer's office—meeting the nurse as she unlocked the door.

"Hi. I'm Mary Templeton," she said.

"Yes. Hi, I'm Sandy," said the nurse. "This must be your first appointment."

"I assume the doctor is on his way?"

"Yes. He usually is on time for these early appointments since there aren't that many interruptions this early."

Mary sat in the waiting room as the nurse flipped switches, turning on the fluorescent lights overhead. One by one, row by row, the brightness intensified the room. The chairs were rigid, covered in artificial leather.

The magazines were a distraction she could not deal with. The images on the covers seemed repulsive with happy and healthy faces. Some were old, some young. All had foot-wide grins, and banner headlines proclaiming "non-fat, low-fat, healthy diets." And of course, there was *Redbook* and "Can This Marriage Be Saved?" Mary thought to keep it and send it to John, but he wasn't worth the postage.

The doctor walked in and directly over to Mary. He said, "Just give me a minute or two to hang up my coat, and I'll be right with you."

Mary sat, with her palms beginning to sweat and her mind in overdrive. She was generating too many thoughts. Her body felt weak. She thought of herself as a condemned woman on her way to that "parrot-green" chair. "The doctor will see you now," the nurse said. "Please follow me."

Mary continued to think of the nurse as an executioner as she led her away. Her legs felt weak. Her vision was blinded by her thoughts. A humming, in her mind, blocked out the sounds and sentences she didn't want to hear.

She walked into the doctor's office. He was seated in a large leather swivel chair. He gestured, offering her a chair just in front of his antique desk.

His paper work was all in a neat stack, with one sheet of paper, a summary of it all, in front of him. It was filled with information from top to bottom. It even had something written in the margin. His voice echoed in the room as Mary's attention turned to him.

"Mary, are you OK?"

"No, I'm not. I'm frightened of this meeting. I'm so disturbed by this meeting. I... I... "

"Would you like a sedative?"

Mary leaned over toward him, lowering the pitch of her voice and gritting her teeth. "Just tell me. Please... Tell me."

"The prognosis established by Dr. Satara in Calcutta is reasonably accurate. However, the technology and benefits of the research hospital that will treat you, are enormous. I feel we have a chance of beating the odds for you, but I do need your help. The state of mind you are in, at this moment, is not going to help."

"Well, what's its name? My disease?"

"Cancer of the pancreas."

"How long?"

"Impossible to say. If we get to work on this immediately, with the chemotherapy and other methods, you could go into remission and live till you're an old woman."

"And if not? How long?"

"I don't... "

She interrupted him, "Months? Like March, April, May, June?"

"Why don't we think years like 2010... 2030?"

"Because I don't know how to... because you are of science and I am of art. Because with me it's agony and ecstasy, and with you it's facts and numbers scrolled across charts—facts, figures, odds, mathematics, equations. For me it's life. My life now placed on a canvas."

And then she wondered... *Will I finish this painting or be deprived of the last stroke that completes my creation? Is this titled, 'Unfinished?' It's my name in the corner!* "Templeton, Mary," she said, breaking into tears.

Dr. Kainer came around the desk and touched her shoulder. The nurse entered the room.

"Can I help?" she asked.

Dr. Kainer shook his head and looked down at Mary with compassion. "I'd like Mary to have an appointment with Dr. Hennis at the hospital—immediately after she rests for a short while."

"Yes, doctor," the nurse said, then left to schedule one.

Dr. Kainer excused himself and said he'd be back in a moment. Mary leaned back in the chair, then forward, holding her head. Her eyes filled with tears—so many tears. They began to roll off her cheeks onto one of her hands.

The nurse stopped what she was doing; she could hear Mary sobbing. She returned with a glass of water. She lowered herself to her knees, holding the glass out to Mary. Mary turned, allowing the nurse to help her take a sip.

This woman, whom she didn't even know, was now sharing the most difficult moment of her life—the fear of death. *No specific dates... just the announcement of its possible arrival.*

They looked at each other, both crying, hugging, and feeling the pain. Mary raised her cupped hand to the nurse to show her the tears in her hand.

"Never catch too many tears in your hand. It's not good," she told the nurse.

The nurse looked at her, not understanding.

"The man I love told me that," she explained. "He's away now. I don't want him to know. Please don't tell him."

"I'll get some tissues for both of us," the nurse said.

Mary held the tears in her hands as another fell—sliding into her palm. She seemed to be collecting them as if to save them as moments, not to disappoint Michael. She took a deep breath. The nurse returned, placing a tissue in her hand.

"I think the doctor will allow me to walk with you to the hospital," the nurse said. "It's just down the bridge. Would you like that? Is that OK?"

"Yes, please."

They stood together and walked out of the office... *the execution is postponed... it's date uncertain.* Her thoughts were vague, casting dark shadows. *The rest of my life... how long? No one knows. The journey, I now face has no known path. How long does it take to die?*

As they walked, the nurse held Mary's arm. Mary recalled the old woman who was helped down the long corridors, by her son, in the hospital in. Young, vibrant people now looked at Mary ; *she* was the subject of interest , the pitied —the "about to be lost." Then she thought of the caring offered by this nurse, a stranger who exchanged emotions too real to alter. It was not like anything. It was her reality.

The bridge connected the doctors and other services to the hospital. Their short walk took them directly to two very large doors, both a brilliant blue with large block letters: H-O-S-P-I-T-A-L. The doors opened automatically. They walked through them. Mary stopped on the other side, with the nurse, and looked around to see which direction she should go in. She noticed the nurse's aide from her earlier visit coming by and pushing an empty wheelchair.

"Well, hi," said Charlene. "How you doin'? I thought you were all finished with this place."

"No, unfortunately," said Mary. "I'm just starting."

"Where you headin'? I'll give you a lift."

The nurse looked intently at Charlene. "Oncology."

Charlene stammered. "Well, let me sit you down here for a second. It's a short ride," she said.

"Not too short," Mary said

The two women said nothing.

Chapter Seventeen

After leaving the hospital, Mary went to the hotel. She was exhausted. Throwing her coat over a chair, her thoughts were of sleep. She went directly to the bedroom. Michael had left her a note placed on top of his pillow.

Hi, I'm glad you stopped by. I will be back by the end of the week, probably late Friday. I will call you here or at home. Have a pleasant stay. Our weekend together was the beginning of my loving you forever. Michael.

Mary took the note to bed with her. She lay on top of the comforter and fell asleep immediately.

It was late morning when she awakened. Taking her time, she showered. Putting herself together and feeling physically better, she thought an appearance at the gallery was a very good idea.

Two young boys held the doors of the gallery open wide. A group of about thirty students made their way into the gallery. Mary was directly behind them.

A little voice was heard from somewhere around the group. "Hey, that's the lady who made the picture on my cast."

Mary looked around. A few children stopped and looked directly at her.

A little girl pointed. "This one?"

"Yep."

"Awesome," said the little girl to Mary. "I liked that the best."

"Hi, it's George." He was standing between the door and some evergreens.

"Well, hi George. How are you?"

Mary placed her hand on the door above his head. George came around with his crutch. He skipped to gain his footing and entered the gallery. They moved aside allowing others to pass.

"I'm fine."

"So, George, is this a school trip?"

"Yes."

Mr. Withers was standing near the Moore sculpture and walked over to greet Mary and her little friend.

"Hi, Mary."

"Hello, Mr. Withers. This is my friend, George."

"Hi, Mr. Withers. Mary is so cool. She drew this picture on my cast in the hospital." Then he pointed to it.

Mr. Withers took a long look. "Well you're pretty lucky, George, because Mary is a really fine artist."

From a distance, the teacher's raised voice was heard, "George... George Michael, you get over here immediately."

"I gotta go. Mrs. Garetty is freaking out. I *knew* you were an artist. Thanks. See ya."

George hobbled away, trying not to use his crutch too much. "Later," he said.

"You like children?" Mr. Withers asked.

"Very much," Mary replied.

"How do you know that young man?"

"We met on the elevator in the hospital. I was there for some tests."

"Nothing serious I hope," said Mr. Withers.

"No, just a checkup."

"Good."

"I just returned from the San Juan Islands for the weekend. A wonderful place... just beautiful."

"How is your work going?" he asked.

"Well, I haven't called the people you suggested, but my work has arrived in crates. That is, at my home. I was wondering how I get to show it to you and the people you referred me to."

"Well, let's see if you can help me on this one. Are they big? Is your work bulky?"

"Some are. I can bring in a few of the smaller ones and perhaps I can take some slides of some of the other things so you might get a feel for them."

"That's great. The timing is good. We're looking for someone new for our summer show."

"I'm excited. When?"

"Well, you can see I'm not hard to get hold of. So whenever you're ready... but soon. Don't miss this timing."

"Should I call those people?"

"Let's see what you've got. Then we can get to the business part. I looked up your file, back in the records. There were very favorable comments by some very influential people. *This,* as they say, 'is a good thing.' I have this feeling about your work. I don't do this too often, but I do have this intuitive feeling about you."

Physically, Mary was beginning to feel miserable, but she was bearing up under the strain. She was trying to look up and positive, not revealing the emptiness she felt. She said, "Thank you," and walked back to the hotel. She stayed the night, after eating a very light dinner. She got a lot of sleep, and early that next morning, she made her way back home and parked her car in the driveway.

She had been home a short while, when she felt an enormous need to see the condition of her paintings. *Their* journey was longer and less luxurious. Mary found a small hammer in one of the kitchen drawers and was on her way to the garage as Uncle Paul drove up, beeping his horn. Then he pulled in behind the Buick.

"Keeping the car out? That's unusual," he said, as he gave her a hug.

"Well, wait till you see what's in here," she said, as she opened the doors wide.

"Well, I'll *be,*" he said. "What are all these crates?"

"My work this last year. It's a lot of my work."

"Are you going to open them with that?" he asked, pointing to the little hammer.

"I thought so."

"Hmmm. Just hang on. I'll be back in a minute."

Uncle Paul walked towards the house. Mary stayed behind, touching the crates. The rough-hewn splintery surfaces were marked by stamps and stickers, scrolled across each of the many-shaped boxes. Uncle Paul returned with a crowbar and other hand tools.

"Which one do you want opened first, Mary?"

"I can tell from the sizes, what some of the pieces are, so I'm only going to open three. These two," she said, pointing, "And this one." She stretched out her arm, strained her voice, and reached up high to touch one on top of the stack.

Uncle Paul carefully began to wedge the crow bar beneath the slats, taking his hammer and gently tapping the metal under an edge of the wood. He pried the nails, and the squeaking made it sound as if the sarcophagus of King Tut was being opened for the first time in thousands of years. He pulled one panel off, then another. Finally, he picked up the crate and laid it flat on top of another, removing the final panel.

"Well, here are one, two, three pieces, all wrapped so well."

He picked up one of the pieces and handed it to her. She pulled away the wrapper as if it were a present, allowing the papers to fall to the garage floor. It was upside down. Mary rotated the painting, holding it at arm's length so she might see it in its entirety.

"Well, that's wonderful, Mary. Did you know this child?"

"Briefly, I did a study of this little person with my camera for a couple of days then used the images as a reference to create the painting. I must have spent weeks on this one."

"You could have told me years. It has so much detail. The texture, in his hair, looks as if I could comb it. And from his expression, it seems as if he is going to cry. He is precious. Are the rest of these crates filled with these beautiful children?"

"Yes and no. Some are not so beautiful and not as sad. Some are angry."

"Angry, sad children. I don't know, but it would seem the artist might have had something to do with that. It wouldn't be a good idea to leave them here too long," he said.

"Well, I don't have much of a choice. Those that we open, I'll bring into the house. The others, I think will be fine."

"Well," Uncle Paul said slowly, "the roof doesn't leak and the floor is concrete. The fact that the crates are made of wood makes the humidity reasonable. I'll take care of this for you very soon, Mary." He paused.

"I don't know that this is the time... " She turned to him, thinking he knew.

"Your Aunt and I had a long talk about you last night... about you and your sadness. I am so sorry." He embraced her. She let the painting come to rest on the floor, in the papers. Then leaning the painting against her leg, she wrapped both her arms around him, remaining very quiet.

"I haven't shed that many tears in my life, but last night was too much. The tragedy of your marriage magnified by this loss is more than you should have to shoulder. For me to be recognized as a person you really love enough to name your child, Paul, is an honor that I will hold in my heart forever. I know that this happened a while ago, but for your aunt and me, it's upon us now.

"Your coming home filled us with happiness, and now this news we share with you is so very saddening. I know you feel our love, but I want you to know, *today,* that we are here for you *forever*. It's going to take all of us to get through this... and we will. We love you, dear. I wish your son wasn't so far away. I'd like to visit with him from time to time. He... well that's enough; I'm going to start again... "

"Thank you, Uncle Paul. It's been a very bad year in too many ways."

"Well, we have work to do," he said, as he bent over to pick up the painting and the paper. Uncle Paul opened the remaining two crates she had selected, looking at each painting intently. He saw children and more sadness. He could see what she was feeling this last year. Being a part of Mary's childhood was a privilege since Catherine and he could never have any of their own. Mary had become their child. Seeing her as an adult, with this degree of sadness, just added to his compassion for her.

Mary carried each of her paintings into the house, placing them along the walls and on chairs. Uncle Paul carefully stacked the empty crates on the outside of the garage.

"How many paintings are there, Mary?"

"I'm not sure. I think about sixty to eighty."

They closed the garage doors and walked inside. Uncle Paul looked at her a little closer.

"You seem very tired honey. I guess all this trouble wrings us all out."

"Yes."

"How is Michael? Aunt Catherine said you were away up in the islands. It's a nice area."

"Very nice."

"Michael is very important to me, Uncle Paul. He is a man I wish I had met years ago."

"Well, I think he's a nice guy. Bring him along for dinner any night."

"He's away, but I'll be there on Friday."

"Is there anything else you need? I've got to get back before your aunt starts complaining about how long it took to get the groceries."

Mary gave him a hug and kiss on his whiskers. "Thanks."

She sat in her room, surrounded by her work, her images taking her back to scenes, places, and faces she had not thought of in many years.

She decided to construct a portfolio of images along with some odds and ends of a bio she once had. *A few pictures, a nice leather binder, a couple of smaller pieces... that's what I'll present to Mr. Withers. But that is tomorrow. Tonight I can't do much more. I am very tired.*

Mary drove in and out of the city for the next few days, struggling to take the photos, resurrecting some others, and searching for that old bio. However, the treatments were devastating. Dr. Kainer had told her that this weekend was to be a rest period and that they'd check to see how she was doing on Tuesday at 10:00 a.m.

Friday night came with Mary having assembled a "show-and-tell" book for her dinner with Aunt Catherine and Uncle Paul. She arrived early. Aunt Catherine gave her a big hug the second she walked into the kitchen.

"That smells like... "

"Yes, it's a Granny Smith pie for you and Michael. I know he isn't coming, but I thought you could bring a piece to him over the weekend or something."

"He's coming back tonight or tomorrow, early," Mary said.

"Well, he is missing out on a baked ham. I've been slowly cooking it in my oven for the past three hours."

"I haven't had that in such a long time."

Uncle Paul came downstairs and joined them in a conversation about old times. They remembered Mary's graduation, her choir practice, and her parents. Mary said she'd be going back to the cemetery the next day and that she had meant to get there sooner.

She showed them her portfolio and explained how she had met the people in the paintings. She explained who they were and how long it had taken to finish each piece. They went on and on until almost 8:30 p.m. when Mary said she had to get home and get some sleep.

"You're not looking so good," Aunt Catherine said. "Maybe a trip to that doctor is a good idea—next week, honey, I'll go in with you if you'd like."

"I'll look into it, Aunt Catherine," said Mary. They exchanged their goodnights and she went home.

Mary could hear the phone from the porch. She hurried, unlocking the door, hoping it wasn't John.

"Hello?"

It was a child's voice. "Hello... Aunt Mary?"

"Yes, this is Aunt Mary. Is this Jiral?

"What a wonderful surprise!" Mary added.

"I like your painting of me and Rose. All my friends come see it. Mommy put it up high, and it is in my room. And I can spell Aunt Mary now."

"Oh that's so smart. Did you use the chalk?"

"Yes, but Mommy got a little mad. Just a second… Mommy wants to talk to you. Bye, I love you."

"Goodbye, Jiral. Kiss my sweet Rose for me."

"We didn't wake you, did we?" Manisha asked.

"No, I just walked in the door from Aunt Catherine's and Uncle Paul's. Jiral sounds like a big boy."

"He is getting big. He talks like a seven year old and in two languages. But what about Dr. Satara's findings? I have been so troubled."

"I've had treatments with a very professional group, and I don't know. I will find out in the next few days."

"Mary it's me... find out *what?*"

"Oh my, Manisha. I'm in such a state of fear... if it weren't for Michael."

"Tell me of the fear first. You're not OK. You're always doing this. I have to pull it out of you."

"Dr Satara told me that I might... "

Manisha interrupted, "That you might *what?*"

Mary completed her sentence. "Yes, that his thinking was a pancreatic condition, which if not reviewed by the people here, could mean... "

"What?"

"It might be... I'm dying."

Manisha choked up and tried to get her words out. "Mary, my Mary, I am... I'm so sad. I want to help you. I can't come there. Oh what can I do... *anything!* Why didn't you tell me *here?*"

"It's not certain. I have been through hell. I have an appointment next week. So I can tell you more. What can you do? You're *listening* to me, my dearest friend. You *called* and you *care* about me. John has burnt me out. I'm frightened to say anything. It's so hard to trust. It's not you, Manisha. It's me. I feel that I'll be hurt even more than before for all these years."

Mary backed against the wall and slid to the floor crying. Her knees were up and the phone was cradled under her chin. She was sobbing.

"As far as Michael, you were right."

"I was right? I don't know him, do I?"

"You said that my flight would be fun... exciting," Mary said. "And it was the most thrilling time, because of Michael who made a trip that would have otherwise been so depressing. It was a *beginning* for the two of us. He invited me to chase time and celebrate many New Year's Eves and the Millennium in one night... all the way to Seattle. We just spent a weekend together... and I... well... I love him. I haven't told him either."

"You love him and haven't told him?" Manisha asked. "Why not, Mary? He should know."

"But I don't know. I don't want to know for sure. I'm so angry and confused. I'm sick... yes. They are treating me... yes. These treatments can turn it all around. I can't lose him. It's selfish, I know, but I don't know what to tell him. And to tell is to admit I am... terminally ill. That it's not treatable . I'm not... I'm... If it wasn't for that jerk's vague analysis , I wouldn't... Well I don't know Manisha. When is it right... for whom?"

"Mary, I wish I were there. You said you would know more next week. Call me... please!"

"I will. I'll call you in the next few days. I promise."

"I love you, Mary. You're right; we don't know. So that means to be positive. Call me soon. Let Michael know. I'm here for you as well. Tell him, Mary. You must."

"Thank you, Manisha. Thank you for being my friend. Give Jiral and Rose a kiss. Goodbye, Jiral," she said louder.

"Goodbye, Mary. Thank you for being my friend. Jiral is waving goodbye."

Mary stood, placing the phone in the cradle. With tears in her eyes, she went up to her bedroom thinking of Manisha, her friend, and her little sweet Rose.

It was late Saturday—a damp, gray day. The doorbell rang at Aunt Catherine's home. She opened the door to find Michael standing there with his big smile. It was a greeting that anyone would welcome. "Come in. Come in," she said.

"I drove up for a little surprise for Mary. I haven't been to my hotel yet, but she's not home. That's a bummer."

"I think she went to the cemetery," said Aunt Catherine. "She mentioned it last night. And here I thought you were coming over because Mary told you that I made my famous Granny Smith apple pie. Would you like some?"

"Well, just a taste. I'd like to drive up to meet Mary at the cemetery."

"Well, you've got ten minutes."

She dished out a piece of pie and poured him a cup of fresh coffee. Michael ate quickly, sending accolades to the pastry chef. "It's delicious," he said, and Aunt Catherine recognized the little boy look Mary had described in his face. "I hate to eat and run, but maybe we'll come back later."

"I want to ask you a favor," said Aunt Catherine, "for Mary."

"Anything!"

"Look at her, and see if you think she is OK. I think she is not feeling well, and quite frankly, I don't like it. Just look at her?"

"I will. Definitely. I thought she was a little tired this past weekend. But yes, of course I will."

Aunt Catherine gave him directions to the cemetery, and he was off, still savoring the taste of the pie as he drove up to the gates.

Michael's car moved quietly up the tree-lined path to a remote portion of the Flower Hill Cemetery.

This January day added little to the setting. The trees were still dormant. Overcast clouds that clung to the tops of the trees muted the grays of the head stones. His car rolled to a stop, just beside Mary's Buick. Michael held the car door back, so it wouldn't slam. He closed it with a quiet click. He walked towards the gravesite which was surrounded by a few leafless bushes. The gravestones of her mother and father dwarfed Mary, who was seated between them—offering flowers to each.

Michael continued to walk towards Mary, who had her back to him. She seemed unaware of his presence, even though he was now close enough to hear her speaking out loud.

He listened to her thoughts, her prayers, and wished not to interrupt. She removed a folded piece of paper from her pocket.

"Mom, Dad, I told you I'd come back and read you this piece I wrote. I promised. I hope you like it." Michael wasn't sure what to do. He didn't want to interrupt, but he didn't want to eavesdrop. She began to read, and though he tried to turn away, he couldn't. In a very quiet voice, she began:

It's been too long since I passed by
Too many times I tried to cry.
To see the tears I should have shed
About the distant life I've led.

I've questioned how I've spent my time
The guilt I feel deep within my mind.
About my life and where it's been,
Nowhere, I guess. Is that the sin?

Hey Mom, hey Dad, I'm over here —
Your only girl
I hope you hear
I'm back you see, but not in time
You spent yours right; I'm lost in mine.

I need to do this for you, you see
I misunderstood all the good
You meant for me
I guess it's too late, a tragedy.

Could you lift me up to touch the sky
So I might reach the reason why
The life you gave, so free, to me
Is now with you, for eternity.

My time is near, I know it's true
So close once more to both of you
I had to tell you now, you see
Too late, I know
That I found you in me.

"Mary," said Michael, softly.

She turned, surprised. "Michael!"

"That was beautiful." He walked closer to her. "But the one line, *'Your time is near.'* What does that mean?"

"Just that," she said, looking down at the graves... Just that... " She walked closer to him.

"Just what? Are you ill? Is that what Aunt Catherine and Uncle Paul have been seeing... your being tired?"

"Very," she said.

"Very tired?"

"No! Very ill."

"The piece you wrote, the one inside for you," he said, beginning to realize what she was saying. "You had told me about this on the plane. You said it was 'not for an audience.' My God, Mary, how long have you known?"

"From the day we met, I was on notice. That night, that afternoon…how long have you suspected?"

"I didn't... I can't," he stammered.

"I can't admit to these thoughts," she said. "It must be denial."

"Why wouldn't you let me help?" he asked.

"You did," she said. "You have. You have given so much to me."

"But I want to do so much more. This is wrong." He wrapped his arms around her.

"Too many questions... I'm sorry. I am overwhelmed!"

"There's nothing to do, Michael. Time is what it is. Time is what I don't have... or do have."

He paused and pulled back to look at her. "How little time is there?"

"No one is sure," she said, "least of all, me, Michael. They're not sure. They're still filling in all the blank spaces on my chart."

He kissed her forehead. Mary held her head against his chest.

"Can we put this on hold?" she asked. "Can I ask you to do that for me?"

"You are the only one in our personal circle who knows... except Manisha."

"Manisha? Yes, your friend in the maternity ward."

"My close friend in Calcutta. She said I must tell you. I don't know what to tell you, Michael, except I have my fear of losing you. If you think I've been deceitful, tell me. I don't know what's right . I'm not... I didn't... " Tears flowed from her eyes, and Michael 's welled up, too.

"I'll be quiet for now until I know more, but I can't stand by and not help you. I love you too much but... deceitful, Mary... no. This burden is too much for any one person. I refuse to fault you.

"Your friend, Manisha... tell her thanks for her wisdom. And if that's what you want, I'll respect that for a while. OK?"

She nodded her head.

"I have to know more," he said. "I'll stay away from the questions until you are ready, but I will help. Would you like to leave?" he asked.

"In a second," she said. She turned and walked to the headstones, remaining motionless for a few minutes. Softly and slowly, she began to speak.

"Mom, Dad, this is Michael. I love him."

She turned back to Michael.

"I talk to them a lot. Is that crazy?"

Michael approached her. Tears were flowing from his eyes. "No, you talk to them all you want, my love. I'm very happy that you talk to the people you love. It's OK."

Michael reached for her hand. He stood close to her for some time but said nothing.

"It's time," she said. "Goodbye for now, Mom... Dad."

They walked back to the cars. They turned to one another and their eyes met. He seemed to have the same expression of caring and sadness that the young man had had toward his mother, in the hospital in Calcutta. *His caring expression is universal,* she thought, *when we see one whom we love, about to be lost... lost forever. Only now—it is myself.*

Michael opened her door. "Shall I meet you at your home, or would you prefer to be alone?" he asked. "I don't know what to say. Mary, this... it's too important."

"Michael, please don't. And please don't leave me alone... no, not alone... not now. Please, I can't," she said. "I just can't."

"Make this go away for a moment. Please be creative. Make this go away, Michael, please."

"No, wait. I've got an idea."

"Good, is it dangerous?" She asked.

"I hope not. Something to eat? A late lunch... early dinner ? A fast trip to, uh... Easter Island, or bungee jumping? Pick two out of three. It's a diversion. I hope it's just that. Am I doing OK?"

Mary managed a little smile. "Yes... bungee jumping... where do we go for that?"

"Really?" he asked.

"Something to eat sounds fine. I know of a little place down the road. You'll follow me OK?" She smiled again.

"I'll follow you anywhere, Mary."

"I know that Michael," she said. "I so much know that."

She drove her Buick out the gates. Michael followed her down the road to a little local restaurant. It had just the right ambiance. A tasteful presentation of quality seemed just right for the two of them.

"An early dinner for two?" asked the maître d'.

"Please," said Michael.

They followed the maître d' into a pleasant room, where just a few people were seated.

"Is this table suitable for you?" he asked.

"Mary?" asked Michael.

"This is fine. Thank you," she said.

The maître d' snapped open their napkins and placed them on their laps as they were seated. "Would you like to order a cocktail?" he asked.

"In a few minutes, please," said Mary.

"I'll leave you with the menus... at *your* leisure."

Michael reached for Mary's hands across the table. She offered them both to him. They touched. She moved her hand slowly around on his. She stared at their hands, intertwined. She looked up to find him staring at her, his eyes filled with tears. His mouth started to move as if to say something. She feared if he did, they would both burst.

The waiter arrived and interrupted them. "Would you like to hear about our specials?"

"Not now, but I've got a fine idea," said Michael, catching his breath. "Maybe you could help."

"Yes sir?"

Michael looked at Mary. "... Cordon Rouge 79... if you have it, please."

"Yes sir."

"Champagne!" said Mary.

"Oh yes, we must," he said. "It's beyond a must. It's a requirement. All members of the NYECOA drink champagne here. You *have* to."

"NYECOA? More of the M.O.B," said Mary.

"New Year's Eve Club of America," he explained.

She looked at him so deeply that he sensed her emotion. He felt the same inside and wanted just to hold her tightly.

"I know you'll take care of me," she said.

"*Forever. However. Wherever,*" he said, squeezing her hand.

The waiter returned with the champagne, and displayed the label: 1979.

"Shall I open the bottle, sir?"

"Please."

He produced two chilled, fluted glasses and began to unwrap the wire and seal, placing them tastefully in his pocket. He twisted the cork ever so gently to release a soft pop of effervescence that had been concealed for seventeen years. He poured a taste into Michael's glass, allowing him to complete the ceremony. Michael handed it to Mary for her approval. She took a sip and began to laugh as the bubbles tickled her nose.

"It's wonderful," she said.

The waiter was about to pour her a glass when Michael intervened.

"I'll pour it if you don't mind," he said.

"Of course, sir. Would you like to wait a while before ordering?"

"Yes, thank you," said Michael.

Once the waiter was at a safe distance, Michael reached over to the next table.

"Drop your napkin?" asked Mary.

"No, I need these special containers," he said, grabbing two coffee cups. He poured the champagne into them and offered one to Mary. She began to cry.

"Then she said, seventeen years ago someone put all this emotion inside this bottle not to be released until today," she said. "I'm not sure if I like that person."

"Let's toast to the best, most loving 'five years' of my life," said Mary, "for without you, I would never have had them."

"*And* to having shared the experience with you... it's all I could have asked for. I'm not sure if I'm on time, but I love you," Michael said.

Their cups touched, and they drank.

"Your timing is perfect," said Mary. "Mine? That's another thing. It's not too late to love. It's not too late to give. If there are just so few 'grains of sand' left in the hourglass... I'm sorry."

"No, I don't want to hear that. You didn't say that. I'm not... " He broke off and filled their cups again. "Oh, Mary, you did nothing wrong, my love. You just... well... you have awakened my spirit, from New Year's Eve until this moment. I have relived our five years again and again."

Mary reached for his hand. "You're so wonderful to have near. Never stop jostling emotions or redirecting the negatives to make it comfortable. I just never thought it would happen... that time could not possibly provide any opportunity for me to find you. But there you were. I guess we were high enough in the sky to catch an 'angel in my cup.' You're never going to be in the attic... never on hold... always with me... always there."

"I'm sorry. I've had too many years of storing emotions and just a few months expressing them," he said.

"Do you think this bottle has a partner ?" she asked . "If it's OK... a light dinner... something quick would be great, and then we could go home. We could make love. You could say 'yes.' Is that OK? And I do like it when you make love to me."

"Stop," said Michael. "Let's do this by the numbers. One... I get another bottle of this wonderful champagne," he said, pointing to the bottle. Two... We enjoy a 767-calorie helium dinner here. Three... I get to talk to the most beautiful woman over dinner. Four... I follow you home, get to drink one half of the second bottle of 1979 champagne, and then I am invited to sleep with you. Did I get that straight?"

"In a word, yes."

"Waiter!" he shouted

"Yes sir," he said, returning in an instant.

"We would like to order, please."

Michael looked at Mary. "Immediately."

"And what would the lady like?"

"I'm not sure," she said.

"Sir, surprise us," said Michael. "Two 'somethings,' quick... easy... you know," he said, motioning with his hands.

He looked at Mary. "Something for people in love," he added. "Oh, and waiter, no organs... no liver."

Mary looked at Michael observing his gesturing, his smile, and his being himself. She was now sure that she loved him.

Chapter Eighteen

It was very early when Michael awoke. He slipped out of bed and sat on the edge of Mary's rocking chair, slowly easing himself down so as not to make a sound to disturb her. He leaned back to support himself, never taking his eyes from her as she lay there. The sheets were flowing as if she were a composition, framing her as the subject of warmth, of women, of a woman at rest.

Yesterday he had shared a part of her life in a way he could never forget. He thought of the weekend. He knew that he wanted to love and be loved by her.

He looked at her again, wanting to absorb every texture, every part of her being, to savor its meaning, because he loved her so much. *Oh*, he thought, taking a deep breath. *She is so beautiful. Life... it makes so little sense that I should have loved and lost and now to lose again.* He hoped it would not be so. *The cards are screwed up. She's OK. It's OK. Mary... shhh... sleep my baby, so that I may catch up with the time we have not spent together. I love you. It's so easy for me to love you.*

The sun broke through the trees and filled the room with warmth. A single bird broke the silence with its constant chirping as if to say, *it's time, enough thinking. Get on with your day—this glorious day we are going to share.* Her finger twitched. Her eyes fluttered than opened. She looked at him. He placed one finger over his mouth as if to say, shhh. She smiled, and he said, "I love you."

She raised a hand into the air and motioned for him to come lie next to her. "No," he said.

She winced. He just loved that look on her face.

"No," he said, "not unless you agree to go to the zoo today."

"The zoo?"

"No, the zooooooo."

"Yessss. Now come here before I melt."

They remained in bed talking for hours, talking about silly things and great things. They discussed problems in the world that needed to be solved, and they solved them. They laughed but didn't cry this morning. She told about John and how she had called him. She

175

told Michael that she flew halfway around the world with the wrong man and flew halfway back with the right one.

Michael told her it took five years—the longest flight in the history of two people who would eventually find themselves in love. He said if she were good and rested, he would go make some coffee and tea and be back before the birds chirped another fifty-six or fifty-seven times.

As he walked to the kitchen, he looked at all the paintings hanging on the walls, propped in the corners of the living room, and leaning against the couch. There was a lot of work, all in a style that was Picasso, Monet, and Vermeer. It was wonderful, expressive, and filled with detail. He thought of taking a few minutes to look, but his mission was focused—coffee and tea, and fifty-seven chirps.

The kitchen was more organized than Michael was, for sure. Finding things was easy, even the thing to hold the tea leaves.

The phone began to ring. "Are you OK?" he shouted upstairs to Mary. She must have answered because she didn't yell back, and the ringing stopped.

She reached for the phone from the bed.

"Mary... it's John."

"Yes."

"I've left you alone with your thoughts these past few weeks, hoping you have reconsidered."

"I'm afraid that's impossible," she said.

"Well, I'm coming back to the states in a few weeks and would like to see you."

"You're welcome to come to the states, but I doubt whether I'm going to make it convenient for you to see me, John. I don't like you."

"I'll call you then. Please don't be this way. You know I do love you, Mary."

"Do me a favor?"

"Anything."

"Look up in the dictionary the word 'love.' Xerox it, carry it with you, then every time you see a couple kissing or exchanging what you think is that word, or even an image of a couple looking at one another, read the definition."

She hung up.

Michael came back into the bedroom with the coffee and tea, steaming hot. He placed her cup on the night table beside her.

"Did you get the phone?" he asked.

She paused a moment. "Yes. No one was there... just nothing."

"That's good. Nothing can be good. Now, let's talk about animals. Or, I've got another idea that I'm guessing is better than the zoo."

"There's nothing better than the zoo. Well, except... well, I got to see more water buffalo than most Americans."

"When did you stop painting?"

"A while ago. I became aware that I was painting a darker side of myself. I went beyond depression. I just couldn't paint anymore. I would want to, and then I stopped. I was so depressed.

"I would find I had painted fear in my subject's eyes and sadness in their mouths. Their backgrounds were forbidding. The innocence I sought was gone. Their faces expressed rejection, neglect, and a feeling of loss.

"All I had suppressed was revealed in their faces. I couldn't paint children's faces. I tried 'still lives,' but they became dark and mysterious, and in the end I just couldn't work at all."

Michael held her tightly. "You have the mind of an artist and this gives you the depth of your emotion. Would you take me on a tour of your art?"

"Oh yes, I'll be delighted."

The excitement of showing her work was not ego but sincerely wanting to share her experience. Mary *was* her work. Each brush stroke, each line, was an expression of what she wanted to say. She loved sharing this with Michael. This was a special occasion—gift-wrapped—with the respect they had for each other.

Her *home* was her gallery. It housed every emotion she ever felt, from a young girl to the woman she was today. The work revealed her sensitivity and a capacity to create captivating imagery—some whimsical, some not, but all with a style that seemed her own. Michael asked when she had shown her work. She told him that many years ago, she had won a very special award and the opportunity to "be shown" in Seattle at the Hartford Gallery. She told him that she went, that her work was well received, and that John and she had met there and that he had purchased a few of the canvases. "That's where it all began," she said.

John had shown the world he was the patron of all starving artists, and that was it. She continued to paint but never showed her work again. She was made to feel owned and inadequate with John, she said to Michael. "He was the keeper of the key and had the power to remain that way."

"Not so. The key, the lock, and John are gone," Michael said. "Your work is terrific."

They went through the house, room by room, looking at sketches and paintings. Each had a little story that Mary personalized for Michael.

They spent all morning reviewing her work—she with exuberance in her delivery and he with honesty, wanting to absorb everything she wanted to show and say to him. At one point, he placed his hands upon her shoulders and stared into her eyes. He told her she was magnificent, and she kissed him. He was launched. His mind filled with passion that he had found at the inn. Mary responded to him as they stood in the middle of her life's expression.

She took his hand and led him to her room and made love. The depth of his sincerity was revealed. He wanted to communicate the need that he now had to be with her forever. He now understood what Mary had expressed to him. He was vulnerable and for the first time in his life—he *wanted* to be just that.

The hall clock labored as it chimed, sluggishly, this morning. Its pendulum was swinging slowly as the sound of the space between ticks lengthened.

As they lay in bed next to each other resting, Mary suddenly grew aware that the clock had stopped ticking. Its silence became the focus of her attention. The pendulum was at rest. The glass-walled clock had hung in the hallway for an eternity. It was now Mary's turn to give it life. Her father—then her mother—had held its key in hand for decades, sharing the ritual of turning it thirteen times each week.

But now it had stopped. The spring was awaiting that gentle twist that would start the pendulum's sweeping motion. Its hands circled the clock face that multiplied *time* into days and nights. It was time shared with Michael. And each moment was so precious that she had no right to deprive it of its purpose. The silence that filled her mind needed attention. She left the bed to attend to it.

"Where are you off to?" asked Michael.

"To wind the clock," she said.

"Now?"

"What time is it?"

He picked up his watch. "It's 11:34."

Mary opened the door of the clock, placed the key in its hole, and began to twist its spring thirteen times to the right. She moved the pendulum to the side with her finger. It returned. She heard a tick, then a tock. She closed the door and returned to Michael.

"I feel better now," he said.

"Good... me too," she said.

"So, what about going to a private zoo? One where it's just you and me and a very special friend?"

"Sure," she said.

"I have to make a few phone calls. I haven't spoken to this buddy of mine in sometime. Do you mind?"

"No."

"Well, it's just as nuts as winding the clock now," he said.

"Sure."

Michael went down to the kitchen and made what seemed to be many phone calls. Finally, he returned.

"Hey, we're on... It's OK."

"Where are we going?"

"Well, can I keep it a surprise? It'll be terrific."

"OK. Let's get going."

The drive took about an hour. Eventually they pulled up to a dirt road with large gates that were closed. A sign read, "Private! No Admission Without Express Permission of the Owner."

Michael pulled up to an intercom, pushed a button, and waited. A man's voice on the other end said, "All right, all right, what's the damn hurry?"

"Is this the craziest Texan I ever met?" asked Michael.

"I doubt it," said the voice. "But you can give it another shot if you like."

"Bret."

"Michael, c'mon up."

The gates began to open.

"Just be a minute," said Michael. "I got the most beautiful woman in the world with me. Ready?"

"I'm combing my beard as we speak," said Bret.

They drove up a steep incline, twisting right, then left, past an open field with a simple building seated on the rise. It looked more like a house than anything else. An older Jeep sat in front of it. Michael pulled alongside it. They got out and walked towards a tall, thin man with a thick beard. He was wearing jeans and a blue denim shirt. As he came towards them, she could see that his boots were worn from years of work. A cigarette dangled from his mouth. He seemed to take one-step for every two that Michael took and *three* of Mary's. The two men embraced each other.

"It's good to see ya," said Bret. He turned his head to cough.

"Same here... you old coot."

"Now watch it. I'm not old, you know." Bret turned to Mary.

"Well, Michael, you're right," he said, reaching for her hand. "She is damn near the most beautiful woman... except for Jan. I'm Bret and hello... old friend of Michael's."

"Jan is his wife," explained Michael.

"Mary Templeton," said Mary, shaking his hand.

"Bret Campbell."

"You men... you've known each other a long time?"

"This man single-handedly built the largest generating plant Texas ever saw," said Michael. "And we're talking big... big."

"Well, I did have a little help," said Bret.

"You still got *him*?"

"Him?" asked Mary.

"My buddy Kato," said Bret. "Yep, he's better than ever."

"OK, Bret. This is my surprise. What's a Kato?" asked Mary.

"She doesn't know? Well, come on up to his house, and I'll introduce you."

They walked around to the back of the building, through two barn doors and there he was. An absolutely live, full-grown Siberian Tiger. He was 16½ feet long, 900 pounds, and taking a little nap.

"My, oh my! What a beast. It's unbelievable," said Mary.

"Want to pet him?" asked Bret.

"Through the cage, I hope," she said.

"No, inside the cage," said Bret.

"You're kidding!"

"Nope."

He began to unlock three very large locks and to slide bolts aside. Bret opened the steel cage and asked Michael and Mary to join him inside. They walked toward Kato. He was lying on top of a concrete slab. Kato lifted his head, recognizing Bret. Bret grabbed its ear and rubbed it, talking to Kato.

"How're you doing, you beautiful beast?" The cat lifted its head high—yawning. Its mouth was enormous. Its fangs were the diameter of a large carrot. He just lay there. Bret pointed to a whole dead calf that was placed in the corner of the cage, intact.

"He isn't hungry right now," he said. "I got the dead calf from the farmer up the road. Kato will eat it later. Go ahead and touch him."

His head was bigger around than the circle Michael's arms would make if he touched his fingers. He was beautiful. His paws were the size of baseball gloves, his eyes intense, glaring at them all. Kato just lay there needing his beauty rest. Mary reached for his nose and scratched it back and forth. Kato's tongue emerged to lick her hand. It was frightening and exciting all at once.

"Now you two walk out slowly," said Bret. "I'll stay here for a second."

Michael and Mary left the cage. Bret petted Kato one more time and turned to leave. The cat rose to its feet, stretching. Kato's paws reached out, and he lowered his head as if to bow. His back arched, then his rear legs moved back. His tail rose high in the air. Then the cat made a clicking sound, which Bret repeated. Kato yawned again, and Bret turned back.

"Stay," he said, in a very deep voice. "Stay."

Kato moved toward the calf as Bret slid one of the bolts closed.

"Has he ever been hostile?" asked Michael.

"No, but he doesn't know his own strength," said Brett. "One cuff from his dainty paws and well... this was his play toy for a few days," he said, pointing to a heavy-duty plastic trash barrel. "That holds about sixty gallons. It was flattened by his weight then punctured a few hundred times with his teeth, and then the thick plastic sides were ripped open by his claws. It looked like machine gun bullets had sprayed it. Look at his mouth. It opened as wide as the base of the barrel, and he squeezed it flat... faster than you and I can say nice kitty."

"What are you planning to do with the ripped, torn, punctured, and flattened 'nice kitty trash can?'" asked Mary.

"Garbage."

"May I have it? It's beautiful," she said.

"Sure but let me hose it off. His scent is all over everything."

"Is *that*, that odor?"

"Oh, that's him all right."

"I'm sure no animal comes near this place," said Michael.

"Not true. We got a whole new eco center here. All the little animals have found homes directly around this building since the predators of those animals won't come near his scent. Old Kato here is their savior."

"What else does he eat?" asked Michael.

"Everything he eats is dead. I didn't want him thinking movement was part of his dinner game. So he eats about two dead deer a week from fresh 'road kill.' The locals know he is here, so the town truck drops off the carcasses down on the road. It's good for him and the town. If there isn't a deer or a calf, I go down to the A&P and buy six cases of frozen chickens. We call'em chicken pops."

"What a beautiful animal," said Mary. "How old is he?"

"Fifteen," said Bret. "They live till they're twenty-five. I've taken good care of him since he was six months old. We're buddies."

"Michael, you have some great friends," said Mary. "They are certainly unusual."

Bret rinsed the barrel off, with some detergent and a hose and asked for Michael's keys. They walked together and placed it in the trunk of his car. Michael and Bret continued to talk while Mary slipped back to the cage. She stood watching Kato, sliding the third bolt closed, slowly, as Kato watched her. Kato moved towards her sticking his face against the cage. His whiskers, long and spiny, jutted out.

He's so big, she thought, and she spoke to him softly as his tongue licked the metal cage. *He is magnificent... a predator. This one has character, style, and beauty. He's one of the last of his kind on the earth. He has been in a cage from the beginning of his life until now. But this is his home.*

She wondered if his instincts were suppressed because a choice had been made to control his life, confine him to this space by one man's will. *He is the last of the strongest and fastest cats ever known to man, a dominant predator, controlled by the cunning mind of man, each using the other in a different way.*

Bret protects Kato from society. Kato suppresses his man-hunting instincts, allowing them to coexist in this society. Both win. Both lose the edge that made the real difference in their roles a hundred centuries ago... who they were, mutated into the submissive.

__The cat needs to hunt, to stalk its prey of choice; it needs to provide its own kind, with instincts and strengths that proliferate the species. Bret keeps himself and his cat tucked away, hidden from the realities of society. They're both a dying species. I doubt there are many more Katos left than Brets.__

"Do you know who you are?" Mary asked aloud to Kato. "I'm sure you do, but so does Bret. Who masters to whom? You think about that today?" Kato yawned.

Michael walked over then. "Well, I can't convince Bret to have lunch, but he promises to have dinner with us soon."

"I'll talk to Jan," he said. "But I'm on a big project in a few weeks, so hey... you know how it goes."

"Well, thanks for the present, and I hope to see you and Kato again," said Mary, who then gave Bret a kiss on his whiskers.

Michael and Mary drove off, Bret waved to them before he returned to his friend. The ride back was filled with conversation about Kato and Bret and the various adventures that had occurred in the construction of the Texas project.

"He's quite a guy," said Michael." A real man among men ... corny, maybe, but a breed that I would place my life with. But just like Kato, don't make him angry. He's one great guy."

"I believe it," said Mary. "How many are left?"

"Brets or Katos? Just one of each, I think," he said.

They stopped talking and enjoyed a brief silence. There remained a sense of wanting to talk. Michael reached for the words, storing the sounds in his throat. He searched for the opportunity. He came to stop at a red light. "Mary," he started, "I know the subject is impossible, but we can't *not* talk about it. I... please, I want to know as much as you will let me know about your condition."

Michael continued, "I know I don't bring up my past so much, mostly because it's a mixed bag of experiences that brought me to Calcutta. But having lost my wife and child, I really begin to get paranoid when I think about you not being part of my life. We need to talk about you. I know I'm a quiet kind of guy, but you have to share what little you *may* know so that I, at least, can help... please."

"It's not determined yet," she said. "It's not good, but I've just started treatment this week. I didn't know the results of anything until we returned from our weekend. Then you went away with me, in the beginning of more tests and procedures, which are not reviewed as of yet. They said they would have some results on the effects this week. So we wait and wait. This last part has been very difficult."

"May I go with you?"

"I... "

He interrupted. "Please. I want to be with you. I gave you my word that I love you, and if *you* need... so *I* need. Let me help, please."

"Thank you," she said.

Michael stayed the night. They lay in bed with Mary's head tucked closely into his shoulder, their bodies intertwined. Michael's eyes were wide open. His mind was fueled by questions to which he had no answers. *Mary, this woman I am touching, may be dying.* He brushed her hair back from her face. *It's not true, he tried to tell himself. Yes, she's sick. Yes, it's terrible, but the tests will show improvement. She'll be fine in a few months.*

I remember my buddy, Tom, who was hurting for a while, and he pulled out of it. He's fine now. And Mary will be OK, too, he told himself. Let's see, she needs attention, lots of attention. Well, she's going to get it. She needs love, a lot of love. Do I give her enough love? Do I care enough? I don't know. He moved his hand across her face again. How do you know that? When does she feel that? But when do I feel that? When she looks at me? When she touches me? Hmmm... letting her love me is part of this communication thing. Accepting love is harder to express than giving love. If I don't allow her to love me, it won't work. How do I know this now? Where the hell did that come from? How do I let her love me? I'm not sure. It isn't taking, it's accepting. She touches my hand. I feel that. I touch her hand, she feels that. But my touching her makes me feel good. I have to let her know that it feels good for her to touch me. Guys should have lessons on this real early, but we would probably cut class and go look for frogs. I think given another decade or so, I might get this down.

It takes a lot of years to begin to understand the feelings of a woman of any age. I can't say I knew this until now... until Mary.

Michael pulled her closer to him. *What special formula has made this come together? It is a gift... a special present, that makes us feel great. Love, when it's right, doesn't rust or diminish. It needs attention, but you just don't mind. It's not work. It's worth giving, no... accepting.* He wondered if he would be up all night thinking. It didn't matter. *Mary is sleeping, and that's good. She needs her rest.*

I love her, and I'll make it work.

Our Father, who art in heaven, hallowed be Thy name. Thy kingdom come, Thy will be done, on earth as it is in Heaven. Give us this day our daily bread and forgive us our trespasses, as we forgive those who trespass against us. Lead us, O Lord, to the hour of our death, amen. 'Death... the hour of our death... not her death... mine. It's easier. I need a little help with this, God. This isn't about me... but Mary. She needs your help. I just want to help you take care of her. We need to take care of her.

The aroma of coffee and toast lured Mary downstairs into the kitchen the following morning. She wished Michael, "Good morning" as he was pouring his second cup.

"Some tea? The water is boiling," he said.

"Thanks," she said. "Sleep well?"

"Really good, thanks." She put her arms around him.

"Aunt Catherine... " he began.

"Oh, she gave me a piece of pie for you. Do you want it?" she asked.

"Later... I had some Saturday. It was delicious. Your uncle, theoretically, should weigh 480 pounds."

"I know what you mean. She's a great cook."

"Should we take them out or something?"

"No, they are tethered to their home. The cord makes it to the city now and then but that's as long as it gets. I can't remember when they ever went out to dinner."

"Well."

"It's not me you have to convince. We will see them later."

"OK. Will they come here?"

"Sure."

"Well, I'll cook," he said. "Is that OK?"

"You cook?"

"Pretty good."

"What are you making?"

"Something basic. How about teriyaki pork, mashed potatoes, spinach ali olio, a Caesar salad, a little white wine. Do you like anchovies?"

"Yes, but not the bony ones."

"And bread."

"We've got some great bread."

"That's it. Where's the store?"

"We'll both go. It's not too far," she said.

"It's a little early to call them," said Michael.

"No, they're up with the chickens."

Mary called and spoke to Aunt Catherine. She asked them to come over at 3:00 p.m. They went to the store and enjoyed collecting the ingredients for Michael's dinner. They returned home, and he went to work immediately. Mary asked to help. There was plenty for both of them to do.

The roast smelled delicious; Michael basted it in a tangy sauce. The potatoes were prepared with chicken broth. The Caesar salad was chilled, and the spinach was flavored with fresh stir-fried garlic.

At 2:45 p.m., Mary offered Michael a glass of wine.

"My kind of girl... yes," he said.

She looked out the window and shouted back to Michael. "They're here!"

"That smells wonderful," said Aunt Catherine as she came through the door.

"Michael did all the cooking," said Mary.

"Big mistake you're making," said Uncle Paul. "You're making the rest of us look bad, son. But well... not to worry. It smells like you know your stuff."

"Would you like a glass of wine, Aunt Catherine?" Michael asked.

"With club soda," she said.

"Coffee, if you got it," said Uncle Paul. "If not, some of that club soda."

"The pie is in the Corning Ware, Mary," said Aunt Catherine.

They shared a toast to "good things" and raised their glasses.

"Are we eating in the dining room?" asked Aunt Catherine.

"Yes, the table is all set," said Mary.

"I haven't sat in that room in a century," Aunt Catherine said.

Michael dished the food into platters and bowls for serving, and they all took their seats. They passed the thick slices of steaming roast around the table. The potatoes were just right. Uncle Paul sliced the bread. Mmmm," said Aunt Catherine, as she tasted her food. "You're right. This man is a bit unusual."

They all raved about the teriyaki and enjoyed the dinner. When it was time for pie and coffee, Aunt Catherine looked over at Michael, while speaking to Mary.

"Do you think you're going to get in touch with your doctor this week, Mary?" she asked. Michael's eyebrows raised as he winced in sadness. Aunt Catherine's thoughts exploded as she read Michael's expression, confirming her suspicions. Mary stood, as an obvious diversion, picking up a dish to return to the kitchen.

"I... " Mary started.

"What's wrong?" asked Aunt Catherine, standing up.

Mary looked directly at her Aunt. "I've seen Dr. Kainer. It's not good."

"Dr. Kainer, that's the same one your mother went to." said Uncle Paul.

"I'm... " Michael started. "Mary just told me Saturday." Then he looked at Mary for approval.

"That they think she... " Mary turned away.

"That she what? How bad it is?" asked Aunt Catherine.

She walked around the table and helped Mary into the living room. They sat down on the green couch together, and the two men followed. Aunt Catherine put her arms around Mary and held her tightly.

"Tell me child, tell me please. Is it the same as your mother? Tell me."

Tears flowed from Mary's eyes, and she nodded. Aunt Catherine burst into tears, too. Uncle Paul removed his handkerchief and handed it to his wife.

"Oh my God, what now?" asked Aunt Catherine.

"She has had tests and some therapy last week, and the results are not conclusive in terms of the effectiveness," said Michael.

"Tomorrow... I'll know tomorrow if the therapy is working," said Mary.

"Oh my child... I knew something. I just knew. My worst nightmare," said her aunt. "We have to get to work fast on this. Is it pancreatic, Mary?"

She nodded.

"How long have you known?"

"A few weeks. I was told, 'maybe,' in Calcutta. I ran, the very next day, away from their vague diagnosis and John, to go through all the tests again. Some were different, most the same here. I didn't know conclusively until a few days ago."

"So that's where you've been," said Aunt Catherine. "Oh my child, you should have told me. I could have been there."

"I didn't want anyone to know. I didn't know what to say."

"Just like your mother. It's OK. We all love you so much. Well, Paul, make some tea. Michael, we have to help our little girl," she said, and started crying all over again. "We have to help her."

Michael walked over to the two of them and knelt, hugging them both.

"I'm here for you both," he said, tears in his eyes. "You know I love her, don't you?"

"You must," Aunt Catherine said. "What time is your appointment tomorrow, Mary?"

"At 10:00."

"Michael, are you staying here this evening?" she asked.

"Mary?" Michael questioned.

"Yes... definitely," she responded.

"I'd like to go with you, OK?" asked Aunt Catherine.

"Yes," said Mary. "I have to have tonight to rest."

"And you will," her aunt said. "So, we'll clean up, and you and Michael rest here. Tomorrow is tomorrow, and we're going to beat this problem back into hell where it belongs."

Chapter Nineteen

The decision to take two cars to the hospital was sensible. Mary and Michael went in one and Aunt Catherine in her own.

Aunt Catherine had discussed Paul's response to hospitals and doctors with him, and as much as he wanted to go, he offered to stay behind. His contribution would be to un-crate the remaining paintings and move them into the house. "I just don't think all that work should be left in that garage any longer."

Aunt Catherine went directly to the doctor's office. Mary and Michael parked at the hotel. They walked from there, lagging behind by fifteen minutes but still early.

Aunt Catherine was standing outside the medical building waiting when they arrived. By now, Mary was familiar with the maze of corridors. She had fully memorized an alternate route as well. The three went in to see the doctor. "Good morning, Mary," said. "I hope you had a great weekend."

"Yes, I did," she said. "This is Michael and my Aunt Catherine. This is Sandy... a friend."

"Thank you. If you will all take a seat, the doctor is coming up from the hospital. He should be here any minute."

They sat down and Michael began thumbing through *Redbook*.

"Chances are no... not in this magazine," said Michael.

"What are you talking about, Michael?" asked Aunt Catherine.

"Can This Marriage Ever Be Saved... see?" He held up the magazine so they could see the cover. "No."

"Once I got a cooking tip out of that book," said Aunt Catherine. "After that, it's good for recycling."

The doctor came in greeting them. "How nice to have this support for you, Mary," the doctor said. "Nice to meet you both. Mary, I'll be with you shortly." He disappeared into an office.

For a moment, the only sound was the air whistling through the heating vents.

"He doesn't look as old as I thought he would," said Aunt Catherine.

"He's kind," said Mary. "But maybe I expect too much from him."

"Would you come in, please?" said the nurse. They all stood.

"The doctor would like to have a consultation with Mary, first, please," she said.

Mary went into the doctor's office while Aunt Catherine and Michael sat back down.

"Good luck," whispered Michael, as she left.

While she was in with the doctor, he began to pace. She was gone a long time... at least twenty minutes. Aunt Catherine sat, holding her pocketbook, tightly, in her lap.

The nurse came out and asked if they would like to join Mary in the doctor's office. They were through the door in seconds.

Mary had been crying. She wiped a tear from her face and smiled. The smile telegraphed a message, relieving some of the anxiety before the doctor spoke.

"Well, Michael and Aunt Catherine, it seems that the tests have given us some very positive news about how Mary is responding to the therapy. This is very encouraging. Mary wanted me to tell you... I guess straight from the horse's mouth."

Mary stood up. Michael wrapped his arms around her. Aunt Catherine grabbed her hand and gave it a big squeeze. They turned and thanked the doctor.

"It's not over," said the doctor. "We have to continue our therapy for some time. However, it will be strictly on an outpatient basis, and my guess here, Mary, is that with these wonderful people at your side, your spirits will be up and positive, like we spoke about. If you check with Sandy, she'll work out a schedule for your therapy."

"Thank you, doctor," said Mary. She went directly to Sandy, who came out from behind her desk to hug Mary.

"I saw the great news. I'm happy for you," she said. "I've prepared a schedule for you over the next month, which is adjustable sometimes, but not all the time. So when you get home, review it and get back to me. I will stay in the loop for you. I really feel privileged to help."

"When do I have the next appointment?" asked Mary.

"Today at 1:00," Sandy said.

"OK, fine. I'm going to the same place?"

"It's always there."

They left the doctor's office and walked towards Michael's hotel.

"How about a little coffee or tea for you wonderful ladies?" asked Michael.

"How about a brief stop at the gallery?" suggested Mary. "And then if there's time, coffee or tea?"

"Sounds good to me," said Michael.

"I've got to call your uncle," Aunt Catherine said.

"There is a phone on the corner," Michael said.

"How are we going to do this? Don't you need a lot of change?" asked Aunt Catherine.

Michael said, "I'll take care of the dialing." He picked up the phone and used his charge card numbers. The phone rang many times when Uncle Paul finally answered.

"Hello."

"Hi, Uncle Paul, this is Michael... just a second."

He handed the phone to Aunt Catherine.

"Paul," she said.

"Yes! Is she OK?"

"Go find that bottle of Port because we're going to finish it tonight."

"Mary is OK! Thank God. I'm so happy."

"Where did you stash it?"

"Top of the hall closet."

"Tell Mary I love her. Get home early!"

"I'll be home before dinner. Bye!" She hung up the phone with a great smile on her face.

"He is very happy and said that he loves you, Mary."

And "I shouldn't have told him where the Port was." I don't drink much. He drinks less. If he has a sip before I get home, he'll be in bed sleeping... snoring his head off. Oh well it's worth it!"

They walked to the gallery, enjoying another warmish day. Mr. Withers was visible through the enormous glass windows. He saw Mary and waved for her to come in. She was more than glad to accept the invitation. Mr. Withers met them just inside the door.

"Mr. Withers, please meet Michael Bowland and my Aunt Catherine O'Connor."

"My pleasure to meet you both," he said. "I am feeling that we have a mutual friend, who has an enormous amount of talent. Can we guess who that might be?"

"Have you seen her work?" asked Michael.

"Yes," said Mr. Withers. "I reviewed many documents from Mary's first show, before I had taken the position here. I reviewed slides only, and I had many comments from some very discerning people, who all agreed that her work was outstanding. I can't wait to see the actual work."

"Thank you," said Mary. "I am putting together a small portfolio of material, along with a few pieces. I would like to drop them off to you this week... if I may."

"My pleasure."

"Do you know the Urbans, sir?" asked Michael.

"The Urbans... the Urbans... I believe they have a lot to do with the Guggenheim, do they not?"

"Yes, they do," Michael said. "They are personal friends of mine. I was hoping to make them aware of Mary's talents on my next trip back to the East Coast. Might I mention your interest?"

"Please do. In fact, if the work I see is as good as I am expecting, I'd like to offer a letter from the board. But of course it remains to be reviewed."

"Thank you."

"She has been painting, sculpting, and writing since she was a very little girl," boasted Aunt Catherine. "I'm sure you'll like her work."

"Well, thank you. May I call you Aunt Catherine?"

"Sure... and what may we call you?"

"Scott."

"My pleasure, Scott."

The three excused themselves, with Mary offering to show them a little more of the gallery and its treasures. The light pouring from the one room attracted Aunt Catherine's attention. Mary was excited to introduce her to the experience. They entered the room, and the light spewed across the walls in multi-dimensional, prismatic fragments. It was undulating. "It likes you," said Mary.

"Likes me?"

"Yes. The work responds to you as you move; it's your infrared image. Look," she said, moving her arms in a circle. "The more we move, the more we are in number, and the more it changes."

Aunt Catherine took a few quick steps. The light undulated again, sending shafts of brightness across the ceiling. Michael moved the crystal, and it exploded in color.

The two of them moved their arms then walked as Mary observed them interacting with an experience neither had ever had. *The artist would truly be happy to see the astounded response his work was having on two strangers, finding their way to the core of his concept*, she thought.

"No two people ever see the same thing," said Mary.

"We're lucky to even speak the same language," Aunt Catherine said.

Aunt Catherine kept talking and moving her hands. She raised her pocketbook with the sculpture convulsing with pulsing colors—reds, then greens; blues, then whites. The colors moved up across the wall, across their bodies, in their eyes, and gently touched each of them in its own way.

On the way out, Aunt Catherine stopped and waved again. The entire room lit up as if to say, "Thank you."

They had just enough time to get back to the hospital for Mary's appointment. The walk was refreshing. Michael and Aunt Catherine waited outside the room while Mary went in alone. But this time she felt the spirit of her aunt, uncle, and Michael, with their love and support, just outside the door.

Mary kept her word and called Manisha, telling her the wonderful news. The two chatted.

Manisha was relieved, sending a hug to all and promising Mary she would be calling back. It was her turn.

The appointments were crossed off one at a time. There was one on a Monday at 10:00 a.m., and then one on a Thursday at 10:00 a.m. Another week, there was one at 2:00 p.m. Then, there was a test—and good news, followed by another month of scheduled therapy. Michael had taken quick trips to Vancouver, sometimes flying up and back in the same day.

Michael had also dropped off the portfolio and paintings to Mr. Withers, who was in Los Angeles at the time, but the assistant swore on a 'stack of Monets' that he would get it.

If Michael wasn't with Mary, Uncle Paul was. And if not him, Aunt Catherine was always there. February was gone and March's schedule lightened a little. Their busy itinerary kept all of them going back and forth from Mary's home or Michael's hotel room to her treatments. Many nights were spent in the city, and they managed to squeeze in some sight-seeing—a trip to the gardens, a walk to the markets, and visits to Pioneer Square and the Space Needle. It was a wonderful neighborhood.

The regulars on the streets, sought out the couple. The Sabrett man, shop owners, and business people began to recognize their patterns—and exchanged their "hellos and good-byes" and their "see you tomorrows," tightening the bonds between all of them. It was a close environment, and each shared Michael and Mary's friendship.

On March 12, Michael was away in Washington, D.C.

Aunt Catherine had stopped at Mary's mailbox and found a letter from the gallery. (Mary had stayed the night at Michael's hotel.) Immediately upon greeting Mary, she opened her pocketbook and handed her the letter. "I thought you would like to see this," she said.

Mary stared at it for a moment.

"I don't know that I want to open it," she said. "I don't know if I'm frightened of the response or if it's because Michael isn't here. I can't open it right now, Aunt Catherine. I'm going to wait. He'll be back tomorrow."

"Well, it's up to you, dear. But why don't we take a walk in that direction? Maybe Scott will be there. If he ducks when he sees you, don't open it. If he waves and invites you in, you don't have to open it. If he isn't there, you can wait for Michael. It's like trying to guess if you got what you wanted at Christmas by shaking the boxes."

"OK, let's walk," she agreed.

Mary wished she had eyes like the eagle so she could see, at a great distance, and know if he was there. As they came closer to the gallery, she thought she saw him, but it was an older man standing immediately outside the windows. They walked closer. The traffic of people began to block her view. She moved her head from side to side, analyzing every face—every suit. *This was a little much... making this journey.*

"I'm just going to open it," she said.

Three people walked through her view. She stepped to the side, glaring at the gallery windows. There he was, looking out, staring in another direction. A woman approached him and tapped him on the shoulder, needing his attention. They moved away from the window then reappeared. Mary and Aunt Catherine were 20 feet away from the doors when he recognized them and lifted his arms to welcome them. As his hands opened wide and a big smile spread across his face, he motioned them in to see him.

"So far, so good," said Aunt Catherine. "My guess is you don't have to open it."

"Congratulations," said Mr. Withers, as they walked inside. "Did you get our letter?"

Mary reached into her purse and removed it. "I was afraid to open it. I just couldn't deal with any rejection."

"Rejection! The board loves the work you left for us and is looking to have a closed review of the remaining pieces you outlined in your presentation, to make a final determination. It's going to take a few weeks because there's a vacation in there, but I knew I was right.

"The style, the detail, and the subjects are incredible, and I must admit the technique is more than I expected. You *do* love children... what an understanding! I get so proud of myself when I find someone like you, Mary. I have done this only two other times in my career. Aunt Catherine, you should be proud of this young lady."

"Are you going to open the letter?" Aunt Catherine asked.

"No, I'm going to have some fun with it. Michael can do it tomorrow night... here, at dinner. We'll have a celebration with some of that champagne I haven't had in quite a while."

Mary leaned over and kissed Scott on his cheek. "Thank you, thank you... wonderful... wonderful man."

"No, thank you, Mary. You are a national treasure. Wait and see."

Michael's return this evening would be even more exciting, now that she knew what was in the sealed letter. The two had become so close that sharing the great news was only half of the thrill. The other half was Michael's response.

She met Michael at the hotel. He took a quick shower, while she tried to contain her excitement. She didn't want him to catch on.

They decided to eat in the hotel dining room, which was lovely, to say the least. But most of all, it was close. The elevator ride seemed to take longer than usual, stopping on nearly every floor. The doors opened too slowly for Mary. The walk down the hall took too long. The maitre d' was too fussy and the wine steward, not attentive enough.

"So, how do you feel? How's my baby feeling?" asked Michael. "How does the most beautiful woman in the world feel tonight?"

"OK, I guess," she said.

"Just OK?"

"Well, some champagne would be nice... in cups... I hope."

"Are we celebrating?"

"I don't know."

"You don't know?"

She removed the letter from the purse. It had grown crumpled.

"I couldn't open it without you," she said.

He looked at the return address. "The gallery! Oh my, the gallery! You waited for me?"

"Yes."

"Waiter... wine steward please!" called out Michael.

"Yes sir?"

"Dom Perignon, please... and as 'tastefully' soon as possible."

"Immediately, sir."

"So, what's in this letter? A ticket?"

"A ticket?"

"Yes, a ticket to success, for you. Finally, the world recognizes Mary Templeton as an artist."

The champagne arrived, and the wine steward removed two fluted glasses from the ice bucket.

"As strange as this may seem, I'd like two coffee cups, please," said Michael.

"There have been stranger requests," said the wine steward. "Are these suitable?" he asked, pointing to two cups on another table.

"Definitely," said Michael.

"Shall I chill them?"

"I don't think there's time," said Michael.

The wine steward released the cork and offered it to Michael, who handed it to Mary. Then he poured some champagne into one of the cups and, with a little attitude, offered it to Michael.

"Please offer it to the lady," said Michael.

As he did, Michael began to open the letter. He ran his finger across the seal and removed the letter, unfolding it slowly.

"Please serve the champagne," Mary told the steward. "It's wonderful."

At this point, the wine steward didn't want to leave. He wanted to know what was in the letter. So he served the champagne slowly.

Michael read the letter to himself as Mary stared at his eyes.

"There must be some mistake," he said.

"How so?" asked Mary.

The wine steward busied himself twisting the wine bottle into the ice.

"What mistake?" Mary asked.

"I don't have my shirts done at the Chinese laundry." Michael stated, "Because, according to this, they're 'overdue.' But how did that get in this envelope?"

Michael reached for his cup and raised it to Mary's. By now, she was completely confused, and the wine steward could find no further reasons to dally.

"To you," said Michael. "The bad news is that my shirts are lost. The good news is that the gallery will make a final decision regarding a show this fall, in the next few weeks. In any case, Mr. Withers said *you're in.* I love you."

"Congratulations," said the waiter. "I'm so thrilled, but the cups?" Then answering his own question said, "For you successful artists, anything goes."

The steward disappeared and Michael smiled at Mary.

"I am the happiest guy in the world. I'm so proud of you," he said.

"I have to tell you the truth," said Mary. "I knew about the good news yesterday, but I wasn't going to open the letter without you. I couldn't. Aunt Catherine suggested that we walk over to the gallery and see if Scott was there, and that if he ducked when he saw me, I shouldn't open the letter. If he waved me in, I wouldn't have to open it. And if he wasn't there, I'd just find out what was in the letter when you got back. So we walked over, and he told me the good news. I just wanted you to be happy with me and read their proposal with me."

Michael laughed. "I'm so pleased for you. It's OK. What a woman you are."

"You're not mad at me for knowing?"

"Don't be silly. I am so very proud that you have received the recognition you deserve. An artist without an audience is sound without hearing, eyes without seeing, and a Michael without a Mary."

"Or a Mary without a Michael."

"Thank you."

"Someday I'd like to have one of your paintings, when I have a real home again. Or better yet, I'd like to have you painting in the home, making dozens of canvases, all fabulous... with New York, Paris, Chicago. Seattle, and Rio... all responding to you... *for* you. That's very important to me."

They continued to enjoy their dinner and Mary's acceptance into the inner circle she had longed for, from the beginning.

They had almost finished their bottle of champagne when a man in a dark tweed suit approached from the shadows, walking directly toward Mary. He stopped in front of her. It was John. Michael had no idea who he was.

"Are you enjoying an entirely new business, Mary?" John asked, "... possibly one of the oldest professions known to man? You seem to be enjoying yourselves immensely."

"And if she were, sir, what business is this of yours?" asked Michael.

"Michael, this is John," said Mary.

"Well, she *is* my wife," said John.

"From what I understand, she *was* your wife," said Michael. "However, she is my friend. Have you flown from London to Seattle to engage in some kind of word game, John? I understand that you had many years to repair the discontent you seemed to generate."

"John, I'd like you to leave us alone," said Mary.

"I don't think I traveled this distance for a second insult," said John.

"My leaving you was not meant to be an insult, as much as a very deliberate exodus regarding my feelings... or lack of feelings, about you and your shallow life," she said.

"And you are?" asked John of Michael.

Michael reached into his billfold, removed a card and turned it over. He wrote something on the back and handed it to John.

John read the front. "An impressive company," he said. "I assume your involvement is some kind of middle management?"

Michael said nothing.

John said, "When this company needed financing on the Aswan project, I offered a significant package to senior management to make it all happen. I doubt you had any awareness of my involvement."

"What companies offered this assistance?" Michael asked.

"The Powell Group."

"Yes, I remember the proposal. It came by my desk, I believe. In fact, I know I refused it because of a credibility question. After all, my level of management has to answer to so many. Move your thumb."

"What was that?" John asked.

"Move your thumb." Michael said again. "You might find it interesting."

John read: "Michael Bowland, CEO, Managing Director."

"Would you like to sit down and toast to your embarrassment or just leave quietly? The names I've written on the back of the card are Mary's representatives as of last week. If you have to communicate with her, either of them will be glad to assist you to the appropriate end and I might add... in your jolly ole tongue... a bloody hell of an end. Until then, Ole Chap, I share Mary's feelings regarding your presence, sir. Tell your story while walking away."

John left, walking to his table, shouting commands to a waiter and then leaving the room, entirely.

"What did you write on the back of your card?" asked Mary.

"The telephone number of Bret Campbell and Kato. I thought Bret might break the rule on Kato's dinners not having any movement."

"You are not to be fooled with," she said.

"Only you, however you wish... but *no one*... no one else... *ever*."

They went for a walk around the hotel, enjoying the wonderful news that Mary had received. Michael was happy that she would now achieve an identity of her own—the recognition of her talent. It had become important to both of them.

The season was changing.

Michael was in Washington for a few days.

Chapter Twenty

Spring was near. Its fragrance teased the senses. Freshness wafted through the morning air. The dew was no longer chilled as the challenge of winter rested. This trusted seasonal awakening of the spirit, which sleeps within us, had kept its promise to return.

Flowering paths appeared as surprises in places planted by nature's hand—the crocuses were the most adventurous as they broke through the wet soil. Their blossoms were so supple, yet they defied the chilled earth to contain their message. Since spring is the only season to welcome these official ambassadors, they seem to offer a "choir of tasteful elegance," silently rewarding our patience as winter moves away.

The kitchen's screen door squeaked, as Aunt Catherine closed it behind her. She wanted to stop by to see how Mary's latest doctor's appointment had gone. She drove up the road and pulled in behind the Buick. Her walk was strong—each step deliberate as she covered the short distance with determination. She walked up the porch steps, through the unlocked front door, and into the hallway.

"Mary," she called out, then a little louder when she heard no response. "Mary? Are you here, darling?"

She checked the living room, then went up to the bedroom, where she found Mary in bed.

Concerned and fearful that things weren't right, Aunt Catherine spoke her name softly, "Mary, Mary... are you OK?"

Mary answered in a weak voice. Her face and brow were wet with beads of perspiration rolling down the sides of her face.

"Mary, you're on fire," she said, putting her hand on her forehead.

"I'm not feeling well," she said. "I'm weak and cold... but still hot all at the same time. I decided to just sleep for a while."

"I'll make some tea."

Aunt Catherine went down to the kitchen and looked for Dr. Kainer's telephone number. *Is it in the drawer? On the chalkboard? No.* Sensing that time was important, she called information, then his office. Of course, he wasn't there, but he could be paged. Before the tea had seeped, the phone rang. She grabbed it on half a ring.

She told the doctor about Mary's condition. He was quick and to the point, and she was off the phone.

She brought the tea upstairs.

"Who was that? I heard the phone," Mary said.

"Yes, it was the doctor returning my call. He wants to see you as soon as possible."

"Oh my, that's not good," said Mary.

Mary quickly dressed, only taking a few sips of her tea. The drive seemed shorter than usual; Aunt Catherine delivered her right to the doctor's door in forty minutes.

While Mary was in with Dr. Kainer, Aunt Catherine stood in the waiting room, attempting to busy herself with reading, absorbing nothing other than thoughts of Mary.

Finally, the doctor asked her to join them.

Mary sat quietly, her arms folded, and her chin tucked into her chest.

"I'm admitting Mary to the hospital now," he said. "I'd like to have her stay at least one day, possibly two, depending on some tests."

"What can I do?" asked Aunt Catherine.

"You could walk her to admitting. The signs are clearly marked."

"I believe I remember from the last time we walked over."

Mary whispered to Aunt Catherine, "Michael is away in Washington," which is all she said.

They found their way there, with Mary more tired than before. A candy striper came and wheeled Mary away from Aunt Catherine, who remained to finish up the paperwork. Catherine felt a sense of parting as the wheelchair took Mary down into the depths of the hallway. She tried to watch as more and more people crossed her view, obstructing it. She saw a glimpse of them make a turn. Catherine paused, then turned her attention back to the paperwork.

Patience was not among her strong points. She paced, watching both the clock and her wristwatch, with increasing frequency. Hours had gone by. Hospital protocol would not allow an aunt up to the room. Annoyed, she made the few people immediately around her aware of her discontent as she verbally attacked the system.

"This is ridiculous. What could I possibly do? I'm here. She's there. This is stupid."

Finally, a nurse arrived to deliver the message that she could go up. Catherine looked at her, wanting to choke her but backed down with the relief that she could finally see Mary. She set off with a gait strong enough to take three others with her.

When she walked into room 538, the drapes were closed—shielding the beauty of what was left of the day. Catherine walked to the bed to where Mary was sleeping. She kissed her on the forehead. Her temperature seemed cooler to her lips. She was in a deep sleep. Aunt Catherine sat in a chair immediately next to the bed and placed her pocketbook on the floor beneath her. The white walls of the hospital room had grayed from the little light that escaped out from the drapes. The quiet was sedating. She closed her eyes to compose herself now that she was finally next to Mary.

Damn rules, she thought. She lifted her hand and placed it on top of Mary's. Sensing that she may be chilled, she pulled the light blue blanket over her hand to warm her. All was quiet and Aunt Catherine rested.

The rustling of paper, and the footsteps of someone entering the room, startled her. Catherine opened her eyes to see who was there. The darkness and the business suit threw her off a little, and she didn't immediately recognize Dr. Kainer.

"I'm sorry," he said. "I wanted to take a look at our friend."

He snapped on the light, filling the room with an explosion of stimulus, causing Catherine to look away for a moment to adjust her vision. The doctor reviewed Mary's chart then picked up her hand and checked her pulse.

"She seems to be resting comfortably. Not much is going to happen in the next few hours, so if you wish, you could get something to eat or remain here. It's up to you."

"Is she going to be here very long?"

"As I said, possibly two days, but we have to see what has gone astray first." He started to leave.

"Wait, I'll walk with you," said Catherine. "I'd like to make a few phone calls."

"Sometimes in these cases a resistance occurs to the quantity of the therapy administered," he said. "We have to watch it under more favorable conditions and controls. That's why I've asked that she remain here. I'll know more tomorrow. Call me, or I will see you then."

"Goodbye, Doctor."

Catherine seemed satisfied with that answer and left to look for a phone. She called Paul and explained what she could. She said she'd be home after dinner and that he had plenty to eat in the refrigerator. And she told him she'd leave a message for Michael at the hotel to call them at home since Mary had just told her he was away.

"Don't make it sound like he has to come home immediately," Uncle Paul cautioned.

She made her calls and returned to Mary's room to find a woman standing at the bedside.

"Hello," she whispered to the stranger. "I'm Mary's Aunt Catherine."

"Hi, I'm Deborah. Mary and I met a few months ago. Shall we step into the hall? I'm the resident psychologist here. Mary and I hit it off right away, when she was here for some testing. I came right up after seeing her name on my admissions screen. We didn't know she was here."

"Yes, she kept all of that inside her. I'm sorry she was adamant about her secret."

"I'm so relieved she has spoken to you. It's very important to be as open as possible. Mary is very special."

"To all of us," said Aunt Catherine.

"She's resting now. I'll be back later. Hopefully, she'll be up, and you'll be around. Mary has become a friend. I will watch over her progress while she's here."

"Thank you very much," Aunt Catherine said.

"It's a pleasure meeting you. but it's unfortunate that it's under these conditions," Deborah said as she left.

Catherine returned to Mary's side. She seemed to be waking up. She sat down next to her again and looked at Mary's face as she began to open her eyes.

"Hi," Mary said. "It looks like I had an extended nap."

"That's good. It's good to get your rest. I'm sure they are going to start doing something with you very soon. I'm going to get back to the house. The nurse said they are going to take you to a test in a short while; then, there will be something else, which she did not elaborate on. Oh, my child, I am very concerned for you, dear. Shall I stay? Or what would you like me to do?"

"I'll be fine. Go home and have a good night's sleep. Say hi to Uncle Paul. I'm not going to be much fun anyway. I feel pretty good right now... I was just dreaming about something."

"I'll stay until they come to get you for your tests, but I did leave my flame juggling torches in the car, so we'll have to think of something to talk about. What kind of dream?"

Mary seemed to have more strength. She seemed determined to convey her thoughts.

"Rio... I remember," Mary said very softly. "Many years ago, before Calcutta, John and I spent a few months in South America... It was a big business deal for him." She stopped to clear her throat. "We decided we would spend a weekend at a resort. It was a beautiful place, but our relationship was on the razor's edge of caring, and not.

"The many arguments had sliced into the center of who we were... dividing us. He had changed. He had begun to spend all his time on the 'business of business,' with me as an addendum to his life. I was trying to understand, to cope. We both had invested many years. I wanted some attention, but he was traveling at a pace faster and faster away from me. It was impossible for him to grasp the simplicity of my needs.

"We went to the beach. It was a gorgeous day. Each wave was a crystalline sculpture— exploding into sound as it crashed on the sand. A young couple, holding each other's hand, stopped and placed a blanket a discrete distance away. I knew John was aware of them. They became the subjects of our interest for too long as we both realized that they were deeply in love.

"He touched her face gently, and then kissed her. She embraced him. He whispered something in her ear, and they laughed. She rose, running towards the surf. He ran after her. We both could feel that this exchange of caring and giving to each other was that "something" we once possessed. I was jealous in a sense, of their happiness, as if they had found what we had lost, and would not return it. It was sad. *I* was sad. Mary coughed; Aunt Catherine offered her a sip of water.

"I'm not sure," she continued, as she cleared her throat "... that considering all things, our relationship would have been any different in the end. But we had a chance to begin to work on it, that day, that moment. But nothing ever happened. We just observed *our loss,* through them. The couple returned from the water, laughing. John looked at his watch and said, 'We have to get back.'

"We walked past their blanket and saw the two of them intertwined in each other's arms. They were aware only of themselves. Our separated shadows moved over the top of their embrace. Neither one of us looked back. Neither he nor I spoke to each other about this couple then, as we observed their love, or after, when our own had been discarded."

Aunt Catherine looked at Mary and held her hand. They remained very quiet.

A nurse came in, carrying a little basket of vials and asked if she could take some blood. Mary responded with a lighthearted moan.

Aunt Catherine felt it was time to get home to Paul. It was later than she thought. "You take care, and I'll see you in the morning," she said.

"Thank you," said Mary. "I love you."

The nurse stopped, watching the two hug. Then Catherine took her hand and pushed a few strands of hair away from Mary's face. "May I?" asked the nurse.

"Yes," said Mary. The nurse proceeded to take many vials of blood. She was just finishing as others started to come in to take Mary to additional tests. They rolled her down the hallways of the hospital, each hall looking exactly the same. The ceiling lights and doorways became a blur. And the people they passed began to look. All were wearing white with the occasional green gown. The voices were never attached to any one person. They sounded like machines. "Drink this." "Hold still." "Roll on your side." Then there was another floor, another wait—each person asking more questions—offering no answers. People were touching, probing, some of them were pleasant; some of them were as cold as the metal that pressed against her.

Now, there was more and more anxiety—so many questions, and not one answer. They were accumulating information at a faster rate than before, adding to the chart, now filled with many pages of numbers, facts, dates and times, concerning her medical history. This story had been translated into technical jargon, an unreadable biography, touched by so many technicians, but not one entry was by anyone who 'knew' her: *Templeton, Mary, female, age 38. Condition: 'as well as can be expected.' Yes, expected! What is that 'expected?' These long waits with nothing... no one. I'm lying here with myself... waiting for an answer... waiting for my life to turn a corner. 'Expected... as well as can be expected.' How much time is left for Mary? What am I? What should I expect?*

They wheeled her back to her room. Deborah was waiting. She looked at Mary and smiled. The attendants moved her on to her bed.

"So, how's my friend?" asked Deborah.

"Your friend has had it!" Mary answered.

"How so?"

"It's too much. I mean the anxiety I have. I'm developing a fear of fears."

"That's not a new phobia but very understandable. Can I get you something?"

"No... Yes, a new body... same life... well almost the same, but a trade in."

"I hear you were doing so well. I'm sure this will pass into a new positive for you."

"A positive?" I'm not so sure. You're not feeling what I feel inside while you make that statement." Mary's face paled.

"What's wrong?" asked Deborah. She turned to look at the doorway.

A man wearing a suit and carrying a hat and raincoat over his arm was standing there.

"Hello Mary. May I come in?"

It was John.

She bent her head down, but her eyes were riveted to him. Her mouth was slightly open in surprise.

"Deborah, this is John, my... soon to be ex-husband."

"I don't believe I've ever been introduced quite like that before," he said. "...interesting."

"How do you do?" said Deborah. "I'm Deborah Harris Penna, a friend of Mary's."

"Yes, I don't believe we've ever met. Would you mind? I'd like just a few moments alone with my 'estranged wife.'"

"I'll check back with you later."

"Thank you, I'll be close by."

John looked around the room and placed his hat and coat over the chair.

"So, why are you here? Dr. Satara called for you shortly after you left , asking if you were feeling well. I told him you were off to the states on some extended holiday. He seemed distant and asked for you to give him a call when it was convenient. And now you're here. It would seem there is much I don't know."

"Volumes," Mary said

"Look, Mary, I'm a lot of things, but I'm not totally insensitive when it comes to you. These months without you have been very revealing. At first I liked the space, then I began to feel your absence, and now I know I want you back. But you're here, and I don't know what to make of it."

"I'm sorry, John. I really am. But no, I cannot. There have been years of neglect... years of time, distancing you and me. A few weeks... a few sentences cannot begin to repair the emotional damage that you have created in me. And I, it's true, have damaged you in return. I'm leaving you as I said... forever. It's done. Finished. Enough. I don't want any more of you and whoever you are. You changed. And yes, I did as well. We were the predator and the prey, each adapting to a new environment."

"Predator... is that me or you?"

"It's interesting, John. I guess it's a little of both. Each of us must acquire the others' traits for survival. Are you staying long? I mean, in the states?"

"As long as I need. I have a few business things, but I'm here mostly for you."

"Then you won't be here very long. It's certainly me then, is it?" she said.

"I'm sorry I said that. I just... "

"I'm not sorry at all, about anything, other than the *time* we managed to waste on nothing."

"Is there anything I can do? I stopped in at the hospital's office and transferred all of your medical costs to my account."

"Well, that's *almost* it then. Thanks for the treat, John. Just please leave me now. Come back if you'd like... some other time. I just can't do this now. Please."

"'*Almost* it?'" he asked.

"Yes. Go see your son. Did you ever bother? I'm sure the answer is no."

John grabbed his hat and coat from the chair. "Goodbye, Mary."

"Goodbye, John."

As he was leaving, he passed Deborah in the hallway. He stopped her.

"You must have known Mary for centuries," he said.

"Well... " Deborah started to speak. He interrupted...

"Because our marriage of thirteen years has hardly left a dent in her caring to see me."

She began to answer again, but John walked away.

Deborah found Mary very angry. "So that's John. Wow! Not an easy thing for you to deal with," Deborah said.

"No, not easy at all."

"He certainly has his own agenda."

"Did you notice which elevator he took?"

"No, I didn't. Why?"

"I thought he might have been going home to the basement."

"The basement?"

"Yes, the morgue. He likes the cold. It suits his miserable self to see some of his competition."

"Mary, it's time to rest. Anger is not conducive to healing. The worst is over. I'm sure he has the message; it's just not processed yet. While he figures it out, you can rest."

"It's not going well, Deborah. It's not, I feel it. I know you don't know, but I need Michael. Where is he?"

"Do you want me to find him?"

"Yes, please."

"Where do I start?"

"He has a secretary, he told me about months ago, who can find him anywhere. He gave me his business card. It's in my bag in the wallet. 'Bowland LTD.' No, 'Bowland Industries.' Don't let him panic. I just want him to be here as soon as he can."

Deborah handed Mary her purse, and she rifled through her cards until she found the one. She handed it to Deborah.

"I'll be back in a short while," said Deb. "Mary, you rest. It's getting late."

"Thank you, Deb."

Deborah went back to her office to make the call, but the timing was off. It would be 11:00 p.m. in New York. No one would be there. She gave it a try anyway.

The phone rang four times and a machine answered.

"You have reached the offices of Bowland Industries. We are unable to answer your call at this time. However, if you would, please, leave a message. We will return your call within the next business day. For European calls and the Far East, please note the time of your call. Thank you."

"Michael Bowland, this is Deborah Penna, a friend of Mary's. My number is 853-5655. Mary asked me to call you. She's OK but in the hospital. Please give me a call anytime. My home number is 234-9765, should you care to use it... any hour. Thank you. She needs you."

Deborah returned to Mary's room. She had fallen asleep. She looked at her friend resting and felt much compassion for her. She picked up the chart and reviewed it for a short time, occasionally shaking her head over the information that unfolded as she read on. She placed the chart back in its place, opened a drawer in the bedside table, and removed a piece of paper to write a note.

"I called him and left a message on his machine. I'm sure, by morning, I'll be speaking to him. I moved the phone closer, so you can reach it. Love you. Your friend, Deborah."

She placed it by the phone where it was easy to see.

Mary awakened much later. She felt it was time to call Manisha. But how? She rang for the nurse. Within moments, she was there.

"Anything wrong?"

"I need to use the phone and call India."

The nurse, in a whispering voice, said, "Did you say India? That's quite a phone call."

"I just moved here from there. It's a very important call. Could you talk to the operator and charge it to the numbers I'll give you."

"Of course."

"I need my purse."

The nurse gave Mary her purse, and Mary removed the information offering the area codes.

"Could you ask for a Manisha Saha, please?"

The nurse went through the process fairly quickly.

"Yes, a Manisha Saha, please."

"Hello. Hello" said Manisha

"Could you hold for Mary Templeton, please." The nurse handed Mary the phone.

Very weakly Mary said, "Hello Manisha."

"Mary, it's you. You sound *not well.*"

"I'm not. I'm in the hospital. I am very tired, but I wanted to call you to let you know I was here. There's so much to tell."

"Mary, what is happening?"

"I called to ask you to help me once again."

"Anything!"

"Will you take care of Paul's grave for me, please?"

"What is wrong that you would ask me this? Are you not coming back for a while?"

"I need you to help me, Manisha. Please."

"I will, of course, but... has John found you? Rumors have it he is in the U.S."

"Yes, but I... it doesn't make any difference. He doesn't matter. Michael is all that matters."

"Can I do... well… is that all I can do, Mary?"

"I'm asking a lot right now. I know you will do this. I trust you, Manisha, forever."

Manisha was crying. "I don't know why. I understand the distance but the time. I'm saying yes, Mary, yes. You don't have to ask."

"Manisha, I'm feeling very badly. I was in remission, but it's back, and I don't want to take a chance now and leave Paul without someone to take care of him... to love him... please."

"I'm... Oh, Manisha, I feel so tired. I'm sure I'm not going to make it back to Paul... my baby."

"Mary don't say these things... please. You're going to be fine. We love you Mary. Jiral and Rose keep looking at your painting of them. Jiral wants to hug you."

"I'm so happy for that but so tired. I need to sleep now... please. Goodbye, for now, Manisha. God bless you. I'm sorry to upset you, but it's for Paul, and you know that is important."

"I'm calling you very soon, Mary, very, very soon. You take care. We love you... "

"Bye."

Mary placed the receiver in the cradle. She felt that she had just disconnected herself from her past and could see no future. This void she was part of—this moment—was more than depressing. The only evidence that others were close by, was sound. But the footsteps in the hall were hollow, lonely, and empty sounds. And occasionally, she heard a distant ring of the telephone at the nurses' station or a beep on one of the other patient's monitors—with another patient moaning. *There's too much dark space in here*, she thought, *too many lonely sounds directing my fears into a world of abandonment. The child in me is fearful... anticipating the unknown.*

Hours had passed when the phone rang. Mary's hand brushed past the note. She reached the receiver, pulling the phone closer, hoping it was Michael. His voice warmed her and filled her mind with emotion. Her lips parted to announce the magic of the one word... "Michael"

"Mary! What are you doing there without me? Did you get us a king-size bed? Tell me you're OK."

"I'm not feeling well," she said.

"I spoke to Deborah and Aunt Catherine, and I'm on my way to you, after playing 'checkers' with a few flights. I'll be landing in Chicago in an hour. I waited a while to call. I didn't want to wake you too early. My girl needs her rest. I fly out of O'Hare and should be with you by ten-ish, for a late breakfast."

"Don't be late," said Mary

"I won't. Get better! Love ya!"

"I love you," was spoken in a weak voice.

Michael placed the phone back and returned to his seat. The sun had just risen behind him and was reflecting off of the wings and rear of the engine cowlings, making it appear that they were as hot as a poker, flying as fast as they could to get to Mary. He sat thinking of her, reviewing the few months that had passed since they met.

His feelings were desperate. He wanted to be with her—to see her face—her smile. To find out she was all right was all he wanted. He questioned how fast he could get to her. *How well organized can I make it?* he asked himself.

Chicago is a half-hour to forty-five minutes. Then there's a waste of time and back in the air. Then there's three hours flying time to Seattle. A car rental would be too long. A car service is much faster. They need at least an hour's notice, so I'll call one hour into the flight. Then into town, and I'm there. Do I make any other calls? No, not now. Mary, I'm making it happen. I'm going to be there, right next to you, very soon.

The Urbans... she'll be happy to know they have an interest and especially that her friend, Scott Withers, is a name they are aware of. That will be a nice 'up' for her. I love her. She has become a big part of my life.

The pilot's voice came over the sound system. "We are making our descent to O'Hare on time. For those of you who will be continuing on to Phoenix, Seattle, and Denver, please see our red-jacketed United representative as you exit the jet port for specific gate assignments. Thank you."

Michael raised his hand and depressed the flight attendant's light. A woman appeared in less than a minute.

"Flight 676 out of O'Hare to Seattle. Could you find out if it's on time for departure?"

"Surely, I'll check," she said.

"Thanks."

She was back in a few minutes to let him know that according to local information, the plane had arrived and was at the gate. However, there were delays taking off because of heavy traffic, and he should expect a wait of twenty minutes or more.

"But I'm sure you're aware the pilots can make that time up fairly easily."

"Thank you," he said.

The plane landed with a hard hit to the undercarriage, sending a burst of groans and 'woos' through the cabin from the passengers. The standard, "Don't get up until the captain has safely stopped at the gate," was relayed as a few passengers began to stand anyway. Michael was the third in line to the exit door; the handle was released and the gangway attached.

As he deplaned, he caught up immediately to a man in front of him excusing himself, and passing him—almost running. Out from the gangway and into the seating area, he spotted the red jacket.

An older woman was standing next to the representative and asking every conceivable question about flights since Orville Wright... *whom she probably knew, personally, as a little girl,* Michael mused.

"Excuse me," said Michael.

"I am talking. I hope you realize that," said the older woman.

"Excuse me, ma'am, but my connecting flight is leaving soon, and it seems... "

"Well... where to?" asked the woman in the red jacket.

"Seattle—Gate 28 W. Tell me it's at the opposite side of this airport, and I promise not to be surprised."

"Yes, you're right."

"I'm not surprised. Do you have communications with that gate? Could you inform them that passenger Bowland is in the terminal?"

"Yes, sir."

"I was saying... " began the older woman again.

"Yes, ma'am," said the red-jacketed woman as she hailed a mini passenger cart.

"Carol, Carol," she called out.

Carol pulled over and stopped. She helped the older woman on and asked Michael to hop on as well.

"Carol, 28 W ASAP," she said, pressing a few buttons on her phone.

"Yes, this is Rosemary, 28 W."

"I'm transporting a Mr. Bowland and a Mrs. Kravitz to you at gate 28 W."

She paused for a moment to listen. The voice on the other end said, "Take your time. We are holding. No one's getting out for a while. We're running fifty minutes in the red."

The representative translated the message.

"They are going to wait for you," she told Michael and the older woman.

"Thank you." he said. "You're off to Seattle?" Michael asked the older woman next to him.

"Yes," she said, holding her hat with her hand. "And your seat number, sir?"

Michael looked at his tickets, hoping not to win the lottery in the next few seconds. "Six A," he told her.

"Fancy pants, in first class. I'm 33 D."

"Oh, too bad," he said. "We could have had a wonderful conversation."

"I'm sure," said Carol

All went well, as the doors to the plane were finally shut. Michael ordered an Irish coffee. It was a reasonable time to get indigestion. The plane taxied down the access to the runway. As the plane turned, Michael saw the traffic backed up. *There are at least twenty planes in line. At three minutes each, that's an hour. And then if they're alternating runway... who knows.* He reached for the attendant's button.

"May I help you, sir?"

"Hey look, I'm an old hand at this, but this flight, this time, is different. I've got a real problem with time. Can you give me your best estimate on the delay, so I can attempt to suppress my insanity? I need to get to Seattle ASAP."

"An hour," she said. "But subtract at least half of that, since we can make up for the loss of time, and you're talking twenty or thirty minutes."

"May I have another coffee?"

"Sure. I'd like one, too, but rules are rules."

Michael sat back and listened to the whine of the engines revving up every few minutes as they moved ahead, one plane at a time, each taking its turn, leaving the traffic behind. He began to think of New Year's Eve. The evening they first met.

Finding her, took a lifetime... A trip around the world, and in a plane over... she was there. We exchanged a gift of time and lavished the experience together. In our happiness, we allowed time zones to express years of excitement as we shared the spontaneity of it all. We counted down the minutes to the next Millennium, repeatedly, confirming our commitment to good times. The second—that first, singular, precious second—we met was the best thing that ever happened.

But now I'm rushing to her, and this journey is offering an entirely different feeling. This would not be a good time. The minutes are painful, the seconds excruciating, and the waiting much too long. Time is an enemy. The emotion is not happiness but anxiety over getting to her as fast as possible. As she expressed to her parents at the cemetery when she read, "My Time is Near," so have I wasted too much time in finding Mary, and it's taking too much time to get to her side. When the hell are we going to move?

Another plane took off. The engines whined. He pressed his head against the window to see ahead of the plane, as it turned, but he couldn't. *She is so beautiful. So, this is hell... waiting. I'm going to explode. Why the do these things happen when you need to get to a place fast? Murphy—you bastard!*

I had spent so many years with nothing... no one. There had been a date, a dinner, but nothing real. It's not fair to find a precious emotion tucked away in the outer reaches of this world and then have it taken away, not for a minute, but forever.

The engines revved, but not as before. They grew in pitch—stronger—louder. The under carriage dug into the runway. The plane moved faster and faster closer to Mary. The pilot's voice announced that they were on their way, and he thanked them for their patience.

"Seattle, here we come," the pilot said.

"Finally," said Michael.

The passengers had settled down and the flight attendants were busy serving breakfast when the first-class attendant asked if Michael would like another Irish coffee.

"It's St. Patrick's Day, you know," she said.

"It is? I'm sorry. I must be ordering these Irish coffees out of instinct. I've been a little crazed on getting to Seattle. My friend," he said, and then paused. "No, my... you see... the woman I love is in the hospital, and I just need to get there as soon as possible."

"Why, may I ask? Was it an accident?"

"No, she is very ill. Or, at least, I hope she's not *very* ill."

"I'm sorry," she said, and touched his shoulder. "I'll check to see how much of this time we can make up. Excuse me."

He looked at the empty seat next to him. She wasn't there. He touched the arm rest. He could think of nothing else but to be with her. He released the phone from its compartment and called the hospital. The phone rang in her room but no answer.

Finally... a voice, he thought. It was a nurse.

"Hi, I'm looking for Mary Templeton," he said.

"This is her room. She is having some tests done and will return in a few hours. I'm not sure exactly when."

"How is she?" asked Michael.

"I can only refer you to her doctor for information regarding the patient's condition. Are you her husband?"

"Yes, I am," he said. "Now how is she?"

"I don't know," said the nurse.

"I'm calling you from my flight from Chicago. I'm on my way to Seattle. I'm very concerned since I can't get there for a few hours. I would really like to have some idea how she's doing, please. I love her. I am very frustrated, and it seems it's down to me and you."

"She's OK, and her condition won't change in the next few hours, so relax," said the nurse. "I'll tell her you called."

"OK. Tell her I'm almost home."

He hung up. Pushing himself back in the seat, he thought, to himself... *bureaucrats frightened by lawsuits. Our society is sick... very sick. We have every contraption imaginable to communicate and no one can talk to each other. So, why bother?* Reaching again for the phone, he made his other calls.

The flight attendant returned.

"They think we'll end up about ten minutes late... maybe fifteen, depending on the weather. It's one of those foggy days in Seattle."

"Coffee," said Michael. "This one's on St. Patrick."

"Top of the morning to you, sir."

Michael's thoughts drifted away again, running through the many moments he and Mary had shared. His mind was dedicated to her. Even as the attendant placed his coffee on the tray next to him, his response was mechanical. He smiled and said thank you, but continued to daydream of his love. It seemed so easy to reconstruct it all. There was the first meeting where she had sat next to him and toasted the New Year. Suddenly he sat up.

"Miss... Miss," he called the attendant.

"Yes?"

"Hey, you've got to do me a favor. I don't want the coffee, I'm sorry. Can I have a split of champagne and two coffee cups?"

"Sure," she said. She removed the coffee and returned with his request.

As he opened the bottle, he said, "I know you can't share this with me, so please humor me." He popped the cork and poured the champagne into one cup, offering the empty one to her. He raised his cup to hers. "Happy New Year," he said.

She looked at him, strangely, but seemed to trust him.

"Happy New Year," she repeated. "I don't know why I feel comfortable doing this with you."

"Because it's St. Paddy's Day, and it's a day to believe in just about anything, especially if you are a little daft. Thank you for humoring me. This was something I just had to do. You're very kind to put up with me."

"If it's something you do with your friend," she said... "the cups and the champagne then I'm glad I could help. Lucky girl. What's her name?"

"Mary. And yours?"

"Marcy."

"Well, Happy New Year, Marcy."

"Happy New Year."

Marcy placed her cup down. "I'll be back later for more of this," she said. "But duty beckons."

This flight is the longest stretch of time ever spent in an airplane, Michael thought. *It feels like a statistic in* The Guinness Book of World Records *for the most airtime ever... for an object in space.* According to Michael's emotional clock, it felt like 654 years on one tank of gas.

The wheels touched the cloud that had consumed Seattle, then, bumped along the runway. There was a screeching sound of the wheels as the flaps went up. He heard the pilot thank the passengers for flying, and Marcy stopped to say goodbye. The door release sounded like a can of "Chock Full o' Nuts," and he was out the door, down the gangway and through the gates, heading to the arrival area.

He searched the little black signs with people's names on them, looking for his own. Aimone, Leister, Safro, Hellmen, Affsa. Bowland... yes Bowland.

"That's me. I'm Bowland," he said. "Where are you parked?"

"Right here, sir."

"Good, let's go, immediately. To the hospital, please."

"You have any luggage, sir?"

"Just this, thanks," he said, referring to his carry on.

The driver opened the door and Michael climbed in. The driver walked around the car, stopping for a second to let another car pass.

Get in the damn car and drive, Michael thought.

Finally, the driver got in and flicked his cigarette into the street, blowing smoke into the air as if to push it outside the car. Michael leaned forward to speak to him.

"Have you ever been in a hurry? You know, when the entire world is in front of you in traffic and the clock's face is wound so tight that you're going to explode because of the pressure?"

"Let me guess, you want me to get the hell out of here and get to the hospital faster than Batman's bat mobile. Is that it?"

"Someone who understands! Please... you got it, sir!"

He started the car and moved slowly toward the exit, paid the toll, and from that moment on, Michael couldn't move his body from the rear of the seat as the car sped off, never slowing until it pulled up to the hospital doors.

"Thank you, and in the interest of time, how much?" asked Michael.

"Sixty bucks."

"Well, here's a hundred."

"Thanks. See you soon."

"I hope so, sir... every day."

Michael walked straight to the front desk.

"Mary Templeton's room... please."

Michael looked as if he had been up all night frolicking for St. Patrick's Day. He wasn't quite himself as the clerk gave him the room number. He was up in the elevator and on to the floor in seconds.

Finally... room 538... a billion hours, planes, cars and here it is.

He walked in. Her bed was empty.

A nurse came in behind him.

"Where is she?" he asked.

"Sir, the visiting hours... "

"Where is she?"

"Sir... "

"I need to know now!"

"She's not back from chemotherapy. And you are?"

"Her husband."

"John?"

"No, her second husband. How long will she be?"

"I don't know. And generally, for this type of therapy, the patient returns very groggy and spends most of the time sleeping."

Michael walked up to the visitor's lounge. A few people were seated in a small area. They each made eye contact with Michael as he took his seat directly across from an elderly man. His back was flat against the seat, his girth protruding well out over his thighs, his arms folded atop of his stomach. He nodded as Michael sat. Without flinching, he began a con - versation, offering his concern for Michael's "family member."

"I hope he or she is doing all right," he said.

The man seemed to be firmly attached to his seat. Michael reached for his hand and said, "Thank you. She's doing fine."

The old man strained to reach Michael's hand, to shake it. His chair was creaking from his weight.

"And your loved one?" asked Michael.

"They tell us she is doing well, but I don't know. It doesn't look too good to me. She's in a coma and doesn't respond to much of anything. We're married fifty four years last month. That's a good run."

"Well, I am sorry," said Michael. "You are very fortunate to have had a wonderful rela- tionship for such a long time."

"Well, I don't know about wonderful but real... very real. We had our ups and downs. We had a lot of hard times, and fortunately more good times."

"Well, I'm sure it will work out for the best," said Michael. "Are these other people with you?" he asked, pointing to the remaining group.

"No, they're just here like us," he said, "for some other unfortunate person. It's a shame."

"How long has she been in the coma?" Michael asked.

"Two weeks," he said.

"I'm sorry."

"Well, there's nothing we can do except wait and pray for the best."

Michael turned and looked out the glass walls of the lounge. Aunt Catherine was just walking by.

"Excuse me, please," said Michael.

He walked to the glass door, waving his hands at Catherine. She didn't see him and continued walking.

"Catherine, Catherine," he yelled, opening the door.

She turned and looked at him, and they embraced.

"Mary is not in her room," Michael told her. "Come and sit in here for a while with me."

They walked back into the lounge.

"I'm sorry, I didn't get your name before," Michael said to the older man.

"Lee... Lee Marin."

"This is Catherine O'Connor, and I'm Michael Bowland."

Michael offered Catherine his seat. "Lee's wife has, unfortunately, been in a coma for the last few weeks," he explained.

Yes, she is not doing too well," said Lee. "But we'll see."

"Oh my goodness, a coma," said Aunt Catherine. "My niece is here for testing for a few days. She's going to be fine."

"I'm sure," said Lee.

Michael leaned over to Catherine and quietly asked if she wanted a cup of coffee or something to eat. She did, so they rose and said their goodbyes to Lee, wishing him well.

The hospital coffee shop was filled with traditional white and light blue or green gowns. The line for coffee was long, so he offered to get the coffee while Catherine looked for a table. A moment later, a nurse approached and asked if Michael were a doctor.

"No, I'm sorry. I'm not... just a very concerned man looking in on a very special person up on the fifth floor."

"Fifth? I'm over on 3 south... sorry. Has she been here long?" asked the nurse.

"A day or so, for additional testing."

The line began to move up to the empty trays and utensils, and Michael assembled a tray.

"And you, how long have you been here?" he asked.

"Six years," she said. "It's been a good stay. I love what I do... well almost all the time. Pediatrics is a great feeling, except when you lose one. They're the most beautiful children.

Their little faces are so courageous. It's a real tug on the heart. It's very sad sometimes. But fortunately, the majority live happy and healthy lives."

The line moved. "May I help you?" asked the server.

"Yes, coffee, a bowl of bananas and oranges, and a side of half and half," said the nurse. She filled her tray with the order and turned to Michael.

"Well, I hope it all works out well," she said.

"I feel it will," said Michael. "I'll be here again, I'm sure. So may I say thank you, and I'll see you again. Bye."

Michael ordered a cup of coffee for himself, tea for Aunt Catherine, and a couple of blueberry muffins. Then he began looking for Aunt Catherine's table. He stood in the middle of the dining room staring, knowing he was probably looking right at her and not seeing her. Finally, he saw her arms waving in the far corner, next to a window. He walked over to her, placed the tray down, and sat, sighing out loud.

"Let's see. It's about two in the afternoon for me, but I'm not sure if it's Wednesday or Monday."

"Well, it's Wednesday," said Aunt Catherine... all day. How are you feeling, Michael?"

"Well, physically, I guess fine," he said "A lot of achy muscles but OK; however, psychologically, I'm just so worried about Mary."

"I know it's not easy, but her mother, God bless her soul, was taken from us having the same illness. It must be something genetic. I hope the difference in time and technology allows us to have a much different ending... please God.

"The tests and treatment are some of the best in the world, right here in this building. One doesn't really think much of it until you begin to see the effort and the caring that these people offer. I hope, I do hope, we can beat this and be done with it. You do love her, don't you Michael?"

"Yes I do. I see her as the most important person in my life and hope she will allow me to share time and a part of her life for as long as we live."

"Marriage?"

"*Anyway* to be with her... a piece of paper offers no real commitment to any relationship. If she would have me, yes, but just to be a part of her day—her thoughts—is fine. I would offer myself as a humble recipient of the gift she continues to give me.

"I hope my openness doesn't bother you. But she has revealed to me feelings I never knew I had. I've had a very good life in business but have managed to hide under tons of concrete, emotionally. That was my problem. But Mary never bothered to recognize the barriers. She reached past them in a way that I cannot begin to describe."

"It seems you're doing a fair job right now," said Aunt Catherine.

"Do you think we're going to make it?"

"I pray to God. I've been to our church more these past few months than in my entire life. The priest and I are the best of buddies. He's starting to put me on committees. I don't know if I have the time for all that, but he is in prayer for her as well, so... "

"What do *you* think about this? Please?"

"I think the best thing we can do is to offer our strength to her, letting her know we are here for her in spirit and in any way she may need to use us in her battle for survival. Unfortunately, that's *all* we can do."

"Well, I want to be a major contributor."

"I know, Michael. If I were ever not sure or if I ever questioned it, I was wrong. You and she are a remarkable testimony to the way life takes mysterious turns. I am so happy for you both and so saddened for us all, that Mary is upstairs fighting a battle for her own life. And we can do so little to tip the scales."

"Shall we go up and sit on the right side of the scale to assure a win for Mary?" Michael asked.

"Sure," she said, taking her last sip of tea.

They went back to Mary's room, not knowing what to expect. She was in her bed sleeping. They quietly walked over to her. Aunt Catherine touched her forehead with her hand, gently pushing a few strands of hair back. Michael just stood there looking at her. He thought to reach for the chart and as he did, the doctor entered the room. Michael's hand fell back to his side. Aunt Catherine turned to the doctor and whispered, "She's sleeping."

"Good," said Dr. Kainer. "She needs rest. I know you're concerned, but she will be staying longer than I initially expected... at least for the next few days. Keep your stays short for her sake. I know we all want to help, but I am appealing to your intelligence in the matter, not trying to scold you for being here."

"We understand," said Michael, using a hushed tone. "How is she?"

"Not good," said the doctor. "We're taking a guarded position at this point. She will have a rather intense next few days and, hopefully, that time will provide a better perspective and the improvement I expect to see."

"What can we do?" asked Aunt Catherine.

"Be here for her, but not, as I said, keeping her from her rest."

"Thank you," Aunt Catherine said.

The doctor shook Michael's hand. "I'll be seeing you, I'm sure. If not, feel free to call me at my office. The nurse's station will provide you with the number, should you need it."

"Thank you," he said.

The doctor left and Aunt Catherine appeared ready to follow him.

"I'm going to leave you two alone," she said. "I promised to run an errand for Paul. I'll be back later. I'm sure you want to be alone with her when she wakes up."

Michael sat down in a chair next to Mary's bed as Aunt Catherine left the room. He leaned back, his head tilted back over the headrest. He loosened his tie and stared out the window. Many minutes passed, as he turned occasionally to see if she had awakened. The sounds of the monitor were the only sounds that were heard. The monotonous "beep— beep—beep" became the focus of Michael's attention, and he wondered if he could find a volume switch and turn it down. *It's enough to drive someone nuts... listening to that for hours and hours,* he thought. He sat up to look at it, just as the door opened and Deborah entered, walking as quietly as a mouse.

She came close to Michael and whispered his name.

"Yes," he whispered back.

"Hi. I'm Deborah. Can we go outside in the hall?"

"Sure." He followed her out, closing the door only partially.

He positioned himself so he could see Mary's face.

"I'm Deborah Harris Penna," she said.

"Oh, thank you for the call. You're wonderful to have done that."

"She is special."

"Yes."

"I'm not going to stay right now," she said. "But if you need me... "

"Well, I know your numbers, and I will most likely be able to leave a message for you somewhere in the hospital, I'm sure."

"Absolutely... I'd like to stay to see her face when she awakens."

"I'll see you later," she said.

Michael opened the door slowly and walked towards Mary. The light from the window was grayer, the room a little darker, hiding most of the shapes in shadow. Mary's sheets were the brightest things in the room. He sat at her side and reached for her hand. It felt cool to his touch. Michael placed both his hands around Mary's, making them warm.

His eyes were heavy as he leaned his head down, touching the bright sheets and a small portion of the blue blanket. His head came to a rest. Mary's lips were parched, her mouth dry. Her eyes began to open, and she turned her head to see Michael's face at her side. Her lips separated slowly. Her mind reached for the most wonderful word in her world. She whispered, "Michael."

He turned his head and their eyes met.

"Mary," he said.

He brought his head upright to see her, then leaned towards her and kissed her softly on the lips.

"Would you like a sip of water?" he asked.

"Yes."

He filled half a glass from a pitcher near the bed. The sound of the ice cascading into the glass was a welcome relief from the beeps of the monitor.

"You're an old sleepy head," he said.

"Not old," she replied. "Did you have an OK flight?"

"No problem, except for my wanting to be here instantaneously. It took forever."

"Well, I've been very busy."

"Hey, did I tell you I loved you today?"

"No."

Michael closed his hand and softly pretended to beat himself up on his chest and his head. "So there."

She smiled. "You deserved that for not telling me."

"I'm bad. I love you so much. You have to do me a favor."

"Anything."

"Get well fast, and let's go to the islands next week."

"Well, I'm... "

"No excuses."

"I missed you. Well, I knew you were away on business."

"I just quit. I'm here and going nowhere without you."

"Quit? How did you quit your own business?"

"Well... " he began, then took a tissue from the box next to her bed and dried her tears. "Hey, you're looking really beautiful to me right now. Your eyes... your face... you know a guy can really fall in love with a girl like you."

"Michael, I don't feel good. I don't feel very beautiful. I feel ugly and miserable and rotten." She turned her head away. "I don't know, Michael, I'm... I feel so bad."

"You are going to be just fine," he said. "And besides," he whispered, "the people in New York at the Guggenheim and your buddy at the gallery know each other. A good match to maybe put the icing on the cake for your show. We'll go there after you get out of here and before we go up to the islands, to firm up the show for you, OK?"

"Wow. My show. I wanted this my entire life. My own show. My work and an audience of people reviewing it. I'm scared they won't like it."

"Of course they will like it. I'm going to be there with a rubber hammer and anyone who doesn't say good things, gets creatively silenced. Not to worry, Mrs. Picasso. I never knew anyone who was truly creative before."

"I'm still scared, Michael."

"Yes."

"I'm very tired. I think I'm going back to sleep. Is that OK?"

"I'll just stay right here, holding your hand. Is that OK?"

"Yes, it's perfect."

She fell asleep. Michael's eyes closed. His head returned to the bed, and they both rested, feeling a strong sense of devotion, that they belonged to each other. The room grew darker. Michael faded in and out of sleep, offering vigilance to Mary. Occasionally a nurse entered the room to see if Mary was OK. Michael heard the door swing open at one point and felt the presence of someone behind him. He lifted his head and turned to see Aunt Catherine.

"I didn't want to disturb you," she said.

"It's OK. She's sleeping again."

He got up and made room so Aunt Catherine could touch her. "I'm going back to the hotel to take a shower and get in some jeans. I'll be back in about an hour. Do you want to stay?"

"Sure. You go ahead and take your time," Aunt Catherine said. "I'll be here when you get back."

Aunt Catherine sat as Michael had, close to Mary, looking at her as a mother would look at her child. This illness had not changed Mary's youthful face or her eyes. It was thirty-eight years last May 22, that she was born, Catherine reminisced: *I was thirty when Mary ar-*

rived. It was such a happy time for her mother and father. Her father had been with them in the hospital all night, waiting for the delivery of their first and their only child. The phone call that morning was filled with laughter. They were so happy to have a little girl, Mary, 7 pounds 11 ounces... so pink, healthy, and the image of her mother.

It seemed a privilege to have watched her grow from the little girl with crinoline skirts and dainty shoes one day and making mud and stone pies in the back yard, another. Mary would ask her father to help serve them to Paul and myself as special birthday size pieces.

Mary's father was such a giving man, so willing to allow her to be creative... to be herself. He felt so sure she would one day become a great success at whatever she chose.

These next days may prove to be a tragedy, a waste, a shame that Mary would find herself united with her mother and father too soon. This price is too dear, having to surrender to this illness... the calendar... this date. None of us are privy to the number that stands reserved for each of us to end our stay, giving to the Almighty our most precious gift of life.

Oh please, my Lord... let the pages of her calendar reach far into this new century, for this child... this talented and loving child... so that she may share the love of a man who will be destroyed if we lose her. Find it in your heart to turn to the business of the world and allow her to slip by the date that I feel is so, closely near... too closely near. It's not for me I ask, but for the spirit, that, I know, has just been reborn within her. I ask that I hold this child in my arms... once more... as I did for the first time those thirty-eight years ago. Please. Turn your head. I will watch over her while you busy yourself with the masses of humanity that need your attention. This child I loved as my own, needs only your blessing and our strength to rid herself of this very bad time. I thank you... please.

Michael returned. Aunt Catherine could not hide the tears in her eyes. They embraced.

"Love her even more in this difficult time, Michael," she said. "Each day is a precious commitment. I fear the worst."

"I'll stay the night and call you early tomorrow before you leave," he said.

The night was long. Mary slept through it while Michael moved from one chair to another, sleeping now and then. The real advantage, he thought, was the three-hour time difference, making Mary's time work in his favor. The nurses all offered their help, bringing him cups of coffee, talking to him out at the nurses' station and peeking in at Mary while he took a break. "Please don't tell the Doctor we were here so much." Michael said.

"What Doctor?" They replied

Michael had not smoked in years, but for a moment he thought it would be a good idea. The first glint of sunrise came across the city. Michael had been examining its profile through the night. One by one the lights in the buildings were turned on as the morning brought new promises. Mary's eyes opened. She looked at him and in a strong voice, said, "I'm hungry, Michael."

He grabbed her hand and kissed her two, no, three times on her lips, her eyes, and her nose.

"You're hungry? Well... eggs, pancakes, syrup, rolls, croissants, soufflés, oysters, a steak... anything you would like... food, glorious food!"

"My guess is its Jell-O, but let's hope for the best."

Michael picked up the phone and pressed out Aunt Catherine's telephone number.

"Who are you calling?" asked Mary.

"Aunt Catherine," he said, just in time for her to pick up the phone and hear her name.

"Michael?" she said on the other end of the line.

"Yes. Mary has just awakened from a wonderful, restful night's sleep and is hungry."

"Oh, thank the Lord," she said.

"I spoke to the nurses last night. Mary has a light day ahead, in terms of tests, so I thought maybe you and Uncle Paul could come in for lunch, and we can celebrate."

"We're on our way, dear," she said. They hung up.

"Don't you want to get freshened up?" asked Mary.

"Oh Mary, I'm fine. I'll catch up with myself later, when they're here."

The nurse came in to check on her. "How are you feeling, Mary?"

"Better than yesterday," she said.

"Good. The doctor said if you would like some juice, a muffin, and some tea, it's OK."

"I'm buying," said Michael.

"That's not necessary," said the nurse. "We can."

"I know, but I'll go down to the restaurant and bring back a bunch of stuff, if that's OK. What would you like?" he asked the nurse.

"Do you really want to know? A jelly donut... and there are three more of us. But hurry, we only have an hour left on our shift."

Michael gave Mary a kiss and hurried down to the cafeteria. He got in line and noticed that the nurse he had spoken to yesterday, was two people ahead of him. She saw him and said, "Good morning. How is your friend?"

Michael opened his eyes wide and smiled big. "She is feeling really well this morning," he said.

"Oh, great. I am very happy for you," she said.

Then it was Michael's turn, and he purchased enough tea, coffee, donuts, and croissants for the entire floor. He hopped back in the elevator, delivered his booty to the nurses' station, and went back to the room to deliver Mary's breakfast.

He placed a cup of tea, a muffin, and juice on a tray for her, and elevating her head, he said, "Good morning, my love. Have I told you that I loved you today?"

"Yes, you did," she said.

"I did?"

"Yes. I don't want you beating up on yourself again. You told me."

"Well, just in case you were delirious, I do love you."

"Come give me a hug," she said.

Aunt Catherine and Uncle Paul arrived then, and Mary smiled at them as Michael moved away from the bed to give them room.

"Caught you!" said Aunt Catherine.

Uncle Paul walked over to Mary and gave her a bear hug. Then the doctor came in.

Well, I see my favorite patient is in a party mode," he said. "I like that."

He looked at her chart and said hello to the crowd.

"Hi, I'm Uncle Paul. I'm sure you've met everyone else."

"Hi, Uncle Paul," said the doctor. Then he turned to Mary. "I'm very happy to see you sitting up. Look at that color in your cheeks. Well, I'll be back later. Have a great day, all of you."

"I thought we were going to get the riot act when he first walked in," said Aunt Catherine. "I guess he was so happy to see you sitting up, nothing else mattered."

Deborah came in next. "Well, hello," she said.

"Hi," said Mary.

"Well, look who's bright eyed and bushy tailed."

"I'm so happy," said Mary, and everyone smiled. "I see someone must have gotten through to the Big Guy up there... to get his OK."

Aunt Catherine just bowed her head in answer.

A nurse came in to ask that they take turns visiting, and she let them know that Mary was going for some more treatments in the next half-hour, so they all might consider returning later.

Aunt Catherine gave Mary a hug, confident that she was on the mend.

"I'll stay until they pick you up for treatment," said Michael. He suggested they all meet downstairs in the lobby in about half an hour.

Michael was just as happy as he could be, with Mary looking so much better. When the nurse came in to get her, he gave her a kiss. She was off again to chemotherapy, a room she was beginning to dread seeing.

Michael walked through the lobby, looking for the others. Uncle Paul was reading a magazine and Aunt Catherine was standing in line, paying for something she had purchased in the gift shop. Michael offered to take everybody back to his hotel, where they could get something to eat and so that he could take a quick shower and change.

They went to the grill, and Michael asked if he could steal half an hour to change while they ordered and stalled for a bit of time.

He was back faster than they had expected. His hair was wet, and there was the fragrance of Polo—a scent, Mary had said, was his very own.

Aunt Catherine and Uncle Paul were feeling particularly good about Mary's "perkiness" as Aunt Catherine called it. They decided that they would rotate a watch so that someone was always with her, with Michael being the "anchorman at night." But it seemed that from the way she looked, it wouldn't be long before she would be home once again.

The next weeks were frustrating: Mary seemed progressively stronger, but the doctor refused to allow her to leave since the quantity of therapy was so intensive that as an outpatient, it would be difficult to monitor the nuances that could be key to her being well.

Manisha had called Aunt Catherine's house. Aunt Catherine told Mary about the conversation.

Aunt Catherine said she had told Manisha the "good news" and that they anticipated her coming home soon.

The message from Manisha was, "Please tell her that Jiral, Rose, Upen, and Manisha send the biggest hug that India could make." Aunt Catherine chuckled.

Manisha also told Aunt Catherine that, Mary was "Aunt Mary," to Jiral and Rose, and from the stories Mary had told them, that Jiral believed that he and Rose loved Mary as much as Aunt Mary loved her Aunt Catherine.

Mary was happy to hear the highlights of their conversation, and she told Aunt Catherine that she would return the call to Jiral, Rose, Upen and Manisha very soon.

Chapter Twenty-One

Each day Aunt Catherine or Uncle Paul would bring in a little "show and tell." Every day there was another performance just for Mary. The pictures from Aunt Catherine's albums were the highlight, with Michael carrying in flowers, cookies, and a few books for Mary and candy for the nurses. The other patients and nurses were all sharing the good times and the booty, and they were becoming an extended family.

Michael and Mary took long walks around the hallways. At the beginning of each hallway, the wall was marked with numbers indicating the distance, in fractions of a mile, that the patience had walked.

They stopped to say hello to the other patients as they exercised, getting to know them well. There was Mr. Simeone in Room 583, Mrs. Zenzinger in room 535, and Mr. Agresti in room 547. Each had family there to support them in their quest for wellness.

Each day Michael and Mary tried to break their record of laps from the previous day, waving and saying hello to their new families. The morning of April 3rd, they walked past room 588 to find it empty. Mr. Edgars was gone.

"Mr. Edgars went home. That's nice. He was such a great old curmudgeon," Michael said.

"I love his stories," said Mary

They stopped the nurse to ask how he had been doing. The nurse was reluctant to answer.

"No," she said sadly. "He, well... a very nice man, but it was too much... he expired... last night on my shift. He was eighty-one years old. It was just too much to ask. His illness was in control."

Mary felt badly and wanted to return to her room. They walked back slowly. She seemed weakened by the news. She sat on the bed—and Michael sat next to her—placing his arm around her. Her head fell into his shoulder. She reached for his hand and held it tightly. Mary spoke in a compassionate voice. Her words were weak, searching for meaning in Mr. Edgar's death. "He died last night when we were talking about tomorrow... or next week... or this summer," she said.

"He just died. It's so sad to die at night when it's dark. The morning, when the sun appears, and there's promise of a new day, is a way of cheating death. You get to use an extra grain of sand. A few more moments of precious time... a look into a new day."

She paused, squeezing Michael's hand, looking for support. He reached up to her with his fingers of his free hand and touched her lips. She kissed them. She continued:

"At night, there is nothing, just the dark, or worse, tacky fluorescent lights above your head... in your eyes with so many lumens per square foot... tasteless illumination defining your space. It's man-made, not made by our God. The light you feel is clinical, cold... delivering you to what? The socket in the wall? No, the morning sun should be there, offering its prelude... its warmth... welcoming another day."

Mary seemed weaker. Michael held her closer. Her voice became quieter. "Then at that moment, a glint of sunrise, will mate the awakening of your spirit that will never have to feel darkness... in your last moments. It can only happen as the morning sun greets your awareness... as a beginning of a promise... and then it fades away slowly... into the silence of death. It has to be true, Michael, even executioners have the decency to take a life at sunrise."

Michael said nothing.

Mary's weight fell to the bed. Michael helped her back. Beads of perspiration appeared on her forehead. Her palms were cold, her eyes sullen. She shook, pulling her legs up under her body. Michael turned pale with fear. He quickly covered her and went for the nurse. She responded to his expression, immediately, returning with him to the room. After reviewing her condition, she called for the doctor. Michael's anxiety level rose as he watched the woman he loved plunge into relapse. Mary had plummeted into a dreadful place.

Within minutes, the room was filled with nurses, and Michael was asked to wait in the visitor's lounge, where someone would keep him informed of what was happening. He sat staring out the window, his eyes flooded with white light, his pupils—tiny dots—seeing nothing. There was a tap on his shoulder, twice. It felt almost painful.

He turned but could hardly see; the light was so bright. As his eyes adjusted, he saw that it was John.

"Well, 'Mary's friend,' I understand that you've been tending to my business... I might add, extremely well, but nonetheless... *my* business."

Michael stood, his eyesight restored. John extended his hand, but Michael didn't take it. John sat down in a chair next to him.

"How is she... my wife of many years... your friend of many months?" he asked.

Michael paused before answering. "She was getting better," he said slowly, "but this moment when you decided to arrive, this very moment, she is having a very serious relapse. And I don't know. I can only hope she is OK. They're in there now with her. I don't know."

John began to rise. "Well, I'll go see about this problem."

Michael walked to the window, still in shock over Mary's condition. As if in a fog, he allowed John to go to her room. In a few moments, John returned.

"They won't tell me a thing and suggested that I wait here with you. It seems there's a lot going on in that room at this moment."

With that, a gurney raced by with Mary on it. The two men looked into each other's eyes.

"She's dying," said Michael, as his eyes welled up. "She's dying. Does that even register in that egotistic brain of yours?"

"Well, I am certainly at a disadvantage," said John. "You seem to think you know so much of me and I, so little of you. Well, with the exception of the fact that you have successfully taken my wife on an emotional roller coaster."

"Roller coaster? No. She has taken me to a place in mind and heart, in four months, that you couldn't find in thirteen years . Look , you're right... I don't know you. You are merely some part of Mary's past. She is everything to me. All I care about is that she lives to be one hundred years old and *you...* if I could... I would replace your shallow existence with her life in a heartbeat. But don't be offended. I'm sure others have voiced their feelings *about* you, *to* you, in the past."

"Not for such a prize," said John. "It seems Mary is on the auction block."

"You've got to be kidding. The auction block? With you, it's all money and a purchase. If I thought I could offer my highest bid, my soul, and in doing so allow her the right to life, I would surrender to your auctioneer on my knees. But my guess is it's not that easy.

"Maybe some day you'll see it, or as a miracle feel it. But, I don't think so. As for me, I have had the most enlightened moments of my life with her, experiencing how one person loving you, and your *acceptance* of that love, can make the difference in being alive."

"I don't like you much," said John.

"Well, it's Mary's not liking you that you should be thinking about, not me. As for me, it doesn't matter. You and I don't matter. It's Mary that matters. Her *being*, her talent, and her love. That's what matters. My fear is that we both lose. The world loses. It's about much more than you. I'm trying not to get angry."

"Nor I," said John.

"I'm going to leave and see what's going on with Mary," said Michael.

"Are you through?"

"I think *you* are," said Michael, emphatically.

"For now," he said. "Why not? But I must say, I don't like you *at all.*"

"Well, just so it's easier for you to remember, the name is B-O-W-L-A-N-D. Don't push me too far," he said, putting his finger on John's chest. "My trip today is longer than yours and not constructive."

"The trip? How so?"

"You have only to go downstairs to the emergency ward, a few floors below. When I get through with you, I will go to jail for assault. That makes my trip a little longer and further away from Mary. So please...don't. Let's not cross each other's path again. Good day, John. Hope for all of us."

Michael left John standing in the lounge as he headed toward the nurses' station. Deborah was standing there.

"Michael, can you give us just a few moments?" she asked.

"Sure."

The nurse and Deborah postured themselves away from him, obviously exchanging information they didn't want him to hear. They looked back at him occasionally. Deborah placed her hands on the nurse's shoulder, then turned as she thanked her and walked towards Michael.

"She's in intensive care," she said. "The relapse is significant. They are working on her now, and you must keep your distance for a short while... please... if you would. I'll stay with you, and we can talk. Shall we go to the lounge?"

"No, I don't think so. John is there."

"Oh my! Can you wait here, Michael?"

Michael stayed behind as Deborah went to the lounge. He could see her talking to John, who was becoming a little more animated now that he was dealing with his specialty—the "inferior woman." Michael could see Deborah's actions grow more and more emphatic. As she turned and left him alone in the lounge, she came back to where Michael was standing.

"That guy is... I shouldn't say this," she said.

"A prick," said Michael.

"Yes. A very tiny prick," she said. "How did they ever *happen*?"

"I've got to go call her aunt and uncle," said Michael.

"Let's go down to my office, and you can relax for a while. We'll sort things out."

Michael made the calls and Aunt Catherine was devastated. She broke into tears. Catherine read between the lines, repeating back most of what Michael was saying for Paul to hear. Deborah picked up the phone immediately after Michael hung up. She announced who she was, and that she would like to know the condition of patient Mary Templeton.

"I see, thank you," she said. "She is stable but weak," she told Michael.

"When can I see her?"

"Now," said Deborah.

"Thank you," he said. "I don't know why I'm even thinking of this, but what about... John?"

"I'll give you an hour. Then if you want, meet me back here, and I'll tell him she's available to see him at that point—but not before—since his presence can only be viewed, in my professional assessment, as detrimental to the well-being of the patient. If there are any legal ramifications that become a part of this terrible story, I'll deal with them."

Michael went to his Mary. The intensive care unit was one large room with glass cubicles skirting the perimeter. The center held a monitoring system for each patient, with many people attentively responding to the dozen or so patients. On the far wall was a series of rectangular, vertical windows. Michael entered her glass walled room. Mary's body was riddled with IVs, tubes, an oxygen mask, and many wires and other devices that shielded his view of her face. She was sleeping in a fish bowl—an environment illuminated by fluorescent lights. There was a profusion of activity as nurses and doctors scurried around the area. It was something totally impersonal but comforting from the standpoint of all the technology that was there to support her. It seemed to make sense.

No one seemed to care about Michael's existence. A single chair was placed, pathetically, next to the bed. That device was connected to her again, making its sound: "beep—beep—beep," sending a sharp wave of anxiety into the room. He insisted there was a volume control on it somewhere.

Michael sat at her side as a nurse entered the room. She quietly adjusted one of the IV's, then, having looked at the beeping device, left the room. In and out they came, each checking something else, each filling her chart with more and more information. The room grew quieter. The shift was changing as Michael looked at his watch.

Fifty-five minutes had passed with Mary never even twitching. He made his way through the tentacles that hung in and around her, carefully kissing her on her forehead. He looked at her intently. He then glanced again at his watch, knowing he had to return to Deborah's office. He was thankful that he didn't have to pass John or exchange as much as a nod as he used the stairway.

Deborah was very kind to Michael. They talked about Mary's coming show at the Seattle gallery.

It seemed so sad that they were both thinking what each would not say. They spoke for some time—praising her talents. Michael wondered where he would catch up with Aunt Catherine and Uncle Paul. Deborah offered to check with intensive care to see if they were there. She hung up the phone and told Michael they were up there, right then. There were only two people in the room, she told him. Obviously, John had left.

"Let me *go* now," he said. "I'll see you tomorrow."

Michael found Catherine and Paul crying at Mary's bedside. He was quick to explain about John and the guarded watch over Mary in the next twenty-four hours. They asked if he needed a break to get some coffee and offered to stay there while he was gone.

Michael got back in line, in the cafeteria, and noticed his nurse friend seated at a table, immediately, in front of the counter. After placing his coffee and a buttered roll on the tray, he stopped by her table.

"Hi, how are you?" she asked. "How is your friend? Ready to leave, I hope?"

"No, she's in intensive care," he said.

"Oh, I'm sorry. I really am. What's the prognosis?"

"No one is sure," he said, slowly. "It just happened a few hours ago."

"I'm sorry. What's your name? I just didn't think to ask," she said.

"Michael Bowland."

"I'm Susan, Susan Ringland. I've got to run right now. I'm sorry. It's just a quick break for me. I hope all goes well."

She touched him as she left, and Michael stayed there for a little while, finishing his roll and coffee.

When he returned to intensive care, Aunt Catherine told him they were leaving. They hugged each other and left him alone with Mary. It was another long night with Mary not moving a muscle. Her breathing stopped momentarily, scaring Michael. He stared at her chest and throat to see if they were moving. If he slept, he was unaware of it. The nurses continued to move about the room, testing and tweaking their monitors that were beeping and flashing—recording Mary's bodily functions. How did this happen? Why her? Look at her!

The night grew old and unbearable, and Michael remembered what Mary had said about the night and death. A code was announced across the room. The cubical overhead lights were turned on and a crash cart raced quickly to the patient. There was a flurry of activity and then silence. One last beep sounded. The man was cheated, as Mary said, by the "darkness of night." The technicians left—their job completed. The tubes and wires were disconnected. His covered body was wheeled away to a place that no one wanted to know about.

Across from the profusion of monitors, charts and clutter, the windows began to take shape as the first light entered the room. Michael sensed the beginning of another day.

He looked at Mary, his eyes glaring at her world—the bed, the tubing, the machines, the IV bags, and the monitors. He was filled with fear. She twitched. Her finger moved. He looked up to her face through the plastic that webbed around her. Her eyes fluttered. His thoughts raced—taking him back to the morning when he sat on the edge of her rocker in her room. The contrast was too much. The flowing sheets framing her composition were now cemented in place. The tubing and IV's pierced her flesh. There was nothing poetic about her presence in this nightmare.

Michael moved closer to her. It seemed she was awakening. Her eyes opened fully for a brief second and then closed. She seemed to sense the early light. An internal clock linked to the start of another day. Her head turned to the windows. Michael was frightened.

Was this it? All the monitors seemed OK. Her breathing? Yes, she was breathing. The oxygen tubes were in place.

"Mary, you're scaring me with this 'morning thing.'" he said. "Mary, are you awake?

I'm here, my darling. I'm here for you. Come on baby, open those beautiful eyes and say hi."

Her lips parted, and softly, so very softly, she spoke.

"Hi, Michael."

He was filled with anxiety, love, and fear. His eyes welled up. His words choked.

"They've... you've got to get out of here, honey," he said. "It's not the place to be these days."

Her hands moved toward his. "I'm working on it," she said.

A nurse entered the room. "Mr. Bowland?"

"Yes?"

"Could you step aside for just one moment?"

"Sure."

"Well, you're awake. That's good," said the nurse. "I'll let your doctor know about this good news."

She went about her business as Michael moved to the other side of the bed, grabbing Mary's hand. It was warm but difficult to hold because of the IV taped to it, preventing her from moving it. She tickled Michael's palm with her finger. He responded gently. The nurse finished and left—saying nothing.

"What time is it?" asked Mary.

"It's 6:15," said Michael, looking at his watch.

"Did you sleep?" she asked.

"Yes, I think," he said.

"I understand."

"How do you feel, baby?"

"I feel so little, except tired, weak... content to just lie here... no interest in getting up. The warmth of the sheets and blankets is comforting."

Michael turned and blew his nose. "But you're going to be ready to go to the islands for sure this weekend, right?"

"Sure... bungee jumping, too."

Michael's mind flashed back to the cemetery. He quickly put it out of his mind, as he couldn't bear the scene. It was so morbid—so depressing.

"Well, look. Do you think you can miss me a little later when Aunt Catherine and Uncle Paul come?"

"How long?"

"Less than an hour. I've got an important mission. It's for you... a surprise."

"Well, if it's for me... OK", she smiled.

Michael moved around to the side of the bed as the doctor walked in.

"Good morning, Mary and Michael," he said. "I'm happy to see you awake, Mary. Now Michael, if you don't mind, I need a little time with Mary. I'll be here a few minutes if you can wait in the hallway, please."

Michael left and stood alone in the hall. He stood against the wall, feeling conspicuous—in the way—as people in uniforms passed hurriedly by. A candy striper, pushing a wheelchair, came directly towards him.

"Excuse me, sir. Are you the man who is with that nice lady? I took her around the hospital a few times... really nice lady."

"Mary?"

"Yeah, that's it. Mary. How's she doing?"

Michael couldn't reply. She felt his sadness immediately and offered him her compassion. Yet another stranger was concerned for Mary's well-being, adding to his feelings for her. Her eyes met his as he tried to speak with a choked voice.

"She's awake," he said. "She's getting better. Thank you for asking. I will tell her you... I'm sorry... your name?"

"Charlene."

"Yes, Charlene, I'll tell her that you asked for her."

She touched his hand and sensed his weakened manner. She could tell that Mary was not in a good place.

"Tell her I'm her friend. Tell her the girls are pulling for her. Tell her I, personally, want to wheel her the hell out of that room, to her car. You tell her that, please." And with that, she left with her empty chair, heading toward someone else in need.

The doctor came out and spoke to him then, allowing Michael little time to compose himself. His strength was disappearing, as one person after another drained him of his resources.

"Michael, in cases such as this one, there is a high percentage of morbidity," the doctor said.

"At this time, it's up to what we call 'stuff,' the person's inner strength—the will to live.

"What that means here is that the more encouragement she receives, the better. Technically, it's a coin toss. There is nothing left for us to do. We have run out of ammunition. All that's left is luck, hope and fate. I'll be here anytime you need me. She is quite a lady."

Michael said nothing. The two men shook hands, and the doctor walked down the hallway. Michael called after him.

"Doctor? Doctor?"

He stopped and turned around. "Does she know?" asked Michael. "Did you tell her?"

The doctor stood alone, an isolated figure in the empty hallway.

"Yes. She's waiting for you."

Michael went back to her cubicle. It seemed like a corporate space—the kind where the boss can watch you—one wrong memo and a new name is on the door. It wasn't that at all, but he still felt as if they were in a fish bowl. Each movement was monitored by the many, who, with a simple turn of their heads, could observe another battle—lost in the tragedies of a dozen lives—in a dozen cubicles, just like hers.

He walked straight up to Mary, and kissed her on the forehead.

"Did I tell you I loved you today?" he asked.

"Yes, Michael. And I love you."

"So, the doctor said you're out of here tomorrow."

"What?"

"He said it's up to you and me to make it work. So here I am the guy who loves you. What can I do to get started?"

"Tell me about the time you first met me. Tell me... no, confess to me now, why you brought me the cup of champagne."

"A confession? Well, bless me Mary, for I have sinned. I saw you get on the plane. Well, actually I saw you in the airport long before I knew you were on my flight. You seemed preoccupied with something. You walked directly to the gate. I crossed my fingers that you would sit next to me. Then I found out you weren't."

"How?"

"I was behind you as close as I am to you now. As you presented your boarding pass to the attendant, I could see you weren't sitting next to me. But the best, second best, would be that you sat next to no one. And you didn't."

"You sound like a pervert."

"No, intrigued. I was captivated by your manner. I wanted to talk to you, to find out about you. I'm just as safe as you know me to be... a little sneaky... maybe. I had a minor problem with the seat assignment earlier. I asked the attendant if all the passengers were ticketed through to the states. She returned with a gift: 'Not all.' But you were off to Seattle."

"Where were you really going that night?"

"Los Angeles. You sat in the rear of first class, staring at *what* I didn't know. I waited so patiently for a reason to meet you. I must have gotten up for the men's room so many times, the attendant must have thought I had a bladder problem. Each time, I looked at you, and every time, you didn't notice me. Oh well... rejection!"

"At 10:00, before one of our New Year's Eves, I took my cups and walked up the aisle to you, and for the first time in my life, you looked at me. You had been crying. I had to reach down into the oceans of phrases, words, and chutzpah, to find the right sentences. I was a little nervous.

"But here we are, my darling. And I wish I had our *cups* right here to celebrate the four months and three days we have loved each other. I know, now, that your gift to me is the one thing I will cherish in my life forever. Thank you for letting me sit down that night. Thank you for loving me."

"I do."

They clutched each other. Michael bent over to kiss her, softly, once again. Aunt Catherine and Uncle Paul walked into the room. Michael moved aside, allowing them to get closer to her to say hello. They were both happy to see her awake. Michael explained his errand and left Mary in the care of her aunt and uncle. He blew her a kiss, slowly, she returned it by closing her eyes and lips as acceptance.

"Not too long," she said.

"I promise."

Michael went directly to the hotel, remembering to collect Mary's little necklace that he had had made in the San Juan Islands. She had left it in the hotel, on one of their many nights together. He showered, changed, and placed the necklace in his pocket. The next stop was the gallery, as precious time passed by. He didn't want to be away from her, but it was so important to see Scott. He made the turn onto University Street, looking at the gallery windows, hoping to see him walking around. He was running when he pushed the doors open. He quickly scanned the room.

"Is Mr. Withers in today?" he asked a guard.

"Sure. He's up those stairs, through the door, and you'll see him."

Michael burst through the door to find him standing next to some computers with his staff busy at work. He turned and smiled at Michael.

"I wonder whether I could have a moment of your time?" asked Michael.

"Surely."

Michael explained about the Guggenheim people and the letter, and Scott remembered meeting them some time ago at a fundraiser. Michael then asked, very politely, whether Mary had a chance of having her show soon.

"Well, I'm quite sure she is going to be confirmed in the next few weeks," he said.

"Please allow me to explain," said Michael. "Whether it happens next week or in the next ten years is not why I am here. Mary, our talented friend, is in the hospital in the intensive care unit, just a few blocks away. Her life is in question. The doctors say it's the flip of a coin whether she lives or dies."

"Mr. Bowland... Michael. I am so sorry. What can I do?"

"Well, the doctors say her spirit is very important for her 'will to live.' I came here hoping to ask, tastefully, if on your letterhead, we can say that the show is imminent, or whatever you think is appropriate.

Since I love her very much and thought... I... well, I hoped you wouldn't mind my being so aggressive."

"Well, a creative person like Mary won't enjoy a letter," said Scott. "No, I'll do that, and I'll do something better. I have a few of her pieces. I'd like it if you would allow me to offer some graphics for her approval? I can do this, but I need just a moment."

Scott turned and walked to a few staff members working on the computers. He asked a few questions and returned.

"I need three hours to rough out some poster concepts. You needn't wait. I'll messenger them over to wherever you tell me, with an accompanying letter. Now that's what Mary would like, something visual. Is two and a half hours OK?"

Michael gave him the information and thanked him a thousand times. He rushed back to the hospital and Aunt Catherine and Uncle Paul greeted him in the ICU.

Mary was laying quietly, her eyes closed. She seemed to be in a deeper sleep than when he had left. He removed the necklace from his pocket.

"Mary, are you awake?" he asked.

She moved. Her voice was weak. "Yes."

"Look what I brought you," he said. He raised it high and out of the way of the IV's.

"My necklace." She raised her hand as if to take it but could move it only about an inch in the air.

"Thank you," she said.

"What a curious stone," said Aunt Catherine.

"It's part of Constitution Mountain," said Michael. "It's the key to the mountain... my gift to your niece a few months ago, when we stayed there."

"How pretty," said Catherine, as he placed it in Mary's hand.

"She's very tired," Catherine said to Paul. "We'll be back later."

Mary mouthed the word, 'Bye' with her lips.

Michael was wired. The rush back and forth had raised his adrenaline level far beyond the quiet composure, appropriate for the cubicle. He felt like a raging bull—confined to a small space—too small for his action. He sat, trying to quiet down.

"Do you want me to talk or just be quiet?"

"Tell me something more," she said. "Tell me about today. Is the sun out? Is it warm?"

"Yes... yes, the sun is out. Yes, it's warm... about 60 degrees or so. It's a beautiful Seattle day. Not bad for April."

"Is it spring?"

"Yes... it's in the air. And we have to get you out of here and into the sun and warmth of the April breezes, so you must think of getting better."

"Tell me what you were thinking when we were on top of the mountain."

"How the hell were we going to get down?"

"Michael," said Mary "But I had no fear, since you were there for me... just as you are now."

"Well, I was fearful *then*, as I am *now* for you."

"No Michael. We have each other... just as we did looking down at the eagles."

"I was thinking that you and I were one. My eyes filled with tears for the first time in my life because I was happy. I had never cried because I was happy. And it was you who had taken me there to the top of where we intertwined our emotions forever.

"Mary?" he asked, suddenly noticing that her eyes had closed. His voice grew louder. "Mary?"

He shot up and looked at her throat—her chest. A nurse came in and looked, too.

"She's sleeping. She's OK," she said. "You should get some air. Go for a walk. She's resting, and that's good for both of you."

Michael walked outside the building and sat on the steps. The sun and the warm air felt so good.

"Michael? Michael?"

He looked up. It was Scott—delivering hope.

"Hi. Here is the envelope. There's a letter and, what we call, comps for her posters, announcing her show. The letter explains it all. How is she?"

"She's sleeping. They told me to get out and get some air, so here I am."

"I'd like to come see her later if they allow me in," he said. "If not, well... send my best to her. If you need anything, please contact me. There will be some contracts and things but not to worry... all in due course."

He left, and Michael noticed the shadow of another man passing by. Suddenly it stopped. Shielding the sun from his eyes, the man looked up. It was John.

"How is she?" he asked.

"Not very good. She's sleeping and in the ICU. Just follow the signs."

John moved on. Michael sat staring out at the busy street. He noticed people moving about—dogs on leashes—and cars in traffic. None held his interest. His own shadow had moved to a lower step when he noticed John skirting away from him, taking the furthest distance from him, to get down the many steps—keeping his back to Michael. He walked toward a limousine, and a driver opened the door for him. He disappeared into the long, black shape.

Then Aunt Catherine and Uncle Paul appeared out of nowhere. Michael asked them to go up and stay for a while. He needed to wash up and would be back shortly. He returned to the hotel, washed his face, and changed his clothes. He seemed to be preparing for the worst. He picked up the telephone and called his office. Heather answered.

"Hi, Michael. Where have you been? I tried calling every number I have for you. I even tried your mobile phone with no success. Did you get the messages?"

"Yes, I did. My apologies. I've had a rather personal crisis these last few days," he said.

"What happened?"

"It's Mary... She's dying. I hope not... I do, but the next few things, I say, will be *it* for a few days. Call me if you must, but to answer your questions, have legal go to contract on that last bid in Vancouver. Tell Mark I need better perspective on those spreadsheets. They are not structured properly at all for a Germanic mentality. They have to be very specific.

"As far as the new business in Bombay goes, send Terry on vacation there for a few weeks. Invent a reason to go... like you're looking for a tiger... whatever. Make it believable. Entertain the heavies. He's good at that. Tell him to stall for time, spend money, and enjoy himself. That's it. Oh, yes and thanks for the help."

"I hope all goes well, Michael."

"Thanks. I need the help, Heather. Bye."

What a change in me, he thought. Three minutes of business in two days, and it used to be the other way around.

He went back to the hospital. When he got to Mary's room, Aunt Catherine was in the chair and Uncle Paul was leaning, quietly, against the wall.

"She's still sleeping. We're going to go and leave you, OK?" asked Aunt Catherine.

"That's fine. I'll call you later if there is any change. If not, I'll call you in the morning to let you know how she is."

Michael brought the chair around to the other side of the bed after they left. He wanted a vantage point where he could look out into the entire ICU and see Mary. He sat, placing his head down upon her bed, waiting patiently for Mary to awaken. He closed his eyes. The sounds in the cubicle and the unit grew hollow as he began to drift into sleep. But the activity was relentless. The windows on the far side of the unit turned black, ending a day that was so very difficult. Mary's hand twitched. Michael lifted his head, awakening. He was quick to check her breathing. Her eyes opened.

"Hi," she said.

"Hi... hey, I got something here for you," he said. "It came from the gallery, from Scott. Shall I open it?"

"Please."

"Shall I read it?"

"Yes."

"Dear Mary," he read. "Please be informed that after careful consideration, the Seattle Gallery has decided to make final arrangements for your work to become part of our permanent collection. I have enclosed some comps for the posters and other visual pieces we may use, should you find the graphics suitable for your work. Any suggestions or changes are welcomed, with final approval made only by you."

"Congratulations," he continued. "I am looking for your earliest availability for a meeting so that the board and I may personally welcome you to the finest collection of art in the Pacific Northwest. Thank you. Scott Withers."

"I'm so happy... thanks," said Mary.

Michael held up the 8½ by 11 comps.

"I hate them," she said.

"You do?"

"No. I love them. They're beautiful graphics."

Michael looked at one of them. The type was bold, with a headline spreading across the top with Mary's painting of the little Indian boy seated just below. The expression, the detail, was magnificent. The other was a variation of the same.

"They look great to me, Mary... really great," he said.

"Is that where you went this afternoon?" she asked.

"Yes. I wanted you to know about this. So here it is. You're famous. Can I still hold your famous hands?"

"*All the time*, Michael... *anytime*... and *no one else*." Mary's eyes closed as she began to fall back to sleep. Michael placed the good news back on a small table next to her bed. He sat looking at her, wanting to do anything to help ease the frustration. Anxiety was ripping him apart. He looked at her as tears trickled down his face. His vision was blurred; he was seething with sadness. His head fell to the bed; the sheets absorbed his tears.

He wept for Mary. *This moment*, he thought *is a gift. Is that why it's called 'the present', because it's a gift? Is it that yesterdays are the past, tomorrows are the future, and this moment... with so few grains of sand falling through space... is 'the present... a gift of time'. These moments with her... my love... are they the last? I hope I'm wrong. Let me be wrong... please.*

Hours passed. The white sheets were still moist with his tears. People outside the cubical quietly talked about the new day. *Spring is here. What a wonderful day it will be. People are talking... just being people,* he thought.

The windows began to lighten as their shapes became more defined. His fears escalated. His mind became filled with anxiety as it did yesterday. The brighter the shapes grew, the more apparent their outline became against the darkened walls. It's *morning. Oh my God, the sun. No... not the sun.* Mary's finger twitched. Her clock, her inner self, sensed this time. Her eyes lids began to move. He was frozen. Don't awaken! Please sleep another day, Mary. Her eyes opened.

"Michael?" she said.

"Yes, my love. I'm here."

"Is the sun up?"

"No, it's very dark. It's still the middle of the night. Go back to sleep."

"But I sense something. It looks like sunlight on the far side of the room."

"It's a light in the room. You must sleep. It's dark... very dark. Let's wait till morning to talk."

Mary's voice was a whisper. Michael moved closer to her, placing his ear aside her mouth.

She said, "It's time to treasure my love for you... silently."

"No, don't. No. Please... it's dark... so dark. Mary... please, Mary... "

Michael reached for her. "I lied, Mary. I'm sorry. You're right. The sun is up. Take it with you. Don't be cheated, my darling. I love you. It's a brand new day... just for you... unwrapped by... "

Her head fell to rest. He placed his head upon the sheets—the moist sheets still chilled from his tears. The florescent light came on. A nurse rushed in. Another technician arrived and grabbed Michael's arm, taking him just outside the room. A crash cart arrived! They called the code. That sound, "beep—beep—beep" consumed his mind. More nurses rushed in, each of them attending to their respective jobs, creating a frenzy of activity. "Stat. Stat," he heard. A doctor administered something. The doctor stood there waiting for a response. Nothing!

The sounds stopped! No one moved! The silence was deafening. Oh my God. She was gone.

They tried to move Michael away, but he pushed towards her. They all moved aside, creating a gauntlet. He leaned over Mary. He kissed her, pushing a few strands of her hair aside her beautiful face. "I love you."

A nurse reached for his arm, holding it gently. They remained at Mary's side a few moments. "Mr. Bowland," said the nurse softly... then again, "Mr. Bowland." Michael turned. She began to walk with him to another cubical immediately adjacent to Mary's. He was weak—his arms limp. His mind was filled with sadness. He sat holding his head with his hands. He listened for the sounds of the gurney to take her to a place he didn't want to know about.

He sat there for an eternity, wanting to go back. He felt like a coward, not being able to witness her leaving. He stood and looked back. She was gone. Tears were still falling from his cheeks. He took the emergency steps down to the lobby. The nurse, he had met in the cafeteria, was walking towards him. She was very animated and was preparing to smile as she began to say "hi," but Michael couldn't see her. His tears filled his eyes. She looked at his face as he passed, and she said nothing. She stopped and turned—watching him walk out of the hospital.

Chapter Twenty-Two

Time and distance take their toll on family and friends. Mary's absence from Seattle for all those years was evident. Michael was sure she had many more friends and not so many relatives. Her family was one which seemed to dwindle. A cousin here or there, but with Mary, not having children and no siblings, this branch of the family tree stopped abruptly. The few that attended her funeral service seemed to come from her mother's side of the family, each of them older than one might expect. Deborah was there, as well as Mr. Withers. All were sparsely placed in a classic setting, a scene that Mary could never paint.

Seattle's weather had delivered the common denominator to a classic cemetery scene—rain. The umbrellas touched each other, creating a black canopy, shielding the container that held his Mary.

I hate funerals he thought... *anyone's... especially in spring. It's a bad time to die.* Michael had been thinking of death for many years now. He realized the product of his age. Mary's illness has made it intense. *It's a toll on all those around her; it runs deep. My own existence means little without her.*

A few weeks ago, on his way to her home, he had witnessed a deer hit by an oncoming truck. He stopped as the other drivers did. It seemed pathetic. At that moment of impact, the deer was thrown to the side of the road; its limp body was quivering, and helpless. It had been brought to its end by a circumstance over which it had little control. Nature, its instincts, and its breeding, kept it alive through winter only to die now that it was spring. This should have been a time to rejoice after spending a winter in the cold and snow... after spending a winter of sunless weeks with unbearable nights of winds that chilled your spine. The deer had made that journey, only to die a few weeks ago, April 4th, at the edge of warm breezes and budding trees, of rich green grass, and the fragrance of new life *this* had to be wrong.

And so, for Mary, this earth, her grave, and this awful place did not need to be disrupted this day. It could have waited 'till fall. A few months more... time for Mary... for us. We were like the trees who, with their memories of glorious summer evenings, had much to share, but now, each leaf helps to blanket the ground as if to hide the flowers that, no longer, are blooming.

I can't think of a time to leave this earth... especially for my love. But the fall is the only season to die. The softened earth is more accepting... your life better spent... a time that mates our feelings as we prepare our thoughts for the cold desolation of winter. I hate winter.

"I loved her so very much," he said, out loud, his eyes welling with tears.

"You must be John," said the older woman next to him. "I'm sorry we had to... "

"No, my name is Michael," he said.

"I'm Vera, an old friend of the family. I sense... *you're* much more than a friend."

"That man standing next to the priest is John," he said. "Mary and I met...a short while ago... New Year's Eve, on a flight back from Bombay. I was not aware that she was ill then. She told no one. A few months ago, circumstances revealed what became this tragedy. She will always be a part of me."

Vera was crying now. "I'm so sad for all of us," she said, hugging him.

The man was dressed in black. His collar was white, and his hair was as thick and dark as his garb. He has a boy's face. It seemed a little awkward for Michael since he was at least twenty-five years older than the priest. He still knew so little about life. Michael wondered how to call him father... and not Jack or Bob.

John knows his stuff. There's something about those who sing the loudest in church, Michael thought. There he is standing right next to the priest, knowing only Aunt Catherine, Uncle Paul, and Michael. For all John knows, he could be at the wrong funeral.

The young priest said all the words that no one wanted to believe were being said. He did well—his delivery undaunted by the rain that seemed to endure throughout the ceremony. They passed a flower from one of the few wreaths that encircled the casket. The priest suggested that the family place the flowers upon it as they left. Michael thought about keeping it. He couldn't. He just couldn't. The priest turned to John and spoke. He removed an envelope from his inside pocket and handed it to him. Michael observed John carefully opening it then removing something. He then opened a folded piece of paper from inside the envelope and read it quickly, refolding it immediately and putting it away. All was quiet as the priest reached into his jacket once more. He reviewed the name on the envelope, and said, "Is there a Michael Bowland here?"

"Yes," said Michael.

He offered Michael a second envelope, his name written in Mary's handwriting across the front. He held it tightly, knowing she touched it. John came towards him.

"Well, Mike, we seem to have each received a parting message. I trust yours is a little more of what I remember of Mary, and our beginnings."

"At this point, I don't know what is in either envelope," said Michael.

"I don't mind telling you. After all, it's over for both of us, isn't it?"

"Yes it is," said Michael.

"I got the ring and a copy of Webster's definition of the word love. I suppose that's the last word in any language."

"I have to say you really messed up. I don't know how you did it... that was your thing, but Mary was well worth fighting for, and you, sir, made a big mistake. You'll have to live with that for the rest of your life."

"And so it goes," said John. "Goodbye, Michael."

John turned and placed his flower on top of the casket. Aunt Catherine stepped in his path. Michael and Uncle Paul moved closer to them. Aunt Catherine spoke, "John, this is the saddest day I shall ever have in my life. But I would like to deliver something to you that Mary *should have*, years ago." She placed her pocketbook in her left hand. John thought she was about to shake hands. He seemed off guard. Without blinking an eye, this loving woman slapped his face so hard, that everyone turned to the sound. "Now get out of my sight." He said nothing and walked to his limousine. John's driver met him with an umbrella. They left.

Uncle Paul said, *"Catherine!"*

"Yes... I know." she said.

She turned to the priest. He was amazed. "Father," she said.

"Yes, Catherine."

"Didn't you say in your last sermon that the Almighty asks some of us to do His work?"

"Yes I did... but Catherine."

"Well, it's done"

The one and only smile Michael had in a very long time remained on his face as he expressed his acceptance of Mary's Aunt Catherine.

Mr. Withers looked at Deborah. He was shocked.

Deborah whispered into his ear, "This is a very good thing."

Aunt Catherine and Uncle Paul delivered their flowers; then they stopped to hug Michael. With tears in his eyes, Uncle Paul offered enough sadness for all of them.

Michael said, "I'm staying a short while, then stopping at her house for a minute. I feel I have to. I'll call you next week.

"Come over later if you like," said Aunt Catherine.

"No, I can't right now. You understand."

"Yes, I do. But now that we have lost Mary, please don't let us lose you, too. One more thing... Mary's friend Manisha called from yesterday. We told her. She was shattered. Evidently, Mary had called her and asked for her to watch over her little one. Manisha will, she said."

"Never to worry, Mary and Paul will always be part of her memory."

"Rose, Jiral, Upen, and I will be there for Mary," Manisha said. "She promised." They walked to their car.

Michael couldn't leave Mary there alone. It seemed an impossible task. He placed the envelope in his jacket pocket and ran his hand through the raindrops that lie atop the casket, then again just beside the crucifix. Time mattered not, anymore. He tried to shield her coffin from the rain—frustrated, then angered, that no one was there to help her.

"Is that what they do? Just leave you here... for how long?"

A hand touched his shoulder gently. Michael turned to find the priest.

"Would you like to walk with me to our cars, Michael?"

"I can't leave her... Father, I can't."

"We'll walk," he said. "Please."

He took Michael's arm. His voice was steady and confident, even magnetic. He sounded as if he had the wisdom of a man one hundred years old. He swept Michael away from her—from the rain—and from her presence.

He was in his car driving out the gate, towards her home, never to see Mary again. Michael passed John's limousine pulled to the side of the road. The window was half down, with a cloud of cigarette smoke, exiting the window. John was attentively reading his letter.

John leaned back against the seat, his left hand holding the letter. He placed the cigarette against his lips, inhaling deeply, then flicking its remains out the window. With smoke still escaping his mouth, he directed the driver to take him to the hotel. The limousine pulled away.

Michael turned the simple lock of the front door of Mary's home and entered. His clothes were wet. He removed his jacket and placed it on a hook next the hallway mirror. He knew it was the worst possible time to be in the house, but he needed to be there. After this *last* time, he would go anywhere, just go. Michael went to the kitchen, looking for a bottle of wine or something to soften the edge of his misery.

He found a half bottle of Pinot Grigio. He thought about drinking from the bottle, but somehow he just couldn't see himself doing it. He poured himself a glass and walked to the living room and sat down. He took a long sip, feeling the wine, cold, running down his throat, touching his stomach. It was good.

He took another sip and remembered the letter Mary had left for him. He shot up like a thief, as if he were guilty of a crime, went out to the hall to his jacket, and pulled out the letter. He wanted never to read it; it was just too much. He walked back and took another sip... one more. He had to read it. It was so unlike him not to do it.

OK, take a seat Mike and read the letter now, he told himself.

He sat down, placing the glass on the table beside him. When he opened the envelope, the paper slid out so easily... too easily. *She had touched this fold... Stop... Mike stop. Do it. Unfold it. She wants you to read it. It's from Mary to you... no one else but to you.*

He placed it down on the table and stood up. His eyes consumed every item in the room. He looked at everything... anything except the letter.

Sit down and read.

He sat down once more and composed himself. He leaned back and unfolded the letter. He could hear Mary's voice.

"Dearest Michael,

Thank you for the most wonderful five years of my life. Your gift to me is a treasure that only you and I can see... that only you and I can touch.

I sat on that plane in fear of never attaining my goal: to offer my love and to be loved in return. I, too, did not know it could be as it has been for us. I never knew. One moment I sat, thinking thoughts of *never*. And within seconds, you were there, offering your 'cup of kindness' to me. Oh, if I were only smarter... to have recognized it then, but it had to grow. It needed time, and we had your gift of 'five more years.'

To say, "I *love* you," is so little. To say, "I *cherish* you," is not enough. But to say another word is meaningless. Yet to feel what I feel is *you*... for all the rest of all the New Year's Eves to eternity. I'll wait for you. Please take your time. I have but you to wait for.

All of what I have left behind is yours. My paintings... everything. I'm sure you can work that out with Aunt Catherine and Uncle Paul. I did have time to be awakened by your spirit of trust, instilled in me with one last burst of creative synapses at the tip of my brush. In the corner of our bedroom, I left a painting for us. For me, it's the knowledge of myself being creative... a second... a precious grain of sand well spent. I feel as if I managed to freeze time. I hope you like it. I guess I'm still a typical artist with her insecurities.

I love you. I love you. I love you... I do! I hope this is OK, but I decided that for the rest of time, that my name is "Mary Bowland."

Michael ran up the steps, two at a time, her letter still in hand. There was the painting. It was in her style—whimsical. There they were, the two of them. It was Picasso's best, at the very least.

Michael and Mary were seated next to each other, atop a wisp of clouds. The sun was setting, rich and full, as the light and color wrapped around them—offering the warmth they always felt when they were together. His figure was holding the same cup they held on their flight from Calcutta. Her hand was outstretched toward his.

He slowly fell to his knees... then rested his forehead on the edge of the canvas. He remained for a while, and then he carried the painting downstairs.

He lingered for hours... finishing the wine. The day grew dark. He locked up the house, placing the key in the secret place they shared... thinking, *Mary will never touch this key again.*

Chapter Twenty-Three

Michael dedicated himself to Mary's show at the gallery. Mr. Withers and the board welcomed her creative genius, offering it to the residents of Seattle and to the world as a very permanent part of their collection.

Michael would go frequently enough to meet all those that Mary knew at the hospital—even Charlene, who took it upon herself to bring all the girls to see the talent of her friend, Mary.

He had changed. His work became a way of absorbing the pain. He immersed himself back into his business. He was committed to this distraction.

Months passed as he tried to cope with Mary's being gone. To see Aunt Catherine and Uncle Paul was very difficult, but they managed to share a few dinners. They always ended in sadness—always the same.

Summer went by quickly: Michael traveled to New York, Vancouver, and the Orient—but never India. He just couldn't. Fall was upon him. His visits to Seattle always included the cemetery. "Work, thank you for work," he would always say.

In December, just after Christmas, the weather was miserably wet and cold. Michael deliberately arranged a meeting in Seattle. His flight traced almost the same schedule as their journey a year before, when he had shared Mary's laughter. Several times, on the flight, he turned sharply away from his thoughts thinking he heard her voice in the empty seat next to him.

How had so much time passed? He wondered. *I don't seem to feel the days as much as the nights... the loneliness. These seasons have passed so quickly. It's as if someone has wound the clocks too tightly, and we are being cheated of time. It seems to be ripped away without meaning. I loved her so,* he thought, as the wheels of the plane screeched, touching the cold concrete runway in Seattle. His only thoughts were of Mary and New Year's Eve 2000. It had arrived.

Headlights pierced the late afternoon fog as they found their way up the serpentine drive of Flower Hill Cemetery. The time was 3:48 p.m. on the cusp of New Year's Eve—London time. Michael's car rolled to a stop. He parked, leaving the headlights directed just askew of Mary's headstone.

His Grundig radio—left on the car seat—was riveted to London's BBC. He carried a small bouquet of flowers, two cups and a bottle of Cordon Rouge, to his love. He could hear the announcer through some static, "It's eight minutes to twelve here in London this New Year's Eve, 2000."

He knelt at her feet and unwrapped the wire and seal, placing them in his pocket. He twisted the cork, ever so gently, releasing a soft pop of effervescence that had been concealed for eighteen years. With his hands trembling with emotion, he poured the champagne into a single cup and began to speak to Mary. The radio became distant as sounds of excitement were absorbed by his weeping. In a whisper that he felt she would hear, he spoke:

"Do you know the difference you made in my life? Oh my God I hope so. Your gift of love, of caring. It's just not fair to love someone and then go away, Mary. Eighteen years ago, someone put all this emotion inside this bottle, not to be released until today. I'm not sure if I like that person, either.

"This place is too cold for you. Oh, Mary... I love you so much. I can't be happy. But from my heart, I miss you so very much... I do."

He lifted his cup, as the radio announcer reached back across their journey, announcing the end of this tragic year. But "five" years, to this moment, they had toasted. Her smiles, their laughter, were still fresh in his mind.

A choir of voices began to sing, "Should auld acquaintance be forgot."
Michael's tears slid down his cheeks, touching the brim of the cup, as he shared their toast, "To Mary, to our love, with your memory lasting with me forever... as Mary Bowland."

From the little Grundig, the music filled the air. The volume rose.
"*We'll drink a cup of kindness dear, to ole lang syne.*"

About the Author

George Cochran lives in Charlotte, NC. He is a retired NYC, DGA Commercial Film Director. He has been a professional contributor to the communication industry in New York City, Chicago, LA, Atlanta as well as many other major centers of advertising and marketing here in the USA and abroad. His companies have been awarded almost every National award the industry bestows on its own.